ANTÓN MALLICK
WANTS TO BE HAPPY

# ANTÓN MALLICK
# WANTS TO BE HAPPY

## NICOLÁS CASARIEGO

*Translated from the Spanish by*
*Thomas Bunstead*

 Hispabooks
Publishing

Hispabooks Publishing, S. L.
Madrid, Spain
www.hispabooks.com

Originally published in Spain as *Antón Mallick quiere ser feliz* by
    Ediciones Destino, 2010
First published in English by Hispabooks, 2014
English translation copyright © by Thomas Bunstead
Design © Simonpates - www.patesy.com

Cover image, *Hung up* © Phillip Schumacher

A CIP record for this book is available from the British Library

ISBN 978-84-941744-8-3 (trade paperback)
ISBN 978-84-941744-9-0 (ebook)
Legal Deposit: M-3995-2014

*To D. N., for all the times.*

The aim, I take it, is to live more
at leisure and at one's ease.

MICHEL DE MONTAIGNE

How much truth can a spirit bear,
how much truth can a spirit dare?

FRIEDRICH NIETZSCHE

The family is one of nature's masterpieces.

GEORGE SANTAYANA

*Tuesday, October 13, 2009*

My name is Antón Mallick and I'm thirty-two years old.
Throughout my life people have always told me that it's a
strange surname. I say, it isn't strange, it's Hungarian. Vidor
Mallick, my great-great-great-grandfather, came to Madrid
at the age of twenty, in 1830, having, he claimed, walked
all the way from Pest. No one ever knew what he or his
family did in the city they came from, maybe because in
the beginning no one could understand a word he said, or
maybe they just never asked. He was a good-looking man,
fairly short and athletic, and bursting with life. Though
generally of a sunny disposition, people also claimed that
he had a terrible temper. He may not have been all that
sincere as a person but at least he didn't show up, like some
people did, claiming to be an aristocrat or a concert pianist.
He picked Spanish up quickly and married a humble local
girl who was by no means attractive, but stuck by him and
knew how to scrimp and save. He opened a shoe shop,
made a lot of money (dealing in everything except shoes),
and died at sixty in the lap of luxury. So, as far as anyone
knows, the first and last person ever to make any kind of
serious money in my family was a Hungarian immigrant.

Until he burst onto the scene, so the thinking goes, our
family had always been poor and middling—as far back

9

as the Garden of Eden. Vidor Mallick also knew how to write, and I don't only mean as in he wasn't illiterate. He recounted his made-up life, as he called it, in fact not very willingly (he thought writing and writers were beneath him) in a notebook entitled *Confessions of a Once-Hungarian Spaniard*. My idiot of a father kept it, and I only have a copy of the Spanish translation, which was commissioned by my uncle Juan. It's a great book, a kind of counter-memoir, if you will, and if we haven't published it, it's only because we prefer to keep it to ourselves, like a painting acquired by dubious means, a canvas languishing behind a pair of curtains down in some basement that the owner proudly unveils only for that special visitor, at night, just the two of them . . .

But Vidor Mallick's story, his affairs with married women and his shady dealings with stolen goods, have not an awful lot to do with this diary. This diary is a kind of chronicle, or a crusade, or chronicle of a crusade, and I commit it to the page with the unlikely aim that it will serve as therapy. Not for the first time, something happened to me today, something horrible and absurd, something that brought on another of my overwhelming anguish attacks. To begin with I was me but, suddenly, I wasn't, I was someone else, and ended up in the strangest state of not-being-me and yet still being inside my body—all in the middle of a bookshop jam-packed with people. Then, terrified, rooted to the spot, as the cashier stared at me uncomprehendingly, unsure whether she should scream or call security, the thought popped into my head that my Hungarian ancestor's name meant "happy," and, on top of that, that he swore he was indeed happy, and then I came back to myself, I was me again, Antón, and it was in that moment that I decided to overturn my woeful destiny.

Enough is enough. I don't want to be a pessimist, or a victim, any more. I reject the status of black hole. This notebook, which I address and dedicate to Vidor Mallick, inveterate gambler and amateur loan shark, is proof of my will to optimism, that is, my great desire to become a man with a sunny disposition, happy, *normal*, one of these guys who springs out of bed every morning and has answers for pretty much every single one of life's many questions. I believe it can be done: there are, they say, many such men sprinkled across this earth—the ones, yes, whom the pessimists (who probably are in the majority) describe as constituting hell itself. I will speak of happiness, or of the search for it, which is really the one thing that matters to us human beings, much as some try to busy themselves with learning, power, or even just with love, pretending they don't know how doubtful these are as ways of attaining it, or at least in the hope of giving the slip to sadness and the certainty of death. I will speak, finally, of my life and of this unattainable ideal, one we don't know how to define without reverting to such vague terminology as "satisfaction," "mood," "pleasure," or "contentment."

May it be so.


*Wednesday, October 14, 2009*

It's a starry night, dear Vidor (do you mind, oh happy ancestor, my addressing you thus?), very clear, the air so crisp it can only mean cold. I've just got home, I'm drunk

11

and I smell of cheap perfume. I've smoked a cigarette out on the balcony, gazing up at the firmament, and I've been trying to imagine what your childhood in Hungary must have been like. You rarely spoke about it. Sheets of ice floating down the Danube, river waters frozen and in motion at the same time. My belief is that you avoided talking or writing about your childhood not, as everyone in the family claimed, because it was so horrible, but in fact because you had such a good time. It pained you to leave it behind. You never got over the happiness.

I rang Bela this morning, but there was no answer. Bela's my sister—I'll fill you in on her soon enough, Vidor, but all I'll say for now is that she's an angel. I was so badly in need of someone to talk to that I even thought about going and seeing Zoltan. I know this wasn't a great idea, but then I've never worried very much about having great ideas; those I leave to Great Men. Zoltan is a psychologist. He specializes in behavioral and cognitive therapy—search me—and has an office on Calle Mayor, not far from the Puerta del Sol. It's a bustling, touristy spot, the roads around there have been under construction for years, and demonstrations, marches and processions constantly go along that way too. Hardly Zoltan's style, but then again, what is?

I went there on foot, something I've been getting used to since I sold my car and my motorbike. Like all Mallicks, when I'm walking I look at people's faces and bodies, and not so much at shop windows or buildings, or the sidewalk or traffic. And once again it was unhappy faces and deformed bodies that confronted me, but since I'm an optimist now, I thought, for example, that the fat woman who had dropped a twenty-euro bill and was struggling to pick it up, and whose dull, teary eyes were crying out for help, was in fact a perfectly happy lady who enjoyed being helped by gentlemen such as I, and that if she hadn't had those hairy warts removed from her unhealthy looking face, it was because she just didn't feel like it, not that it had never dawned to her to try and make herself look nice, not that she had no one in her life to appreciate the change, not that she was too poor to afford the operation . . .

I took the stairs at number 31 two at a time, asking myself why on earth Zoltan hadn't moved his office somewhere calmer, or at least somewhere with an elevator, bearing in mind he charges an arm and a leg, and business had been booming lately. Maybe there was something perverse in it, maybe he liked his patients to turn up feeling not only insecure and beset by troubles, but also sweating and out of breath.

His secretary Linda opened the door for me. Given that *Linda* means *good-looking* in Spanish, she strikes me as one of the few people I know whose name I can honestly say fits her perfectly; I had an aunt called Milagros (Miracles) and the only miracle she ever performed was dying; Sol (Sun), my grandmother on my father's side, was the unhappiest, gloomiest character imaginable. Linda's twenty-five, she has dark, lustrous black hair, a broad nose, and is otherwise very well proportioned. She's black, I should add; her parents are from Equatorial Guinea, part of the first wave of immigrants who really integrated, and she speaks extremely good Spanish. She seemed pleased to see me, though something in her eyes told me she wasn't especially looking forward to telling Zoltan about my showing up unannounced at his office.

13

I left my jacket and was led to a small waiting room where there was a middle-aged woman with Botox lips and several inches of makeup who looked like what she needed, more than anything, was a good roll in the hay (or even two or three). Just as, whenever I go to hospital, even if I'm ill myself I eye the other patients nervously—thinking they must be in a much worse state than me, or they must be suffering terribly, or that they're unhygienic, or highly contagious—the few times I've been to Zoltan's office his patients have unsettled me too; I feel like, if they're here, they must be raving lunatics, and maybe they're going to leap up and take a chunk out of me. I know how ridiculous this all is, Vidor, given it's probably me who's in the worst state of all, but still . . .

I took a seat in a corner and had a look at the magazines on the low mahogany table. Confirmation of the idea that the presence of out-of-date magazines in doctor's waiting rooms is some kind of cross-clinic tradition, as entrenched as that of surgeons chatting about their weekends whilst they prod around in your major organs. I had to content myself with an antiquated *Hello*; another guided tour through the mansion of a millionaire who could afford everything except good taste. Meanwhile, the parrot sitting across from me—Botox Lady—kept on glancing at me, and my fear levels began to escalate. Would she sink her dentures into my arm? But just then Linda came and rescued me, showing me into Zoltan's office.

Zoltan. Aside from the cartoon supervillain name, he's tall and slim, forty years old, and has the look of a man who's lived abroad for a long time, which is in fact the case, and that of being a nice guy, which isn't. Some women find him attractive, above all when he gets annoyed and arches one of his bushy eyebrows, but that isn't very often; rather, women tend to find him dull and inaccessible because he's married and, unless I'm completely wrong, faithful to his pain-in-the-neck of a wife, María, who's a nice, good-looking woman, just as dull as him, though pleasant and a little less aloof. Then there are their twins, who are from another planet too, but a planet where there's such a thing as laughter at least. To be clear, dear Vidor, Zoltan and his family are either sympathizers with some political party, or they will be, they believe in democracy and in the fight against climate change and any other nonsense associated with the well-being and progress of mankind.

The moment I set sight on his perfect, classically proportioned face, his blond hair and his blue eyes, I knew I shouldn't have come; there was nothing more humiliating or unpleasant than being vulnerable, even if it was only going to be temporarily. Nothing more infuriating than depending on others, needing help, begging for comfort. Nothing worse than to be pitiable, a moral creditor, or the type of person who deserves extra from the world and its revolting inhabitants.

"Hi," I said, failing to muster a smile.

"What brings you here, brother?" asked Zoltan, seating himself at his desk and pointing me to the black leather couch, smiling but making clear with an impatient flick of the hand that visiting during opening hours wasn't entirely convenient.

Yes, Zoltan is my brother. He, like my sister Bela, has a Hungarian first name to go with the surname. The family tradition that the eldest child should bear a Hungarian first name has only been broken once, which was when a bankrupt Mallick (one of our great-grandfathers who as well as being slow-witted and extremely overweight was a spendthrift) named his first daughter Lola, just for the hell of it, fed up, on top of all his debts, with having to bear our supposedly glorious Hungarian past. My idiot of a father, on the contrary, as well as naming my elder brother Zoltan, also decided to name Bela à la Hungary. But when I came along, my mother put her foot down: two children being teased all the way through school was quite enough. My father, Lajos, is the eldest of two brothers—his brother, Uncle Juan, an exceptional man, was my mentor. Because his name has the word "ajo" in it, which means "garlic" in Spanish, he suffered years of garlic jokes through school and, remembering these, he was immediately persuaded to call me Antón, short for Antonio. According to him the name comes from florid Greek, the loveliest of languages, and is more than acceptable therefore.

"What brings you here, Antón?"

I don't know what was wrong with my brother, he doesn't usually show his impatience like this. He learned to repress his base instincts, every possible trace of spontaneity or bad temper, during his upbringing in the US. I just decided to go for it.

"I'm going to be a father, Zoltan."

My brother lurched back like he'd been shot in the stomach.

"What! You? How?"

I told him how, the previous day, being the free spirit that I am, a man without attachments, I'd spent the afternoon in one of the cultural shops in Callao, just off

Gran Vía. I was just browsing, really, and, though I hadn't planned to buy anything, I ended up consuming, like I usually do. I'd picked up a couple of old Westerns and joined the queue.

"So *that's* what you've been spending your time doing? Watching old black and white movies?"

I was standing in line behind a young woman wearing a tweed jacket. I stood very close to her, to try and make her hurry up. I noticed she had all four *Lethal Weapon* DVDs and thought how oversubscribed this world is when it comes to intellectuals. When she'd paid and was leaving the shop, just as I was handing my card to the girl at the checkout counter, this woman turned around, called me by my name and said she was going to have my baby.

"Jesus, Antón!"

My vision went cloudy. I was petrified. Before I had time to respond, or to get a proper look at her, I had one of my anguish attacks, my mind fled my body, in the same way that the soul does when a person dies.

"Get to the point Antón!"

The flustered cashier was talking at me but I couldn't hear her, I wasn't there, I was outside, away, and a couple of interminable minutes must have passed with me plunged in the void, and when I came back to myself a security guard had caught hold of me and a very nice, Parisian-looking girl was staring at me with horror in her eyes, and the cashier was speaking to someone on the phone, and, without really wanting to, I half smiled at all of them and said I was okay now. Mystery Woman had evaporated, like the shadow of a dream, not a trace, and I paid for the DVDs and . . .

"Antón, mind telling me where this is headed?" said Zoltan, barricaded behind his antique wooden desk. "You've got me keeping Señora Jarque waiting for this? Have you lost your mind?"

I told my brother, yes, that was exactly what I was saying, and that I'd had my first severe anguish attack in months. But he didn't believe in Mystery Woman; easier, far less uncomfortable, to think it was just me talking nonsense. When it comes down to it, he already thought I was out of my mind before I told him about the encounter with Lady Upsetter, but if my story was true and I really was going to have a child with her, then it would be fair to think that his brother (yours sincerely) wasn't *a little bit special*, but that in fact someone (the Devil or the Fates, let's say) was taking a hand in his destiny. But this—me having a little bad luck, me being normal—would be a defeat for Zoltan the Peabrain who, being a died-in-the-wool believer in Cognitive Behavioral Therapy and all things rational, couldn't possibly bear the idea. He asked me if I was still seeing Domínguez, my psychiatrist, and I had to confess that I wasn't. Domínguez is a person possessed of huge amounts of emotional intelligence, I believe he could fill several liter bottles with the empathy that oozes from him; maybe that's why he's so well-known. But when it comes to intelligence intelligence, the normal kind, let's just say he isn't the brightest light on the Christmas tree, and I gave up on him after several sessions of making zero progress—except downwards in terms of my bank account. Plus the fact he ended up just prescribing me drugs, and for that I can always ask my brother.

This made Zoltan angry. I'd never get anywhere, he said, with that attitude; the recovery process wasn't some quick fix. I shut him up by promising I'd find another psychiatrist, then asked for a prescription of Alprazolam and one of Paroxetine. He went to his partner's office for the prescriptions—he, as a psychologist, isn't allowed to prescribe—and when he came back made it clear these were the last ones he'd be giving me.

"I could go to prison, you know that? I've got a family to think about! I want you to start seeing Domínguez again, ask him to get you your pills, he's your doctor. What, think you can just self-medicate?"

He obviously wasn't listening to me. I explained that I'd decided to become an optimist.

"What? What the hell are you on about now? Optimist? You?"

Zoltan realized I wasn't joking, and possibly found this unsettling because he stood up and turned away so I couldn't see his expression, and then went over to a bookcase and took down a number of books. My brother and my parents are never sure whether to admire or pity me, and they are usually ashamed of me. Which goes for me with them—as in I cringe when I'm with them, because I've never felt pity or admiration for them. Zoltan brought over some books that he said would help me in becoming an optimist, and then started surreptitiously ushering me out. That's exactly the way he is. That's his life, or at least that's how it seems; there's a simple, practical prescription to cover everything. So you *wanna be an optimist? Here, take some books.* But no time to talk, no time for a little chat with his brother, never mind the terrible state he happens

19

to be in. In Zoltan's world, schedules are kept to, and visiting hours—particularly if it's a thorny issue—start at nine o'clock in the evening, when the kids are asleep and it's okay to let the monsters out from under the bed.

"I've got to get on, but let's make a plan to do something together one night soon, okay? Need any money? When Linda told me you were here, I thought about hotfooting it down the fire escape! Seeing as you said the other day how broke you were . . ." This was Zoltan's attempt at a joke. "I almost prefer the pregnant woman story . . . Sure you haven't made it up?"

That hurt. The last bit. That was below the belt. Blood rushed to my head, I thought it might explode.

"Are you really asking that? Are you really asking whether I made it up?"

"Yes . . ." He was a little taken aback; he might have crossed a very dangerous line. "I thought it could have been a joke, you know, unconsciously asking for a little attention . . ."

"Right," I said, putting on a smile. "I'll answer that if you answer me one thing."

"Sure, shoot!"

"ARE YOU FUCKING YOUR SECRETARY?"

"Jesus!" he said, lowering his voice, glancing furtively in the direction of the reception. "Linda? No! You're sick, Antón, you know that?"

"SICK?" I shouted, really losing it now. "It would be perfectly normal, dear brother, seeing Linda, to imagine getting her in the sack. That would be the healthy thing to do, why talk shit? Are you telling me YOU HAVEN'T EVEN FANTASIZED ABOUT FUCKING HER? Never even thought about STICKING YOUR TINY COCK INSIDE HER?"

Was this what it was like when you lost your temper, Vidor? Zoltan turned his back on me, incensed and ashamed, and I headed for the exit. When Linda said goodbye I detected a note of compassion, that unbearable *poor Antón* look that's followed me everywhere this last year, and as she handed me my gray jacket I asked for her phone number, to get my own back on the both of them. She didn't seem to mind, but it's also quite possible that, if she'd heard me shouting before, she would have made something up out of sheer fright.

Coming down onto the street I felt so ridiculous about the scene I'd caused, and for having asked for Linda's number, that I headed straight for the nearest bar. It was a dingy place, the floor filthy covered with prawn skins and all manner of leftovers, and there were various lonely drinkers keeping themselves to themselves. Normal people, or good people, or people lacking imagination, have no idea just how easily day turns into night, or dreams into nightmares. How do they survive, I asked myself, how can there be so many people in the cities doing nothing at all, just vegetating, people who no advertising campaigns would ever target before one o'clock in the morning? I ordered a whiskey. Then another. There was a moment when I remembered having sworn to try and be optimistic and that I had neither right nor reason to be so immature and antisocial, which was when I ordered yet another. Nothing is sadder than bland post-adolescence, than the ruins of adolescence, I said to myself. I didn't cry. I didn't complain. I didn't tell my life story to the drunk next to me. I just drank. And, as I drank, I thought, what's the point of drinking, I'm not even an alcoholic, I've never even felt the desire to obliterate myself, at least not consciously.

I should go to bed now, it's past five o'clock in the morning and I'm exhausted. The sky's covered over, there aren't any stars. Just the cold and a deceitful quiet. I hope sleep comes quickly.

*Thursday, October 15, 2009*

The world we live in pretends to be better than it really is. Countries, governments, businesses, products, people, everyone and everything only put their best foot forward (and all the same it's appalling, outrageous, sick). Here on planet earth our prime concern is to sweep the shit under the carpet and carry on regardless. If we explained to future generations what life's really like and then asked them if they still felt like joining us, none of them would choose to be born, or only the worst kind, the masochists, the dimwits, the scatterbrains, or the saints, who definitely come within this sorry confederation. *And?* Well might you ask, Vidor. Where's this little speech of mine headed? I, a twenty-first century individual who's already here, who was never consulted about wanting to be born, am making an effort to be an optimist, and the point I'm coming to is that maybe that isn't so strange. It's the appropriate, *the elegant thing* to do. Don't cry, smile. Keep on smiling, brother, keep on smiling!

Bela still isn't answering. I left a message. Maybe she's had another fight with John Grant, her partner, if I can call him that. There's also the time difference between Spain and the US, which is such a pain; you have to schedule in phone calls. At midday today, when I got out of bed and went to the fridge for orange juice, seeing the dull daylight coming in from the balcony, the cardboard boxes encroaching on the living room, the wires hanging down from the kitchen ceiling, the general disarray, I decided enough is enough. If I plan to get my act together and put my days as a pitiful victim behind me, the first thing is to make my apartment vaguely liveable. There can be no happiness in doing nothing, or in untidiness, neither for the ascetic nor the devil, both of whom are experts in their respective fields. I showered, had a breakfast of coffee and toast, put on a CD of *Nora* (the opera), and started putting things in order. I ought to get rid of everything I wasn't able to throw away when I moved. Make the apartment memoryless, clear it of anything that binds me even more strongly to the past. I also ironed a mountain of clothes and I swept the floor.

At six o'clock in the evening I went to buy some lamps from Simsum and, at about seven, having set them up in the kitchen, I came across the books Zoltan gave me (or lent me? Must check: You never know with him). Let's see: *The Psychology of Optimism* by Susan C. Vaughan, ingeniously described as *Glass Half Empty or Glass Half Full; The Power of Optimism* by Luis Rojas Marcos; *Your Erroneous Zones* by Wayne W. Dyer, also brilliantly described, *Step-by-Step Advice for Escaping the Trap of Negative Thinking and Taking Control of Your Life; Alain on Happiness* by Alain; *The Conquest of Happiness* by Bertrand Russell. The titles alone were enough to make me want to vomit, Vidor, but

I haven't forgotten my promise; I mean to keep it. After all, it would overall be a good thing if these idiots were right and happiness were nothing but a question of personal discipline, of iron will plus agreeable disposition, and if luck had nothing to do with it, nor circumstances, nor genes, nor a lack of intelligence, nor a combination of all of the above.

I've made myself a dinner tray and started reading, beginning with Ms. Susan Vaughan's monstrosity. Suzy has another bestseller to her name, *Viagra*. Mmmmm ... Can't wait to rush out and buy that one. I picture her in the company of her girlfriends, in some loft, all very Manhattan super-Manhattan eating super-sushi, everyone super-happy, ha! ha! ha! go on, a little more sake, oh okay, pass me the Viagra, and a Lexatin while you're at it! Ha! *Fascinating* ... After giving myself indigestion with a hundred pages of that, I threw it in the trash and gave *Your Erroneous Zones* a go ... Back to cleaning, until one o'clock in the morning.

Nothing in the world makes me feel a charge of optimism like getting rid of a book I can't bear, and feeling not a jot of guilt, only pleasure. Who ever said we shouldn't throw books in the trash? Who ever said there's *anything* that isn't better off in the trash?


*Friday, October 16, 2009*

Now to pick everything up, and open all the envelopes, the piles and piles of letters, all the condolences, invitations, bank statements and bills, as well as the tremendous prizes I've won merely for having the name Antón Mallick; a whole year of throwing them in a pile in the room that I'd intended as my study but ended up becoming a trash can instead. Bela finally rang. She and John are fine, she swears. Her students still aren't paying attention in her classes. The other staff members at the University still consider her an efficient and valuable member of the team. Pau Gasol's Lakers beat The Celtics. John's still working on his novel. She doesn't feel Spanish, but she doesn't feel American either.

Nothing new, Vidor. Bela, without quite being an optimist, is a reasonably happy woman, or at least she was before she went to the States and moved in with John. She has a lightness about her, and she's witty too, with a touch of malice and an infectious laugh, like a flea-ridden dog. Unlike me, she's a fighter, she has this capacity to make light of her problems. We've always leaned on one another. I've always told her everything and it's never been an effort to convince her I'm telling the truth. And what she says in this case might be right: maybe Mystery Woman is nothing more than a Fury, or a Clown on the Loose—but it's still a bit worrying that she knew my name. It's also fair to say that I've encountered quite a lot of people lately when I've been somewhat worse for wear, and often in the dark too. It's altogether more likely that they'd remember my name—and not at all fondly—than I would theirs or them, and possible as well that I might have had relations with lunatics without knowing it, or only half-knowing it, or thinking they were only circumstantially lunatic, or simply mobile distributors of prohibited substances. Bela's view is that if this Mrs. Fury or Mystery Woman or Lady Upsetter really is pregnant by me, and wants something from me— money, most likely, let's not kid ourselves, Vidor, I can't

25

fathom she'd want "responsibility" or that other word, the one they use in romantic novels, in films, in advertising campaigns, and in hushed, earnest conversations, that four-letter word, "love"—she'll track me down soon enough. She's wise, my sister. Talking to her always calms me down.

She laughed when I told her about my diary and about the books Zoltan lent me. She promised to send me some books of hers that touch on optimism and happiness, even if only in passing. They're bound to be better than my big brother's self-help books.

It's two o'clock in the morning and still sleep won't come. My personal ghosts have decided to intrude on me. I've just finished *Your Erroneous Zones*. When I read essays, I usually underline phrases and make notes in the book itself. Now that Zoltan and Bela have decided to set me off on these text adventures, I've decided to include some notes in my diary on what I'm reading. So, I'm going to tell My Story and, at the same time, The Story of My Ideas (two things that, naturally enough, might be at odds). I want to know how I read these books, what reflections they prompt in me, whether reading them really changes my concept of happiness. Is happiness possible? We'll see. Repeat ten times before going to sleep: "Yes, yes, it's possible, yes."

NOTES ON ZOLTAN'S BOOKS

On *Your Erroneous Zones* (1978) by Wayne W. Dyer.

Okay. This is the first self-help book I've ever read, Vidor, though I have come close to buying one on numerous occasions in the past. The idea of *Your Erroneous Zones* is to help me be happier, to combat my systemic pessimism — to be more like you, right? If someone is trying to transmit a certain optimism through the book, the first thing that person should do, so as not to drive the readers up the wall, is understand how to think and how to convey ideas. Wouldn't you agree, Vidor? *Do things properly.* Unfortunately, Mr. Dyer doesn't seem to be of this opinion. I also suspect he may have been translated into Spanish by his very worst enemy. But he couldn't care less. He doesn't give a damn about his readers, he doesn't give a damn about the dictionary, grammar, philosophy, anything, and meanwhile, he's on top of the world, just like ol' Suzy Vaughan (I can very much see the two of them settling down to a nice bit of super-sushi together). To whet your appetite, he claims his book is amazing (which says a lot about his humility, his manners, etc.). Self-help books, Vidor, are a kind of electroshock therapy for people who are marginalized, insecure, desperate, ignorant, innocent and losers (like me). Mr. Dyer approaches optimism with the shabbiest and most degrading kind of mental plastic surgery. How can I put it, Vidor? At six o'clock in the evening I took a break from reading my backlog of emails and watched half an hour of a porn movie I bought the other day at the newsstand. Okay then: porn is to sex what self-help books are to thought. And Dyer's book is something akin to the kind of porn flick where a dying slut gets humped by a guy with a nutsack as big as an elephant's. If you see what I mean.

Writers cited by Mr. Dyer: Herman Hesse, D. H. Lawrence, Lewis Carroll, Tolstoy. These are to be grouped together under the heading: WRITERS NOT TO BE TRUSTED. And in Einstein's case, whom Dyer also quotes, PHYSICIST NOT TO BE TRUSTED, or maybe, if you like, UNTRUSTWORTHY GENIUS.

Aggressive, threatening undertones, a lack of subtlety, extremist behaviorism. He tricks the reader with swindling syllogisms to prove where there's a will there's a way; he attacks honesty, values, friendship; he extols one hundred percent sincerity; he makes fun of suicide: Self-help *strengthens* the ego via childish prescriptions. It's all about not needing anyone else to make you happy, not feeling guilty, not worrying, boosting your creativity (as easy as reheating pizzas, possibly, given that Mr. Dyer's ideas of "creativity" could just as well be applied to apes), breaking with the past, living in the present, being free from other people and all forms of responsibility . . . How is this different from the shyster simplicity of advertising? A + B = C. Easy as pie. Better not let chance into the equation, better not mention anything about life moving mysteriously, or the profound complexity of relationships and feelings . . . Mr. Dyer's readers might well end up being happy, their disposition might indeed become sunnier, but they'll also end up alone, turned into monsters, psychopaths surrounded by chopped-up bodies, including, sooner or later, their own.

Vocabulary used by Mr. Dyer, a man dubbed by his (many) enemies as the Bulldozer of Language and by his (not very many) friends, Linguistic Murderer:
- self-fulfilling and self-defeating behaviors
- anti-growth

- self-acceptance
- self-veto
- underappreciation systems
- scapegoat messenger (who blames everyone else, mind you)
- mini-depressions . . .

What can I tell you, Mr. Dyer? You, sir, are a swine. A few more books like yours and there's no way I'm getting out of this rut. I am trying to be an optimist, and you are a champion of people's desire to be optimistic, so in a way we should be brothers, bosom buddies, but I'm afraid that if you and I ever met, I'd find it altogether necessary to spit in your face. I'm sorry to be so blunt but I find everything about you and your scheming deeply depressing.

*Sunday, October 18, 2009*

Vidor, I've been to see my nephews today, I've just got home and I'm exhausted. Let's chat. In your memoirs, you said you loved your wife "profusely." Every single day, unless you were away travelling (which was actually rather frequently), you'd "literally" prostrate yourself before her, sometimes you'd even kiss her feet, something she didn't appreciate in the slightest, to the point that she once kicked you in the face. You also say that you used to play guitar for her on the afternoons and evenings when you didn't have to attend to "pressing matters of business." But when you did go out, clearly very often it was to visit your many lady friends; "these Señoritas and Señoras from Madrid and the provinces, with their *mantillas* and *peinetas*, so traditional, who whipped off their clothes with surprising acuity, and who knew more about sex than they dared to admit but still less than everyone, them included, would like."

I wonder if you ever loved women other than your wife, or if you never really loved any of them, including her. Sometimes, when you describe your mistresses, it seems as though what you really loved was winning their hearts, the very fact of being intimate with multiple women at the same time, being able to converse with various ladies in various states of undress lying in various beds around the city. You probably paid, or at least had to shower them with presents. They were your safety valve, your only way of avoiding death by boredom or overwork. As for me, Vidor, I was only *truly* in love once. The other times it's been mere obsession—unhealthy, harrying desire; brutal, all-encompassing compulsion—which lasted until I finally possessed the woman in question; at that very same moment, as she was only an idea in my head, she vanished. What you had with your mistresses was always playful; my relationships, especially lately, have been darker, less free, more compulsive.

Obsessed. That's what I am with Lady Ghostgirl. I know she has dark hair, light skin, and I think she was attractive, although I could just as well have made that part up. Flat nose. Big mouth? Not sure . . . I'd be willing to bet she wasn't fat, short, and she wasn't a heffalump either . . . I've racked my brains for who she could possibly be. It hasn't been fun. In fact, it's been rather painful. I want to find some calm now, and going over and over everything I've done this past year really doesn't help. I know I've been to bed with about twenty women. To be precise, I've fucked roughly eighteen, stayed over with only a couple of them. Hardly a world record. But the problem is I've only got the phone numbers of the two I had a more or less "normal relationship" with. Chat, make a date, have dinner, see a movie, copulate, see them again, don't see them again (if something like this can really be considered "normal," bearing in mind I felt nothing for any of them aside from a certain disdain because they were attracted to me, because they put up with me, and, at the same time, because I knew they were unable to save me). And neither of those two were Mystery Woman. I scrubbed the rest from my memory, including their phone numbers, if I ever had them. All that remains now are encounters, moments, flashes, a line, sounds, an unmade bed, a laugh, loving whispers, dirty talk, but . . .

I thought briefly that it might be Kris, an engineering student, addicted to every drug on the market, but I seriously doubt it. We had one repeat (comatose) encounter, and I'm sure she had green eyes like a cat. I remember she was a good dancer and had a sense of humor . . . I also thought it could have been Teresa, a brunette who went on and on about her son; but no, it definitely wasn't her either. Who then? The worst, and, why not, funniest thing was unearthing one conveniently repressed memory: the time I was getting a blowjob from some woman in some dive, and me virtually asleep standing up, her really going for it, suck suck suck, to no avail, until suddenly she stopped, lifted up her head and looked at me with her dark eyes and silicone lips, and said: "You know I'm a guy, right?" And I almost fell over laughing, we both did, and I gave him a fifty and got the hell out of there. I didn't count *him* amongst my twenty brief encounters . . . But so who the hell are you, you Capital Bitch? And where the hell are you? What are you doing? Why do you want to make my life a misery? Isn't it enough to know that I'm a wreck? Who told you to go and have my baby? Why don't you go and jump off a cliff?

ADVICE AND CURIOUS PHRASES FROM
*CONFESSIONS OF A ONCE-HUNGARIAN SPANIARD*

"Once upon a time there was a pair of twins named Hunor and Mogor, a valiant and vigorous pair. One day, strolling through the forests, they laid eyes on the handsomest stag in the world. Since they were both hunters and not poets, they decided to slay it, but every time they tried to come near, the stag evaded them. Without realizing it, enthused with the chase, they came all the way to the mouth of the Don on the Black Sea. The stag vanished in the mists. Then, seeing what a wonderful place they'd come to, the brothers decided to stay and settle there. Hunor and Mogor were the first Huns, and from the Huns came the Magyars. Now, how's that for a nonsense founding myth? And not just any founding myth—our founding myth."

"If you walk down the street and see a woman smiling at you, it can only be one of two things: either there's a child holding your hand, or the woman's a prostitute."

" . . . and to this very day Madrid, with its air of a large happy barn, and its heavenly skies, still captivates me."

"Nothing is useless, but many people are."

"If you want to abduct Señora S. you won't need a Turk in a pirate ship. Books, damn them, will suffice . . . "

"Love, according to what I've just been told by a street peanut vendor, is man's invention to align himself with the universe and forget death for awhile."

"I only had to glance at the other players at the table and I knew already who was going to end up with strawberry cake, and who'd have to make do with the crumbs."

"For charm, only a woman with a fan can do better than her."

"Another historical Hungarian whom I respect even more than myself: Lél, a tenth century military commander. There was a Bavarian uprising against Emperor Otto I, and they asked the Magyars to assist them. In 995, at the Battle of Augsburg, the rebels were crushed. Lél was brought before the German sovereign. They offered him wine in a hunting horn. Suddenly, he shouted: "In the next life, you will be my slave!" and before anyone could stop him, stabbed the horn into Otto I's neck, killing him on the spot. Naturally, he was put to death that very same day."

"Every circus needs its clowns."

"At home, so no one will understand me, when I get angry I let off steam by shouting in Hungarian. This was until, one night recently, a maid who I thought was mute and, anyway, half out of her mind, turned beet red and answered me, in Hungarian, using some very ugly words to boot. Then I knew she was no mute, nor was she half out of her mind: she was one of my wife's spies. She knew everything. I had to pay her handsomely to make her disappear. I imagine that, wherever she is now, she must be known as The Hungarian Duchess."

"My father used to say that between a great idea and a decent goulash, he'd chose the goulash every time. This gives an idea of my father's wit, as well as how hungry he was."

33

"You can't be off work for a year, Antón. We need you."

Silence. It's eleven o'clock in the morning and by some miracle I'm awake. The voice at the other end of the line belongs to the Director General of reinsurance multinational Apri's Southern Europe Division, a German. Why German? What does a German know about Southern Europe? What do I know about Germans? What on earth's going on?

"The department's made a start and it's absolute chaos. No one knows a thing about satellites. We've already signed the confidentiality agreement with Hispaniasat."

Silence. I have no idea what to say. Am I ready? Not yet? Will I be able to bear it? Can I afford to miss the boat? Am I, as Bela thinks, "capable of anything, at any time," or am I actually done for at thirty-two years of age?

"We can't do it from London, Paris or New York. It has to be from Madrid, and you know it, Antón. *Right next to* the client."

Silence. All this work to try and become an optimist and when your boss rings begging you to come back, you're totally unable to utter one single word. What kind of idiot . . .

"Fine, I'll leave it with you. If you decide to come back to us, give Ken a call. And whatever you need, Antón, just ask. One step at a time. I'll let you go now. I've got another call coming in, *un abrazo*, bye-bye."

Click. Klaus Richter hung up. The Bavarian Whale, as he's known to the more rebellious of the Southern European employees, hung up. It isn't every day The Whale gets down on his knees for you. Clearly it must have been the client who asked for me to act as go-between with the insurance people. I'm the only one in Apri South with any experience of satellite policies. My employers aren't all bad, but they're hardly a charity either. I know full well that the only way to construct a reasonable life is by introducing a semblance of order, a routine to enable you to find some balance, a structure to keep the madness at bay. In other words, you have to work. Stand still, and the ghosts will devour you. The Whale needs me, and I need to work to focus myself, plus I'm way into my overdraft. I need to *pénzt keresni*, as you'd put it, Vidor: earn some cash. It doesn't seem like a complicated equation. You were the one who said: "Walls shouldn't be attacked head on, in the manner of a ram, but side on, in the way that sharks attack." I'm going to have to take side bites.

I spent the rest of the day putting my apartment in order and weighing up my answer. I'd accept if they let me work from home and only have to go to the office for meetings. Richter won't mind, as long as I agree to a medical including a psychological evaluation. It isn't as if insurance multinationals are known for exposing themselves unnecessarily to risk; it's their job to quantify the stuff and turn it into profit. One step at a time. I was going through my wardrobes and, just as *The Miraculous Mandarin* came on and I'd finished filling two trash bags with clothes, I found my running shoes. They were covered in a clayey, orange-colored mud, and I knew full well how and where they got like that. I remember who was running alongside me. And her laughter at seeing me covered in sweat. One year, two months and twenty days ago, it was.

This was sheer treachery on the part of my memory, and I knew another of my anguish attacks was coming. My brain couldn't have cared less about the ten milligrams of Alprazolam I'd taken not long before. Here it comes, said my brain, here it comes. I looked at the clock. Twenty-five past seven. And on it came ... Suddenly I wasn't me, my soul or my spirit or my consciousness or my being or whatever it is departed my body and set up in the roof above me, watching me, or, more precisely, watching my empty-of-me-body, like from a surveillance tower. And that was when I wanted to die, or explode, or dissolve, no, no, no, no, I'm no-one, no, I don't exist, what's happening to me, *noooo* . . . One minute and twenty-five seconds. You didn't come into my mind, Vidor, it was a memory of Uncle Juan I reached out for to save me. I don't know if my cry for help worked. The attack stopped as suddenly as it had begun, just like that. Who was the first troublemaker to measure physical time? Does anyone know of a way of timing horror? No doubt it was an optimist, someone who believed man was going to be able to put the universe in a box and study it until all the questions had been answered; some eminent sonofabitch. One minute and twenty-five seconds of not being me is equal to the horror an optimist experiences in the course of his or her whole life, and that's probably being generous. Anyone who's passed through the terror of that emptiness can never be the same when they come back. With every attack, I'm convinced that a part of me dies.

Then I put my sneakers on. And I saw two Antóns when I looked in the mirror—no trick of the mind. My mother says that an obese person is not one, but two people; there's the one we see, and there's the one that's locked inside, swaddled in fat, the latter being the true person but also the one who, having been kidnapped by the evil, exterior one, can never talk or stick up for itself. There are thin men who we see, out in the open, and there are also thin men under the lock and key of obesity, defeated, imprisoned inside the body of a fat person. In my mother's eyes, all fat people are bad, even though they have good, slim, healthy people inside them. This is why when my mother speaks to anyone who's fat, she tries to make it so her voice reaches the thin person trapped inside, she encourages them to free themselves, to destroy the fat person, and then she starts shouting. This makes for fairly surreal conversations between her and fat people, who usually end up putting their fingers in their ears. But that's my mother for you. Me, I'm 5' 5" feet and 180 pounds, and the exterior Antón is controlling my body, enveloping the true Antón, suffocating him. My mother wouldn't be able to stand seeing me like this.

Antón#2 must be destroyed. Work must be resumed. The crisis mustn't spiral. Mystery Woman must be found.

I have a full agenda.

## NOTES ON ZOLTAN'S BOOKS

*On The Conquest of Happiness* by Bertrand Russell (1872-1970)

I've been reading Russell by night, whiskey in hand, classical music in the background. He's an honest man who speaks of happiness and optimism in measured tones. I don't advise that anyone read him after a couple of drinks or while drinking. You'll find yourself overwhelmed by the urge to commit torturous acts upon him, to desecrate his grave, to rampage amongst his lovely flower beds, to humiliate his butler, to stamp on his wife's poodle's testicles.

R. calls for you to reflect on the happiness that comes about through calm and honesty, through having respected a few basic values. The happiness of being able to look yourself in the eye, of having confidence in yourself while staying humble, of accepting yourself, including your defects. That is, the happiness of common sense, which isn't actually happiness, which has a touch of mere survival, of honorable defeat, of glass-half-full, of a mediocre life, no spice in it. It's like visiting a psychologist of Zoltan's ilk: it feels good, but don't even think about expecting to feel any intellectual pleasure, or inspiration, or courage. Russell's weapon of choice is common sense, like people who are always quoting bits of popular wisdom and old adages, and never come to any remotely interesting conclusions, or show you a different perspective. Common sense has its uses, for the common man it can even be a great resource, because, paradoxically, it isn't all that common: but *it isn't enough, it falls short*. Most of Russell's advice is sound, and he often has a point, and there's a nice touch of mischief. He never achieves great heights, but he does walk in a straight line. His idealized concept of the Soviet Union is pathetic (you wonder if he had any idea what really went on there, or if simply he was a hypocritical pig), and the way, among other nonsense, he talks about the ambience of factories being humane and calming.

*Thursday, October 22, 2009*

Clea. The last time I left her she was dancing to some insufferable song, eyes shut, a frighteningly taut smile on her face, and I swore I'd never see her again. But I wouldn't exactly define myself as a promise-keeping kind of person. It got to nine o'clock last night and I couldn't stand staying at home a moment longer. I felt very lonely. I missed my sister, my mother, and I missed religion—or, to be precise, I missed having faith in God, in Paradise, in Supreme Goodness. I didn't even change clothes. I walked the fifteen minutes to Calle de la Reina, a spring in my step. It's a nice walk, up my street, which is Calle Moratín, turning on Costanilla de los Desamparados and strolling through the Letras and Cortes neighborhoods as far as the Gran Vía. Each person I passed, I tried to make eye contact with: when they returned my gaze, I looked away. Time and time again that's how it's been, my whole life, as long as I can remember.

I got to Del Diego's, sat at the small table in the corner and asked for a virgin cocktail. I don't remember which one, I've chosen to forget it. Should it really be allowed—virgin cocktails calling themselves cocktails? I took out a paperback, well thumbed by Zoltan: *Alain on Happiness*, by Alain, a gossipy French philosopher. Him, his trifling adages, three glasses of water and two highly elaborate juices helped me kill time. I finished the book at two o'clock in the morning and called Clea. The conversations were so loud in there that I could barely hear the ringtone. Part of me didn't want her to pick up the phone, a feeling I have quite often when I call people, a kind of terror in the face of the imminent conversation, in the face of the so often ramped-up expectations of the person receiving the call. But she picked up.

"Hello? Antón? Is that you? Damn, you're still alive, you sonofabitch!"

I went by my usual bar to buy the cocaine, chatted music with the numbskull dealer and by three o'clock Clea was at my side and we were knocking on the door of one of these unwholesome dives where I/we used to hang out. They opened the peephole and as they looked us up and down before letting us in, I thought this was all back to front, that it was us who should have been deciding whether we wanted to let that which lay on the other side of the door enter our lives. But perhaps we'd already made that decision, and a long time ago.

I passed Clea the wrap and, in the words of my friend Carlos, "I abstained." I watched her as she snorted a couple of lines. Clea the coke fiend. Was she really a nurse? Maybe she was, a locum, a replacement here and there for a few months, that sort of thing. Or she'd been ten years in the same job, salary raise after salary raise. How would I know? She wasn't pretty, which in fact had nothing to do with her features but rather the fact her face was constantly gurning. Many nights Clea had been my guide, in exchange for which I paid her way. At that time I still believed that going out all night it was purely a sociological pursuit, or nocturnal tourism, or a way of combating stress, of forgetting myself, or unwinding, or finding myself by losing myself, never realizing that what I was doing was falling apart. We'd go to a bar until two or three in the morning and we'd go to an after-hours club. She showed me the Madrid of tense jaws and ludicrous conversations, endless nights of trailing from bar to bar, almost always the same ones, round and round on the merry-go-round, and on, a day, two days, three. The sun might come up and the light of day filter through the cracks in some barred-up window, but the nights never ended, they went on and on, until the drugs ran out and you'd pull up suddenly, head home to knock yourself out with a tranquilizer . . .

"I knew you'd be back," said Clea, smiling. "You're no fucking tourist, you're—"

"You have to help me," I said, interrupting her.

Clea glanced across at me, half intrigued, half shocked, as she applied bright red lipstick.

"Seeing planes or something?"

I told her about Mystery Woman, and Clea burst out laughing.

"This another one of your stories to keep you awake at night? Why does weird shit always happen to you, Antón? Trying to stand out, or what? You don't need drugs to get messed up, do you? You're pitiful."

Clea, strangely, has an excellent memory. We ran through the nights I'd been out with her, and she could remember every single one of the girls or women we'd spoken to, all the more if there'd been any incidents in the toilets, or if I'd left the bar with a girl. It was fun, just as it was unnerving, trying to piece it all together with her.

"It was her, the one with the light blue glasses, you got it on with her because of the coke. It obviously wasn't because of your pretty face. You talk so much bullshit, you come out with so much nonsense . . ."

41

Clea babbled on, and she'd already made sure that the wrap was safely stowed in her tiny silver purse. I started to feel worn out by all the squalor, all the absurdity. What was I doing asking after the person who might be the mother of my child in some almost pitch-black dive, everyone around me off their heads? What was the world on about? What had happened to me?

"I'm leaving, Clea."

"Huh?"

"I said I'm out of here. Bye."

"You know best."

It was cold outside. End of October, Madrid, cold. Who'd made me go out in shirt and cotton jacket? In the end my tale had shrunk to the point where I'd become a complete retard, or, sorry, *special abilities*—wouldn't want to offend anyone. I turned the collar up on my sports jacket and walked along hunched up, casting around for a taxi on that deserted street. But then my phone buzzed. A message from Clea:

*Lucía. Pounced on you in El Chino. Brunette. She wanted hanky-panky. Bye.*

I was about to go back and try to find Clea again, to get her to expand, but just then an empty taxi miraculously came by and I hailed it. Who knows. Maybe I knew that if I took that taxi I'd never see Clea again, and that cheered me up.

Lucía. In El Chino. Could it be her? Brunette, flat nose, neither particularly fat nor thin . . . Unfortunately, that particular night I was stoned out of my mind, and for all I racked my brains as the taxi drove down Gran Vía, I came up with few details. Only that it was a very strange night.

She didn't ask for a drink or anything and, just as Clea said, pounced on me suddenly, dragging me off to the toilets. I reacted to the experiment like a mouse in a lab, submitting in the name of science. But after that . . . Did we do it there? I've got an image of this Lucía with her elbow propped on my chest, in the half-light. Crying? Why was she crying? Where, when? Was that the same night? Lucía. At least I've got a name. Not Mystery Woman any more. Being positive about things, it would be best just to call her Lucía from now on. The woman who's going to save me.

*Saturday, October 24, 2009*

One day a well-known banker went to his country estate, accompanied by several of his advisers. On the way, there was a hundred-year-old oak tree, and when they came past it the banker pointed and cried: "This oak tree must be insured!" His advisers, intelligent men but not very brave, though they asked themselves why their employer might want to insure the tree, kept their mouths shut. They endeavoured to find an insurance policy that would cover the venerable old oak. They moved heaven and earth, alas no such policy existed, but they managed it nonetheless. Pleased with their work, they informed the banker, only to be greeted with incomprehension on his part. What he'd meant was that the trunk and main branches should be propped up to prevent them from falling down: he wanted to ENsure the tree, not to INsure it. He wanted a gardener, not an insurance broker. But how much did it cost to insure the tree?

On another day, in one of the matches in the "Copa del Rey", a player from a second tier team broke the leg of a player from a La Liga side, the top division. The La Liga player was from a powerful club, plus he was first choice, a striker, famous—a top player. The assailant was a part timer, a plumber. It was an ugly tackle, studs up, borne out of envy maybe, maybe helplessness. The referee showed the plumber a straight red. Early shower for him! The forward was operated on, but never got back to his best. Anyway. The victim's leg was insured. What happened?

I actually have no idea how much it cost to insure the oak tree, or how things turned out for the injured footballer, but what I do know is that I've always enjoyed working on strange policies like these. Legs belonging to famous soccer players or to models, hundred-year-old oak trees, election defeats, your children suffering career setbacks, a child losing its milk teeth prematurely, box office flops, unexpectedly deflated erections, you name it. The line between insurance and betting is vanishingly thin. When I studied Law and Economics I looked for work in a company that would cover strange risks, but they only exist in London, that kingdom of insurance, and even during the years I spent working there, I never got to process such juicy policies. It can sometimes be shocking to recall why you chose your profession, but now that I want to be an optimist, I am indifferent to the fact that I might have become a judge, an accountant, an astronaut, and that I wouldn't have liked being an artist, singer, actor or any of your "creative" type jobs. I've got my own house (mortgaged, but, in my eyes, mine), I'm good at what I do and, all things considered, I work with pretty unusual insurance. My profession isn't the problem.

I've signed off policies on artworks, on bank clerks revealing confidential information, on kidnappings and terrorism, to name a few examples. And for a couple of years I also worked in contaminated products. Germany, I assure you, is a swindler's paradise when it comes to adulterated products, as in intentional, malicious, not at all accidental contamination. They'll spoil children's shampoos, jars of sausages, tins of sauerkraut, frozen pizzas, pickles—anything—regardless of whether the products are made there or imported; when it comes to business there are no nationalists, unless it's profitable to be one. They'll use glass, nails, toxic products—no holds barred. And, knowing that, for companies, public image is everything, they can call up demanding ridiculous sums. Sometimes they get what they want, sometimes people don't pay out, and sometimes they get thrown in jail. I've also drawn up policies like these in Spain, but my speciality in recent years has been satellites. There are two currently in orbit that I've worked on and now, if all goes according to plan, I'm onto my third.

They told me yesterday that I'd passed the medical, although I have to see the company psychiatrist once every fifteen days for a while. I stopped by the office on Calle Mejía Lequerica and it felt strange, after six months away, seeing the building's pale pink façade, the plaster cornice, the entranceway with the receptionist Marga in it, my office and colleagues. Fran, a buddy of mine at work, was angry at me for having been out of touch for two months, even after The Whale rang. He's right in a way, but I've been so worn out. When they left me on my own, I was on the verge of breaking down, but managed to contain myself, because I refuse to be a same-as-all-the-rest victim, your everyday contemporary Western orphan, frail, understanding, tolerant, sensitive and hypocritical. They've given me the laptop, the mobile, the passwords, a shared secretary and a work agenda. Back to having an identity.

I celebrated by dining alone at La Vaca Verónica, on Calle Moratín, a short walk from my house, near the Plaza de la Platería. Water, T-bone green pepper steak with roast potatoes followed by chocolate mousse. I spent half the meal chatting on the mobile with Bela, using the headset, and I suppose the other clients in the restaurant must have thought I was a madman who talks to himself. Bela's thrilled at the news and has promised to send me the box of books straight away, which she's already prepared.

Fran and I have arranged to meet tonight to go looking for Lusty Lucía. The idea that the embryo of a child of mine is growing, and that, furthermore, it's doing so inside a sociopath who is probably hooked on every toxic substance in the market, is enough to make my hairs stand on end. We'll see.

NOTES ON ZOLTAN'S BOOKS

I almost forgot about my reading session at Del Diego's, with the virgin-pseudo-cocktail and mineral water, pleased with myself for being able, at least for a few hours, to concentrate while surrounded by drunkards and loudmouths, by people apparently at ease in the world.

*Alain on Happiness* (1928), by Emile Chartier, pen name Alain (1868-1951).

Alain, minor French philosopher, best known for his "propos" or short reflections, of which he wrote no less than 5,000. Simple, personal, you could almost say folksy, finding inspiration in other's works. An outdated journalist writing for an outdated newspaper.

Trifles such as: "And there is more intention in happiness than is generally believed." Or indeed: "I would even dare to suggest, that a kind of civic crown be awarded to men who put their minds to trying to be happy." I don't plan on getting that crown myself, Alain. I'd feel silly. Anyway. Being French, a nice guy and a philosopher is all fine and well, but it doesn't score you that many points. What you do, when it comes down to it, is self-help with frills, 1920's style. Claiming you're a philosopher, when your starting point is the idea that it's better not to think . . . Chin up, Antón, don't let the well-intentioned type and nice guys drag you down! Some wicked soul will be along to save you soon enough!

*Sunday, October 25, 2009*

"Right, so, this is the place where . . . ? You're sick, Antón. This is too much, even for you."

Fran Hidalgo spoke these words to me yesterday, Saturday, as we were relieving ourselves in the sinister washroom of El Chino, the after-bar in which I believe I fucked Lucía the Uninhibited, or at least where she and I met. It's a dark and pretty trashy bar, full of mirrors, old-fashioned, with an air of having once been a hostess bar. I'm not sure if the amorous encounter itself happened there or elsewhere, going back didn't refresh my memory. I do remember now that she had a short boyish haircut, that she looked about twenty-five, and that we were both stoned out of our minds. I asked the waiters about a Lucía fitting such a description, but she can't have been a regular and no one remembered her. Even bringing out a twenty-euro bill like in the movies failed to jog their memories.

"Forget about her, Antón. It was all a bad dream. The only beings that can be conceived in places like this are . . . goodness knows! Freaks, monsters! Fuck! Put her out of your mind once and for all, focus on your work and on getting yourself a normal woman, you've given enough to this now, God, spending the whole day cooped up by yourself, shit, turning it over and over in your head."

If society could speak it would say that Fran, as well as needing to wash his mouth out, is a model citizen, a little over forty years of age and an upright individual, a good husband and father, and a great friend. And in a sense this is all true, but it's also true that he feels stifled by his wife, Sandra, and their three kids, that all he thinks about is sex, that he's becoming more and more prejudiced with time, and that any day now he's going to cause some scandal of front page proportions. He's a lawyer at Apri, he heads up the legal department, and he was one of the main reasons I decided to go back. Since we met, four years ago, when I first took the job, he's been like a father to me.

"The trouble with you, Antón, is you're a romantic. So you obsess over things, you stew, you think you're different, but when it comes down to it you're just a poor wretch like me, or like this guy," he said, gesturing to one of the truly unwashed, a guy asleep in one of the cubicles, his head in the lap of a deeply unattractive woman with a face like a wrinkled clove of garlic. "But if you've got a Hungarian last name, fuck! Can you imagine? Life is really just about grinning and bearing it, staying on the straight and narrow, sticking to the path. And not wanting to puke every time you catch a glimpse of yourself in the mirror. And your wife and kids not feeling sick either when you walk in the door . . . What's the time? Let's get out of this hellhole, shit!"

What I like about Fran is his directness, his high-mindedness and his loyalty. His blond, strawy hair, his clear, drooping eyes, his rosy skin, always squeaky clean as though he's just stepped out of the shower, his thick, welcoming figure, and his tailored suits—not overly elegant—make him look slightly like a Saint Bernard (the dog, I mean). In a bar after work on Friday, I confessed to him that it looked like I was going to have a child, the circumstances of the conception, my encounter with the mother, and that I'd decided to try and find her. He nearly wept. In fact it was me who had to cheer him up. Downing a couple of large whiskeys, he kept quiet until I pointed out that it wasn't the end of the world, that I wasn't the first person something like this had happened to.

"Before, you had a family of your own," he said, literally holding back the tears. "Now you're off pursuing another

49

one you don't even know. Jesus, Antón. You don't do things by halves."

My response, partly because I wanted to show my fortitude, partly because I believed it to be true, was to call him old-fashioned. The idea of family, I said, had evolved (NB, Vidor, the use of this optimistic term, the kind of positive phrase that someone who believes in progress would use). I argued that nothing was set in stone, and that families, just like every other supposedly sacrosanct institution, would have to adapt to the changing times and come up with original answers both in terms of modern relationships and abiding emotional needs, and that perhaps I was going to form just such a twenty-first century family.

"That's if you manage to track her down," said Fran, still deadly serious.

"Clearly," I conceded. "Of course."

"Which remains to be seen, right? For now all there is, and god knows where, is a little sprog floating around in a belly, deaf, dumb and blind, with an absent father and a mother who is probably a basket case."

"Lovely picture you've painted there, Fran. You forget that she could be perfectly normal. She could even be a really wonderful person."

"Honestly, Antón, I don't get how you can think about becoming a champion for optimism just at this particular moment. Antón Mallick wants to be happy!" said Fran sarcastically and, spelled these words out on the air with a finger, as though blazoning them up high like a neon advert. "You, you're a pain in the ass, you're a social misfit in disguise. Me, I'm an optimist, but then my life hasn't gone totally to shit like yours."

"Much appreciated, Fran."

"I've got my own place, a manageable mortgage, good salary, adorable wife, great kids . . . Whereas you . . ."

"Congrats, old pal. Not sure an attack of sincerity was precisely what was needed here. My round?"

Naturally, my speech didn't convince Fran, but at least he had to admit I was showing some guts in facing up to the problem. But that was Friday, and now it was Saturday, we were leaving El Chino and the drinks were slowly taking their toll on my friend, and he was getting more and more worked up.

"And this is the night you lined up for me? I haven't been out in a month, I've eaten in every single weekend with my wife's girlfriends, all of them ugly as sin, the only saving grace of these witches being that they're much smarter than me, funny sometimes too. I've had five years straight with one or another of my kids being ill at home, every single hour of every single day. And you, for my one night off, bring me to some shithole to try and find some queen of the night you've knocked up. Now, unless you want us to become eternally depressed, let's go to a bar near your house, or to Tony 2, at least they mix a decent drink there."

In the 1960's timewarp that is Tony 2, we took a seat at the bar, not far from the door, surrounded by curious old cranks, careful not to bother this one very aggressive gambling addict who was glued to his slot machine and constantly itching for a fight. To Fran's astonishment, I ordered mineral water. That calmed him down: proof of my good intentions. The conversation drifted onto work matters and we ended up talking about "the sixty million chicken thingamajig," which is his name for the satellite because it's worth as much as sixty million roast chickens, that is, three hundred million euros or so, or six hundred million cans of Coke, or, if one felt inclined to carry the analogy further, fifteen top soccer players like Ruud Van Nistelrooy, whose transfer fee was a piddling twenty million euros. All of a sudden Fran remembered he hadn't told me that I had a meeting in London this coming Thursday, with the Apri broker and thirty specialist insurance companies, to present the satellite project to them. It was going to be a real squeeze getting ready for it in time, so this bit of news brought our night to a close.

Lucía hadn't come up again in conversation and I found this encouraging—I don't want to become obsessed with a ghost story. I walked home along Paseo de Recoletos and Paseo del Prado. The frozen, deserted street, with its bare wiry trees and unforgiving asphalt, bore witness to another quiet conversation between myself and Vidor, my confidante. Remember, Vidor? I told you a couple of anecdotes from my and Bela's childhood, and you were bold enough, for the first time, to talk about your mother, "that big, black, imposing woman from Pest who always walked hunched over, tottering, drawing laughter from the children all down Vaci Street, calling her *goblin* and throwing stones." How you loved her, Vidor, how you loved that woman, that good, obtuse, cruel, tender, monstrous woman. You parted from her in order "to be born again, but with a heart dyed black, walls full of cracks, and the veins and arteries empty, crying out, in happiness or in pain, who knows?" "Two," you said, "there were two things I missed—two holes, gaps, chasms: one, the Tokaji

Aszu wine with its delicious bouquet, like female wisdom, and the other, my beast of a mother."

So, if you missed her so badly, why didn't you bring her with you, Vidor? Were you ashamed of her? Was that it? You wanted her to die far away so that, in the city of your success, you wouldn't wish she were dead again?

*Tuesday, October 27, 2009*

"You can't go on like this, Antón."

This encouragement comes from my brother and personal coach, brains-of-Spain Zoltan. He's pissed off, which is the only reason he called, making time for me between two neurotics—one menopausal, one mysoginist.

"You can't just pick my kids up from school and leave them irrevocably traumatized. It isn't fair. If you want to crack up, do it on your own, alright?"

Zoltan is referring to Friday, the day when I had my medical. He's waited four days to have a go at me. When I came out of the hospital, around four o'clock, it occurred to me to go and pick up the twins and spend the rest of the day with them, take them to the movies or something. At half past four I was waiting for them at the school gate. Seeing me, they ran over and hugged me, winning me a look from one of their teachers like I was some kind of pedophile. Anyway. I called María, who said it was fine for me to take them to Retiro Park. We went and were playing soccer when, suddenly, I felt indisposed. I needed to go to the toilet urgently. I lay down on the grass. I held on. But at one point I wavered, I let go, I relaxed, I stopped fighting it. The next thing I remember is opening my eyes and seeing the twins' little faces over me, wide-eyed.

"Uncle Antón, you've pooped yourself," one of them pointed out.

"Uncle Antón, have you pooped yourself?" the other asked.

I cleaned myself up as best I could, crouched down behind some bushes, hailed a taxi, took the boys to their mother's office and fled home.

"It isn't my fault, Zoltan, for the love of God. Do you know what a colonoscopy is?"

"Yeah? right. Still painting the town red every night? Still getting high on the regular?"

"No, I'm back at work. I started back this week."

"Don't lie to me, Antón."

"Up yours."

And I hang up. Why do these things happen to me? Have I lost the twins' respect for good? Whatever. For the first time in a long time, my house actually resembles a house. I'm taking forward steps. Happiness is possible. Happiness is possible. Happiness is . . .

*Wednesday, October 28, 2009*

**To:** Antón Mallick
**From:** Zoltan Mallick
**Subject:** RE: WORDING MEETING

Very nice, Antón. I don't suppose your employer would be thrilled to know you're forwarding me confidential company emails, would they? GROW UP, WILL YOU?

---

Dear Benoît,

With regards the meeting on the 11th, I've just spoken with José, and we agreed that in order to move things on as much as possible and close on the subject of wording, the best thing would be a working lunch at the Hispaniasat offices.

José also mentioned that because of issues with their flights, Juan and Ignacio will join us later in the day. They'll be arriving from Toulouse after a meeting with the satellite manufacturer.

I therefore suggest a start time of two o'clock.

Regards, Antón

This message is intended exclusively for its recipient and may contain private or CONFIDENTIAL information.

---

**To:** Antón Mallick
**From:** Zoltan Mallick
**Subject:** RE: WORDING MEETING

Ho ho ho, Antón! Don't send me your work mail! FINE, okay, I BELIEVE YOU, THEY'VE TAKEN YOU BACK, GREAT, CONGRATS. And, by the way, YOU AND YOUR COLLEAGUES WRITE TERRIBLY, it's barely Spanish, you ought to take a bit more care. Either that or go back to school.

Zoltan

---

**To:** <pfarrarr@apri.com>, <amallick@apri.es>, <csethsmi@gyc.es>, <lerryc@repis.com>
**cc:** pdominguez@arrows.com.br, lprado@hispaniasat.es, bnaranjo@hispaniasat.es
**Subject:** RE: WORDING MEETING

Antón,

This is to say that, as per what has been discussed between the parties, we confirm that myself, Colin, Georgina and Mark will be available at whatever time is suitable on November 11 in the afternoon for this work meeting at Hispaniasat. Please let us know what time we should be at the offices. What are the current comments on wording in the US and English market?

Regards,
Benoît

This message is intended exclusively for its recipient and may contain private or CONFIDENTIAL information.

*Thursday, October 29, 2009*

It's half past three in the morning and, after running through the presentation one last time, I smoked a cigarette leaning out on the balcony, shivering in my boxer shorts, and then I sat down to write. The flight to London is at half past seven, which makes sleep hardly worth it. Working this hard, it's amazing how many issues you can solve in just a few days. I'd almost forgotten. The satellite is gradually becoming a part of me. The meetings with Hispaniasat's technical and finance directors, and with their insurance adviser, have helped improve certain points in the presentation. Aside from the meetings and the calls and emails, I've been going over the paperwork, mainly to pick out the truly important parts and cut out the background noise. The good news is that I should be able to do most of the work from home, which is what I wanted.

Vidor, I like the idea that my being called back to work by a satellite wasn't sheer coincidence. That it wasn't only down to my experience with this kind of policy. That it might be a symbol of my recovery. I'd like to think that after its launch in five month's time, once it's set on its geostationary orbit, when it's revolving at the same speed as me, watching over me from up in the sky for a few years at least, stationary in relation to me, loyal, sending and receiving signals, that it will be my own personal bodyguard, guarantor of my future happiness, proof that some things can turn out all right. A shining silver point in the heavens, almost twenty-two thousand miles up, keeping me company. Proof of the triumph of technology, of science at the service of mankind.

I'd like to think like this, even though to others it might seem like nonsense. If I have this hope—that a communications satellite be anything more than a money-spinning gizmo—if I go so far as to write about it, it's because I've always liked being told stories, and stories— including those that look to represent reality—or create reality, have always been brimming with symbols, with images from the past, with contrived interpretations, knowing winks between know-it-alls, quite pathetic attempts to put the universe in order, as well as of a lot of imagination. Like Korolev's story. He had nothing to do with my choice to specialize in satellites, but when I heard about him and read his autobiography, something changed. No longer was a satellite merely one body revolving around another. A transponder became more than a cluster of transmitters. An antenna was no longer merely for sending and receiving electromagnetic waves. GEO was more than the abbreviation of Geosynchronous Earth Orbit. Korolev became a symbol for me, but I've never been clear what exactly he represents. Victory? Defeat? Genius? Effort?

Suffering? All of these at once? What Korolev makes clear is that, in every story, what matters is how and by whom it's told. A child dies, and it's a different tale if told by the parents, or by the larvae of the worms set to eat his corpse.

Now that I am set on being an optimist, I should be capable of telling Korolev's story from such a perspective. And that's what I shall do, Vidor—a therapeutic exercise to go hand in hand with this diary. I'm going to narrate Sergei Pavlevich Korolev's story as though, to him, life had been a thing worth living, as though he'd enjoyed every minute, as though he'd been happy in the moments leading up to his death. If I manage this, it will serve as definitive proof of my ability to become an optimist.

It's half past four in the morning now, and I'd rather not go into how I've come to this conclusion, nor the reason why my obligations seem to be stacking up.

KOROLEV 1

Korolev was born on December 30, 1906, in Zhitomyr, a city in western Ukraine, bathed on one side by the River Teteriv, a tributary of the Dnieper, and surrounded by dense forests. One of the trade routes between Constantinople and the Baltic Sea passed through Zhitomyr, and the city was ruled in successive ages by Russians, Lithuanians and Poles. The year before Sergei's birth the Jews, who made up half of the population, were subject to a pogrom instigated by the authorities: eleven young students died, and it would be the first of many pogroms throughout the twentieth century that would leave tens of thousands dead. Anyway. Back to Sergei, who—incidentally—wasn't a Jew. Three days after he was born, Korolev's parents separated, and the baby was left in the care of his maternal grandparents. It's nearly six o'clock in the morning. I ought to get ready for the trip. Let's imagine that the pogrom had no effect on the cultural life of Korolev's town, that his parents' separation was all for the best, given that they argued so much and had even come to blows, and that his grandparents were affectionate and kept him well nourished. A happy childhood. To be continued.


*Saturday, October 31, 2009*

I'm at Heathrow airport, two hours before boarding. I read in a book by Marc Auge that airports were "non-places" in the sense that no one can really *be* in them, people just vegetate until the onward journey to their destination, be it a hotel or their own house or a bar with happy hour. So airports are transitory places, by their very nature provisional. Time tends to be wasted in "non-places," contemplation becomes difficult, and you become tired more easily, because of being unsettled, waiting for something over which you exert no control and that, it seems, will never arrive. In such places, one doesn't *do*, one simply *waits*; one does not *make*, one *kills time, life*. Other "non-places": train stations, waiting rooms in doctors' offices, elevators, the subway . . . I'd add that there are also such things as "non-situations," with similar characteristics, that you attend under duress: baptisms, wedding receptions, opening ceremonies, speeches at official or corporate events, midnight mass, testimonials, funerals of people you didn't know all that well, certain family gatherings, conversations with bores who get on your nerves.

London's a big place. Each time I've visited, whether for long stays or short stopovers, I've had a great time. It's a far cry from a "non-city," as many a small city ought really be known—the places that, unluckily, aren't able to absorb tourism and have become nothing more than stages, urban theme parks. The term *city* is too broad: there ought to be a different word to encompass places as different as Paris and Bruges.

My presentation worked out well, no serious blunders, though of course it also generated more questions, and a lot more work, for when we get back. It was held in our offices in the City, London's financial district, whose motto, "Domine, Dirige Nos"—"Lord, guide us"—refers not to the fact that executives turn to God to reveal unto them the way of righteousness, but that they hope He'll help make them filthy rich, give them a private jet, a butler, and their very own flesh and blood goddess to play with. Protestantism to a tee. There were several familiar faces among the executives, and I was pleased to see Peter Farrar again, Apri's English broker specializing in satellites. In his forties, tall, fair and slim, with an aquiline nose and a bearing that's more sarcastic than ironic, dressed in his striped, white-collar shirts, seemingly aloof, itching for everything to be over with so he can get to the pub, have a few gin and tonics and talk about his beloved Arsenal, plus a bit of financial gossip and armchair politics for good measure. But that Thursday we didn't have time. I went back to the

Chamberlain Hotel, in the Minories, near Tower Bridge, at around ten, without even having had dinner, and went straight to bed.

At six o'clock the next morning I put on my running outfit and took a maroon colored taxi down to Hyde Park Corner. The city seemed to be asleep, but you could sense something brewing in the mist. Alarm clocks starting to ring, kettles being placed on the stovetop, someone checking the temperature of the shower water, deliverymen shutting the doors of their already loaded vans . . . It was still dark, and it was cold, but the sky was clear of rain and dawn wasn't far away. I don't know why but as soon as I got to the park, as soon as I set out running, I felt powerful. Maybe it was because I felt heavy, yes, but not horribly fat, or because I was almost the only person in sight, or because I heard birds chirping and the sound of my footsteps on the sand, or because the dawn light was beginning to silhouette the trees and reveal the frost-covered lawns, or because I knew I wasn't going to hear anyone speaking my own language, or because the simple sensation of forward motion is pleasant, or because it had been so long since I'd felt good and the time had simply come to enjoy something. I don't know. The fact is that I began to sweat and felt like shouting for joy, like telling the whole world that I, Antón Mallick, was alive. Yes, Vidor, I know why you're smiling. You know there's no way this could have lasted for long, and you're not wrong. Precisely twenty-five minutes it lasted. Suddenly I felt a stitch in my chest and I stopped, feeling slightly uncomfortable, not far from Grosvenor Gate.

I walked to one of the gates holding my side, taking deep breaths to ease the pain. Morning had broken by then, and other runners were jogging along the tracks. And that, Vidor, was when Lucía burst into my mind. She reared up suddenly. It was you who pointed out that "women always make sure they know you're coming in advance, but don't like to announce their arrival, because they long for control, and they are masters at the art of surprise." Anyway. What came to me was a detail from the night of the crime, after the after-hours bar, when this Lucía and I went back to a cheap hotel on a seedy street behind Gran Vía: that was where we went to bed. A medley of mixed-up, somewhat demented images came into my mind: junkies sitting in an entrance stairwell; a woman at a reception desk, with a curly red wig, whom Lucía paid with a bill for the room; black prostitutes clucking at me as I passed; Lucía locking the door once we were inside. Was she a whore? As far as I remember, she didn't charge me. So why did we go there? Why didn't I suggest my place, or she hers? Was she still living at home, did she share an apartment with four students from Cuenca, did we mistrust each other for some reason? It definitely wasn't me who suggested the hotel, that's for sure.

We had sex and after that I fell asleep. I can't dredge up a clear memory of her face or her body. When I woke up, it was just me. Of Lucía, neither hide nor hair. I suppose that's the way she is, she likes vanishing, a lady of the theater, the vanishing circus lady. Still drunk, I dressed, staggered along, leaving that particular non-place (in a different sense to an airport, but with the same capacity, and just as determined, to cancel out life). Instinct directed me to Gran Vía, and

I hailed a taxi. Approaching Calle Moratín I realized I didn't have any money on me, even though I always go out with two hundred euros in cash and there was no way I'd spent that much. Had I given it to her, had it fallen out of my pocket? It didn't occur to me to let the taxi driver know and look for a cash point. I wasn't even embarrassed to stop the taxi, open the door and run off with all the awkwardness that comes with being semi-obese. I know that the taxi driver shouted insults after me, but not why he didn't run after me and give me a beating. Taxi drivers aren't what they used to be. Anyway. Until now it's never occurred to me but, a few days later, I noticed I didn't have my ID card. At the time I thought I'd lost it, but what if it was Lucía who stole both my money and the ID? And so what if she's a thief, someone cleverer and even more degenerate than me? To go to bed with me at that time in my life she must have been pretty sick in the head. To steal from me, lacking in the scruples department. Lucía the Dishonest Deceiving She-Devil. Now we're getting somewhere, I thought as I left Hyde Park to hail a taxi on Park Lane.

It was Friday and, after another exhausting day with Brits, Germans, Yanks and Frenchmen, like something out of a children's joke with characters of all different nationalities, each one stupider than the last, Peter Farrar and I left together. He took me to his favorite pub, a Victorian place called The Ship, with a red brick façade, on Talbot Court, down a winding alley. We ate sausages and mash and he drank several bottles of London Pride ale. He was surprised that I wasn't drinking, but didn't make a thing of it. Three gin and tonics later and he was lit up, if you can say that of an Englishman. I told him I was going to have a child. That was when I realized I knew barely anything about his life, only that he was single. Peter didn't ask who the mother was, or anything of that kind. He just looked at me poker-faced, piercing me with those gray, metallic eyes of his. It possibly also occurred to him that I'm out of my mind, although I have the advantage that he must think that of anyone with Latin blood. We clinked our glasses without very much cheer, and I went on: I had no idea who the mother of my child-to-be was, that she was probably a thief, a drug addict and slept around. Peter jumped forward off his stool like he was spring-loaded. I believe that was the first time I'd ever seen him laugh properly, a southern European laugh, unchecked, with all of his body and all of his face.

"You ... bastard ..." he said a few times, eyes streaming.

After that he did begin offering enthusiastic toasts, and even went so far as to pay the bill. I went back to the hotel on foot, jacket collar up, relishing the icy wind as it reddened my cheeks. This morning, after breakfast, I went to the Keats Museum before coming to the airport. It's in Hampstead, in an attractive white cottage with a garden where the poet resided for a couple of years. He wrote *Ode to a Nightingale* there, the one that starts: "My heart aches, and a drowsy numbness pains ..." *How* romantic. He fell in love with his neighbors' daughter Fanny Brawn, and they were due to marry, but Keats contracted tuberculosis and had to go to Rome, to a milder climate, and a year later, in 1821, he died, at twenty-five years of age. I wasn't the slightest bit moved by his story, oh so romantic, oh so tragic. Really, the Romantics are all optimists—though admittedly they always also come to bad ends—and in this sense they're contemptible, all of them, because they make themselves out to be the victims they really aren't. They love life, and they thrive on passion, and chance encounters, exchanges, humankind, pain, flowers, and death . . . They are part of history.

In the museum they told me that they ran activities for children. One, for instance, called *Be a detective!* in which six to twelve-year-olds hunted the museum for objects, at the same time learning and becoming better people. How optimistic and how adorable the English are, or how hard they try to appear so. All that brazen optimism really got to me and I left the museum in a foul mood, I wanted to smash the face of the first Londoner I came across. Which isn't as easy as it might at first seem—meeting a Londoner in London, I mean. You, Vidor, would have wanted to do the same. I remember the time you were walking along the Paseo del Retiro at night, on your own, swiftly, beneath the streetlamps' uncertain light, angry because an eviction had, in your view, cost you too much. Just then you saw a man sleeping on a bench, an elegant-looking gentleman, and you whacked him on his shin with your walking stick, just to let off steam. Then, when he woke up, you offered to help him, and he turned out to be a young man with a broken heart, and you ended up going for a bite together in an excellent eatery, I imagine washing down the vittels with various pitchers of your beloved Valdepeñas wine. Well, Vidor, the first Londoner I came across turned out to be an elderly woman with a blue rinse hairdo, wearing a brown jacket and matching skirt. A fitting candidate, doubtless. But when she saw me she smiled, and I was surprised to find myself returning the smile, utterly disarmed by this classic cat-loving, charity-addict, crochet-aholic little widow.

Anyway. Let's see if the plane manages to take off on time. If it doesn't, I'll be obliged to read *The Power of Optimism;* by Rojas Marcos, and I fear I may not survive that.

NOTES ON ZOLTAN'S BOOKS

On *The Power of Optimism* (2005) by Spanish psychiatrist Luis Rojas Marcos.

Just as I feared, the plane was delayed. I've just got home. Nobody was here waiting for me, which, Vidor, though to you it will seem like nothing unusual, to me it was an unpleasant surprise. But let's focus on the readings. I had no option but to read *The Power of Optimism*; I didn't have any other books with me. The title's a bit overcooked and forbidding—makes you feel like hiding in the wardrobe. It's a "light" self-help manual, just the thing for anyone willing to be convinced of the superiority of optimism as regards pessimism. Better than you might expect. But let's look at a sentence picked at random: "Nonetheless, it has been shown that disproportionate realism, under adverse conditions, comes at the cost of demoralization and indolence." Excuse me, Doctor Rojas . . . What was that? *Disproportionate* realism? And what might that be? Once again, the optimist is found to be harboring a pessimist inside. *If you're a realist, you're a pessimist*, he tells us. Watch out for that!

For R. M., optimism's main selling point is its usefulness. I have a sense that those who call themselves optimists are nothing more than pessimists in disguise, or people straining to be optimists, people who find both reality and pessimists unbearable. They've already been through this realist phase, this time when everything seems bleak; now they prefer to smile even though they don't really feel like it, because doubtless it makes it easier to survive in the jungle, to roll with the punches and just hang out. Their imposture means they can't stand self-confessed pessimists. In fact, R. M. applies the word *pessimists* to people who are really resentful, inept or failures. He comes to us and says: "Being an optimist is better." So what? Being Olympian gods or men of independent means would also be better, but happens to have nothing to do with it. They'll end up in my situation: wanting to be an optimist, but really just being a cryptopessimist. And on top of everything else they'll hate people who are openly so. It isn't "the power of optimism" but rather "power-fed optimism." Sad.

R. M. calls Kierkegaard "sinister" and is forever quoting Russell and—NB—SuperSusan C. Vaughan! Sure sign of a refined literary taste.

Happiness, according to the philosopher Julián Marías, consists of thinking that one day you'll be happy—the hope of being so. So there's no such thing. It simply does not exist, nor will it ever exist. Now there's a useful idea.

Once again, four books deep now, the defenders of optimism, of happiness and good vibes, have let me down. Either they're stomach-churning (self-help), or unconvincing (Russell and Alain), or merely enjoyable (Rojas Marcos). Why why why? Is it that optimism doesn't hold water or, rather, that there's no such thing as an optimist who is lucid *and* ludic *and* ludicrously convincing? Are the doom merchants, melancholics and depressives in the right? The future's hardly bright. Let's see when Bela decides to send some more books . . . Now, I should get some sleep. No pills, straight up. Not stopping to think about the World Health Organization, according to whose statistics more people committed suicide in 2000 than were killed in homicides and wars put together. Chin up, Antón. Happiness is possible. Happiness is . . .

*Sunday, November 1, 2009*

At the end of the afternoon yesterday my friend Carlos and I went to Ikea to buy a desk, and some shelves and filing cabinets for my study. The shopping experience was hair-raising and exhausting, it left me feeling like the meekest lamb in a whole flock of deeply meek lambs. Today, on opening the boxes and seeing the amount of pieces, screws, washers and the like, on looking at the instructions (seemingly straightforward but full of booby traps), and on realizing that the tools in my tool box are as cheap as they come, I seriously contemplated jumping out the window. I began putting together the furniture at eleven o'clock in the morning. Bit by bit, taking my time. Slowly,

I got to grips with the way it all worked. When I finished, around five o'clock, the afternoon had slipped by and I was a new man. Fleetingly happy, but happy, in the final analysis. Working with my hands, after such a long time, did me good. Start something simple, and see it through. The return of primitive man. Hmm.

*Tuesday, November 3, 2009*

A couple of hours ago, after dinner, I set about organizing all the papers piled up on various shelves. Among them were a fair few written in the last year to vent things in particularly difficult moments, handwritten with the blue and silver pen that Uncle Juan gave me when I finished school. That reminds me, I ought to spend some time on him in this diary, but all in good time. One says, for example: "Are we in fact nothing more than information transmitters? We consider ourselves to be unique, unrepeatable beings, when most likely we only exist in order that the species may continue. We are merely shoots, excrescences, abortions whose objective is to maintain an invisible process, disoriented runners who huff and puff during the short time that's ours to live. Thanks to individual consciousness, our capacity to choose, our detachment from the immediacy of experience, we want to be different, to stand out, and this improves the performance of the species, and this is what really matters. Good. Let's accept it. We're links in a chain. The only thing we know for sure is that we will die one day. The Universe—including our darling Mother Nature, the flowers, the lakes, the meadows and all the sweet little animals—is utterly indifferent to our poeticizing, our obsessions, our declarations of love, our sadness and our murders. Even if we plant a tree, or write a book, or have a child, oblivion is inevitable, permanent death is what we're all heading for, even people like Cervantes or Shakespeare or Hitler or Stalin. We're alone. We aren't so special. The Earth is a cold ball of silicate and iron. We're mere stardust and our true mother is not called Conchi, nor Itziar, nor Rosa, nor Carmen: it's a white dwarf whose whereabouts we don't even know. God doesn't exist, he's just another of our pathetic fabrications. Don't even talk to me about superheroes. And our hosts on Earth, when we're born, are not our parents but the dead, those who have already come and gone. And less of the save-the-earth chat, because, in case people haven't worked it out, it's a well-worn concept bought at a second-hand shop. Now, let's go out, let's drink, dance and be merry."

Okay. Going back to writing such things again is strictly off limits, though my actual intent is greater: to flee from the state of mind that prompts them. For now I've put them in a folder called "Downcast notes to cast out," but I feel confident I'm not going to be adding any more. I've also come across the Hungarian dictionary that Uncle Juan gave me when I turned eight (Bela also still keeps hers). The covers are blue, the whole thing is well-thumbed, missing two pages. It has pencil drawings of mine, representations of words here and there. They're wonderful little drawings, now that they've lost all meaning.

If someone were to ask what my favorite place is in Madrid, I'd have no doubt in answering:

"The Royal Botanical Gardens, 2 Plaza Murillo, 28014 MADRID."

"Why's that?"

"Because I've spent twenty-seven years wandering its paths, beneath its trees' canopies. I was six the first time my uncle Juan took Bela and me, and after that we went back with him hundreds of times. There, among many other things, I've been told stories, I've read books, played cops and robbers (just me and my sister), had lunch, been sick, had popsicles and ice creams, got bored, learned the names of the trees and plants, stolen vegetables from the patch and walked hand in hand with beautiful young ladies. Naturally, I'm a friend of the RBG, and I always pay my membership fee, even if I'm totally broke. And the main reason that I live at 22 Calle Moratín, which with its wine and white-colored façade is in itself an unremarkable place, is because of its proximity to the RBG.

"And have you ever been to the gardens with your parents?"

"No, never."

"That's strange, Antón. Why not?"

". . ."

The interview could have carried on in that direction, along the personal, more intimate side. If we draw conclusions about someone on the basis of a single preference, or because of a penchant, or some single indifference, or a mania, perhaps we'll arrive at the cardinal facts of their life, but it will also be an altogether spurious summary, reassuring, as a rule, and always self-satisfied. *What Are We? Where Do We Come From?* Yesterday, November 4, I went for a stroll around the Botanical Gardens. I was in the Apri offices, hysterical, writing a message to Mark Wocynski, the broker in New York, at the same as speaking on the phone to a German imbecile of an insurer who was claiming that the data I had sent him about the satellite was "meager, mediocre and garbled" (how can data possibly be "mediocre"?) when my gaze came to rest on a world terrorist attack risk map that had as part of it, I've no idea why, a calendar. I saw, highlighted in red felt-tip, yesterday's date, and I remembered that I'd forgotten the third anniversary of my uncle Juan's death. I finished the message, put the phone down on the mad German, left the office, bought a couple of cigars at a tobacconist and went to the Gardens.

In all favorite places there's a favorite spot, or at least one for every occasion. On this occasion I headed to a little clearing-cum-square near the far west edge of the Villanueva Pavilion. This was my uncle Juan Mallick's safe haven, and it's been mine as well ever since he showed it to me. It's a small circular clearing, unpaved, the surrounding hedgerow interrupted by just the one entrance. Nowadays there's a granite pedestal in the middle bearing a bronze sculpture of a cutesy, obnoxious little girl holding a rose. Five leafy linden trees give shade almost year-round, making for an oasis of peace that's rarely frequented by Madrileños. There my uncle Juan said that he felt himself to be "away from the world, in a magic place." In the first week of November, 2005, Bela and I scattered his ashes at the foot of one of the lindens, the one whose trunk sports a wisteria coiled like a serpent, constricting it. After this simple ceremony, Bela and I looked at each other and smiled. Barely ten days had gone by since his death and, even though it was so soon, it was already dawning on us that thoughts of our uncle would not always be sad ones. This, among a good many other things, was what he'd left us: to be lifted by his memory, to make us think that life, thanks to people like him, is, sometimes, worth all the trouble.

When I got to the clearing I sat down on one of the wooden benches, took the metal Davidoff cigar tin that I'd just bought out of my coat pocket, and smoked one in his honor. Juan Mallick smoked Davidoff cigars and Dunhill cigarettes, the ones that comes in little red and gold packs. As with other very austere people, he only liked luxury products. He was one of those men whom the epithet "gentleman" fitted well, and, as any grandmother you care to ask would say, "they don't make them like him anymore."

He was born in Madrid in 1937. He studied law and, with a university colleague, set up a corporate law firm, Mallick and Alonso, that he kept up until the day he died, fell in love with and married a woman from Santander, becoming a widower a number of years later when she died in childbirth—the child also died only a few hours old. He never remarried, and nor did he have any known mistresses, although perhaps he had some, or perhaps he preferred to frequent brothels, whatever. He remained constantly committed to his firm, which was highly respected, to his partner, whom he also counted as friend, though he only ever saw him in a strictly professional capacity, to his other friends, a select few, to his well-stocked library, which he left to me and I keep in storage, to Hungary, a country he never visited, to his collection of antique coins and tin soldiers, which Bela inherited, and to his team, Real Madrid. He knew how to cook one dish and one dish only: *goulash*. Moreover, he was a father to Bela and me.

My parents went to live in the US in 1981, taking Zoltan, the oldest, with them, and leaving my sister, eight years old, and me, six, in Juan's care. My father's reasons for abandoning us (which my mother didn't want to do, as far as I understand it, though she went along all the same) are still murky to me, twenty-five years later. They left two years after the death of my younger brother, Luisito. To this day I wonder if my parents' sudden flight had anything to do with his death, and with the fact I was present at the accident, impossible though it seems. That they went because my father was offered a fantastic job is fair enough. That they left Bela and me behind, unjustifiable.

Anyway. Juan Mallick, younger brother to Lajos, my father, welcomed us into his apartment at number 18 Calle Velázquez, and there we lived, among classic furniture and walls lined with books, crossing the blackish parquet flooring which creaked, filling the house with phantasmagorical groans, until we were old enough to move out. He dressed us, bathed us, attended parents' evenings at school, took us to the doctor, consoled us in times of sadness, gave us wonderful birthday presents and brought us up with the same care and attention he would have lavished on children of his own. When he got truly angry, he'd give us a smack on the backside, though his stare—intense and icy—was scarier. He was a reserved, caring man who didn't find it easy to let himself go. He loved it when Bela and I jumped on him and smothered him with hugs and kisses, and he always spoke proudly about us to others. We only ever saw our parents on summer holidays, always in the States (they've never set foot in Spain again), and never for the whole three months. When we weren't with my uncle, we missed him so badly that we'd write him long letters. We'd always include scathing observations about our parents and Zoltan. And when we'd return home, Uncle Juan, always proper, would tell us off, though I suspect the letters made him laugh. As for a dark side, he had one too. Why had he and my father fallen out, what was the origin of that silent, years-long struggle, lasting all the way until his death? And what was he doing during all those hours he spent locked up in his study at home, mainly at night and during weekends, year after year?

I spent yesterday afternoon in that clearing, smoking cigars and making an effort not to cry. When it was coming up to six o'clock, closing time, I left the bunch of white daisies I'd bought at the entrance beside the linden tree, and once more bid farewell to Juan Mallick. He was the one who gave me *Confessions of a Once-Hungarian Spaniard* to read, when I turned eighteen. Three years ago he died of a heart attack. Now, with every day that passes, it makes me happy that my uncle never got to see me falling apart, never heard me cursing life, didn't get to witness any of my anxiety attacks. Dying at least saved him from that.

KOROLEV 2

Sergei Pavlovic was a pampered and lonely child. His grandparents adored him. He didn't have friends, but that meant he was able, from an early age, to devote himself to thinking. Unhappy, stubborn and clever, he missed his parents, who had abandoned him, but this was no bad thing, no: it only made him stronger. One day, when he was six years old, he saw an aeroplane in flight, piloted by the famous Sergei Utochkin. It changed his life. From that day on, he knew that he'd dedicate himself to flying machines. He went to live in Odessa with his mother and her new husband, Bolonin, an electrical engineer, training to become a roofer but never taking his eye off the prize. At sixteen he'd already flown in a plane and, at seventeen, he'd designed a prototype and had met the woman who would become his wife, Layla Vicentini, who to begin with wouldn't give him the time of day. The pieces were beginning to fall into place. The Moscow State Technical University awaited. TBC.

*Friday, November 6, 2009*

The box of books from Bela has arrived. Beautifully presented in blue cardboard lined with orange paper. Epicurus' *Principal Doctrines.* Leibniz's *Theodicy.* Marcus Aurelius' *Meditations,* Rousseau's *Emile, or On Education.* Seneca's *On the Happy Life* and *Consolations.* Boethius' *The Consolation of Philosophy.* Voltaire's *Candide, or Optimism.* A considerably higher standard than Zoltan's, for sure. The books came with a note: "Hey little brother. A bit of optimism fieldwork for you. Beautiful day today. It's snowed—weather's crazy—it's six in the morning and no one's been out yet to ruin the scene by tramping through it. John's asleep and I'm correcting homework. Couple of really bright students this year, real gems. Are you happier yet? Love, Bela."

*Saturday, November 7, 2009*

There's something odd about Zoltan's house, it's a dead giveaway for my brother's American past, in spite of the fact it's been decorated according to María's tastes, and she's a Madrileña, a pharmacist's daughter. It isn't like there are baseball bats hanging on the walls, and they don't have Halloween pumpkins all over the place, and they don't celebrate Thanksgiving; you just feel like you're in a home somewhere else, somewhere artificial. They live in Calle Costa Rica, not far from the Bernabeu stadium, in an impersonal but well built apartment block. It's a sizeable apartment with four bedrooms, and has a terrace where they can have dinner parties and tend to their beloved plants. When I got there they were putting the twins to bed. Being their uncle, I can tell them apart, but not easily. To start with, they're always dressed alike and they have the exact same haircuts. They're six years old, blond, slim and tall. They were born in Spain, two years after Zoltan came back from the States, already married to María, who'd done a Masters there in something to do with her work in the banking sector. The boys are called Maks and Felipe. There were problems in the hospital when they were born. No one was sure who was born first, and for Zoltan this was essential information. Which one would get the Hungarian name? Who would be the heir, the one to continue the saga, the new Mallick of the brilliant future?

"This is outrageous!" screamed Zoltan, beside himself in the hospital ward, his two tiny sons asleep in a perspex crib and María smiling groggily. "If they don't tell me, I'm calling a lawyer. I swear, Antón, I'll sue them shitless! I swear! Bastards!"

And, still shouting:

"What now? How could I be so unlucky? Who made me have twins? Would it really have been so hard just to have one Mallick, give it a Hungarian name, and off we go?"

And, indeed:

"How about if I give them both Hungarian names? As though they had literally been born simultaneously. Bye bye problem, right? Shit! Why does everything have to be so complicated!"

The tragedy lasted four days, the time it took María to recover from the caesarean in the hospital. My brother claims that the nurses ended up figuring out which was the first born, but I don't believe it. They didn't have a clue. Zoltan named them at random, it was he who decided who would be oldest and who youngest. The flip of a coin. Betraying his principles, lying like a knave and being deceitful, and thereby emulating Bela and me, his little underdeveloped Spanish siblings whom he'd always called "compulsive liars because of a mix of innate character, and Latino, quasi-third-world upbringing." Nowadays it's easy to tell who's the eldest because Maks calls the shots, nonstop. In spite of the fact they're forever fighting, Felipe has accepted his brother's dominance. Maybe this is why his gaze is slightly melancholic, and why he frowns when he speaks. He's by far the most mischievous of the two. I'm not entirely certain what the defining characteristic is that enables me to tell them apart in an instant.

"Uncle Antón! Uncle Antón!" cried Maks, leaping from the bed.

"Uncle Antón! Uncle Antón!" Felipe said, echoing his brother. "Are we going to play?"

Naturally, Zoltan didn't let us play. Two kisses, I read them a story, and off to sleep. The dinner was, to a degree, to lighten the mood after my and Zoltan's recent encounters, or clashes, I should perhaps say.

"So," began Zoltan, smiling, serving himself wine but not offering me any, "work going well? They paying you the same? Do they think you're going to be able to handle the satellite job? They aren't worried you'll collide, the satellite and you?"

I sometimes ask myself how my brother can possibly be a psychologist. I also wonder how long it is, once he's seen them, before his patients are in need of a decent psychiatrist for the rest of their days. María, though, always backs me up. She's thirty-four and has so far always done what's expected of her, in every stage of her life. She's already bagged herself a husband, a decent job, a house, kids. I wonder what's left for her to do. Divorce my brother, maybe? Try to seduce me, her brother-in-law? Stuff herself full of cupcakes when no one's looking?

"You are such a brute, Zoltan!" she says, grimacing. "Antón's the bomb. They need you, isn't that right, Antón?"

Halfway through dinner my brother tells me our father isn't doing very well. He's been bouncing from one illness to the next. It seems like he's frightened this time, though this in itself isn't exceptional (hypochondriac that he is, one of these men who wears a scarf all year long, who, instead of a pipe, always has a thermometer stuck in his mouth, and who, instead of kneeling down before God, does so in front of his medicine cabinet). My mother, though she isn't saying as much, is worried. They live in Columbia County, two hours by train north of New York, in a belt of prairies, forests and fishing lakes that's gradually filling up on weekends with well-to-do New Yorkers fleeing the asphalt and the potholes. The other Hamptons, they call it. Six years ago, when my father retired, they bought a little white wooden cottage there, complete with a garden that had a fishpond with organically-fed ducks, and moved there from Houston, Texas, which was where they'd lived previously. My father's an engineer and worked for over twenty years in an American renewable energy and waste treatment company. They picked the house out of a catalogue. It was sheer bad luck my father couldn't get them to send it by mail; he can't get enough of shopping in that way. Nowadays he spends hours at his computer, ordering all kinds of useless junk online, hardly ever venturing out from his den. I don't know how my mother puts up with him.

"If he isn't feeling well, I suggest a trip to the doctor," I say.

"A little respect," says Zoltan, raising his voice. "You now how the old man is. He *hates* doctors, he's afraid of them."

"Really? Well that's hardly the cleverest attitude for someone who's in his seventies, wouldn't you say?"

María lets out a little laugh. Zoltan impales me with a glare. Now, as part of the usual family survey, it's Bela's turn. To Zoltan, she isn't just "Bela." It's "poor Bela." Or "Bela, poor thing." Like *she's* the halfwit.

"And your sister?" he says, as if she wasn't also his. "How is she, poor thing? Hasn't she ditched that drunk yet?"

That drunk being John, her husband. He was orphaned as a child. He calls himself a writer, though no one's entirely sure he's ever actually written anything, whether it be homework, graffiti on a public toilet wall, or an autograph on a girlfriend's derriere. He inherited a lot of money, though we don't know exactly how much, he doesn't throw it around, and he's always muttering and giving us all lessons on literature and similarly pointless things. I'm not a huge fan of John. Bela's a professor of Spanish Literature at a university in Boston, Massachusetts. She went looking for work in the States to be near our parents, and she ended up in Boston, alone, married to some pretentious drunk. You could say that in my family we play at trying to escape one another, swapping places on the board. Not that anyone talks openly about the fact.

"No, she's still with John," I say. "It would seem he's going through a dark patch, let's say. We ought to look on the bright side though, right Zoltan? There's always the chance that John will employ a ghostwriter to get his novel done, and that way become less embittered. Or maybe he'll drop dead: alcoholics don't have great life expectancy. Maybe we'll have our sister back before we think, and everyone will be happy."

Another chuckle from María. Another murderous glare from Zoltan.

"Sometimes you really don't get it, Antón. Don't you realize that other people's problems can be just as serious as yours?"

"You mean 'Poor Bela'? Yes, I know she was dealt a bad hand with John, but she's been with him for years and she seems to be doing alright, wouldn't you say?"

"You and Bela," growled Zoltan, "so lovey-dovey, oh so attached, practically Siamese twins and yet neither of you has the first clue about the other."

María cleared the plates and we all stood up to get the second course.

"And you . . ." and now Zoltan smiles, with that open, good ol' Texas boy smile, so sure of himself. "What happened with that lunatic, that woman? See her again? Work out if she really exists?

María's head sprouts two little antennae.

"A woman, Antón?! Wonderful! High time! Come on, fill me in!"

We sat back down at the table. María hasn't the slightest inkling that I've fucked approximately twenty women this last year. Or that more than half of them were whores. Or that half the whores were streetwalkers, immigrants exploited by gangs, by their pimps and, in a sense, by guys like me, their despicable clients.

"Is she pretty? What does she do?"

María keeps on firing questions at me, not giving Zoltan time to even introduce the story. All the better. I don't want him to tell the story, I don't want to hear a word of what he has to say about it. In fact, I change the subject and, though María insists, Zoltan, for once, maybe to annoy his wife, comes out on my side and asks me questions about work. I don't know if I want to go looking for Lucía. I'm starting to doubt the story myself. Did she really say she was pregnant with my baby? I know that something happened, but it's been two weeks and now it seems like some far-fetched nightmare. You don't find out you're going to be a father in a queue in a bookshop, from a stranger's mouth. Or you shouldn't, at least. Plus, if I do find her, what do I do, beg her to get an abortion? Say to her there's no way I'm having a child with her? Or that I want to be not just the biological father, but the actual father? As I listened to María and Zoltan, who recount stories about the twins, I come to the conclusion that I shouldn't go looking for Lucía. I've got quite enough problems as it is. Better to forget all about her.

When dinner's finished, María asks if I want a drink. But we're all tired, and I decline. We make plans to meet tomorrow Sunday, in the Retiro, with the children. Before I leave, Zoltan takes a couple of pictures of me. I know they're really to send to my mother (now that she doesn't see much of us, it lifts her spirits to see what we look like). I say goodbye, and walk home. Now, having written this down, it's almost two o'clock in the morning. Time for bed.

*Sunday, November 8, 2009*

I didn't fall asleep. And I didn't agree to meet today with my sister-in-law and nephews. I woke up in the bathroom, sprawled on the floor, with a nasty headache, grasping a condom in my right hand. I came out of the bathroom: no sign of any woman. Let's have a recap. When I was about to go to sleep, Carlos called. He and I were neighbors when we were children, and he's a close friend of mine. His father was a con artist, and because of him Carlos went through some very entertaining, and many very sordid and violent situations. He's thirty-three, he works in marketing at Microsoft, and the ladies really go for him. He asked me to go with him to a singles party. There were going to be two women there he'd had flings with, and I'd be helping him out if I could come and distract them as he tried to get it on with a third, a certain Ms. Paloma. I said I wasn't single, I was cursed, an altogether different thing. Give a shit, was his view.

"I'll pick you up in fifteen minutes. And whatever you do, don't wear that polkadot sweater."

The party was in a pretty ramshackle apartment in Calle Fuencarral, near the Market. Plastic glasses, almost empty bottles of booze, indie music, politically committed people. We poured ourselves drinks and off went Carlos. Paloma wasn't about, but the two women he'd previously been involved with were. They were both thirtyish, friends, and worked as salesladies in an accessory shop. Ana was good looking and fairly sullen. The other one, Pepa, average-looking and very sweet. I tried to get Ana, the good looking, not so sweet one, on her own to talk to but Pepa, the nice one, wouldn't give us an inch, she kept a close watch on us, demonstrating the talent that certain women have for not allowing friends the chance to get it on with anyone, not even when they go to the toilet.

Satellite insurance wasn't hugely interesting to them. We talked about movies.

"*Blade Runner?* Awful! I like period movies," said Pepa. "I can't stand violence."

"You really like *Gladiator?*" countered Ana. "I don't get it. Doesn't add up. Woody Allen and *Gladiator*, I mean, come on."

Anyway. At night you can find yourself exposed to all kinds. Like Clea, the coke fiend nurse, said, "it's cold like an Arctic glacier." Things got better when Carlos, who hadn't managed to find himself any women of interest, joined the conversation and handled the whole thing like an ace, coming out with all kinds of nonsense, much to their delight. Pepa and Ana were devouring him with their eyes—it reminded me of when we were sixteen and he'd always ended up with the best looking girl. The party was fizzling out. Carlos picked Ana, or she picked him, and away they went. Pepa and I left together. Out on the street, she suggested we get a drink. It was about four o'clock in the morning. I was stone cold sober and that made me feel odd, like an impartial bystander. We went on to Tranvía, a late bar, and Pepa had another two drinks there. She kept going on about what a bastard Carlos was, what a pig, what an utter son of a . . . I didn't disagree. I was starting to get bored, but then again . . . It was almost six and Pepa was starting to look quite tasty. Desirable, too; just the thought of taking off her clothes, caressing her, fucking her, was turning me on. At least that was how I was thinking at the time, in that bar crammed with people straining to seem interesting and up for it. The worst thing was I could hardly blame the alcohol. Out of the blue, I groped her, and she smiled at me like, you little devil you. She suggested we go back to *my place*. Excellent, I said to myself. I'm going to give her more pleasure than Adam did Eve, and I don't need no apple . . .

As soon as we set foot in my apartment we had a long, bland kiss, and as she fumbled for my belt buckle I pawed her breasts beneath her bra. Not overly sexy, to be honest. Pepa undressed; she had a pear shaped body. If anyone was to give us scores on our physiques, it would be a tie. Or, to be a little less gentlemanly, 5-4 in my favor. Anyway. I undressed. My libido had foundered during the taxi ride. But she was horny, goodness knows why. We tumbled into bed.

"Have you got condoms?"

I went to the bathroom to look. I only found one, but thought that would be more than enough. I suddenly needed to pee. I took a seat. I passed water. I couldn't be bothered to turn my mind to erotic thoughts, and I put the rubber on as best I could. I shut my eyes and . . . I woke up the next day. I must have fallen asleep in a flash. I think my somewhat exaggerated excitement in the bar was a deferred side effect of the aforementioned Alprazolam, my medication. Although I stopped taking it fifteen days ago (now I'm only doping myself up with Paroxetin, an antidepressant), whenever they've prescribed me it I've always been horny for the ensuing months. Yes, it's true, not all medication makes you impotent. Anyway. And the sudden somnolence wad own to the antidepressant, and my usual exhaustion. Not very nice for that Pepa woman. At least she didn't break anything on her way out. She didn't leave a note either, or any flowers, or a lipstick kiss on the mirror. Who can blame her.

# NOTES ON BELA'S BOOKS

*Maxims*, Epicurus (341-270 BC)

Nighttime. I spent all day lying in bed, watching TV, reading, sleeping. I'm done with sinking lower and lower. I'm done with behaving like a guinea pig. Done with waking up in the bathroom alone, unused condom in my hand, done with fraternizing with people I couldn't care less about. Okay, Epicurus, let's see: who are you, what have you got for me? You've been insulted, you've been called a pig, a letch and a pervert . . . The Christians, since they decided to do away with the body, to mutilate it, have had you on their hit list. And so what do you say to that? Are you a pervert? No, you're not, unfortunately. Are you into scandalous pleasures? No. You are the exact opposite of what people normally think you are, someone who speaks softly, you're fairly boring, melancholic and gloomy. You're that weirdo who decided to live in the countryside having had enough of people and of family around him. I picture you with a prostate the size of a football, reminiscing on your days as Mr. Screwmaster, lying around most of the time, fed up with visitors, with young people who look up to you, women who fish around under your toga . . . What have you got for us, Epicurus, what's the story? Epicurus proposes the happiness of the wise man who lives for himself, a happiness that comes from not being afraid to enjoy life (though his philosophy issues precisely out of fear, which is what made him cut himself off from the world). Self-government and serenity are the fundamentals of this kind of happiness, and of wisdom and friendship, its allies. Prudence defines the limits of pleasure, since excess results in agitation. Epicurus suggests one can find pleasure every day in the simplicity of the "hidden life," removed from politics, from social recognition, from competitive ambition, and from consumerism. Epicurus' philosophy entails a disavowal of struggle, an elegant withdrawal, an attempt to forget everyone else. His is the happiness of the fugitive. It's a utilitarian way of thinking, mere advice. He doesn't seek "the truth," he doesn't ask complex questions, nor anything in between. Another charming philosopher.

Epicurus' proposals set out some very clear, exclusive, unsubtle lines. In this he resembles you, Vidor. The problem being that life consists of combinations, contradictions, blurred lines. This, for example, explains why there's such a thing as pleasurable pain, something that both you and Epicurus conveniently neglect to mention in your discourse.

*Wednesday, November 11, 2009*

Nothing.

*Friday, November 13, 2009*

> "I do not believe that being happy is a complex affair."
>
> WAYNE W. DYER

Work, work, work. Read, read, read. I've been out running the last two days. I've lost three and a half kilos in a month. I'm down to seventy-nine.

I've begun interspersing my diary entries with quotations from the books I'm reading. This way it will be more edifying if I read it in twenty years' time.

*Thursday, November 19, 2009*

> "Men who are unhappy, like men who sleep badly, are always proud of the fact."
>
> B. RUSSELL

Thursday, six o'clock in the evening. A street off Princesa, a little way up from Plaza de los Cubos, with its movie theaters and hamburger joints. 15 Luisa Fernanda, apartment 2D. I call on the intercom and they buzz me in. The doorway is old. I climb the stairs. There's a sign over the door: "Milano Private Investigators." I ring the bell and a young woman opens, smartly dressed, although she's chewing gum. I can't stand people who chew gum. She's in a hurry.

"Good afternoon. Please, come in."

She's the receptionist. Her desk is in a wide, bright hall, with twelve or so desks in it, functional, modern. On one side there is an office with French windows and filing cabinets covering the back wall. Apart from the gum-chewing girl and me, there's nobody. Maybe private investigators don't work Thursday afternoons, either that or they're all out on special missions. The secretary is rifling through some documents at her desk.

"Client?" she asks, not looking up.

"Possibly," I reply, playing it mysterious, imagining myself a character in a detective novel.

The girl picks out some documents, heads towards the door, and then she remembers I'm here. She turns and gives me a smile.

"The photocopier's down, as usual. I have to . . . You'll excuse me, yes?"

Off she goes, leaving me on my own. That's private investigators for you, I guess! Leave a stranger by himself in their office full of secrets. I flick through a copy of the Association of Spanish Private Investigators magazine. I come across an ad of a smiling man. It reads: "You haven't got a calling to be bishop of Toledo. You think the interviews for city councilman might be a little competitive. You don't know how to sing so you can't qualify for Star Academy. You couldn't care less about becoming a civil servant, an altar boy, a newscaster, journalist, film maker, shirt-ironer or dog walker. Why not become a private investigator, even if a trilby or a trench coat aren't your style? A profession for independent people." I cast my eye over the front cover, but this isn't any satirical publication; it isn't parody. No. Oh-ho, aren't these private investigators of ours creative and witty. Philip Marlowe and all those other tough guys can get stuffed. Damn right. Just as I'm about to leave, the buzzer rings. I open the door. A lanky young man stands looking at me, somewhat surprised. But he recovers quickly, pushing past me and coming inside.

"Hi. Rosa not here? Quiet afternoon, huh?" he says, seeing the empty desks.

"Looks like it."

"Hi, Félix Ramirez, Milano Private Investigators. And you are?"

"Antón Mallick," I say. "Potential client."

The young guy—I almost wrote "young idiot," but look on the bright side, look on the bright side—smiled and held out his hand.

"How can I help?" and sits down behind a desk, gesturing for me to do the same.

"I'm looking for a woman."

"Right, who isn't!" jokes the comedian Félix as he opens a drawer but then shuts it straight away. "Shit! I'm out of cigarettes . . . Mind if we carry the conversation on in a bar?"

"Of course not. Working out of the office is like a Milano Private Investigators tradition, I'm guessing?"

We head out and Félix takes me to a fairly strange bar, an English pub but not at all English. There are only two customers, propped up on the bar, drinking brandy or something similarly horrible. He buys cigarettes and orders a whiskey. Finally, something that suggests he might actually be a private investigator. I get a coca-cola. We sit at a table.

"So, you were saying you're after a woman, that right?"

Before telling him anything I ask how these things work. He gives me the official agency plug: they're the best, they solve most cases, and so on. He tells me the minimum charge to initiate a case is three hundred euros, and they charge fifty euros an hour, plus expenses. There's a contract. All information, naturally, is confidential. They do not investigate crimes (now I see why there are barely any private investigators in Spanish films today). They usually work in pairs, particularly if surveillance is involved. The relationship always ends with a report and payment at the end.

"If there's two of us, we charge double, got it?"

Got it. I couldn't say whether Félix is a genius or a moron. He smokes compulsively, particularly when he's listening, and his face is inexpressive, like he has no clue what you're saying.

"Why do you want to find this woman?"

"She told me she was expecting my child."

I try describing Lucía the Unknown. Twenty-five-ish, brunette, flat nose, slim (possibly), average height (possibly). In principle, three months pregnant. Possibly a drug addict. Possibly a night owl. Possibly a whore. Possibly a thief, possibly an average person but erring on the slightly odd side, possibly desperate, possibly . . .

"Hold it, hold it Antón," he said, interrupting me. "Forget the *possibly*'s. All we want are the facts. How do you know her? Tell me everything you know about her."

I tell him everything I know, or at least everything I've managed to remember. The night, the drugs. The cheap hotel, the ill-fated fuck, my ID disappearing, everything. And then, the encounter in the bookshop.

"Phhheeeew!" whistles Félix, inexpressive as ever. "Unsettling, right? So we don't have her full name, correct?"

"No. Just Lucía."

"We can forget about the Chino . . ."

"Who?"

"The Registry Office."

Félix says nothing for a few moments. He carries on staring at me. We drink. He takes a long sip of his whiskey, sucks on an ice cube. Suddenly, a flash of intelligence clambers into his eyes.

"Remember if you charged it to your credit card?"

"Yes, I paid on a card."

"And did you keep the receipts?"

"That's how I was brought up."

"So," he says, his facial muscles still in stasis, "she might be ours. She's the woman who bought something just before you. If the woman paid on a card . . . I know someone who works there. I need the precise details of your purchase, including the time. You on email?"

Félix takes out a notebook—every inch the detective!—and takes down my personal details.

"Good. All in order. Maybe we find her tomorrow, maybe not. Time will tell. Anything else?"

I feel a bit bad mistrusting Félix, but also don't feel I have any choice but to ask to see his private investigator license. I also do it just out of curiosity.

"This is me," he says, showing me an ID card with his photo, him looking like a little kid wearing a short hair, jacket and tie. "Three years at Law and Criminology college and, boom! Hit the street!"

We get up. Félix makes no move to pay, so I just go right ahead.

"I'll email you our bank account details, right?" he says once we're outside. "Want to come up so I can introduce you to Rosa?"

Félix smiles now, for the first time, and I realize why he doesn't do so very often. He has ugly teeth, yellow, and an old man's smile.

"Next time, thanks. I'll settle for you finding Lucía."

"Okay. See you then, pleasure meeting you, Mr. Mallick."

And off I go, walking towards Calle Princesa, pleased at how easy it's all been, that soon I'll know who Lucía the Perverse is, at having found a private investigator who's wily as a fox.

Yes, Vidor, I've hired a detective. Five days after deciding *for definite* not to look for Lucía. But, Vidor, know what?, I'm fed up of living with ghosts, of thinking about ghosts, of feeling I myself am slowly turning into a ghost. I've had enough. And this child, or this embryo, or fetus, or whatever it is, could persecute me my whole life, show up during sleepless nights, who knows. If we work on the basis that it's true that I'm going to have a child, is it fair that I forget about its existence? Is it fair that "it" will have no father? Should I not care that within a few years there will be a child with my genes walking around Madrid, probably on drugs, kissing schoolgirls, reading Dan Brown, having anguish attacks? Is that what it is to *be modern*? Is it fair that it have a father like me, who either isn't or doesn't want to be the father, though biologically I am? Can I really *be* its father? Do I want to be? Do I want it to be born, or to die? Am I being selfish trying to find it? Is it a good thing that there are new families in which the father—or the inseminator, or whatever—has been deliberately struck off? Why, why not? What do such children say when people ask about their fathers? Do they say Dad's just a little egg? A spermatozoid? An onanist who sold his semen to a lab? A jerk who got coked up and banged his or her mother in a cheap hotel? Don't children have rights too, or what's going on in this world? Does a child have the right to have a father, a mother, grandparents? Now that we have a right to decent housing, among other niceties, have they got the right for their parents to have legs, and a penis, and arms, and breasts, and a vagina, and hands, and a head, that they be *real*? That they talk, if they're mute? Have children got the right to know the origin of their genes? Are the questions getting overly difficult? Muddled? Almost illegible? Stupid? Do you know what I'm going on about, Vidor? Is there anyone there? Am I going crazy, or is it actually not that strange to want to know if I'm going to have a child without anybody having consulted me?

Right now, Vidor, the embryo exists, at least in my brain, it is an idea, a rather powerful ghost that stops me from settling, that reminds me I can't just stand there doing nothing if I don't want it to visit me in my dreams. It grows, and it's demanding its place in my mind. That's all. That's the way it is. I didn't choose for it to be.

KOROLEV 3

Sergei studied engineering. He lived at number 38 on Alexandrovskaya Street, with his mother and Bolonin. The family dining room also acted as his bedroom and his study. This, instead of being a pain in the neck, meant he learned to be able to concentrate in any situation. Sergei graduated and took up work in Factory 22 as part of an aeroplane and rocket design team. On

August 6, 1931, Korolev married Layla Vincentini, who worked at the time as a health inspector in Kharkov. The courtship, which lasted several years, comprised a few letters and brief meetings. There were just two guests at the wedding. A hurried glass of champagne and Layla dashed back to her own city to do the paperwork needed for her transfer to Moscow. Not that it was a sad or dull wedding, nor loveless, but simple, swift, modern. Years of struggle then followed, years in which Korolev worked on promising experiments with the most promising Soviet engineers of the day, years in which young Sergei acquired experience and began to climb the greasy pole . . . To be continued.

*Friday, November 20, 2009*

> "Either thou livest here and hast already accustomed thyself to it, or thou art going away, and this was thy own will; or thou art dying and hast discharged thy duty. But besides these things there is nothing."
>
> MARCUS AURELIUS

I've transferred the sum of three hundred euros to the private investigator, and sent back the signed contract. On top of that, I've had calls from a couple of women. This is going to work, I can feel it.

*Saturday, November 21, 2009*

> "We have been born once and cannot be born
> a second time; for all eternity we shall no longer
> exist. But you, although you are not in control
> of tomorrow, are postponing your happiness.
> Life is wasted by delaying, and each one of us
> dies without enjoying leisure."
>
> EPICURUS

What things make me happy, what do I enjoy *a lot?*
Drinking half a liter of orange juice every morning. Putting
things in order and throwing them away. Running. Going
for a stroll. Cooking. I've found that I ought to rediscover my
hands again, action, doing things, not just thinking of them.
It doesn't overly matter how well you do them, or if they
seem ridiculous when you tell others about them, or if they
aren't going to get me anywhere in the long term. It's about
*enjoying the immediate experience.* Maybe, that way, I'll find a
way (nothing of course definitive, but liberating, refreshing).

*Sunday, November 22, 2009*

TRANSCRIPTION OF A CONVERSATION WITH
MY MOTHER, PEPA ('JOSEFA' IN OFFICIAL
DOCUMENTS), THIS VERY NIGHT

For the last month we've spoken almost every night
using Skype, online, on the computer. It costs nothing.

I have no idea how, but father somehow managed to show my mother to use it. She's seventy, not part of the Digital Age—a profoundly analog woman. When she prepares her gardening projects—which she refuses to call "landscaping"—she has a hard time with the plans, which my father draws up for her. Now he wants us to install cameras on our respective computers so we can see each other's faces when we speak, but I'm against that. What is this? Are people out of their minds? We want to put cameras in our bedrooms now? We enjoy being spied on?

I answer (by clicking, of course).

"Son? Son? Are you there? (not letting me get a word in edgeways) Son? Son?"

". . ."

"These gizmos! Damned cables! Antón? Can you hear me?"

"Hi, Mom. I can hear you fine."

"Really? I can hear you too!"

"I know Mom, it's almost as though we're talking on the phone. No need to shout. Unless you're shouting to the thin man inside me."

"It's unbelievable! You in Madrid, me in Hudson . . . Every time we speak, I just can't believe it. Now I understand why young people today spend all their time . . . How are you, darling?"

"Really well, Mom. I just had dinner."

"What did you eat? Are you still just as fat, Antón? I saw your photo, you're quite chubby, sweetie."

"Thanks, Mom. Your man in Madrid send it to you?"

"What do you mean? Who?"

"Zoltan, Mom. Your spy."

"Don't be silly, son. Zoltan just likes taking pictures of you, having a few memories of his siblings. And don't change the subject: half your problems are because you're overweight. No doubt about it. Half or more."

"Of course, at least half."

"And the worst thing is, since you carry on like that, you'll become a bad person. And people say we eat badly here . . . No bread, no fats, no pastries, no fried chicken, no marshmallows, no . . ."

"I know, Mom. Don't worry, I'm working on it. I have a healthy lunch and then salad and fruit for dinner. And I've been going running in the Retiro Park for more than a month now."

"Just running? No other sports? Your father and Zoltan used to play baseball, soccer, they swam, they did Swedish calisthenics in the gym every day."

"Good for them. We Spanish aren't so sporty."

"They're Spanish too, don't be nasty. Well, it doesn't matter, forget it, I didn't say anything. You might be fat, but you're still handsome, *very*, Antón, as you well know. More than Zoltan, I'd say. It's so lovely to hear your voice, dear, though it is still a little strange . . . like . . . like you're far, far away."

"I am a long way away, Mom. The sound comes through with a bit of a delay on the internet."

"Sure, I'm sure you must be right, you'd know. So how are you? Have you bought your plane tickets to come for Christmas?"

"I already told you, Mother, I don't know if I can come. I'm working, you know that. And this thing with the satellite is an utter fucking . . ."

"Son, watch your language."

"Sorry . . . At the moment I'm waiting for the insurers to send me the opening offers. Once the game's afoot, I'll get them to fight it out amongst themselves, get a decent premium, cover for possible disasters and hope no one pulls out . . ."

"To tell you the truth, Son, this is all Greek to me."

"I know, Mom, I'm just trying to give you an idea of how busy I am."

"Yes but *you have to come*. Christmas is sacred, Antón. If not, when is this family ever going to get together?"

"I'll try, Mom. I don't know why you call Christmas sacred if we're all non-believers—all apart from Zoltan and the happy family."

"What's sacred is getting together at Christmas, dear. Plus, I'm a non-believer, but I believe in spirits and supernatural forces, don't forget that. So, coming or not?"

"You guys could always come over here, couldn't you? I've got space for you, planes fly from New York to Madrid as well . . ."

"Us? (Long silence, uncertainty at the other end of the line). We can't set foot in Spain, son, you know that."

"No, I don't know that. Why not? Has Father got some pending criminal charges you haven't told me about?"

"What a crazy idea! And? What else? Still not interested in finding yourself a nice girl?"

"Thinking about it, Mom, thinking about it, but no wedding bells just yet, if you catch my drift. Women aren't exactly the easiest subject at the moment. All in good time. And Father? How's he? Zoltan said he's ill, kicking up even more of a fuss than usual."

"He's fine. Nothing's hurting, so . . . I can't put him on, he's in his den just now, with his computer. You know how he gets if you interrupt him. He and I are still having fun together, as usual. We go on a lot of outings, he helps me with my gardening projects . . . I had a maple tree die the other day, poor thing. The one outside the kitchen window. Strangely, Ms. Schnee rang me that same day with a commission for a garden."

"Oh? And what was that?"

"One tree dies and others are going to go and live in a lovely environment . . . I don't know, maybe it was a sign, or a message, or who knows. I *don't have powers*, Antón, I've told you a thousand times. How I'd love to be fully clairvoyant! Oh, I'm *so* pleased you're back working, darling. You should call more often!"

". . ."

And so on for half an hour, more or less. She never tells me anything of any importance. I, an edited version.

NOTES ON BELA'S BOOKS

*On the Happy Life* and *Consolations* by Seneca (4-65 BC)

*The Meditations* by Marcus Aurelius (121-180 BC)

What a pleasure (and what a disappointment) to read the Ancients. I owe my discovery of them to Bela (my discovery, that is; their works are probably among the most well-read of all time). Theirs is a moral philosophy, tackling personal issues and giving advice, which makes them the precursors to monstrosities of self-help. But you can hardly blame people for having degenerate descendants, generations down the line—wouldn't you say, Vidor? What happened to them? Why are they all so unhappy, why don't they leave any margin for hope? Did they think too much? The Epicurean, feigning playfulness, flees, shuts himself up in his comfortable golden cage; the Stoic, proud, severe and resigned, tries to stay on his feet as the blows rain down. Both of these are jaded men. Full of fear of feelings. Fear of facing life as it really is. I don't want to be Epicurus, nor Seneca, nor Marcus Aurelius, much as I admire them. They're pessimists, the poor bastards, in spite of doing everything humanly possible to mitigate our suffering and achieve a state of quietude. I don't want to die in life, Vidor. I want to live, LIVE, to look, even if I don't like everything I see. I want to fall in love again, to care for someone, I want the cells in my body to leap for joy, what do I know . . . to LIVE!! Is it so hard?

*Wednesday, November 25, 2009*

> "But I cannot stomach thy daintiness when thou complainest with such violence of grief and anxiety because thy happiness falls short of completeness. Who hath so entire happiness that he is not in some part offended with the condition of his estate?"
>
> BOETHIUS

102

Vidor, Félix rang, the private investigator! He's located the Supposed She-Carrier of a new Mallick! We've agreed to meet in Café Comercial, on the Glorieta de Bilbao, in half an hour. I'm a nervous wreck. Your dizzy spells when you asked our great-great-great-grandmother for her hand have come in to my thoughts, though they have nothing to do with this.

Seven o'clock in the evening. Félix's anxiety levels are roughly the same as mine, but for different reasons: Café Comercial is no smoking. He bites his nails, squints offputtingly and chews top and bottom lip alternately, a mannerism I find exasperating. I prefer to be in the street so he can smoke, even if it's freezing.

"Come on, let's go outside. We can smoke out there."

It's dark now, and it seems that the few passersby still around are hurrying to take refuge at home. We stand by the newspaper stand, smoking and stamping our feet to loosen up. Félix is just as nervous as before. Most Wanted Woman has turned out to be one Lucía Gómez, full stop. A name like any other. How prosaic everything becomes when put prosaically.

"Damn," says Félix. "The Registry would have been useless. She's a 'Polish'—we were lucky about the receipt."

"Like you, right? Félix *Ramirez* is your name, unless I'm mistaken."

In Spain some of the commonest surnames—Pérez, García, that kind of thing—are called "Polish". And her name is Lucía Gómez. Lucía is twenty-eight and is a manager in the admin department of a transportation company. She works at Mercamadrid, Madrid's central market.

"At least she'll be able to bring you back decent fish, right?"

This hilarious comment is by Félix, who's turning out to be a real hoot, or an aspiring writer of comedy monologues, or simply a deeply unfunny blundering fool. Lucía is more than three months pregnant and lives on Calle Barco, surrounded by whores and pushers, in a part of the old town, not far from Gran Vía, where the police never show their faces and where one day someone will make a fortune knocking down and rebuilding.

"She lives with a Romanian, Señor Mallick. I'm sorry."

His calling me "Señor Mallick" is starting to annoy me—it's as though he actually does have manners and I'm demanding this out of place, old-fashioned treatment. The Romanian blow, on the other hand, I don't mind, at least for now. What was I expecting, that she be Ava Gardner sixty years ago, when she was beautiful and single, and her smile was enough to make a man's head spin? Though, in a way, it is funny that he's Romanian rather than anything else, Romanians historically being the enemies of Hungarians.

"The Romanian's a hustler, younger than her, not much over twenty. He deals in stolen goods, bit of fraud, probably pimps part-time, fingers in different pies. Who knows how she ended up with him, she herself is quite normal. She's well-thought-of at work, and her family, who are from Soria, are good people, hard-working. And, at least according to her neighbors, she isn't into drugs or anything."

"How have you found this all out in a week?"

Félix allows himself a smile. I am confronted once more by his yellowing, holey, sorry teeth.

"It's my job. I tailed her, really went for it, and I put in a decent shift too—as you'll see on your bill . . . Look, that's Lucía."

He shows me photos on his digital camera. They're indescribably bad. They confirm, as well as how poorly decent technology can be put to use, that she's less good-looking than I remembered, or imagined, and she has terrible taste in clothes. Félix hands me a piece of paper on which he's written the phone number of Lucía Gómez.

"So. What are you thinking? Want me to be there when you meet?"

I don't feel much like talking. I don't feel much like standing around in the freezing cold with some guy with yellow teeth who makes me want to kick him in the balls.

"Maybe you'd rather see her on your own. She often goes for breakfast on a Saturday at Colby's, a bar on Calle Fuencarral. Between ten and eleven."

I give a weak smile, turn and head up Calle Sagasta. Félix shouts something about a bill, but I don't look back. It's odd. The Lucía story has made me get my act together, but at the same time is constricting me. Now I know a little about her, I start to realize this isn't a mystery, and it isn't the start of a happy story, but another unhappy accident that good fortune has brought my way, one more obsession. And as soon as Lucía becomes a real woman, with dumbo ears and lizardy skin, as soon as she stops being part of the comfortable, playful realm of imagination, everything will take a turn for the worse.

My friend Fran is probably right. The best thing is to stop chasing the carrot, and simply focus on not becoming a mad hare. Forget Lucía ever existed and turn over a new page. When I get home I take an Orfidal, turn off my phone and get into bed. Fully clothed.

*Friday, November 27, 2009*

**From:** Little sister
**To:** Antón:
**Subject:** Gloom, gloom and more gloom

Hey Antón, what a gloomy email, I wonder if you finally made up your mind—what about the whole becoming an optimist thing? What, you thought Lucía Gómez was going to be like Scarlett Johansson in eight years' time (I mean so you two would be the same age, though I know that makes no sense . . . )? I mean, the thing about her Romanian Mafioso boyfriend is a handicap, but . . . I still think SHE ISN'T PREGNANT BY YOU, YOU'RE NOT GOING TO HAVE A BABY WITH THIS SHIT STIRRER and that, even if you were, IT SHOULD BE HER WHO TRIES TO FIND YOU. Don't get annoyed, but you don't have the right to go after her since you don't know how much of the story is true and YOU AREN'T STRONG ENOUGH TO TAKE RESPONSIBILITY FOR YOUR SUPPOSED OFFSPRING. By the way, brother, ever heard of contraceptives? These are TO AVOID HAVING PROBLEMS LIKE THIS ONE and, easy, VIRTUALLY ALL WOMEN KNOW HOW TO PUT THEM ON THEIR PARTNERS. Some—not me, unfortunately—can even do it with their mouth; your lady, most likely, even with her toes.

Okay, sermon over. The one good thing about your email is that you haven't totally lost your sense of humor. I found it funny what you said about the Llorente guy, your client, and what you were saying about having trouble keeping up when he goes on about the satellite's attributes even though you've studied those infernal contraptions to the nth degree. My IQ's closer to a chimp's than his as well, so don't you worry about that. Jeez, he's an aerospace engineer, and us, we're just ordinary run-of-the-mill speculators. You're a great insurance seller, and I'm a

106

more than brilliant Lit Professor! According to current parameters, we're two utter ignoramuses! We don't belong to the universe of Science! An aeronautical engineer *knows* things—in theory, yes; when people here argue against the quality of an author—always European writers, I might add—sometimes it's all I can do to stop myself from shouting YOU'RE RIGHT, YOU BASTARDS, HE'S TERRIBLE, I DON'T KNOW WHAT WE'RE DOING HERE, THOSE WHO WANT TO THROW THE BOOK IN THE BIN PLEASE RAISE YOUR HANDS? Oh, yeah, by the way, what about the books? DON'T THINK TOO MUCH. As you know, thinking will only tire you out and confuse you. And it gets a bad press. It's an antisocial activity, the only one that's still rebellious, the only one that our ultra-advanced society can't accept. Let the intellectuals cultivate it, that's why they get grants. By the way, don't hold your breath for me joining in at Christmas, I'll be staying with John, he's got doctors' appointments. And I can't respond to the SOS from the Houdini Couple, the Great Escape Artists (been a while since we called Mother and Father that, hasn't it?). I am a little worried, in spite of everything. They're really old now. Why don't you go for Christmas? I'd owe you one, or two.

Love and hugs and kisses—miss you like crazy!

PS. I'm sure you've noticed I'm a bit hyper, right? We're such peas in a pod, you and me.

> "Those whose outlook on life causes them to feel so little happiness that they do not care to beget children are biologically doomed. Before very long they must be succeeded by something gayer and jollier."
>
> B. Russell

There's a woman. I come across her every week, usually at night, when she's out taking her German Shepherd for a walk. She's a little younger than me, quite short, fair, with brown eyes, elegant but not at all classic-looking. I look at her, and she holds my gaze until we pass one another. The other day when I was out buying bread we bumped into each other. When she saw me she smiled, somewhere between facetious and lascivious—terribly sexy. I almost dropped the coins I was about to pay with. We stood looking at one another for a few seconds and the braindead assistant went and interrupted us, the owners' idiotic daughter, she didn't get what was happening, the clot, either that or she's so mean she fully intended to spoil our little game.

I obviously said nothing to her, my state of mind, more animal than human, prevented me from articulating a single word, or even thinking articulately. I managed to hold back from biting her on the neck there and then, no thought for the blood stains all over the bakery floor, or the more than likely hysterical cries from the shop assistant and the rest of the clientele. The interesting thing is how long it's been since something like this has happened to me: ages. With any luck, it could be the start of something. I was convinced that these sensations had withered, that they'd never bubble up ever again. Neural pathways—shut off or clogged up or forgotten—wanted to reconnect, or something. I can't admit it to my mother, but this diary, yes. This woman is what you might call full-figured, although I'd say plump, something you can get hold of. Yes, Vidor, I like them buxom, all curves, wide hips and soft skin, whitish, milky if at all possible, and that their cheeks light up, that they flush and roll their eyes and touch the tip of their tongue to full lips when you whisper something in their ear. Of all my relatives only Bela knows my secret: I like 'em chubby. Yes, Vidor, you heard me right, cards on the table: chubby.

*Saturday, November 28, 2009*

> "The art of living is more like wrestling than dancing, in so far as it stands ready against the accidental and the unforeseen, and is not apt to fall."
>
> Marcus Aurelius

Colby's is on the corner of Calle Fuencarral and Calle Hernán Cortés. It was half past nine in the morning, they'd just opened and there were barely any customers. I took a table next to a window, ordered coffee and toast, and began reading Boethius. I only slept four hours last night. I was at work late trying to settle some outstanding issues with the French insurers, who are holding back from making offers, as well as demanding a meeting that I'm trying to avoid. This morning I was exhausted, but alert. With the priceless assistance of Boethius, who irritated me after just a few pages, and of the nicotine in the cigarettes and the caffeine in the coffee, lifting my gaze from time to time, I kept an eye on the door. I recognized her straight away. At around eleven o'clock, in came Lucía Gómez, and she was chunkier than Félix's photos had suggested, and different to how I remembered that night, maybe because of the pregnancy, or because the light of day transforms us all, or because my memory deceives me better and better all the time. I don't want anyone to think, Vidor, that I was attracted to her merely because she happened to be fat. Word of caution to all the knuckleheads, the dimwits and the dickheads: not all obese or buxom women are the same. Anyway.

Lucía, who must have been about twenty-five but looked more than thirty, was dressed in black. PVC thigh-high fuck-me boots with heels. Fishnet tights. Skirt knitted in such a way that I can only describe it as an eyesore. A loose fitting blouse that gave her considerable paunch room to breathe, and invited us to admire her cleavage and immense drooping breasts. The wrists, stacked with fake artisan bracelets. She had a silver or silver-plated chain around her neck with a stunted, undernourished Virgin Mary hanging from it. Over her shoulder she carried a shiny brown leather handbag with a triangular sticker bearing the endearing legend: BABY ON BOARD. She was wearing green eyeliner and her eyes were small and far apart, calling to mind a pig in drag. And her skin was pretty awful. Prepare yourself, child of mine, I thought: you're going to be ugly as sin. I also asked myself if the Romanian, as well as being a delinquent, had problems with his eyesight, or if it might be that Romanian taste in women has evolved more than ours, or mine. And I felt pleased that a woman with such looks could be head of an admin department in a company whatever the business happened to be, as not only did it confirm once and for all the decadence of the West, but also that tolerance has reached its peak (both positives, no doubt).

The waiter and Lucía knew one another. She sat at a table nearby and they served her a *café con leche* and a generous portion of greasy *porras*. To my horror or happiness or both at once, she took out a copy of *The Psychology of Optimism* by Susan C. Vaughan. Lucía and I already had something in common other than a child on its way: shared literary tastes, a desire to be optimistic and, very possibly, shitty lives. I watched her as she read. She was one of those people who mumble as they read, as if this would help the words make their way more quickly or more securely from paper to brain. A habit that makes my blood boil. I couldn't get my head around how, as drunk and high and desperate I'd been that night, I could have ended up with this woman in a cheap hotel, and having sex with her, and impregnating her on top of everything else. Picturing my child as a teenager looking at me with the bovine expression that Lucía had mastered to perfection, I almost threw my coffee cup on the floor. I tried to calm down, I tried to avoid burying the poor woman—for all I knew, an angel—under a mountain of prejudices and murky rumination. "Damn, Antón, she's the mother of a Mallick! Give her a chance! People can be beautiful *inside!*" I said to myself. Not entirely convinced.

I walked over to her table and stood in front of her. After a few seconds she lifted her eyes from her book and looked at me suspiciously. She didn't seem to recognize me, nor did the slightest sign of intelligence show in her eyes, though that was probably totally normal for her.

"Hello, Lucía. It's Antón Mallick."

She gave a start, screwed up her face dementedly, glanced around as if someone might catch her doing something illegal, took a piece of chewing gum from her handbag, put it in her mouth, chomped on it viciously, before directing a forced smile my way. All in under five seconds. By some miracle, I held back from giving a standing ovation.

"Hi, Antón. What brings you here?"

Now there was a question. I asked if I could join her and took a seat at her table. She fiddled nervously with one of the horrible rings on her right hand. I hadn't noticed before: Lucía wore a dark ring on every one of her sausage fingers, skulls and hideous monsters' heads. Awesome. I'd only heard her speak the once, but I already knew this one other fact about her: she had a high shrill voice, like a rat that's been stomped on. And she chewed gum. I've already mentioned that I detest people who chew gum. I always have. Ever since I was a little boy.

"I don't know what to say," she added, seeing I wasn't going to answer her question.

"Don't say anything then," I suggested, feeling suddenly enervated, annihilated. I'd been waiting for this moment for two months and, now that it had come, everything suddenly felt very uphill.

"It's eighteen weeks old already," she said, stroking her generous paunch.

More like eighteen years from the look of it—and that's being kind. Neither of us said anything for a while. She, I suspect little given to reflection, or introspection, or truly fallow silences, started shovelling down her *porras* like they were peanuts. Still with the gum in her mouth. If my Mother ever met her, oh, they'd get on like a house on fire . . .

"Would you like anything else?"

"Weeeeell . . . Wouldn't mind a few more *porras!*" she smiled.

My co-begetter (I can't think of any other name for her without resorting to insult) was loosening up. Seeing her close up was no better than seeing her in terrible photos, nor much nicer than watching her from a distance.

"What a coincidence!" she said smugly. "I mean! Pretty different from the first time we saw each other, right? What a night! And from the last time. When I saw you in the shop I lost it. Just ran off."

She was acting as though she'd run into an old school friend, some smart aleck who bullied her into letting him copy her homework and would grope her tits every time she went by.

"Yeah, happy coincidence," I lied, drearily, stuck at the bottom of the well, finding it hard to breathe. One thing, yes, there was one thing to feel optimistic about. Seeing the black spider, future mother to my child, close up, hadn't brought on one of my anguish attacks. We were served more coffee and her more *porras*. Seeing the size of her, I guessed there was nothing to be done, but I asked anyway:

"Are you sure you want to have it?"

She gave me a look of pure indignation, as if I were a heartless bastard and not some poor wretch testing the water, casting around for a way out of the labyrinth, in spite of the dishonor, in spite of the fact I might regret what I was saying for the rest of my days.

"Of course, you asshole! It's a few inches long already, you piece of shit!" she shouted. Great. Now everyone else in the place was looking at us. "Who d'you think I am?" she asked, touching the revolting little Madonna on her necklace. "It's a person already, a little boy, and he already has a name: Dragosi."

Charming, I thought. Half Dragon, half tuberculosis; half Drag Queen and Sissy; half Dracula, half . . .

"Oh, and I couldn't say a word to Cosmin about you. He'd kill us both. He thinks it's his. When I told him I was pregnant, instead of hitting me he broke down crying. Tears of joy."

Sure, I thought. The Romanian murderer's deliriously happy. Of course.

"And Cosmin is?" I asked, feigning surprise.

"My man," she said, very dignified now. "He knows what he's about, not like you. He's Romanian, from Bucharest. He was in the Secret Police, the Securitate. You know, torturing people and stuff. Here he's a dealer— antiques. We've got a place together on Calle Barco. The night you more or less raped me I was really, really upset because Cosmin was with this other girl. That's the only reason I let you do what you did to me in that shitty hotel. No word of a fucking lie!"

Luckily, eating porras calmed her down a bit. Note to future self: keep a few porras in your pocket in the event of meeting up—you never know. Possibly also worth mentioning to our child once it grows up. Another note: Dragosi was going to be a foulmouth, that was for sure. Plus, with that name, the most bullied of all the Mallicks. Dragosi trumps Lajos, Zoltan, Bela; it trumps the lot. Maybe this was a silly thought to be having, this was the very least of my problems, but think it I did, sitting with Lucía Gómez, grieving as I watched her chug down her coffee like a legionnaire would a canteen in the Saharan desert.

"Why did you tell me I was the father, Lucía?"

Lucía looked worried for a moment and assumed that lunatic expression of hers. I was starting to get used to it.

"I saw you, out of the blue, and . . . I just blurted it out. Wished I hadn't afterwards. 'Do I really want to make my life more difficult than it already is?' I said. 'Do I really want Cosmin to get his switchblade?' "

"And how are you so sure it's mine?"

"Cosmin's infertile. He doesn't know, I went and checked at the hospital on my own. We were trying for over a year. And you're the only pig I slept with outside of the relationship. Want to take the test, asshole?"

"All in good time. While we're about it why did you rob me? Including my ID."

"I took the ID to check out who you were for real, just in case. I was frightened, you seemed really weird to me. And the money, because it was me who'd got the coke, or don't you remember?"

Not exactly the answers I wanted, but she had come straight out with them. When my breathing had more or less returned to normal, I gave her my number and said I was off. I thought that was enough for our first meeting. Not quite . . .

"What's this, Mr. Mallick, think you're getting away that easily? You put your dick in me, fuckface. You made your bed, mister. Got any coke on you?"

Jesus! Harlot from hell! Magnificent in her meanness! What had I got myself into?

"No, Lucía," I managed to say. "I'm clean. That wasn't just any old night, as you well know."

"Yeah, well I need some money. Cosmin and me are going through a rough patch right now and, what with your kid on the way . . ."

I felt floored again. She opened and shut her mouth rhythmically, her jaws snicker snack. The only thing I wanted in the world was to get this woman out of my sight.

"Don't you both work?"

"Yeah, I do data entry. But we've been on a bad run. Five hundred euros should cover it."

Right, so not exactly the manager; "admin" in the data entry sense. And married. And a total bitch. Félix is a star, yes sir. Half his facts were wide of the mark. I felt waves of rage washing up through my body and crashing in my mouth.

"Come on, come with me to an ATM," I said. "I'll give you the money if you take that damn gum out and don't open your mouth again until I'm out of sight."

"What did you say?"

"What are you, deaf? I said, get rid of the gum and shut your trap, you bitch, and I'll give you the money."

And that was that. And so it went, my first meeting with the woman who was going to be mother to Dragosi, my son. I have no idea how I managed to make it home. I unplugged the landline, turned off my mobile, shut all the windows and collapsed in bed. It was one o'clock in the afternoon and I wanted to know nothing more about the world.


*Sunday, November 29, 2009*

> "To this end were you born—to lose, to perish, to hope, to fear, to disquiet yourself and others, both to fear death and to long for it, and, worst

of all, never to know the real terms of your existence."

Nothing. Didn't leave the house.

*Wednesday, December 2, 2009*

DIALOGUE DURING A PARTICULARLY BAD SLEEPLESS
NIGHT BETWEEN MYSELF AND MY UNBORN CHILD

"Hello, little Antón, how you doing in there? Can you
breathe surrounded by *that many* greasy porras?"
"Dad, I don't have a name yet. My name's not Antón, it's
not Nothing either. But I have a sneaking suspicion they're
going to call me Dragosi."
"But Antón's a really cool name, right? Doesn't it have a
ring to it? You've got the Saint Anthony frogs, they're really
pretty, bright green, then there's the Antón Pirulero song,
and . . ."
"I don't like that name. I don't like Dragosi either,
which is what Mom wants to call me. I don't want to be
Romanian. I want to be called Istvan, like the first Magyar king,
Istvan I, crowned in the year 1000, called Vajk until he was
baptized, canonized in 1083, patron saint of Hungary. He
dismembered Koppány, his rival for the throne, and sent his
body parts to the other warlords as warning of what would
happen to them if they didn't become his vassals. I want to
be ISTVAN THE TERRIBLE, or ISTVAN THE UNMERCIFUL,
or ISTVAN THE DESPOT.

117

"Goodness! . . . That's . . . that's . . . great, kid . . . And why a Hungarian name?"

"To piss somebody off."

"Who?"

"You, motherfucker. You, dear Daddy of mine. You, who only knocks on doors where no one wants to let you in."

NOTES ON BELA'S BOOKS

*The Consolation of Philosophy* (524 AD) by Boethius (ca. 475–524 AD)

I want to get Boethius out of the way. The only positive thing I can think to do today. There are some very beautiful passages, particularly when he's complaining. Boethius had it good—so what if he died in prison, disgraced and beaten: he at least had the chance to address Philosophy directly, one on one, like a sexy lady on a date in a bar . . . Anyway. Bye bye, Boethius. You're no good to me. Take care of yourself.

*Thursday, December 3, 2009*

> "The good life, as I conceive it, is a happy life."
>
> B. Russell

I go out for a walk. I look at the faces of the people passing by, and it strikes me that they are all children to someone. I'm not the only one to be condemned. Thousands of millions of fucked up little children. The mind never stops, over and over, I carry on looking at them, they pass me by, the slim woman, the sad man, the bored executive, the teenager talking on his mobile. An old man shouts abuse at a lunatic who's thrown his newspaper on the ground, a man with no arms begs at a crossing holding the collecting plate between his teeth. Now it strikes me that they are not all children, they are the living dead, carrying death about in their very gait, in their sagging flesh, I see them all as sullied skulls and then a ten-year-old boy crosses the street and nearly gets knocked down by a car and grabs hold of my jacket for an instant and I look at him and see his skull, still so soft, and I stop. I look at him. Can't muster a smile for him. His eyes very wide, he's still alive, alive, alive and frightened. I double over. Retch. Retch again. The boy walks away. I vomit. I wipe my mouth with my coat sleeve. The boy's gone. Vanished.

I carry on walking. Again. Again. I carry on walking. Now not looking at anyone, but at the blue Madrid sky instead, I throw my head back, I want to take in all the air there is, all of it, all the air in this whole galaxy, and I breathe in deep and my lungs expand but, by some misfortune, instead of exhaling it I swallow it and then there's a presence within me, it is not air, it smothers me, something that presses on me and leaves me breathless, and I walk and I go back to inhaling all the air and I so want not to vomit again, the air inside me to escape without making any noise, a little at a time, without destroying me, and I walk and I walk until, walking and trying not to swallow more oppressive air, I arrive at my front door and I take out my keys and my hand shakes and I open the door and I say hello to one of my neighbors forcing a smile that lets in too much air and I launch myself into the elevator and when I'm finally safe, on the fourth floor, in my home, on my own, no one with me, alone, I realize that the anguish attack I've been expecting hasn't arrived, my consciousness is still in its rightful place, inside my head, forcing itself not to leave me, to make me believe that I exist, and that I am whole.

I'm Antón Mallick and I sell insurance, and I take a lungful of air and let it out slowly, making small noises to make sure I exist, I think I've saved myself and so then, yes, then I can dance, I can be an optimist again and open the fridge and take out some orange juice with added vitamins and drink a glass of life without my hands hardly even shaking at all.

KOROLEV 4

First thing in the morning, June 27, 1938. Four men—two secret police from the NKVD and two "witnesses"—entered Sergei and Layla's apartment and arrested the engineer. He wasn't even allowed to take a change of clothes. Nor say goodbye to his three-year-old daughter, Natasha. The testimony that led to his arrest for treason carried the signatures of three of his closest work colleagues. There was no trial. They tortured him until he "confessed." After being shunted from one prison to the next, in October of the following year Korolev was transferred to Siberia's Kolyma region, one of the hardest parts of Stalin's horrific gulag system. Thirty percent of prisoners would die there every year. He worked in one of the gold mines for nine months. His teeth fell out, he had heart problems, his jaw

120

was broken; he'd never be in good health again. But he survived. And had a bit of luck: Stalin needed him in the war, to overcome another monster, Hitler. His case was going to be reconsidered. A few days before his death Korolev recounted that, on his journey back to Moscow, after two days without food, waiting in Magadan for winter to pass so they could continue their journey, one night when there was a full moon and it was forty below zero, he came across a loaf of warm bread in the snow. Yes, just baked. Overjoyed, he wolfed it down. Another day, he saw a butterfly. You, Vidor, can suspect Korolev of hallucinating all you like, but I think, simply, he was a lucky man. In 1940, he arrived at his new fate, a *sharaga*, a prison for scientists and intellectuals. There Sergei the Slave worked designing war planes. He was allowed visitors, and to stretch his legs in a small, barred courtyard known as "the monkey cage." Now wasn't that a bit of luck, Vidor? TBC.

*Sunday, December 6, 2009*

> "Every man passes out of life as if he had just been born."
>
> EPICURUS

Carlos has bought a place in Cava Baja. It's an old house and an architect friend of his has restored it really nicely. I spent today helping him with the move, sweating like a pig. At eight o'clock in the evening, anesthetized by the physical labor, he and I went to a bar for tapas. Do things. Gym for the body. Don't have expectations. Survive.

"Almost everyone will agree on what we consider to be a tragedy or a disaster. When it comes to what's worth celebrating, we disagree. This gives a pretty accurate idea of what we are like."

"The only good thing about flowers, apart from their beauty and their colors, is how quickly they die, and in people's homes, when they're dry, they remind you of those skulls in baroque paintings. Just to see them makes you want to rush out and indulge in all sorts of pleasures. Therefore, placing fresh flowers all around a home is a salute to the world's purity, and clearing them away when they're withered means you are keeping death at bay."

"Leave no offspring and you're lost. How can anyone renounce the single unconditional love, the one that will gush out of you, the one that will *really* make you suffer until the day that you die?"

"My grandfather died in the same way as Count Miklos Zrinyi (1620-1664), general, military leader in Croatia, Hungarian nationalist and poet. Zrinyi wrote *The Siege of Sziget*, an epic poem of great beauty that tells of the heroic fight and death of his ancestor the commander of Szigetvar, which fell in 1566 to Suleiman the Great, that bloodthirsty and respectable Turk. So Count Zrinyi, the one known as "Phoenix of the Age," was killed by a wild bear, much to the Austrians' solace. Gobbled him up. His remains were buried in state, in a stone sarcophagus. As for my grandfather, he went to the woods one fine day and all that came back was his inert body, torn apart by the fangs and claws of another bear. The difference being that when my idiotic family buried him, they failed to dig a very deep grave, and they didn't spend a florin on a coffin. After the bear, the pigs also got to chow down my grandfather. His burial site was promptly forgotten. And here you have it, the difference between a poor man and a Count: the poor man always dies more than once."

"The child who imitates you must be harshly punished; the one who fails to imitate you, thrown out of the house."

"Don't start having thoughts about death as soon as you wake up in the morning, because you'll never get out of bed. Do it at night: the worst thing that can happen that way is that you don't get to sleep."

"A small coffin containing the corpse of your child is the greatest insult you can   possibly receive. 'It's all over between us, Mother Nature,' you say. 'Lose though I may, I declare indefinite war on you, and I shall give no quarter. We'll see who laughs last, and who laughs longest.' "

"When I realized that my daughter had lost her mind, I did not have her locked up. She was still my daughter, but now she was my mad daughter."

"If you find yourself in darkness, light a candle."


*Wednesday, December 9, 2009*

Today at around midday, just when I'd managed to get down to do some work, my office door opened.

"Antón, do you happen to know which is currently the happiest country in the world?"

"No idea."

"Nigeria! Can you believe it? Nigeria, in Africa, the lost continent! We're more or less average, we're in twenty-second, along with all the other boring countries."

And who is it giving me these crucial, definitive facts, Vidor? My friend Fran. Ever since he found out about my

Optimism Crusade, he's been dropping by the office and bombarding me with dubious pieces of information about happiness, dredged up online. He tells me about mathematical formulas for measuring it, made up by psychologists and educationalists. He tells me that, apparently, the man who has discovered the secret of happiness is a Hungarian-American scientist named Mihalyi Czikszentmihalyi (of course he had to be Hungarian, wouldn't he, the charlatan, siding with Hungary's detractors, promoting false and unmerited national stereotypes). He claims that it's all down to "flow," that is, activities that we concentrate on so much that we forget everything except for what we're doing: playing the violin, writing, masturbating with nobody in particular in mind . . . Over time, if we *flow* quite often, we will achieve a state of psychological well-being (since I began writing, I flow more than I used to, when all I did was masturbate—must be doing something right).

Fran speaks to me of studies carried out with monkeys. In the one with Harlow's baby monkeys, the monkeys hugged a felt doll, a mother substitute; in Brady's "executive monkeys" experiment, two monkeys periodically received the same electric shock and only one had any way of stopping it, with the result that the executive monkey, responsible for its companion's well-being, developed terrible stomach ulcers, and died. He speaks to me of studies with rats. Weiss's studies, in which the rats were submitted to the same torture as the executive monkeys, and came through it better, with fewer internal wounds; those carried out by Richter, in which rats died suddenly and inexplicably when their whiskers were shaved off. The whiskers thing killed Fran, he laughed until he cried, he finds it hilariously funny. And then in terms of studies with dogs, a certain Seligman put some in harnesses, and tortured them, giving them electric shocks. The canines, apathetic, defeated, learned to live in helplessness and defencelessness, and didn't even try to escape when the harnesses were removed. Scientists really are nasty pieces of work sometimes. Were they really surprised by any of their findings? Sad tales all, but I don't know what the fuck they have to do with happiness, or why on earth Fran sees fit to tell me them.

He speaks to me of endorphins and he speaks to me of dopamines. Of the fact the best scientific method for measuring happiness is to ask people to score their state 1–10, full stop, no frills, no clinical studies, nothing. The other day he said, utterly convinced, that it is "scientifically proven" that someone's pessimism or optimism depends fifty percent on genes. According to certain "renowned scientists," external factors aren't as important to happiness as some people believe. Money, for instance: it doesn't make you happy, but, rather, unhappy if your basic needs aren't covered. Health isn't that important either. Nor sex (thank goodness). Nor what you look like. Nor upbringing (I've always thought of rude people as happier because other people's rudeness doesn't get them down; and that goes for ignoramuses, too, because they believe themselves to be far less stupid than the erudite, and, essentially, they couldn't give a fig about anything). Nor climate (the link between sun and good mood, all in people's minds). Other circumstances do have an influence, but not that much: marriage (for better or for worse?); living in a developed democracy (like Nigeria?); religious faith, avoiding traumatic events (ie. always crossing at zebra crossings?), having an intense social life and enjoying friends' company.

Anyway. Today I came to the conclusion that being with friends doesn't always help either. Fran's great, and I know he's only doing it to try and help, but his investigative zeal has become a real ballache. Today when he came by to tell me that magnetic resonance has been used to discover that a positive, enthusiastic state of mind is associated with increased activity in the left prefrontal cortex, and that the amygdala is associated with fear, the insular cortex with being unhappy and worried, and that the striatum mediates aggression, that cocaine and ecstasy and orgasms have a bearing on the orbitofrontal cortex, which is where pleasure and reward-experiences are generated, and that women are more inclined to depression, all in a jumble, I threw him out of my office:

"Out! Out! Enough's enough, Fran! I've had enough!"

"Hey! Calm down, relax. Don't be rude! You could at least say you appreciate the effort . . ."

"I don't appreciate it! You're making me depressed. Out!"

And I shut the door. I'm writing this to cheer myself up, because really all it was was an anecdote, and if life consisted of a series of anecdotes, it would be cause for uncorking the bubbly, for getting happily drunk, for laughing until you fall down.

*Thursday, December 10, 2009*

> "And I declared that the dead, who had already died, are happier than the living, who are still alive. But better than both is he who has not yet been, who has not seen the evil that is done under the sun."
>
> ECCLESIASTES

Lucía called. Wanting more money "for the baby." No way was I giving her another cent until the birth, and only after consulting with my lawyers, I said. She threatened to tell Cosmin the Romanian. I've only got myself to blame: it was me and no one else who introduced my head into this wolf's jaws. I'm getting on average thirty text messages a day from Dragosi's mommy. "Bastard" is about the most endearing term she uses. It's great having a mobile phone, but some people have also learned to use them as instruments of torture. I couldn't go out running today. I feel lousy when I don't go out running.

WORDS OF ADVICE FOR DRAGOSI,
MY FUTURE SON

Dragosi, my son. It's going to be difficult for me to address you because I can't stand your name, though I suppose that this, and being able to stand lots of other things about you, Nature will see to, Nature which is wise and all powerful. My first piece of advice to you is DON'T BE BORN. Stay where you are in limbo, along with the rest of the unborn, who are legion.

Exercise your rights, no one can force you to come into this world, to be the child of Lucía Gómez and me, start off on such the wrong foot along such an obstacle-laden path. There, in that nothingness in which you float, which is something without being anything, you can be happy. Many wise men agree with me, your non-place is fertile land, a simple paradise. Maybe that is the much-vaunted Happiness, floating without being, not being, having been able to be. And if you are born, don't throw these words back in my face. It wouldn't be worth hating me before you've even met me. There will be plenty of time for that, child. By the way, your mother is a monster.

*Friday, December 11, 2009*

> "If, therefore, the happiest lot is not to be born, the next best, I think, is to have a brief life and by death to be restored quickly to the original state."
>
> SENECA

Nothing, absolutely nothing. I've watched Blake Edwards's *The Party* again, but even with that, nothing.

NOTES ON BELA'S BOOKS

*Emile, or On Education* by Jean-Jacques Rousseau (1712–1778)

An insomniac reading is always a different reading: weighed down, absent, aggressive. Dragosi, my pseudo-son, like a monster in a horror movie, shows up in my nightmares and, in my waking, insinuates himself into the pages of the book, meddles in *all* my affairs. Rousseau. Why don't you bring Dragosi up, you bastard? Why don't you take him off my hands? Why don't you turn him into a perfect little man, a mini robot like Emile?

At least three things need to be borne in mind when it comes to Rousseau's biography. He isn't French, but Swiss, a native (or anti-native) of Geneva. He killed his mother in childbirth (which gives an idea about how early his repugnant misogyny arose) and abandoned his own children in orphanages (he, the great tutor, the philosopher of freedom and education). *Emile* is a treatise on education written by a monster, with certain modern ideas that are still being applied today, written in a style that is arrogant, pretentious, perverse, manipulative and misogynist. Disgusting. He has a disturbing idea of happiness: a perfect world in Rousseau's eyes would seem like a dystopia to us. Human androids grimacing constantly but trying to pass these off as smiles, women dressed in innocent pastoral dresses, chained to trees, waiting to be whipped, men seeking their non-existent mothers, provosts in dingy cells masturbating while spying on their servants, cities in ruin, fields in flower . . . A Happy Hell. The optimism of the defective, of the unfulfilled, of the bitter, of . . .

*Sunday, December 13, 2009*

Vidor, you arrived in Madrid in March of 1830. The way you tell it, when you arrived on the Castilian plateau on which the city sits and saw the dusty, yellowing, ochre landscape, you couldn't understand what the locals had done with all the grass. Had they eaten it? Maybe the land was cursed? Your spirits recovered when you got to Madrid, walking the streets in search of a hostel in which to rest your head. In those days the city had around two hundred thousand inhabitants. The serious, sober aspect of the Madrileños appealed to you, but also the festive air in the streets, the impression it gave of a gigantic village, uncouth, poor, happy. Your early excursions led you to the conclusion that the city had barely any foreigners, just a few glove makers and tailors over from France. The population was comprised of native Madrileños and migrants from the provinces, water sellers from Asturias, buggy drivers and nightwatchmen from Valencia, beggars from La Mancha, handmaidens from Santander, grocers from Catalonia, butlers from the Basque country, pastry chefs from Galicia . . . Whereas in Pest, Obuda and Buda—which half a century later would come together to form Budapest—you had Magyars, Slovaks, Saxons, Croats, Gypsies, Romanians, Slovenians, Ukrainians, Germans, Serbs and Jews—among others.

You'd be surprised at how Madrid has changed. There are over four million people now, and it is very much a city in the modern sense of the word. Fortunately it still feels like a free place, not at all introspective. Still as uncouth, active, happy as it was in those days, only full of foreigners. Money and job opportunities attract those who are most in need. You've got your Dominicans, your Argentineans, your Poles, Moroccans, Central Africans, Russians, Chinese, Ecuadorians, Paraguayans, Bulgarians, and even a good few Romanians ... I went for a run in the Retiro today. When you got to Madrid, Vidor, were people allowed in the Royal Gardens? Had they rebuilt them, or were there still signs of the devastation they suffered in the War of Independence? Did you know that even today you can still see French bullet marks on the Alcalá Gate? What were the trees like, stunted or splendid? Did you walk its paths with your wife, you wrapped in a gray cloak, she with a *peineta* and a *mantilla* covering her head?

When I got to Calle Alfonso XII, the parked cars formed a second wall, a multicolored metal one. Behind it the Alcalá Gate, already festooned with hundreds of lights, was just one more Christmas decoration. The flower beds, the paths and the area surrounding the lake seethed with people idling, most of them immigrants. Children were playing in the playgrounds, couples were walking hand in hand, tourists were having their pictures taken next to the statue of Jacinto Benavente (wonder if any of them have read his books?). I did a circuit of the perimeter of the park along the dirt tracks. I overtook some runners and myself was overtaken by others, long-legged athletic types that reminded me of flamingos in shorts. I really don't feel like telling you my troubles today, Vidor, or how bad things are with me. I want to escape, to flee. That was why I went to the Retiro, and the regular rhythm of my breathing, the brownish-gray color of the remaining leaves, the sweat that bathed my skin, the sound of my footfall on the ground, the singing of the birds and the pain I began to feel in my legs after the third mile—all of it helped me forget myself for almost an hour.

The only thing keeping me grounded at the moment is the satellite insurance policy. I get home and I carry on working, even into the wee hours, until I fall asleep, refusing to allow insomnia to rule my nights. And if I don't feel capable of working, I read, trying to find a rational justification for this optimism which now seems to me nothing but a chimera. Wednesday I'll go to Paris. It was only two weeks ago that travelling seemed like a drag to me, but today I feel like the trip is a kind of truce. There, in Paris, the city of lovers, or of light, or of wide boulevards, I'll be safe from Lucía's threats. And from my own feebleness.

*Wednesday, December 16, 2009*

Paris. The Air France flight is delayed. I'll land in Madrid at around half past ten tonight if I'm lucky. Yesterday, afternoon meeting in the Apri offices, in the Quai Anatole France, *Rive Droite*, near the Musee d'Orsay and the Place de la Concorde. They're in a gray stone building set inside in a cobblestone courtyard, climbing plants up the walls and paintings strategically situated behind the windowpanes should anyone look up.

I hadn't met Anne Landrin before, the broker working with me. Brunette. Fortyish. A bit cold. Attractive. Divorced. It annoyed her that I don't speak good French. The fact she doesn't speak a word of Spanish didn't bother me in the slightest. She had trouble with her red high heels when she walked. My shoes on the other hand are comfy. It annoyed her that I smoke. Me, I didn't mind that her perfume was a little intense. She was annoyed by my habit of not taking notes in meetings. I understand perfectly well that not everyone has a memory they can rely upon, like mine when I'm working. She was annoyed not to be the one in charge of the insurance contract. I'm delighted that the client is Spanish and is running things. She was annoyed by the cold. I, wrapped up nice and warm, appreciated the freezing air, the cutting feeling of it on the face. She was annoyed at not finding a taxi immediately. I found the wait entertaining, watching passersby, the way they walk, the expressions on their faces . . . She was annoyed . . .

Anyway. Anne is extremely Parisian. A darling, deep down. After dinner in a top (or at least expensive) restaurant, I suggested a drink. Purely out of courtesy. I didn't expect her to say yes. I wanted her to go to bed happy. To think: "I knew it. It was written all over his face: he really thought he had a chance with me?" But she said yes. When we got outside, I pretended I didn't feel well, I felt a sudden dizzyness, and saved her from me, or from some maudlin conversation, in English, between a French divorcee and a Spanish widower.

The next morning at about seven I went for a run in the Luxembourg Gardens, known as the "Luco," on the other side of the river in the sixth arrondissement. Nobody there was reading or playing chess or *petanque*, nobody was out for a stroll. No children, no old people, no couples. Only joggers. The day consisted of meeting after meeting, me dragging my suitcase around. Insurance executives, no matter where they're from, are like wolves. They sniff around, they stare at you with their yellow eyes, trying to detect any weakness, their smiles are fanged, they sniff your backside. They wonder what's happening with the premium, how much they should offer. Fifteen percent? Twenty percent? Seventeen percent? Market, souk, emporium, haggle haggle haggle.

It's two o'clock in the morning already. When I got home I found a note on the floor from the doorman: "Antón, a young Romanian was asking after you on Friday morning. He didn't say what it was about. I didn't tell him when you were getting back. Thank you for the crate of wine." Sleeping pill.

*Monday, December 21, 2009*

> "Art thou dead, art thou corrupted, art thou playing the hypocrite, art thou become a beast, dost thou herd and feed with the rest."
>
> MARCUS AURELIUS

On Gran Vía, near the Casa del Libro bookstore. What could be more dispiriting that a beggar, dressed up as a clown, holding up a sign that says: "52 years old. Schizophrenic. Cannot work." Your typical street clown: the careless makeup, the long eyelashes, the red clown's nose, the two-day-old stubble flecked with white, the black-toothed ear-to-ear smile, the plastic plate with a couple of coins. Second to none for desperation, this mix of clown, madman and beggar. A hair-raising combination. I stood trembling, literally, and crossed to the other side without any thought for traffic. I'm putting too much in at work, craving for everything to turn out well. I'm overdoing it. Sleeping pill.

## KOROLEV 5

Let's kill Korolev off, Vidor. It's simply not possible that I could (or would want to) recount his life in this diary as if it had all been a bed of roses. It would be totally absurd. Yes, Korolev's biography (*Korolev, How One Man Masterminded the Soviet Drive to Beat America to the Moon* by James Hartford) had an impact on me. I read it when I was put in charge of my first satellite insurance job, when I was devouring any book I could find on the subject. So what? Time to kill him off, Vidor, right now. Korolev died of cancer on January 14, 1966 at the age of fifty-nine, in a Moscow hospital. Two days later *Pravda* published an extensive obituary, complete with photos. On the third day a magnificent funeral was held, ending in Red Square, with a speech by the great Yuri Gagarin, another patriot. In death Korolev went from anonymity, from running the Soviet space program for twenty-five years in the shadows, from being one of the Russians' greatest secret weapons against the Americans, to being a world-renowned hero, a titan synonymous with the space age. He developed and launched the first man-made satellite to go into orbit, Sputnik; he sent the first living being ever into space (Laika the dog), the first man, the first woman, and the first group of men; he was in charge of the first "space walk"; he created the first Soviet spy and communications satellites; he built the first space shuttles and ships to ever reach the moon and Venus, and the first to ever travel farther than Mars . . . But the life of this man— this brilliant, egoistic, stern, solitary, tirelessly hardworking, choleric, manipulative, cynical, opportunistic man—was sad, like most lives. I still wonder how he can have stayed loyal to the successive Soviet dictatorships after spending those seven years in prison as a victim of Stalin's purges. Seven years in which Sergei Pavlovich Korolev, future hero, future victor, patriot, must have died a number of times. But, Vidor, this story doesn't interest me any more. Let's finish off killing off Korolev. Goodbye. One less fire to fight. I've just received another incendiary text message from Lucía. "Bastard" is as sweet as she gets. I've still got Leibniz left to write about. No time for any nonsense.

NOTES ON BELA'S BOOKS

*Theodicy: Essays on the Goodness of God, the Freedom of Man and the Origin of Evil* (1710) by Wilhelm Gottfried Leibniz (b. 1646, Leipzig, d. 1716, Hannover)

Back to school, back to studying, homework, yawns, the pen that slips from your fingers when you doze off for a second. I don't want to say a single word about Leibniz, I really don't feel like it. But this diary, and all my efforts to be optimistic, become nonsense if I don't persevere, if I don't keep playing to the final whistle. I must read. Think. Even if my head is pounding, even if what I really want is to burn down libraries and kill butterflies.

Leibniz dedicated his life to the *Theodicy*, a term he coined to describe an ancient philosophical problem: that of reconciling God's goodness and omnipotence with the presence of evil in the world. That is, rationally, evil poses an insuperable obstacle to the admittance of divine providence; only faith can accept it. A simple idea, any child could come up with it. In *Discourse on Metaphysics* (1686) he stood against "the opinion of certain modern writers who boldly maintain that that which God has made is not perfect in the highest degree, and that he might have done better." Anyway. My head hurts. I'm not going to enlarge on the ways Leibniz found to resolve these problems and help God save face. There are plenty of textbooks on it, my dear Vidor. If you're interested, look it up. You're a ghost, right? Well off you go, wing your way to any respectable library and get studying, I don't have to chew it all up for you. And if you don't get it, up yours, you could have spent some time reading instead of stealing, eating lamb, running after women and generally having a jolly good time. Leibniz's answer, naturally, as brilliant and elegant as it may be, is a total scam. He applies entirely unverifiable rules and employs "logic" to reach irrational conclusions, which is nonsense. Hey presto, wizard's tricks, smoke and mirrors. Yes, of course, he doesn't talk about optimism as such. The best of possible worlds need not be a happy world. Maybe the existence of such a happy world is impossible: freedom and knowledge come at a price. For Leibniz, man's happiness depends on his perfection. And for man to be perfect he must love God not only with his heart but also with his mind; he must have both passion and illumination. Leibniz's idea of happiness makes me doubly unhappy. On the one hand, I'm not a believer, I'm an atheist, so I don't have access to faith. And then on the other, I can't achieve happiness by way of reason, since reason leads me to be an atheist. My double condition as atheist, according to

Leibniz, condemns me to hell on earth. Damned is he, and damned am I. Many consider Leibniz to be an optimist; me, I just think he's a spoilsport. A smooth operator.

*Thursday, December 24, 2009*

Christmas Eve. I cooked a poularde, put candles and flowers on the table. A linen tablecloth had its first outing. I put the lights on the tree and unleashed the horrible sequence of colored bulbs. I hung up the presents, mixed a White Lady, opened a bottle of wine and waited, listening to a Bartok piano concerto. Why all the fuss? Maybe because I'm one of those people who hates Christmas but also find it depressing if no one makes any effort, if we don't even make an attempt to fool ourselves for a couple of days. My parents and Zoltan are in Hudson, Bela's in Boston. I left the computer on and Skype connected, ready for them to call.

My guests arrived at nine o'clock. I could hardly complain. Fran and Carlos were coming for dinner with me. Fran used me as an excuse—Antón's depressed, he's all alone, might kill himself any second, won't leave the house—to come and escape his in-laws. His wife, who's a calm, kindhearted woman, loves humanitarian gestures, and other people's misfortunes really get to her. Carlos didn't have any friends or family in Madrid either. They were both heartened when they saw the Christmas decorations and the flowers, the food and the White Lady. They probably expected to come and find all the lights off, nothing to eat and me in bed. Plus the two of them have a soft spot for Christmas, they're peculiar like that.

"Whoa! You've even got a tree! Aren't you an atheist?" joked Fran, who was wearing a coffee colored suit with a loud, sky blue tie.

"What, him?" said Carlos, in black velvet jacket, white shirt and jeans, pointing an accusing finger my way. "I bet you, what with his depression, he's converted and he's going to Mass daily. And what's this music? Beethoven? Rostropovich? Something a little more upbeat, Antón, come on!"

As well as presents, they came bearing whiskey, chocolate cake and cigarettes. All extremely healthy. The two of them get along well, though not *that* well. They met years ago, through me. The three of us have been out together from time to time and, as far as I know, if I'm the first one to head home, they've never stayed out. Although we didn't know it then, that night was going to bring them together irrevocably. Fran's a family guy, goodnatured, upright, a conformist, at least on the surface. Carlos, on the other hand, is slightly wild, slightly unscrupulous, slightly arrogant and . . . a total riot. They can both be a little jealous of each other in relation to me. Fran calls Carlos the "Persian Tomcat" because of his affected appearance and because, according to Fran, when Carlos checks out a good-looking woman he'll actually lick his lips, like a cat with a sweet tooth. Carlos just refers to Fran as the "Altar Boy" or the "Party Pooper." They tend to argue over politics; it doesn't take a genius to guess which party each of them votes for. Also, I'd say, there's something that both divides and unites them, which is that Fran is married with children and Carlos is single. They each complain about their respective situations, though neither of them are that uncomfortable, and each enjoys teasing the other, whilst secretly envying him. If there is one thing they have in common—something beyond dispute, something sacred and eternal—it's that they're both Atlético Madrid fans and therefore see themselves as noble losers, romantic warriors, brothers in unfair but epic defeat.

We started off in high spirits: it isn't every Christmas you get to have a meal with your buddies. They drank a number of White Ladies with the aperitifs. I was still finding being teetotal really hard going, but it at least let me think I was on the mend. We opened the presents. Why wait? I gave Carlos a cocktail set, complete with shaker, two glasses, a small bottle of gin and an even smaller one of vermouth. So he can drink martinis on his romantic picnics. To Fran, who loves antiques, I gave a letter opener from late nineteenth century Russia. I admit I was nervous when I opened my presents. Fran gave me a pair of stratospheric running trainers, with air-cushioned soles, and Carlos gave me gift vouchers for one hour massages. Way to go, guys.

They got through two bottles of wine. They began slurring their words. At around midnight I spoke to my mother and I felt she was very faraway, as she often puts it: in another galaxy.

"Son! Son! Son! Son? Son? SON? YOU SOUND VERY FAR AWAY! VERY, VERY FAR AWAY! MERRY CHRISTMAS! Your father can't talk, he's on the computer, and Zoltan's with the children, teaching them the Hungarian national anthem. We're having a poularde, like always, and vegetable soup. How did yours turn out? Did you remember the pine nuts ? Don't eat too much, son, be strong. Remember how skinny Christ was. Are you coming for New Year?"

The evening wasn't going too badly though. But when Bela called, hearing her sweet, cheerful voice, I very nearly cracked, I came this close to telling her all about Lucía the Extortionist. I managed to hold back, but when I went through into the living room again, Fran noticed my red-rimmed eyes.

"What's up, Antón? Bad news?"

Carlos handed me a White Lady. "What the worse that could happen?" I thought. Bye-bye more than two months sober. I downed it in one go, looked at my two friends, and knew the confession was coming. Who was I to try and play the tough guy? Why bear it alone? Was I expecting a medal?

"I'm being blackmailed," I said.

The bombshell had its effect. Fran lit a cigarette, placed it in my mouth, took me by the arm and sat me down in the green armchair. Carlos changed the reggae CD for something less frantic. The two of them took up positions on the orange couch, pitcher of White Lady and cigarettes ready to go.

"Spit it out!" commanded Carlos, who had by now assumed his true bearing, that of someone far more decisive and courageous than me, at least when it comes to facing problems like blackmail. Since his earliest infancy he'd spent as much time at police stations and in court helping his father, Luis "The Lawyer," with his scams and escapades as he had in school. It was only when his mother left "The Lawyer" that Carlos was able to lead a relatively normal life.

"That girl Lucía, the one I told you I'd got pregnant? Turns out she's even worse news than I thought. Her and her boyfriend, some Romanian gangster, they've been threatening me. They've got a shitload of money out of me already."

I told them how, when I'd refused to pay up, Lucía had begun blackmailing me. By the time I'd decided to face up to it, I'd already given them three thousand euros. I had almost nothing left in my account.

"Dickhead," said Carlos encouragingly. And he was being serious. "Utter dickhead. Carry on."

I also told them that "a Romanian youngster" had been round asking the doorman about me when I was away in Paris. This had to be Cosmin. And that same Romanian had left a number of messages on my mobile threatening to kill me if I "didn't pay what I owed them." For now that was all. Fran, very anxious, kept pushing his hair back with one hand, over and over, not even looking at me.

"Jesus, Antón! You've been living a very peculiar life! This is what you get for hanging around with strange people. What are you going to do now?"

"I'm sobering up," said Carlos. "God! Those bastards are ruining our night."

We drank some more, no one saying anything. The White Lady had gone straight to my head. None of us wanted to be there, sitting in my house talking about blackmail and the fact I was going to have a son called Dragosi. There was something unreal about the whole thing. Finally Carlos got up and went for his coat. I thought he was calling it a night but I was wrong.

"Let's go," he said.

Fran and I looked at each other. We had no idea what he meant.

"To that slut's house. You've got the address, haven't you? They'll blatantly be there, stuffed turkey, tree, bubbly, just like everyone else. Let's go and put an end to all this."

Again Fran and I looked at each other. We didn't understand anything. Carlos, coat now on, took out a wrap and racked up a line on the table.

"If our idea is to out scare the shit out of them," he said, "at least one out of the two policemen has to speak without slurring his words."

He offered us some, but Fran and I refused with a vague wave of the hand. My colleague looked appalled.

"What's up, Altar Boy?" said Carlos, noticing Fran's look. "It's the one and only vice I picked up from my dad. He had just about every single other one, I can assure you. Come on, up with you, we're out of here."

We did as we were told. Once we were all in the car, Carlos told us the plan. We'd pretend that I'd reported Lucía Gómez earlier in the evening. Carlos and Fran, the police detectives, were going to pay the blackmailers a little visit, threaten them with arrest if the blackmailing didn't stop. And if that didn't do the trick, Carlos knew an old school police inspector who had helped his mother keep his father away from the family. They still met up once a year. Carlos always thought that the inspector, by now pretty ancient, was hopelessly in love with his mother. I thought the plan was flawless, which may have been because I was drunk. It didn't even occur to me that Carlos and Fran were far too elegant to be policemen, and I didn't feel frightened of Cosmin either, the Romanian, who was a genuine bad guy. Carlos was so assured, there was no way to disagree. In those moments he was my hero, my one hope of ending the nightmare.

"We might need to slap them about a bit," said Carlos. "Ever slapped anyone about, Altar Boy?"

This I think Carlos did to make things easier for me, but also because he found it funny putting Fran in a difficult situation.

"This is madness, Antón," said Fran. "Why risk making it worse? Why not go to the police? Why not leave it until the morning and you, Carlos, what with all your contacts, give this inspector of yours a call?"

"Because I say so. It's Christmas Eve, am I wrong? Right, well no motherfucker's going to ruin our damn Christmas. Lucía Gómez isn't going to be calling Antón Mallick any more. We are going to make that ve-ry clear. And Antón Mallick," he said, glaring at me in the rear-view mirror, "is going to forget all about Lucía Gómez, and about little Dragosi, his so-called son, whether or not he is actually his. Got it, Antón?"

"Got it," I said, one hundred percent convinced.

It was around one in the morning and a few cars were out on the streets. Carlos parked the car in Calle Barco itself, on a zebra crossing, no prisoners. A couple of tenants had their windows open and a deafening noise was coming out, a not hugely harmonious mix of merengue and rap. There were a few African prostitutes and several drug dealers standing in their spots, in the hope that their clients would finish dinner and want to carry on celebrating, or simply wallowing in vice or in desperation, elsewhere. We got out of the car. Carlos took off his tie, folded it carefully and put it in his jacket pocket. When Fran loosened his too, Carlos stopped him:

"Not you. You're the arrogant, tough, hard-bitten detective, pissed first of all because he got stuck with the Christmas Eve shift and then, to top it off, someone's piddling blackmail case stopped him from getting fed at the police station. All you have to do is look unfriendly, stare straight back at them if anyone looks at you, and keep your mouth shut. You can huff and puff a bit if you want; might as well make use of that stupid face of yours for once. And by the way, you're a Real Madrid fan. As for you, Antón, only talk when I speak to you."

"Real Madrid? Why do I have to be a Real fan?" asked Fran, genuinely indignant.

The entrance of building number twenty, where Lucía lived, was shut. Carlos pressed a buzzer at random. A woman's voice answered.

"Hello?"

"Lucía, it's me. I've got the cigarettes. Will you buzz me in?"

"Wrong apartment."

"Sorry," said Carlos. "I thought you were Lucía from 4D."

Carlos waited a few seconds, then pressed the same buzzer again.

"Hello?"

"Hey, sorry to bother you again, but Lucía's intercom isn't working. Mind buzzing me in?"

And in we went. No elevator. The place smelled of piss. We climbed the stairs. Four floors. Door was bright red, with a peephole. We could hear laughter, music. Carlos took a deep breath. Fran was breathing heavily, his glassy eyes looking straight ahead, expressionless. I stood to one side, behind them. Carlos rang the bell.

145

The laughter stopped. Someone put an eye up to the peephole.

"Police!" said Carlos. "Open up!"

There was some whispering, then quiet, then more whispering. Another person at the peephole. Carlos pounded on the door. They opened. Petrified, Lucía Gómez and a sickly-looking boy of about twenty looked at us. Carlos pushed the boy aside and in we went. It was a one-room studio apartment, and a real mess. Dinner, or what was left of it, was still out on a coffee table, with plastic glasses and some bottles. There was a young girl with blond hair sitting on the floor, joint in hand, gaping at us like she was hallucinating.

"Lucía Gómez?' asked Carlos, addressing the pregnant one.

"Yes," Lucía managed to say, even more frightened now she'd realized who I was. "What do you want? Don't you need a warrant like in the movies? Have you got badges?"

Ignoring all this, Carlos introduced himself as Officer Luengo. Fran was Officer Malo, and Carlos said they'd all be better off not looking at him, not saying anything to him, one because he was crazy and two because he'd been drinking. Carlos shut the door, turned the music up— so the neighbors wouldn't hear, he explained with a half smile—and in a weary voice set out my complaint, the reason for their visit.

"You Cosmin?" he asked the sickly-looking boy. "The Romanian pimp, right? Show me your papers!"

"No, I'm Ruben, I'm Spanish, from San Juan in Alicante," he said, and brought out his ID. "I don't know who Cosmin is, sir. I've got nothing to do with any of this, I swear."

146

Carlos handed back his ID.

"You like soccer? What's your team, Ruben?"

The boy hesitated before answering.

"Real Madrid!"

Carlos slapped him hard. Just once. No one had expected that, including us. Now they really were frightened. The young girl started to cry.

"Where's Cosmin? Does he abuse you?"

Carlos went over to the girl, who hadn't moved, he took the joint out of her mouth (it had gone out by now) and dropped it in one of the plastic glasses.

"This is bad news, little girl, really bad news. Where's Cosmin, you little slut? When's the last time you gave him a blowjob? Since you're not giving me anything I'm going to give this pigsty a good going over. I'm sure we'll hit the jackpot."

Carlos could be genuinely unpleasant when he put his mind to it. Now he began turning the place upside down, throwing things on the floor. Lucía, blubbering, screamed at him, "Leave them alone! They're just my brother and his girlfriend! They've got nothing to do with it. This motherfucker got me pregnant! It's his fault!"

Up until that moment Fran and I had been mere spectators, suitably impressed by our friend's performance. But to my surprise Fran, possibly fired up at seeing Carlos taking CDs out and smashing them on the floor, and no one raising a finger to stop him, or too drunk and anxious to carry on doing nothing, or starting to get into character, or angry because this harpy had just said it was all my fault, or pissed off at having been saddled with being a Real Madrid supporter, picked up the TV, which luckily

147

wasn't switched on, tore out the cables, lifted it above his head and brought it down on top of the coffee table with the dinner on it. Lucía stifled a cry. Her brother covered his face with his hands, expecting another slap from Fran, the sloshed psycho detective. The girl looked on openmouthed.

Just then I noticed Lucía glancing nervously at one of the doors, the only one off the living room that wasn't open. Carlos caught the look too. Why hadn't we thought of it before? It had to be the bathroom door; that was where Cosmin was. Carlos looked at me and I saw a flicker of fear in his eyes. We'd gone about this all wrong. There was nothing in the plan that covered taking on an armed Romanian, and now we'd given him more than enough time to prepare himself. Damn that White Lady, I thought. The two kids and Fran, who hadn't picked up on what we were thinking, were staring at the remnants of the TV and the table covered in smashed glass, dumbfounded. Lucía was biting her lip so hard it had begun to bleed; she knew her glance had given her boyfriend away. Carlos, suddenly ashen, picked a knife up off the table and moved toward the closed door. I went with him, even though my temples were throbbing and my legs trembled. Not him. He knew how to stop his fear getting the better of him. He looked at me, smiled (with his mouth, not his eyes) and jerked open the door. The bathroom was small, with a toilet, a mirror and a stool. It stank of smoke. The shower curtain was pulled, hiding the bathtub and shower. Carlos flicked on the light switch, picked up the stool with one hand and, instead of pulling the shower curtain back, threw the stool straight at it.

We heard a cry, and Carlos pulled the curtain aside. A man, crouched down in there, removed the stool that had just landed on top of him. It wasn't Cosmin, but Félix Ramírez, the private detective. Expressionless, as if this were the most normal situation in the world, he picked up a lit cigarette stub from the floor of the bathtub.

"Félix!" I cried. "What the fuck are you doing here?"

"That isn't Cosmin?" asked Carlos, as surprised as me. "You know him?"

Félix deigned to lift his gaze and look at me. It all suddenly made sense. My adrenaline drained away in an instant, and I felt terribly tired.

"He's the private investigator who found Lucía for me. But he isn't actually a private investigator and he didn't find Lucía and there's no such person as Cosmin."

"I am a private investigator," protested Félix as he stood up, watching us carefully with his small eyes, clearly worried about being hit again. "It was unfortunate. The real Lucía had paid in cash. There was no way of tracking her down, I'm sorry."

I came out of the bathroom. Fran gave me a questioning look. Lucía, now that everything was over, took out three cigarettes, lit one and handed the other two to Ruben and his girlfriend. Carlos and Félix came into the living room after me.

"Who's a clever bastard, Félix?" I said. "Don't let one go by, do you? And the beauty queen here is your lady, am I wrong?"

"Absolutely," said Félix, forcing a smile. "Her real name's Lucía too, crazy as it seems. And she is actually seven months gone. It's a boy."

"Yeah, I thought it was weird how fat she was. Well that's an ugly cow of a girlfriend you've got yourself there, Félix, I'm not sure I'm going to say congratulations, and that's even though I quite like them a bit plump myself. And the person leaving messages on my mobile, and coming to my house pretending to be Cosmin, that was your boy Ruben, huh?"

No one answered, which could only mean I was right on the money. Carlos smacked Ruben on the head, and he whimpered like a child, gibbering. Carlos had clearly had a few smacks he'd been needing to dole out for a while.

"I'm sorry about the threats," said Félix, ostensibly quite calm. "The thing is we're totally broke, and what with the baby . . ."

I went into a rage: my turn. Everything in the living room that Carlos and Fran hadn't yet broken, I threw on the floor. I even smashed a mirror and tore down several posters, something I've always wanted to do, ever since I was a kid. I swung from two lamps on the ceiling. I smashed a jug and a few plates against the wall. In the end, I'd worked up a sweat, and I felt satisfied.

"Let's get out of here," I said to my friends. I didn't feel like spending another second amongst leftovers, broken glass and those two-bit blackmailers.

"Just a second," said Carlos. "They have to give you back your money."

"You aren't policemen really, are you?" said Lucía—or whatever the pregnant one was really called—scornfully. "I knew it, the moment I saw you."

"Well I don't know why you wet your pants in that case, genius. Come on you," said Carlos, grabbing

Félix by the shirt. "We want that money. Malo, get their wallets."

Fran, embarrassed by his previous outburst as well as by what he was about to do now, extended his hand in the direction of Lucía and the others like a beggar. And, against all expectations, out came two hundred euros. This put the wind back in his sails.

"Broke, are you? Going to be a good night, was it?" he reproached them, frowning like a stern priest. "Well there's going to be no drugs tonight, no crazy party, no TV, no nothing."

"Only six thousand to go," said Carlos and, as Félix was looking outraged, added: "A thousand for me, a thousand for my colleague, and four thousand for the victim. Consider the two hundred interest."

And out we all went. Félix in front, with Carlos shoving him. Asked what team he supported, and answering Atlético, he got another slap. I really couldn't say why my friend wanted to take the detective with us. When they stopped at an ATM near Gran Vía, I got it. Félix had three cards. One thousand euros was all he could take out.

"You're five thousand short," growled Carlos.

I put the bills in my wallet, with the two hundred Fran had already given me. None of us said anything, we stood motionless. The tension had taken it out of us, including Félix, who slumped with his back against a building. Without thinking, I lifted my hand to scratch my head, unconsciously, and Félix flinched, protecting his face with his hands, and ended up squatting on the floor. Fran, Carlos and I looked at one another. I'm sure the same thought occurred to the three of us: if one of us hit Félix, then it would turn into a free-for-all, and we'd give him a real kicking, beat him, knock his teeth out, crack his head open. Like Seligman's dogs, he was beyond defending himself. I looked at my hand, as if it were already guilty of something. We all felt bad, however well it had all turned out. How close we are to real violence, to cruelty. None of us needed to say anything. Félix was still cowering, eyeing us. The cigarette in his mouth had gone out. I got my lighter out to offer him a light, but changed my mind: the devil take him. We turned and walked away, back to the car.

"One more drink back at mine?" I said, not wanting that crazy, almost mythical night, to end like this, with all of us feeling pensive and downhearted. "There's still some White Lady left over."

"What time is it?" asked Fran.

"I've told you a thousand times, don't ask *the time!*?" said Carlos. "It's just after one o'clock. I'm with you, Antón."

"Me too, you bastards. My wife is going to kill me. Hey, Carlos, where'd you get the 'Malo' idea from? Couldn't you think of a more ridiculous name than 'Bad' for the tough guy?"

"What's your team?" joked Carlos. "Who do you support, eh?"

We burst out laughing. Calle del Barco was busier now. The rats had come out of their holes. And I was going to be free again. It's six o'clock in the morning, and I still don't feel like sleeping. I'm going out for a walk.

*Saturday, December 26, 2009*

**From:** Zoltan Mallick
**To:** Anton Mallick, APRI Sur Director
**Subject:** You leave me no choice but to intervene

We're not going to beat about the bush here, Antón. I spoke to your sister Bela yesterday (who seems like she's on drugs, or sleep-deprived, or something). She told me, laughing—I never have understood your sense of humor, you two—about your encounter with the criminals. According to her, you referred to it as A CATHARTIC ESCAPADE. Have you lost it completely? Then, when I brought up the subject of the weather, how little it's been raining (for a lighter note), she said, and I quote, that "human beings are shit" and "I don't get it why people are so bothered about global warming, the only piece of good news Mother Nature's had is Mankind's imminent disappearance." Seems we have another optimist in the family. Am I the only one in his right mind? Can I remind you you're thirty-three (you were born in 1975, right?) and Captain Thunder and Spiderman comic books are all in the past now—there are no superheroes, Antón, and Santa Claus is your parents—are you ever going to settle down? Agreed, you went through a tragedy, it was hard, it was terrible, it was horrendous, but is the answer really to throw your whole life out the window? YOU'RE NOT GOING TO HAVE A CHILD BY ANY MYSTERY WOMAN. THE WOMAN DOES NOT EXIST, THE CHILD DOES NOT EXIST. THE WORLD IS NOT A STAGE. FACE UP TO REALITY: YOU ARE ON YOUR OWN (though, for instance, you can count on me).

You've got a strange way of going about it, this trying to be optimistic. FIRST RULE OF BEING AN OPTIMIST: THERE'S NO NEED TO MAKE UP IMAGINARY PROBLEMS, WE'VE GOT PLENTY OF REAL ONES TO BE GETTING ON WITH. Have you read the books I lent you?, which, might I remind you, you still haven't given back, like the professional electric shaver you took from me. Sometimes I don't know how I keep on being so generous. There's a handful of good advice in those psychologists' books, based on good work, work with unbalanced people like you. You mustn't hope for miracles, but for a dignified life, why not? The life of a man who can look his loved ones in the eye, and his work colleagues, and not feel ashamed, the life of SOMEONE WHO DOESN'T CONSORT WITH FAKE PRIVATE INVESTIGATORS, FAKE PREGNANT WOMEN, JUNKIES AND PSEUDO-FRIENDS WHO GO AROUND THREATENING AND DESTROYING AND DEMOLISHING THE HOMES OF THE LUMPEN PROLETARIAT. You left me no choice but to tell Mom and Dad everything. You've broken their hearts—and not for the first time. You could think about giving them some good news for a change: play the lottery, or get a season ticket for concerts at the Auditorio, or go and volunteer for a soup kitchen for ex-junkies. It's about sowing seeds, not laying waste.

María and the kids send their love. Why do you have to ruin everyone's holidays, and this year too, just when I shut the office for Christmas and New Year, with the distinct possibility that it means things could go badly for my patients, and the certainty that my income will take a hit? I'm signing off now, we're going on a boat trip along the Hudson, all of us together. WE ARE A NORMAL FAMILY.

PS. It turns out Dad isn't all that great, but my sense is that it's just mood swings, nothing too serious. But he's holding up. Even though he doesn't want to see you, you ought to visit him, he'd like it.


## Sunday, December 27, 2009

**From:** Antón Mallick
**To:** Zoltan
**Subject:** Re: You leave me no choice but to reply.

Thank you for all your advice, brother. All's well here, I'm pleased you're all having a great time and that I'm in your thoughts. By the way, I'm thirty-two. My Santa Claus was my uncle, not my parents. And your parents, saving some considerable revelations, are the same as mine. I'm sorry that I won't be able to give you back your books: they were so awful I THREW THEM IN THE FUCKING TRASH YOU MENTAL MIDGET! And the professional shaver—I've just now thrown that in the garbage as well. And yes, the escapade with the blackmailers was exactly what I said and, as such, in that it was born out of action, EXTREMELY POSITIVE AND CATHARTIC. See you soon, in Madrid.

Love to all, Antón.


**From:** Antón Mallick
**To:** Sis
**Subject:** Hello hello

Hello, Bela. Why did you have to go and tell Zoltan the genius about the blackmail? Now Mom won't stop going on about it, I had to say you were overdoing it, not that she believes me (plus, she can't get her exceptional brain around the idea of me having sexual relations with "just any" woman): she's saying I ought to go and live with Zoltan for a while, or "try my luck in the US," nonsense like that. So she's got her favorite subject for another year. Anyway. How are you? Been a while since you've written. I'm thinking that your depressing opinions on humankind weren't entirely serious—you were pulling Zoltan's leg, right? Another box of books has just arrived: *Passions of the Soul* by Descartes, the *Bhagavad Ghita*, the *Tao Te Ching* by Lao Tzu, *The Life of Reason or The Phases of Human Progress* by Santayana, *The Art of War* by Sun Tzu, Swami Ramda's *Sayings*. A very Far Eastern little collection, sis. Seeing as you keep on sending me all these books, the average number of books read in Spain is going to rise dramatically.

Lots of love.
(I found the pack super kitsch, sis, but there's no need to line the box with silk paper, you force me to keep it. Recently I've been getting most of my kicks by throwing things in the garbage.)

## NOTES ON BELA'S BOOKS

*Bhagavad Ghita (Book of Devotion), Mahabharata,* Anonymous
(third century BC)

Let's refresh our memories. Putting it this way—*memory refresh*—I
give the impression that what I'm really doing is re-reading these
books, Vidor. Some might say that this whole exercise, making
myself out to be interesting and well-read, is ridiculous, particularly
doing it in a diary that only you and I are ever going to read. They'd
say *I'm fooling myself*, but my answer to that would be, at least I'm
not such a hypocrite not to know *I'm fooling myself constantly*, from
the moment I get out of bed in the morning, and that I consider this
diary one of the healthiest and most coherent things that I spend my
time doing, far more noble, for example, than that of *fooling others*,
something everyone else seems to value so highly. Let's, then,
refresh our memories. The Bhagavad Ghita is an episode in the
Mahabharata, the great Indian epic, written around the third century
BC. It deals with the conflict between two rival families, the Kurus
and the Pandavas. As I was I reading it I couldn't avoid thinking
of Bela and me as the Pandavas and Zoltan as a fuckface Kuru.

What does not exist, is not, and what exists, cannot cease
to be. I found reflections like this relaxing to begin with, because
of the way they don't invite you to think, but to splash around in
the water, to get lost, to digress—a release from the tyranny of
Reason. But the Yogi state, free from desire and intellect, is very
similar to being dead (or what I think of as dead: without curiosity,
nor intellect, nor desire, nor conscience, nor a lovely bit of young
flesh to enjoy, you're dead). This idea of being Nothing in order to
be and participate in the All, this Community in Negation, the true
Great Orgasmic Affirmation, I don't find at all convincing. Strangely,
if I go back over what I've read up until now, from the pre-Socratics
to Russell, the whole idea of happiness or optimism is a way out,
a fleeing from reality, a juggling game—interesting or depressing,
depending on the person putting it forward. My Annus Horribilis is
about to come to an end, and I refuse to hide: I still want TO LIVE.

156

NB: I flicked through Swami Ramdas' *sayings*. I came across phrases like: "Pain does not originate in external circumstances, but in the ignorant, slavish mind," and, though I know what Ramdas is driving at, I still have strong urges to squeeze the Hindu sage nice and tight by the balls until tears come to his eyes. The egoism implicit in Ramdas' model of liberation is probably what attracts your average "successful" Western snob—the annulment of guilt, the suppression of ideas of good and evil (though, once suppressed, we tend towards the good), the relativization of feelings towards those close to us, and liberation from people who essentially get on our nerves, know-it-alls, employees, servants, that kind of thing. Taken *a la carte* (leaving aside celibacy, total suppression of desires, complete and absolute submission to God, etc, ie. leaving aside the essence of this philosophy, sticking to nothing more than its vulgar surface), it's both comfortable and comforting.

### Friday, January 1, 2010

> "Whoever complains about the death of anyone
> is complaining that he was a man."
>
> SENECA

New Year, the Year I've Been Waiting For. I welcome it in front of the TV, with the twelve grapes, one for each of the chimes at midnight. Uncle Juan always remembered at the last minute to take the skin off the grapes and remove the pips. That only left him time to deal with ours and, when he ate his, he would choke, cough exaggeratedly and go bright red. Now I realize that it was a joke, his way of making sure that, for Bela and I, the New Year would begin with laughter.

*Saturday, January 2, 2010*

I had an aperitif with Carlos and Fran in La Dolores. Camaraderie. We haven't come up with another escapade to get our teeth into.

*Tuesday, January 5, 2010*

> "The best plan of the universe, which God could not fail to choose, required this. One concludes thus from the event itself; since God made the universe, it was not possible to do better."
>
> LEIBNIZ

Bela's birthday. She isn't picking up the phone, and this is worrying me. Months since I've seen mouth-watering dog-walking woman. Maybe she moved? At least my encounters with her went to show that something inside me still moves.

NOTES ON BELA'S BOOKS

*Candide or Optimism* (1759), Voltaire, François-Marie Arouet (1694-1778)

The house is silent. What a pleasure to turn on the lamp on the bedside table, put on my pyjamas, go to the kitchen, pour myself a Coca Cola Zero, fill a bowl of potato chips (sorry Mother), come back to the bedroom, get under the duvet and pick which book to read next. A couple of hours, maybe more, stretch out in front of me. The one that most appeals is *Candide*, a satire. I need to laugh. I need to stop thinking so much, if I'm to be able to think properly tomorrow or the day after or maybe never again. I skip the prologue. The book is presented as having been translated by a certain "Monsieur Dr. Ralph", which is a pseudonym for Voltaire, which itself is a pseudonym for François-Marie Arouet, hidden as usual behind masks and disguises. And straight away the title of the first chapter brings a smile to my face:

*How Candide was brought up in a magnificent castle; and how he was driven from thence.*

The adventures of Candide, brought up to think the world was a nice place until his life was taken over by evil and bad luck, provides Voltaire with the opportunity to poke fun at Leibniz's "best of all possible worlds," at anything "a priori," at cause-and-effect, at optimism and at my beloved Rousseau. Though, like Leibniz, Voltaire plays with marked cards, the Frenchman is more to my liking: less solemn, more penetrating. There is, for example, this hilarious description of a battle: "There was never anything so gallant, so spruce, so brilliant, and so well disposed as the two armies. Trumpets, fifes, hautboys, drums, and cannon made music such as Hell itself had never heard. The cannons first of all laid flat about six thousand men on each side; the muskets swept away from this best of worlds nine or ten thousand ruffians who infested its surface. The bayonet was also a sufficient reason for the death of several thousands. The whole might amount to thirty thousand souls."

A social upstart, refined, flighty, intelligent, audacious, polemical, landowner, righteous, anglophile, clown, cynic, elegant . . . But happy, was he happy, Voltaire? I think not. He was too well acquainted with the ills of the world, as well as his own. For him optimism was an insult to intelligence, a cruel joke. But I do believe he enjoyed *living* (every now and then). He died at the height of his fame, acclaimed and surrounded by the great and the good in Paris. Himself a sycophant, surrounded by other sycopanths, he received Death fearfully, alone, divested of all his masks. As does everyone else. Isn't that right, Vidor? What a shame you weren't able to recount your death, that your counter-memoir stops abruptly, five years before your death. Did you cry out before you died? Did you die in bed, prostrate with pain? Did you grab hold of your wife, petrified?

*Thursday, January 7, 2010*

How does the moon travel? Does she plot a perfect ellipse through space? No, she's more coquettish than that, not as aloof as she seems. She sways, gives little jumps, dances, vacilates. Even she, so out in the open, is far from pure. How can a satellite possibly keep to its orbit in space? We find ourselves on top of a mountain, above the atmosphere. We are holding a ball in our hands: we throw it. The force of gravity attracts the ball towards Earth, and it falls. The harder we throw it, the further it goes. If we were able to throw the ball at seventeen thousand miles per hour, it wouldn't ever fall. It would be moving quickly enough laterally as to avoid the orbited object, the Earth. It would be in orbit. A satellite above the atmosphere continues travelling at this speed—there's no air resistance to hold it back. In a few months, our satellite, Transat, will be in orbit.

Straightforward facts like the gentle sashaying of the moon, or what it is to be in orbit, are what make my job entertaining. Ramon Llorente, the aerospace engineer, is the person who provides me with them, who treats me like an inquisitive child. When he notices I'm feeling tired or distracted, he gives away anecdotes or explanations to do with satellites like they were candy, to make our sterile meetings sweeter. Gorostegui, on the other hand, the finance director, is more boring. Maybe because he's a bit stuck-up. Here we are in the third millennium, and he's still using hair gel, calling every woman he meets, even fifty-year-old ones, "my little lady," and he's that kind of executive who think they're entertaining because they wear apple green motorbike jackets and loud ties. Ha. Then there's Gozalo, the insurance consultant, who used to work at Telefónica specializing in telecommunications: an overweight guy accustomed to the daily menus in cheap eateries, a real smart aleck, a very sharp guy. He always wears the same outfit: a dark gray lightweight suit, a crimson tie, plain shirt and loafers. I don't know if it's that he only owns one suit, which would make him a neurotic, or if he has several identical ones, in which case that would still make him a neurotic. The other day, in a restaurant, Gorostegui used his knife and fork to eat an olive. I swear, Vidor. He is that pretentious. Throughout the whole absurd, complex operation, Gozalo observed him in silence. Once it was over, Gozalo said, in his characteristic monotone:

"Gorostegui, I'll be damned! God only knows what you get up in bed. The mind boggles."

Anyway. 2010 has landed, Lucía Gómez overcome, Dragosi abandoned to his fate, private investigator Ramírez exorcized, and I've come to grips, at least in part, with the fact I'll never know if there will or won't be a new Mallick walking the streets of Madrid, and I allow my routine, my freshly squeezed fruit juices and my runs in the Retiro to cradle me once more.

*Monday, January 11, 2010*

> "The anchorite who shutteth his placid soul away from all sense of touch, with gaze fixed between his brows; who maketh the breath to pass through both his nostrils with evenness alike in inspiration and expiration, whose senses and organs together with his heart and understanding are under control, and who hath set his heart upon liberation and is ever free from desire and anger, is emancipated from birth and death even in this life."
>
> ANONYMOUS, BHAGAVAD GHITA

One of my gifts, Vidor, is my very fine sense of hearing. Unfortunately, though, it isn't all that refined. I'll never quite be a lover of music, though I did toy with trying to become one for a time. The flooring at my office is parquet; it creaks. From my office, which gives onto a long corridor, I can make out the footsteps of my colleagues when they pass by. There are the high heels belonging to María V. from marketing, who stomps along, rat-a-tat-tat on the varnish like a woodpecker; Pedro M. from HR with his rubber soled shoes, gliding along like a tiger on the prowl; master photocopier Mario, whose trainers screech as though trying to twist the slats up out of the flooring; Ana from finance with her classic flats, no heels, boring, shuffling along like an old age pensioner; then there's Fran in his English loafers with their stitched leather soles, which sound like their wearer is a bear attempting to tap dance. As for my shoes, Vidor, they're Budapest style, a pair of perforated Bluchers, very Hungarian. I'd go so far as to say they're musical: they make a happy, singsong noise.

A couple of weeks ago I heard a new sound in the office. High heels and a slow, deliberate gait, sated, like a lioness that has just devoured her prey. It was accompanied by a melodious voice, with a Canary Islands accent. All these goodies belonged to Yaiza, our boss's new PA, an exotic, dark-haired beauty, very young, always smiling and a smoker. Well then. It's become customary to hear the dancing bear, when it encounters the self-satisfied lioness, to stop and chat for a few moments. Then the majestic lioness returns to her desk, clicking her paws with an intoxicating rhythm. The bear, gabbling, in a dither, either stops by to see me or walks over to the coffee machine.

I sometimes hear the bear opening the door to his lair, poking his head out and, not seeing the lioness, going back in again. Then there's the times he contrives to bump into her. I haven't said anything to the bear, not about these little chats, or the way he keeps watch over the lioness' movements, and I haven't asked after Mrs. Bear or the cubs either. I've said nothing about the dangers associated with felines. Today, by chance, I found the two of them out on the balcony, which is where we smokers take refuge. The bear was typing a number into his cellphone, presumably that of the lioness. Seeing me, he jumped. The lioness gave me a smile and shot off. The bear, caught with his pants down, pretended someone was calling his phone, leaving me alone with my cigarette, looking scornfully down at a woman who in turn looked down, gloatingly, at her pretty little dog as it loosened its bowels on the sidewalk of Calle Mejía Lequerica.

*Friday, January 15, 2010*

> "Optimism," said Cacambo, "what is that?"
> "Alas!" replied Candide, "it is the obstinacy of maintaining that everything is best when it is worst."
>
> Voltaire

The buzzer rings. I go and open the door. I find Bela on the landing, a very large suitcase at her side. At first glance all does not appear well, though I don't immediately grasp what's the matter. Her golden mane is short and swept to one side, and she's wearing a classic trench coat, jeans and white Converse. I look her in the eye: she's not looking at all well. There's no sign of the usual flush in her cheeks, or the way she normally just looks healthy, like a ripe apple. Plus she's put on weight. And she's got her sweater on back to front. No one's said anything to her? What's going on in the world? Can't people show a little sensitivity any more? Are we such cowards, or so on our guard, or so indifferent, or so rude as to not step in and tell a stranger they've got their top on the wrong way round? We hug, and Bela begins to cry. It's been nearly a year since we last saw each other, since she came and stayed with me for a while, looking after me or putting up with me until she thought I was ready to fend for myself. We go into the apartment. I take her suitcase, an object that asserts her arrival almost as forcibly as her presence itself, and put it down in the middle of the living room. We sit down on the couch, side by side, staring at the lone piece of luggage. Bela dries her tears with the back of her hand, and sighs. I break the silence:

"Alexander Korda, George Cukor and Michael Curtiz."

"Filmmakers, makers of *souffles*—Hungarian sitcoms. Way too easy, brother. Don't worry, you don't have to let me win. David Swarz."

"End of the nineteenth century, invented the zeppelin. I don't plan on letting you win. Karoly Gundel."

"Chef, maker of the legendary Budapest Gundel. Miklos ..."

"You have to say two more recipes! That's the rule, remember?"

Bela breathes.

"All right. Hargitai pork chop, and Gundel stew ... Happy?"

I nod and she carries on:

"Miklós de Nagybánya Horthy," she says, spitting the name out like an insult.

"End of the nineteenth century to mid way through the twentieth, nationalist dictator, Nazi sympathizer, troublemaker, oppressor, murderer, opportunist, the Hungarian Fouché. Paul Newman ..."

Bela gives me a baleful glance like I've offended her now.

"*What* did you say?"

"*Mindenki Magyar,*" I say defensively. "Everyone in the world is Hungarian. I read it somewhere—the great Paul Newman was Hungarian. Didn't surprise me, actually. He had the weirdest accent . . ."

"You lose."

"No, I was just kidding. Remember that thing we used to do, *kidding?*"

"You lose."

"No. Eric Bernat."

Now she really gives me a look. With her eyes on fire—though, after a few seconds, extinguished, the anger fades. But she doesn't laugh either. Bernat used to be one of our surefire laughs. He isn't Hungarian, of course, but Spanish—he invented Chupa Chups, one of Spain's most important contributions to global progress. When we were kids we'd roll on the floor if one of us put Bernat's name forward. We'd hoot, we'd writhe, our stomachs would hurt, we'd end up with cramps. But Bela isn't laughing.

"Fine, fine, I see you left your sense of humor back in Boston. Meter C. Goldmark."

"That's enough, Antón! You got that off the internet! It doesn't count, you can't play like that!"

"Sorry, Bela, but the temptation's pretty huge. You have to bear in mind that I live alone, and I get bored. The internet's killed our game, it means finding new names is hardly fun any more, and the other ones we both know by heart."

166

I decide to wrap it up.

"*Bluebeard's Castle.*"

"*The Wooden Prince*," she fires back.

"*Romanian Folk Dances.*"

"*Allegro Barbaro* . . . That's enough!" she exclaims. "It's a draw."

"That was quick."

"I suspect it might be the last time we play."

"Yes."

Neither of us says anything. After a few moments, Bela says:

"God, Antón! I find it amazing that you wouldn't let me win."

"Coffee?"

"Turkish?"

"What do you think?"

The suitcase is still in the same spot, thumbing its nose at us, full of clothes and belongings that expect to be put away at once. But we aren't going to open it all that quickly. It can wait. Today everything can wait.

NOTES ON BELA'S BOOKS

*Tao Te Ching*, by Lao Tzu (sixth century BC?)

Bela is asleep on the couch, fully clothed, under a Scottish patchwork quilt she gave me once. There's the sound of the washing machine. I'm reading in my armchair, and every now and then I look up from the book at her. I try to create some link between what I read and what I see, or feel—between the words and my sister. I find this surprisingly easy with Lao Tzu, I slip softly in and out of his pages.

No one knows if Lao Tzu, the supposed author of the *Tao Te Ching*, really existed. I like the Tao because I don't know if I like it; I understand it because I'm totally puzzled by it.The Tao is poetic and puzzling. But not Western puzzlement, the kind we've arrived at via reason, after the great truth-seeking escapade, after wanting to get to the bottom of everything and ending up crashing into a brick wall. This is a centuries-old puzzlement, content, beyond time, contemplative—that of seeking without seeking. It is not my puzzlement. Mine pains me. Like it pains me watching Bela as she sleeps.

*Sunday, January 17, 2010*

> "Be broken to be whole.
> Twist to be straight
> Be empty to be full.
> Wear out to be renewed.
> Have little and gain much.
> Have much and get confused."
>
> LAO TZU

Today is Monday. I didn't write on Sunday, but it would have been worth it (though I don't know if "being worth it" is quite right to refer to what happened yesterday). I'm at work, alone in my office, I've read the news online already (how uninteresting it all is, the obligation of turning everything into a show for the masses, how I pity those poor journalists), and the very last thing I feel like doing is working. I prefer to turn my thoughts to my beloved Zoltan.

Zoltan has always made an effort to play his role, that of the older brother. But Bela and I have always found him to be ludicrous, over the top, backstabbing, cowardly, opportunistic and just plain lucky. After he went to live in the promised land, the United States of America, with our parents, we only saw him during vacation. We'd arrive at their house, a prefab duplex in a middle class residential area in Houston, and he'd take us up to his room. It was your usual scatterbrained jock's room. The walls covered in photos of his idols, a cabinet full of trophies, another one with a collection of superhero figures, model airplanes dangling from the ceiling and, in the wardrobes, aside from the clothes, all kinds of games, many of them electronic. All that space, all those toys, all the bright colors—Bela and I felt profoundly jealous. But the worst thing, what really got us, was that he had a color TV all to himself, and it had a million and one channels too. Our bedrooms in Madrid were almost monastic by comparison. His desk was always neat and tidy. If you really looked, if you were able to step back a little from this veritable toy fair, you'd realize that everything had its own place, and that even then my brother was a neat freak to the point of obsession. He'd shut the door, invite us to take a seat on his bed and, year after year, without fail, ask us:

"Like my room? Like my toys?" And since we tried to annoy him by not answering, he'd say: "Well it's *my* room, you little Spics. And this is the first and last time you're going to get to come in here during all the vacation. Got that?"

As Bela and I would routinely pretend to vomit, he, true to tradition, used to give us each a genial slap on the neck before kicking us out. Then, poor him, he'd get bored. At least as bored as us. He didn't have any friends (he always said they were away but we never believed him; he pretended to be very proficient on the friend-making front, when in fact he was quite shy) and as he wasn't bookish he'd spend hours in front of the TV.

Bela and I were always out in the garden. Our parents thought of us as city rats, always shut up in Uncle Juan's apartment, our clothes stained from the clouds of dust that came tumbling off his books and our nails smog-black, so they'd make us spend time outside. After a few days Zoltan would come looking for us but would keep himself discriminatingly apart, pretending he had far more interesting things to do. As soon as we saw him coming, Bela and I of course began laughing non-stop, talking in code and using all the words we knew in Hungarian, which was our secret language. The point was to make him see what a good time we were having, that we could get along perfectly well without him, as well as the fact he was a dolt. I'd be dying to play baseball with him, or football, or with any of his toys (I remember one summer he had a wonderfully noisy remote controlled car, and every now and then he'd rub it in my face by playing with it near us), but I never did, not even on the few occasions when he swallowed his pride and asked me.

Seeing as he couldn't convince us to let him enter our world through fair means, he'd try to force himself into it. He'd spy on us. He'd snitch on us to our parents. He'd hit us (me more than Bela, who once caught him with a well-aimed kick and, another time, when he'd pinned her down, showed him her flat little breasts, after which he was scared shitless of her). He'd put pepper in our food, he'd stain our clothes, he'd lock us in our room. It wasn't that he was particularly intelligent or crafty, he just always got lucky; he was born lucky. My parents would never catch him when he played tricks on us. Mother never found where he hid his porn magazines—she didn't even notice them when Bela and I laid them out on his bed with the pages open. Father never noticed when he stole money from time to time. He was Little Mr. Goody Two Shoes.

Our relationship improved at a distance. He began getting into girls, passed his driving test, took whatever job came up (as a waiter, a shop assistant, a gardener—he was always hardworking and reliable—the prick), and we'd only see him at mealtimes. He went off to university. In the blink of an eye he went from being a teenage bully to thinking himself all grown up. Zoltan joined our parents' team—that is, that of the immature-apparently-respectable-owners-of-a-razor-blade-and-a-current-account-and-a-car-and-a-bunch-of-bitter-friends—though in his case, he always kept his feet on the ground and didn't drift off into unfathomable, delirious parallel universes, in the manner of Lajos and spouse.

From then on he thought of himself as a good example to us, the lighthouse directing the feckless sailors (Bela and I) through the storm (life in a third world country, Spain) to safe port. He didn't hit us any more, he stopped giving us punishments; instead, he talked to us, gave us advice, understood us: he pretended to listen. I don't think he really did it for us, but rather that he already had in mind to become a damn shrink, and we were the guinea pigs. Every single day we began having "family reunions," as

171

he called them, which consisted of shutting us in a room and trying to coax our secrets from us using veiled threats and supposedly brainy interrogation techniques he'd learnt from some obscure manual. So—understandably enough—we made fun of him. Maybe the fact that he knew nothing about us, the failure to work us out, in spite of his prolonged and systematic attempts at it, was more than anything what led him to choose his profession, one in which all kinds of secrets rain down on him continuously without him even trying—plus getting paid for it. Family reunions were far worse than being hit. And still it goes on. Yesterday, when he found out through my mother that Bela was staying with me, he convened a "family reunion." At my house. He provided his own invitation. And didn't bring a cake, or wine, or anything.

"You've put on weight, Bela. Well? Want to tell me what we're all doing here?"

"Because you imposed yourself on us, Zoltan," I lashed out at him "Bela and I were having the most Sunday-like of Sundays, reading, watching TV, taking it easy . . ."

"So mature, Antón! Like it or not, I'm your older brother, and that is never going to change, *never!* Got that? *Never.*"

The last thing my sister needed just then was a family reunion. We'd prepared for the interview as though it were a negotiation between government dignitaries (us) and a Chinese spy (Zoltan). We decided that the two of us would sit on the orange couch and Zoltan on a cushion on the floor. That way we'd be looking down on him.

"Aren't there any chairs, Antón? Been selling off your furniture?"

We'd hidden the chairs and the two armchairs in my bedroom. We'd also sprayed the whole apartment with a nauseating flowery-smelling forest air freshener. It wasn't much fun for us, no, but Zoltan's allergic.

"What's that smell? Mind opening the windows, please?"

And lastly, I made Turkish coffee. Bela and I love it, but since watered-down coffee is his poison, he hates the real thing.

"Haven't you got any coffee that doesn't resemble cement, Antón?"

Bela and I were yet to touch on what had prompted her, from one day to the next, to get on a plane and come to Madrid. I preferred not to put pressure on her—to let her come out with it when she felt ready. But that isn't Zoltan's way. Once again he tried to coax our secrets from us, to intrude on our world. Bela resisted, coming back at him with vague answers. Her and John were apparently going through a bad patch.

"You don't say, little sister," said Zoltan impatiently. "Even in romantic novels women don't run away from their husbands because everything's fine and dandy and they are blissfully happy. What's going on with you? Does he insult you? Hit you when he's had a drink? Is he having an affair?"

I imagine that Zoltan can be subtler in his sessions. But not with us. He was short on time. After one fairly brusque push-pull, Bela gave in. Really gave in—screaming, suddenly—as though she were a firearm and Zoltan had inadvertently pulled the trigger.

"WE DON'T FUCK! WE HAVEN'T FUCKED IN OVER TWO YEARS! WE DON'T EVEN TOUCH

EACH OTHER—NOTHING! THAT ENOUGH INFO FOR YOU?"

Bela had never shouted so much—at least not since she was very small. It led to a genuinely uncomfortable silence—one that paradoxically managed to flatten but also bring closer the sound of the street through the open window. Bela stared straight ahead of her, her mouth pressed shut. Zoltan looked at the floor. I looked from one to the other. How could my sister have been so weak? And was what she'd said true, or a trick for Zoltan? Then I got angry. If Zoltan carried on in this vein, if he didn't leave Bela in peace, I would punch him in that designer face of his . . . But I saw how he was gaping, like the words truly wouldn't come. Finally, whimpering, he managed it. Bela and I could hardly believe our ears; my sister's angry confession had also pulled a kind of trigger.

"I know how you feel, Bela," said Zoltan, hanging his head. "You have no idea! I . . . I . . . I . . . I have to tell you guys! María and I don't have the normal kind of sex. . . ! Only perverted stuff turns us on . . . She . . ."

Zoltan lost his thread, and Bela and I broke down in hysterics. This was too much. The family reunion had got totally out of hand. Once we'd finally composed ourselves, my sister interrupted him:

"Shut up, Zoltan, please! We don't want to hear about what you get up to in bed! God! Has the whole world gone mad? Is everyone's family like ours?"

Zoltan said nothing, tears in his eyes. He looked spaced out. Bela and I had no idea how to react to our older brother's attack of sincerity. Had he crumbled in the face of our innocent humiliation tactics? Or was it Bela's screaming? Or had suddenly finding out one of our secrets left him defenceless, at our mercy? Little Mr. Goody Two Shoes down in the mud, sharing the stables with us, his piggy wiggy siblings. It wasn't fair. Another wave of anger hit me.

"You are a complete moron, Zoltan!" I shouted. "You said it yourself: you're the older brother. And you aren't allowed to fall apart, come here telling us about being some pervert!"

"That wasn't what I said, Antón! What I said was that María . . ."

"Shut up!" I said, jabbing a finger his way, to sound more convincing. "Bela and I are on antidepressants. You aren't. I'm trying to be an optimist. You already are one, or at least you seem to be. That's all there is to it. Stop acting like a coward—you can't change sides just like that."

Zoltan shot me a murderous look. He still had one last bit left in him, one last attempt to forge this impossible alliance.

"I'M HUMAN TOO! DO YOU BOTH GET THAT? EVERYONE'S GOT ISSUES, NO MATTER OUR CREED, THE COLOR OF OUR SKIN, WHERE WE WENT TO SCHOOL, AGE, BODY SHAPE, HOW MUCH WE EARN! But you," he continued, more evenly now, "you two have always thought you're special, ever since they left you behind. Well you aren't. No one is."

And that was that. Fortunately, Zoltan realized how stupid he'd made himself look and that, to us, he was indeed a human being, but not the human being he wanted to be. There was no need for him to air his bedroom secrets, least of all now, at forty years of age, when everything was more likely to be depressing. At least he could have told us when he was sixteen, or twenty—then maybe it would have been of interest. We could hardly kick him out, especially knowing he would be feeling truly embarrassed, so I suggested we watch a film. He accepted.

I picked an oldy—Pedro Almodóvar's *Tie Me Up, Tie Me Down*. Not actually very much sex in it, but a nice, thought-provoking title. It got dark outside, I turned the projector on and the three of us breathed a little easier, as if for a little while the shadows, by smothering everything apart from the screen, helped us forget about ourselves—and everyone else.

*Monday, January 18, 2010*

> "Democritus said: 'If you seek tranquility, do less.'"
>
> MARCUS AURELIUS

Work. Bela sleeping. Nothing to report.
*Tuesday, January 19, 2010*

> "We can still live in the family and realize Him."
>
> SWAMI RAMDAS

A little context: we're at home, I'm back after a hard day's work (a disappointing one—lots of delays, no resolution), and now I've got a session with Bela. You give up on one problem and, straight away, another rears its head.

"Have you read *First Snow on Fuji* by Kawabata?" says Bela, who looks solemn, slightly shrunken.

"I haven't."

"There's a story in it, *Silence*, with an elderly writer who suffers from a neurological disease that means he can't communicate using words. His daughter tells a visitor, also a writer, the plot of one of the father's novels. The main character, of course, is a boy who wants to be a writer. The young aspiring writer goes insane and is admitted to a psychiatric hospital, where he sits at a table, apparently writing non-stop. But when his mother visits and the boy shows her the sheets of paper, they're blank. Over and over, every time she visits, the son shows his mother pages with nothing on them. The madman believes he's written something interesting, and anxiously awaits his mother's opinion. In the end it's her who writes the novel her son's supposedly written, and she tells it back to him every time she visits, as if he really were the author."

"And?" I say. Bela sometimes has a hard time getting to the point.

"Right, right," she says, cracking her knuckles nervously. "And *Warrior's Rest* by Christiane Rochefort, too. And *The Shining*? Right, in that, Jack Nicholson, who's supposedly writing a novel, actually writes the same phrase over and over, filling hundreds of folders, remember?"

"'All work and no play makes Jack a dull boy.' Yes, his wife reads them and realizes he's off his rocker, but they're all alone in a hotel in the mountains, miles from anywhere, so there's no one she can tell. And an axe features somewhere too . . . And?" I say again, hoping to rein in the digressions.

"Well, my story isn't all that different. As you know, John's a writer, but, sadly, unpublished. What he did or didn't do never bothered me, I only felt bad for him, pretending to be something he wasn't, all those hours shut up in his office with the computer on. He never showed me a word. Plus, he said he hated printers, he wasn't prepared to use up paper and kill all those trees. There wasn't one single folder in his office, and the only books in sight were by other writers."

"A man who feels solidarity with the trees, a conscientious man," I say. "I like that."

"It hasn't been as though he doesn't do anything, he does errands, he cooks, house-husbanding, planning trips, helping me with my lit courses . . . I even got a bit worried he was doing so *many* things! So. For the past two years he's been saying he was working on a novel, and a month ago he told me he had a first draft. I was over the moon, I was desperate to read it, particularly because of how sarcastic he can be when he's critizicing other writers' work, even the classics. And then, seeing as he held back from actually showing me anything until it was totally finished . . ."

"You decided to sneak a peek," I said, finishing her sentence. My sister, who's wonderful in so many ways, is somewhat prone to nosiness; it wasn't hard to imagine what had happened. "You had no right, Bela. You had no right to go into his computer and breach his privacy."

178

"What? Who said anything about rights? Have the Chinese got rights? Have American Indians? Or half the women in the world? He's my husband, and it was hard enough stifling myself for almost two whole years! The motherfucker's got a business card that says *John Grant. Writer. Fiction!*"

"Your husband isn't lying. It says "*Fiction*," doesn't go into specifics. John's referring to the fact that he writes—which is pure fiction. Maybe the business card is his best and only work until now. Magnificent, a small masterpiece."

"Are you taking his side?"

"Forget it. And?"

"I went into his study one afternoon just as he was typing his password."

"What was it?"

"*Hell.*"

"Ooh. Go on."

"It got to the weekend and at one point John went out to buy some light bulbs, and I took the chance to go on his computer. We've been like owls for months—all the lights blown. You have no idea," she said, burying her face in her hands.

"What? Your house with the lights off?"

"No, you idiot, what was on his computer!"

I waited.

"I logged on, thinking I'd find dozens of folders, not just with his novel but everything else he must have written, holiday journals, reflections, his aphorisms, everything, and . . ."

"I know what happened! Nothing, it was all empty! How awful!"

"No! Way worse than that! Just the one folder. It was called *WORKS*.

"And?" I said again, finally about to find out the reason why Bela had fled, my curiosity stretched about as thin as it would go, trying to stop myself from grabbing Bela by the shirt and shaking it out of her.

"Just one sentence. Just one."

"What?" I shouted, losing it now. "Spit it out, Christ's sake!"

"*Bela is a bloody bitch.*"

"No!"

"Yes!"

"No!"

"Yes!"

"Jesus!"

"This was three weeks ago. I tried to forget about it, to act as if nothing had happened. But every time I looked at John, every time he smiled at me . . . I couldn't stand him touching me, kissing me . . . Then the other day, I exploded. I threw the computer at the wall, bought myself a ticket and packed my things. And here I am.

Then a silence between us for a few moments—a semi-silence, because Bela began to cry. I couldn't think of what to say. Should I play the whole thing down, or go all out at psycho John and help her find a place in Madrid? Was it that bad? Aren't *all* our secrets unsettling? Wouldn't everyone be thought insane if we aired all our quirks and foibles?

"Maybe John knew you were going to go nosing around in his computer, maybe it was just a message to make it clear you don't mess around with his privacy."

"Are you taking his side?"

"No, I'm just saying maybe that's all there is to it."

"There's also the possibility that he's totally insane and hates me, and one day you'll find me dead with an axe stuck in my head!"

"Bela, come on! Don't go overboard! John isn't violent, is he?"

"No, not yet. I've hit *him* a few times."

"Drunk?"

"Him? Of course."

"I doubt he'll hold it against you. With how wasted he gets, he's hardly going to remember. And everything else— how are you guys otherwise?"

"Dunno. All right, I guess. He isn't getting drunk as often. We sometimes make love. He's stopped bugging me about having kids. He loves me, in his way, and I thought I loved him, in mine. '*Bela is a bloody bitch*'," she said again. "Such a horrible ring to it. '*Bela is a bloody bitch*.' Can that really be the one thing that came into his head sitting in front of a computer screen for ten years?"

"I know, sis. Horrific. Three b's in a row. Let's see how it all turns out, shall we?"

"I've just turned thirty-five, Antón. I've been in America nine years. A few more, and I won't be coming back. That will be that. Or I'll be coming back alone and lost and not a clue what to do with myself. I can't see myself spending the rest of my life over there, but neither can I here, really, teaching at some private university, shitty pay and students who think literature's for freaks. It isn't just the thing with John. The time's come when I'm going to have to decide what I want to do with my life."

"Come on, dry your eyes."

I hugged my sister, but I knew the conversation hadn't entirely played out. When you have two people sitting together on a couch, and it's just the two of them, and the lights are down low, and they're there to share secrets, both are going to have their turn. It doesn't tend to be that one tells his or her story and that's it. Usually the interlocutor, much as he or she pretends to be listening, is really just thinking of the moment when the other will finish so he or she can begin with his or hers, with his or her stories to keep you awake at night. An unstated pact; you listen, you get to speak. Though I wasn't feeling at all like unburdening myself, I knew Bela would ask. And I'd be forced to give her an answer. Our situation was the exact opposite of what normally happens; if you tell, you have the right to hear the other's tale. You talk, you get to listen. When Bela stopped hugging me, then it was my turn.

"And you? How are you? I see you haven't got a single photo up."

"Ever the optimist!" I said.

"No, really. Do you think about Ana a lot?"

I swallowed. Strange as it was to hear my wife's name, I didn't feel struck dumb. Stranger still was to hear myself saying the word, or writing it down here now.

"Yes, I think about Ana every day," I said.

"Is the diary helping? Do you write things about her?"

"No, not in the diary. I don't know why. Maybe the diary is the 'post-Ana me'."

And so, talking to one another quietly, largely stationary, we carried on for hours, until we realized that our words were no longer our own, that they'd begun to sound strange, that instead of explaining us they'd end up leaving us alone again, in the middle of a mist—mute, disoriented, speaking to no one.

"One of my favorite Hungarian characters is Kálmán, known as the 'book lover' because he was so refined. At the beginning of the twelfth century he plucked the eyes out his nephew's head—Béla, the future king, whom when he ascended the throne was of course dubbed 'Béla the Blind.' Béla was also a hunchback and had a stammer. So, the stuttering, blind little hunchback made the most of his uncle's lesson, going on to conquer Dalmatia, Serbia, Bosnia and Croatia. Without being able to see them, just imagining them. That's something, yes indeed. And all thanks to his uncle, who was also a *visionary*."

"Yes, that's it, she said to me. You're wicked. Now don't you dare miss out on any of the pleasures I have to offer. Because not everyone who's wicked knows how to live."

"Money attracts pests. Poverty attracts flies."

"Some say that governments, in Spain, will never meet the people's needs. That may be. But it's also true that Spaniards love injustice. They love complaining, getting up on their high horses, wallowing in their wretched fates, raising their voices, letting their passions loose. With tyrants, they grieve; without them, they get bored. And the Hungarians? They're still lords and serfs. Their emperor, Franz Josef, lives elsewhere, isn't Hungarian, doesn't want to be, and never will be."

"There's no jewel so precious as a truly good person. Or more exceptional. I myself am yet to meet one. My wife, for example, seems like a good person because her lack of imagination prevents her from going any further than that."

"I've never understood people's respect for those who want to better themselves. If someone isn't good at something, or isn't talented enough, the best thing they can do is not to invest thousands of hours in overcoming their flaws, and dedicate themselves to something they're actually cut out for, or are at least better suited to."

"The world wants to be deceived. Therefore, my friends, let us deceive it, and let us not waste a second in doing so."

## Thursday, January 21, 2010

Bela has taken up residence in my study, which I've moved to the poky little room I was previously throwing junk in. I've taken the opportunity to throw away the six cardboard boxes I'd kept from my previous life, plus two chairs, a chest of drawers, my university textbooks, horrendous mementos from my travels and other crap. I sold the exercise bike on eBay. Little as I like to admit it, Bela bursting into my life like this, depressed, disoriented, by shifting the focus from me to her, has done me good. Plus she keeps me company. In terms of my alleged son, there's not much I can do now, unless the mother gets in touch. Another ghost that will jump on me in its own sweet time.

NOTES ON BELA'S BOOKS

The Art of War by Sun Tzu

Reading Sun Tzu's treatise, I asked myself what might have prompted Bela to send it to me, what link she could possibly have found between it and optimism or happiness.

She gave me a somewhat cryptic answer yesterday. "That book teaches you how to wage war. What more do you want, Antón?" The strange thing is that there's a certain nobility to his theories, mixed up with cruelty. The end is always victory, but at the lowest cost for all parties, even the defeated (a *truly* noble idea).

*The Life of Reason or The Phases of Human Progress* (1954) by George Santayana (1863–1952)

The philosopher George Santayana was born in 1863—in Madrid! Surprise, surprise. He writes with considerable common sense, and even goes a little beyond that: light, he does shed some light, though we find ourselves not in front of rough seas but a calm lake, not the slightest wind to ruffle it, weeping willows reflected on the surface of the water. For him, happiness is the only thing that can prevent life from being an altogether unfortunate experience. This, though, doesn't help clarify whether or not such happiness exists. If it doesn't, and if, like any other ideal, it proves to be unachievable, life would then *de facto* be simply unfortunate which would in turn make Santayana a pessimist who's got his discourse in a muddle, but a pessimist when all is said and done. George promises us a birthday present, but leaves us without a cake, and without a song. It's late, nearly two o'clock in the morning. What a shame I can't leave the house, go to the cinema, buy some popcorn and sit down in front a stupid comedy for a couple of hours.

> "But away with thy thirst for books, that thou
> mayest die not murmuring but with a good
> grace, truly and from thy heart grateful to the
> Gods."
>
> MARCUS AURELIUS

One of the things I find most surprising about you, Vidor, is the respect you have for melancholy. It seems out of character. You were someone who devoured life, you grabbed it by the throat. You were active, happy, brazen and you were cruel. But if you encountered someone who was truly depressed, you didn't kick them while they were down, you didn't try to take advantage. This respect for subjects prone to sadness, which in you is almost fear, probably has its origins in your childhood in Hungary. Several months back, I wrote in this diary that you were terribly happy there, but maybe I was wrong. And your mother? Your mother, "that mare," didn't even have time to think about whether she was happy or not. As soon as she went past you, busy with her endless chores, you immediately understood how she was feeling; if she gave you a bear hug and a wet, noisy kiss on the cheek, she was in a good mood; if you found yourself on the receiving end of a slap, she was angry. Was your father melancholic, as well as a drunk? The few times you mention him, he's shut up in his room, "crying with a rather unhappy happiness for hours on end." I don't know. The strange thing is that anyone given to melancholy, rather than making you angry—like people who are happy, or dignified, or serious, or jokers, or pretty much anyone else—brought about a desire in you to celebrate, but not a selfish type of party, individualistic, all on your own, but an expansive kind of revelry, generous, with wine and champagne for all.

And you didn't try to make life more fun for people who were given to melancholy, either. They just reminded you that, though you lived well, tending pretty much daily to your vices, there was still more you could do, more pleasure to be had. And you feared them, too—you feared catching their illness, their black moods? Of the fact they might exert power, like your father, that they were fallen or accursed gods, constantly capable of harm? That you, so sure of yourself, so optimistic, might have been a melancholic in disguise, teetering on the brink of the cliff? Were you afraid they'd figure out you were an impostor?

In our family we haven't been especially inclined to melancholy, but no one's ever totally safe. Bela's going through a dark period. Poor Bela—as the savvy Zoltan would put it. She hasn't even settled down in her room, her suitcase is still open in the middle of her sleeping space, nowhere near being unpacked. She doesn't read. She barely leaves the house. Rejects any plan I put forward, spends the time playing Playstation, pretty violent games—the kind I've barred myself from during my optimistic stage—she's disconnected her phone so she can't be contacted by John, who's turned his obsessive efforts to find her toward my parents, who have also disconnected all their phones and can only be reached by Skype. I at least managed to make her talk to her manager so she didn't instantly lose her teaching job in Boston. It seems she was lucky: she was owed time off and one of her colleagues is going to cover her until she gets back. I'd got to the point of thinking of Bela as an *anthropological optimist*, or a vocational one, or at least a pessimist who kept her mouth shut—but I don't think that now. She's got her war axe out now and, since I'm the one closest to her, I've been on the receiving end of a few hacks. The other day, after a fairly gloomy supper, while I was in my room reading Descartes, I heard shouts.

"ANTÓN! COME HERE NOW!"

I went into the living room. She was holding Confucius' *The Four Books*, one of the volumes she'd sent (which, by the way, I'm not going to make notes about, having found it extremely boring; all I get from his convoluted stories, full of Chinese names I have no chance of retaining, is dizziness). Seeing me, Bela flushed with anger.

"What have you done to my books, little brother?"

"Nothing," I said, a little taken aback.

"Nothing? NOTHING? AND WHAT ABOUT THESE FLY DROPPINGS, WHAT ARE THEY?"

Bela held the copy of Confucius up in front of my face, open at one of the pages.

"That isn't fly shit, Bela. That's my writing. Those are my notes."

"I KNOW THAT, ANTÓN! You've written in *my* books."

"Sorry, sister. I needed to for my diary."

"For your diary? Oh, your diary, yes of course! Know what diaries are? Hiding places for crybabies. Just so you know, I'm never going to lend you one of my books, ever again."

Bela huffed, threw the book on the table and sat down in my armchair.

"So, apart from violating my books, you're still trying to be an optimist?"

"Yes."

"What a load of shit!" she roared, when a few weeks ago it was her urging me to keep on with it. "You're *never* going to be happy. You're pure uppers and neuroses, and you know it. Let's see, where have you got to? Make a case for optimism, for happiness, go on, give it a go, shrimp."

Taken aback by her words, and the unprecedented evil smile on her face, I got up and asked if she wanted a drink. She said yes. I poured two drinks—becoming a teetotaller till the end of my days wasn't my top priority just then. I needed backup. Bela, when it comes to anything to do with literature and, why not say it, wisdom, is a few steps ahead of me. I handed her a whiskey and ice and, in one gulp, she killed it off. Not a great start.

"Go for it, little brother, let it all out. Don't forget what your beloved barbarian Vidor Mallick had to say: 'Only idiots waste time. Lunatics save it!'"

"Fine. Most of those who make the case for optimism point to its usefulness . . ."

"Despicable!" said Bela. "Instant hair growth for bald people would be useful too, as would an IQ detector that works, but there's still no such thing! Come on!"

"Okay, okay . . . They put it down to a simple problem of people's attitude to life and character. And if we consider proper thinkers, the paradise of optimists has become a wasteland." My sister smiles, pleased at this. "They use all kinds of bargain basement arguments: happiness is in living, not in life; happiness is believing happiness exists—in a sugar-coated past, in an imaginary future, in limbo, before we're born or after we die—if we believe in an afterlife—or in fleeing from life, in withdrawal, in salvation by way of annulling conscience. That is, happiness *can be* everywhere, except right here, the one place in which you and I find ourselves. It is, therefore, an *invention*, an imaginary refuge, a mirage in the middle of the desert, and it vanishes the moment you get close. It might be looked on as a healthy thing to aspire to, a valuable stimulus, but also an invitation to be disillusioned, frustrated, further proof of mankind having lost its way, of being unable to accept itself as it really is. And the optimist, he's either lost his mind or he couldn't care less because he's never been dealt a bad hand, or he's a complete fool, or he's taking the easy way out, the bargain basement solution. An optimist would simply be someone who purports to be happy, that is, willpower is the main factor that determines whether you are an optimist or not, gritting your teeth come rain come shine, smiling when your arm's being chopped off. The optimist doesn't believe he lives in a perfect world, he doesn't even think everything he sees is perfectly wonderful, but at least *he wants* it to be, he tries for it to be. So we're clear, I'd be a model optimist, one of the top ones, if only it weren't for what it meant for my career."

"Ha! At least you don't kid yourself. And, apart from all your exemplary trying, where would you say you're at?"

" 'I'm a pessimist because of intelligence, but an optimist because of will', as Gramsci put it. I haven't come to any definitive conclusions. For me, surviving's plenty, and I'm making an effort to try and be happy. Glass half-full and all that."

190

"Mm," said Bela, somewhat placated.

"Then there's Vidor's way of looking at life: drown yourself in wine and roses, uphold suffering just as much as pleasure, leave ethics and shame aside . . . But I don't think I've got it in me, I'm too honest, either that or too much of a coward."

"Super."

"There's more: I've rediscovered the usefulness of the primitive, of going back in time."

"Which means exactly? . . ."

"Going back, to the time before Man thought of himself as Man and formulated a hugely complicated idea of what being a Man is. I mean reminding ourselves that, when it comes down to it, we're no more than hairless monkeys. I mean doing without always intellectualizing, using our hands, toiling, stopping and enjoying . . . *Doing*, leaving *analyzing* aside. Not having goals—it feels good."

"Whoo—congratulations. I discovered all of this ages ago, *way earlier* than you. The future is in action, in simplicity, in what's at hand, in the things *you can touch*."

"And you?" I took the bold step of asking, as Bela poured me a second whiskey. "I bet you'll feel great mixing alcohol and pills."

"Shut it, shrimp! I'll mix whatever the fuck I . . . Me? Me? What's it to you . . . Where am I at, you're asking?" Bela gave me an enraged look, took a swig, crunched an ice cube in her jaws and—not what I'd expected—smiled. "I'm remembering some sayings, by some Greek thinkers, between the eighth and fifth centuries BC." In Bela's case, if I haven't mentioned, memory really was a tool, something she could make use of, and not, like mine, a mere crutch. "Selected excerpts compiled by one of my colleagues at the university. Homer: 'Since among all creatures that breathe on earth and crawl on it/ There is not anything more dismal than man is'; Hesiod: 'Countless plagues wander amongst men; for earth is full of evils and the sea is full'; Mimnermus: 'There is no one mortal to whom Zeus does not assign many ills', Solon: 'Count no man happy until he be dead'; Bacchylides: 'Not to be born 'twere best' . . ."

"Enough," I said, cutting her off "please! Jesus, Bela, I get the picture. And those are just guys from those few centuries, and just Greeks, that is, a selection of a selection? Makes me wonder why I'm reading so much."

So you'll understand now, Vidor, what my reflection on melancholy was about. I made up my mind that, whatever the cost, I had to get my old Bela back. She was clearly in a worse way than I was, though her problem might be short lived and mine was possibly a structural one. If I couldn't get her out of the rut, then living under the same roof as her was going to sink me forever as well.

NOTES ON BELA'S BOOKS

*Passions of the Soul* (1649) by René Descartes (1596–1650)

You get a very good idea, reading *Passions of the Soul*, of the origin of the adjective "Cartesian". It is a strange work, maybe because of its highly ambitious, slightly frustrating and also frustrated, touching, even, attempt to classify, methodically, authoritatively, *precisely*, all human passions. Descartes, like the good Frenchman he is, comes across as both boring and playful.

Descartes is a believer in happiness: whoever is virtuous will be happy, that is, anyone who tries to do what is right and who has a clear conscience. In my view, he isn't actually talking about happiness, but serenity, spiritual peace, which isn't the same thing. Happiness is active; serenity, passive. A person seeks happiness throughout his life; serenity is more associated with the final phase of life, as death approaches and there's a sense of a job well done. Some very old people, as well as people who are terminally ill, seeing that death beckons, manage to accept it and accept themselves, becoming visionaries of sorts for the rest of their time. But the fact is, no one would ever use the term "happy" to describe them.

*Wednesday, February 3, 2010*

> "Happiness is the only sanction of life; where happiness fails, existence remains a mad and lamentable experiment."
>
> SANTAYANA

Bela still won't engage. Yesterday, tired of having her around the whole time, and of her constant snide remarks, I forced her to go out. She hadn't left the apartment at that point for nineteen days straight. I took a bath with some lovely bath salts, collapsed on the couch listening to a Françoise Hardy record, and settled down to some work. She showed up four hours later carrying several plastic bags full of books.

"For you, Antón!" she smiled. She looked totally different: the color was back in her cheeks, the pinkish tone itself quite a change. "For being so nice to me, brother."

Bela gave me a couple of kisses. Thrilled, I went for the bags. They contained: Cioran's *The New Gods*; Kierkegaard's *Diapsalmata*; Leopardi's *Thoughts*; Nietzsche's *Ecce Homo* and *The Genealogy of Morals*; Pessoa's *Books of Disquiet*; Montaigne's *Essays*.

"I have a feeling," I said, "these aren't the happiest thinkers ever. Am I right?"

"Oh, but of course they are! You'll see! Enough of the soft-liners, Antón. Purely hardcore now. And no complaining: Montaigne's in there for a bit of fun. Now, you can destroy your own books, not mine."

I didn't know how to react to the present. A group of notoriously pessimistic writers had just walked in through the door. Further provocation on my sister's part—it had to be. Now that her good points had been buried, frozen, her not so good points were coming to the fore. For the first time in my life I had a strong desire to get away from her as soon as possible and for more than just a few hours.


*Friday, February 5, 2010*

> "Then turn to the morals of those who live with thee, and it is hardly possible to endure even the most agreeable of them, to say nothing of a man being hardly able to endure himself."
>
> MARCUS AURELIUS

The satellite contract is at a crucial juncture: we've got firm bids from almost all of the insurers, and the insurance policy and the collocation slip are both well-advanced, and that's the basic document for the project. I've decided to do full days in the office for a while, a sandwich for lunch in front of my computer, from eight to eight.

I'm lying. It isn't just because of work, Vidor. It's Bela too. She scares me. What a temper. Her snickering laugh, which used to be contagious, I find awful now. She calls me "shrimp" like when we were kids, viciously, in a teasing way. When she gets in a rage, wow does she ever howl. Probably, Vidor, we've all inherited your wrathful gene, the destroyer, the demon in you. I don't even want to think about the day when Zoltan's going to blow up—he who allows rage no space, the sweet little angel, the family superhero, *Wonderboy*. I hope when it happens the police won't be too far away. With Bela, there have been constant close shaves—the apartment's far too small for one tigress and one temporarily castrated tiger. Vidor, I feel like I'm in the same position as your wife, who would shut herself up in the dressing room when she saw the signs of one of your imminent explosions: teeth clenched, a frenzied look in your eyes, stomping around whilst you spoke, yanking on your own earlobe to the point of almost pulling it off, swearing in Hungarian ...

I have no way of anticipating Bela's attacks, maybe because they come so frequently. I'd never have imagined that setting up budget meetings with Gorostegui, or witnessing the way he adjusts his brightly colored tie every five minutes in an obviously neurotic gesture, or chatting about money and genealogies with him, could possibly be relaxing and, even, fun.

*Saturday, February 6, 2010*

"Pessimism, and all the moralities founded on despair, are not pre-rational but post-rational. They are the work of men who more or less explicitly have conceived the Life of Reason, tried it at least imaginatively, and found it wanting. These systems are a refuge from an intolerable situation: they are experiments in redemption."

SANTAYANA

I finally managed to get Bela out for an evening. I organized dinner with Carlos and Fran at Zara, the Cuban place on Calle Infantas. The food's good, but the daiquiris are the real draw: they could wake the dead. It was odd to see, once again, how people are transformed after a couple of drinks in the company of a member of the opposite sex. Carlos and Fran were sparkling and obsequious. They both taunted each other, but really these were signals to Bela. My sister, who bought a dress for the occasion, flirted with them non-stop. Our table resembled a runway, but instead of aeroplanes it was daiquiris constantly coming in to land. I was drinking water, and enjoyed waiting in the wings—until, that is, when we were on to desserts and Bela, sloshed, made me sing the Hungarian national anthem with her.

Though you know it perfectly well, Vidor, though it was the single song you taught your children (not translating it, as though it were some kind of spell or charm), I'll transcribe part of it here. It was composed by Ferenc Kölcsey (1790–1838) and translated by Laszlo Korossy. Whenever I sing or hear it in Hungarian, I become emotional. Though the words have lost their meanings, they smack of childhood to me. Uncle Juan taught it to us.

*O Lord, bless the nation of Hungary / With your grace and bounty / Extend over it your guarding arm / During strife with its enemies / Long torn by ill fate / Bring upon it a time of relief / This nation has suffered for all sins / Of the past and of the future!*

*You brought our ancestors up / Over the Carpathians' holy peaks / By You was won a beautiful homeland / For Bendeguz's sons / And wherever flow the rivers of / The Tisza and the Danube / Árpád our hero's descendants / Will root and bloom.*

*For us on the plains of the Kuns / You ripened the wheat / In the grape fields of Tokaj / You dripped sweet nectar / Our flag you often planted / On the wild Turk's earthworks / And under Mátyás' grave army whimpered / Vienna's "proud fort."*

We were a real hit in the restaurant, though, given that when I sing it I'm usually drunk, I felt pretty embarrassed. Also, being reminded of Uncle Juan didn't feel good in this instance. When we finished eating I headed home. For the first time, Fran and Carlos stayed out together without me and, indeed, so did Bela. I left them arm-in-arm, swaying, looking for a bar. It's eight o'clock in the morning now and my sister still hasn't come home. Should I be worried, Vidor? Meanwhile, here's a little present for you, some Hungarian proverbs.

HUNGARIAN PROVERBS AND SAYINGS (from the internet)

"A Hungarian is someone who enters a revolving door after you, but still manages to come out before you."

"Adam ate the apple, and our molars are still hurting from it."

"The first thing you do to make a Hungarian omelette is to steal six eggs . . ."

"A Hungarian is always prepared to sell his country, his wife, or his soul. He knows he'll never actually hand any of them over."

"Metal bracelets make a sound if there are two of them."

"If the stone falls and hits the egg, tough luck for the egg. If the egg falls and hits the stone, tough luck for the egg."


*Thursday, February 11, 2010*

> "Between birth and death,
> Three in ten are followers of life,
> Three in ten are followers of death,
> And men just passing from birth to death
> also number three in ten.
> Why is this so?
> Because they live their lives on the gross
> level."

> "He who knows how to live can walk
> abroad without fear of rhinoceros or tiger.
> He will not be wounded in battle."

LAO TZU

198

Signs of improvement: people seem all the more insufferable to me, if such a thing were possible. Most of all, naturally, family, friends and (to open it out a bit) TV presenters. The pills are doing their job, helping me out of the rut. Bela has reacted too. She's a strong woman (both mentally and physically), and her depressions, at least when in the critical phase, would appear to last no longer than a month.

When I got back from the office, she was out, and the apartment was sparkling. She's *doing things* now. She showed up at dinner time, with the air of the active woman I admire so much. She had one of my jackets on. It was too big for her, but ever since we were young Bela has liked to wear my clothes. She'd been running around all day. Among other things, she'd been to the Botanical Gardens "to have a chat with Uncle Juan." Since he died, Bela has always talked a lot with him, asking his advice, telling him her problems; she does with Uncle Juan more or less as I do with you, Vidor. When we have a ghostly interlocutor, a confidante from beyond to talk to, what's interesting is that we never tell them jokes and we never tell them good news: we use them only to throw our detritus at. If they really were listening, if they were there (and I include God, or the idea of God, in this), the first thing they'd do would be to get their hands on a decent pair of earplugs. Is that what you do, Vidor? Plug your ears when I speak? Anyway.

Over dinner, as we were having a plate of lentils, Bela told me off. She'd found a wrap of cocaine in the inside pocket of the jacket she was wearing. Drugs are bad for you, Vidor, you know that. Naughty naughty. I wouldn't say it's a good thing going rummaging around in other people's pockets, either, but . . . I managed to calm her down, telling her it must be from months ago, because I'm clean now. Then, looking at the jacket, which is made of gray wool, I remember it was the same one I'd worn on the night of my encounter with Lucía the Disappeared.

"Yes? Really?" asked Bela, excited, and looking at the sports jacket with a very strange look on her face. "Are you sure?"

"Yes, no need to get nervous, I doubt you'll catch anything. Or get pregnant—that seems even less likely."

"Yuck, Antón! You're disgusting!"

Yes, maybe I am, but, again I say—and happily now—I can't stand people.

"And have you remembered anything else?"

"No," I said, about to explode. "There's nothing *to* remember. That's all folks. If I am going to have a child, let it ask its mother, and let it come looking for me when it turns eighteen and needs drinking money."

"Antón!"

"I'm perfectly capable of living surrounded by ghosts! Luis, who was the first, Uncle Juan, Ana . . . I'm starting to think it's better to put up with sporadic visits from ghosts, who are family, after all, and usually show up at night, and only cause insomnia, than real, flesh and bone people, people I've never had the pleasure of meeting, like hypothetical baby Mallick."

"Ok, ok," said Bela, not unaccustomed to my outbursts. "Pass the salt?"

"What? The lentils bland all of a sudden?"

The doorbell rings. I've had enough of the doorbell ringing. I've bought nothing online. I haven't ordered takeaway. Never in my life have I had a courier come with a message. My friends aren't the kind to show up at home at eleven o'clock at night without calling ahead. I don't know my neighbors. It can only be another problem. I open up. And sure enough. It's Zoltan. Smiling. Pretending he's feeling awkward.

"Hi, Antón. Mind if I come in?"

"As if I had a choice. What are you doing here?"

"Oh, nothing. I was just in the area and . . ."

"Come off it, you're never *just in the area*. Go on, come in then."

We have a few beers, the three siblings, and we complain about the weather, about politicians, about the Orwellian road signs ("We can't drive for you," I shit you not), about being taken for complete fools . . .

I felt fairly involved, I screamed and shouted a fair bit. Luckily, Bela and Zoltan didn't fall out. They're both back to fearing me a little, deferring to me a little. Zoltan took some photos of Bela and me before he left, the moron. Like my mother says, to remember us by. Yeah, right.

*Thursday, February 18, 2010*

"For our soul to have this means of happiness, all it needs is to pursue virtue diligently. Anyone who lives in such a way that his conscience can't reproach him for ever failing to do something he judges to be the best (that being what I am here calling 'pursuing virtue') will get from this a satisfaction that has such power to make him happy that the most violent assaults of the passions never have enough power to disturb the tranquillity of his soul."

I'm just back after four days in New York. When I travel to cities other than New York, I feel like I want to relate what I've done, rather than anything about the city itself. With New York it's the other way around: I don't feel like talking about the meetings, or my runs in Central Park, or the restaurants I ate at, nor how good the play I went to see was. I don't want to say anything about my *actions*, but about the *character*, about the city. Why? What makes it play *such* a leading role? It isn't just its skyscrapers, its special energy, its material and spatial grandiosity, its lights, its multicultural feel, etcetera. It isn't purely for its so very well-known and, ultimately, so hackneyed, attributes. There's more than that.

To start with, if you've been there a few times, you come to believe that you own it. It reveals itself to you immediately, it guides you along her streets, her avenues, her symbols; it makes you believe it's easy to read. It's been called the lighthouse of the West. Rather, I think of it as the West's best work of fiction, the most elaborately wrought. Like a good book, first of all it grabs you and then it deceives you, for your own good, leading you to a place where your horizons will widen and grow. It transmits life, and life just *is*, it can't be questioned, much as we try to explain it. It can be read in infinitely different ways, and though it never ceases to transmute, in essence, it's always the same, there's no alteration to the text. Hers is the sweetest trap, because she doesn't claim to provide answers, rather to make you ask yourself better questions. And that's why, like good books, it can also destroy you if you aren't ready to be alone, which is the one irrefutable truth. No book will ever make your dreams come true. No city will give you something for free. Not even New York, that work of fiction.

NOTES ON BELA'S BOOK AND ON BOOKS BOUGHT IN THE AIRPORT

*Essays* (1595), Montaigne, Michel Eyq (1533–1592)

I finished reading Montaigne on the flight to NY, where I had no sleep. I got excited, but this time because of the gem I was holding in my hands. What's the opposite of fanaticism? Montaigne! The modernness and the simplicity of that Frenchman's vision are astonishing. He wrote it in the sixteenth century, Vidor, when your family's wits were still duller than the foxes robbing your chickens! His "thinking self" has its feet on the ground. His prose is fluent, like his thoughts. Or like a river with more quiet pools than turbulent currents. His good judgement transmits a comforting kind of peacefulness, a reassuring calm. He's as pleased to be in doubt as he is to be certain of things (not for nothing was his family motto "Que sais-je?"—"What do I know?" or "How should I know?"). Humor isn't left aside. He knows how to read. He defends happiness, not happiness of life, but of living. A wise man. And on top of all this, hard to believe, he is truly humble. He is proof that it is possible to be simple and profound, his work goes far beyond common sense: it's pure wisdom. Wisdom for the populace, but that doesn't mean *popular*. It's a nice feeling being able to defer the pleasure of the next two volumes. I enjoyed reading this one so much that I would even say that it's people like him, and their work, that make life worth living. They don't make me feel more optimistic, but they do reconcile me with living. Viva Montaigne! Viva the oldies who beget the youthful spirit! Viva!

*The Most Beautiful Story of Happiness* (2004), Andre Compte-Sponville, Jean Delumeau, Arlette Farge

This one I bought in the Barajas airport bookshop (very odd, they don't usually stock anything but bestsellers), when I realized I was half-way through the Montaigne already. The book is set out as an interview (confusingly, though, the reader almost never knows who's speaking) with three French intellectuals on subjects related to happiness, paradise, and religion. They're all chauvinists, they back up their arguments with quotations from fellow French thinkers (including the "philosopher," Alain), and the optimism they propagate is forced at best. Compte-Sponville's view—that, taken as a whole, philosophers, from the Greeks onwards, show that philosophy is an aid to happiness, that improving the way we think helps improve the way we live—is highly debatable. As is his idea that anyone who doesn't commit suicide loves life: it's perfectly common, my dear friend, even if you have a loathing for life, not to commit suicide— cowardice being a fairly common complaint. There are many shades of gray between love and hate. Anyway. I also didn't like the fact that the list of hell on earth, of the worst ills of the twentieth century, didn't include Mao or

Stalin. The most interesting thing in the book is the idea of happiness as the opposite of the experience of sadness—a not-sadness. This is a doleful, realist way of interpreting life. Nonetheless: there is such a thing as intense, passing bliss, not-everlasting, more all encompassing than the not-sadness, and you shouldn't give up searching for it every day of your life. The search itself would be the spice of the not-sadness. It also pleased me to see the word "love" mentioned (for the first time) in relation with happiness or optimism. That's been lacking. Without love for others, for the human being, whatever form it takes (brotherly, passionate, filial . . . ) happiness is inconceivable, whether it be everlasting or passing—and that includes not-sadness, too. Love makes you suffer, yes, it isn't all sweetness and light, but it is *an uplifting* suffering.

*A Pelican at Blandings* (1969), P. G. Wodehouse (1881-1975)

I bought a Wodehouse novella in Strand Bookstore. It isn't a philosophy book, but it has plenty to do with optimism. I asked myself: will I still find Wodehouse as funny as I did when I was sixteen? Am I still alive? He's one of the few authors ever to have had me in stitches and, before I embarked again on this adventure of Lord Emsworth's, half way over the Atlantic, I knew that if I didn't find it funny, there wasn't going to be any point trying to be an optimist any more. The best thing, simply, would be to kill myself, make official the death of my soul. Luckily, Wodehouse won me a deferral. His characters still make me cry with laughter. I'm alive, I can aspire to being happy. Thank heavens.

*Monday, February 22, 2010*

Good (?) news, Vidor. Bela has officially been given two months off work and for the moment she has decided to spend them in Madrid. She's informed John that the separation isn't definitive, but it could be. To ensure he doesn't show up in Madrid, she's told him she's going to *tour* Europe (a very American thing to do, which is why he believed her, poor fool). And seeing as Bela can't stand being idle, she's decided to set up some conferences on the Spanish Golden Age. The reading rooms at the National Library have become her home away from home.

## TRANSCRIPTION OF TONIGHT'S CONVERSATION WITH MY MOTHER, PEPA (REAL NAME JOSEFA, MUCH AS IT PAINS HER/US)

I pick up (using the mouse, obviously. This is a Skype call).

"Hi Mom."

"Son? Son? Antón? Are you there? (Not letting me get a word in edgeways). Son?"

"... ..."

"Damned Skype! Antón? Can you hear me?"

"Hi, Mom, you're coming through fine. Loud and clear."

"What? What are you clearing?"

"Nothing, Mom. No need to shout, I can hear you fine."

"And I can hear you! It's incredible! A real miracle! Seeing how far away you are!"

"The only miracle is that it's still free, Mom. Now let's try and calm down a bit, shall we? How are you?"

"Is Bela there?"

"Yes, she's clearing dinner away. I'll put her on after."

"Why don't you clear the table? We've never had that kind of sexism in my house. What did you have for dinner?"

"Fillet of chicken and tomato salad with a lemon dressing. Strawberries in orange juice for dessert."

"That's good, son, very good. Lost a bit of weight now, haven't you?"

"Zoltan been sending you more photos, right?"

"How much have you lost? Four kilos? Five?'

"Six, Mom. Six and a half."

"You're lying, son, but it doesn't matter. And now there should be some punishment for having let yourself get so fat: throw some clothes away. Don't even think about keeping those fat person's clothes, son, because you'll only fall down again. It's a temptation knowing they're there in the wardrobe, hunkered down in there, waiting for you. Also, no one has to know you misbehaved. Imagine a woman shows up in your life, imagine she peeks inside your closet—all those fat clothes she'll find. Throw it all in the garbage, son. Destroy the evidence."

"I will, Mom. I'll go and donate them to a center for the obese."

"Whereas Bela's put on weight. It's just like you conspire together to torture me. Instead of an apple, now she looks like the little pig that eats the apple. Do you think she'll get back together with that bum?"

"With who?"

"With John, son, use your brain. On one hand I'm delighted she's ditching him, but then again I worry so much about her being alone. Zoltan's right: poor Bela needs someone around, someone who'll look after her."

"She's a big girl now, Mom, don't worry yourself. And John isn't exactly a bum: he's a fiction writer."

"A what?"

"*A fiction writer.*"

"I can't stand it when you do that pretentious British accent . . . That's good to know about John, son, I had no idea. I just had him down as a lazy good-for-nothing. You two should come and visit, your father's not been so great lately. Apart from being on his computer, he does nothing. He barely comes out of his den."

"I can't come, Mom, I've got work. And with Dad, what's up exactly? Have you taken him for a checkup like Zoltan said?"

"Every time I think of Bela and you . . . What are you two up to, in Madrid, always together? I find it *most unusual.*"

"It isn't that unusual for two siblings to live in the same city for a while, Mom. And for years it was just the two of us, because you guys abandoned us, remember? And this time, it's been almost a year since we've seen each other, and Bela's come because of the breakup. Mind telling me what the hell's going on with Father?"

"No need to get like that, son. You're so on edge. You ought to do more sport."

"I run pretty much every day, Mom. And you? Do you do sport?"

"Me? You mean me? I'm not overweight, son, and I don't blow my top at the slightest thing, and I don't rattle like a viper, and I don't let more than a week go by without calling my mother ... You're so ungrateful."

"Okay, okay, Mom. Don't get angry. You know I love you. And Father? How is he?"

"Hold on a moment, son, the teapot's going, I'll go and take it off the stove (and my mother stops speaking for thirty seconds or so, though I can still hear her breathing, perfectly clearly, at the other end of the line, and I know full well she hasn't gone to take the teapot off the stove). Here I am! You have no idea the lovely herbal teas I've been making, Antón."

"Is that right, Mom? There's a really great new shop here in Madrid ..."

And so on, for half and hour. And then, another half an hour with Bela. And then, bed.

*Wednesday, February 24, 2010*

> "This is what happens in laughter: Blood coming from the right-side cavity of the heart through the arterial vein suddenly and repeatedly inflates the lungs, forcing the air in them to rush out through the windpipe, where it makes an inarticulate, explosive sound. The swelling of the lungs and the rushing out of the air both push against all the muscles of the diaphragm, chest and throat, thus causing movement in the

facial muscles that are connected with them. And what we call 'laughter' is merely this facial expression together with the inarticulate and explosive sound that comes with it."

DESCARTES

Until the entrance of my sister into my room, nothing much had happened. I'd got back from the office at about nine, been for a run in the Retiro, had dinner and gone to bed to read. Then, at around midnight, Bela knocked on my door and let herself in. She was wearing white pajamas patterned with little blue elephants. It occurred to me that the only thirty-year-olds in the world who could possibly go around in that kind of get up are US residents. She looked very serious, and when she sat on the edge of my bed, though I knew something was up and that she had something important to say, I'd never have expected what I was about to hear:

"Antón, I've found her."

I said nothing to this, so she did the talking. The wrap she found with the cocaine in it was an invitation to a season opening at a place called Udth, a vintage clothes shop on Calle Almirante. She'd thought about going and having a look around, just in case, but then forgot about it—until today.

"There was a stockman mannequin in the window with an awesome emerald green silk dress and a gray felt Swiss army jacket with silver buttons. Next to that, these red pumps with all these impossibly bright socks . . . I could have bought the lot. Well, in the end I only got the jacket. Shall I show it to you?"

I still didn't say anything. I was trying to stay calm. If my sister said she'd found Lucía, she'd found her. Bela wasn't like the idiotic private investigator, or like me, who hadn't managed to find Lucía either; Bela never failed. Therefore, this meant that the woman claiming to be the mother of my child had finally materialized. My temples were pounding, I could hear my heart, and it felt like someone was dragging a rake around inside my stomach. But no anguish attack came. I didn't break down. I didn't have an out-of-body experience: Antón didn't leave Anton's body, but stayed right where he was, with me.

"Crazy, right? Does it suit me?"

My sister had put the gray jacket on over the sweet little elephants. What a shame not to be able to stomp all over them, send them packing, chop them up into pieces. The jacket was lovely and Bela looked beautiful but, Vidor, just then, I couldn't have given, to put it crudely, a flying fuck.

"You look great, but . . ."

"I'll tell you everything . . . I confess! Three hundred euros! It's a Swiss Army jacket, but also kind of civilian, because Switzerland, proverbially, is a neutral country, peace-loving, right?"

"Yeah, their way of swindling others is very ethical, very civilized. All you're missing is the white gloves."

Bela skipped around the room, checking herself out in the mirrors on the door and my wardrobe. I felt like murdering her.

"And when you and I go," she said, not looking at me, facing the mirror, pouting, "I'm thinking I'll buy the dress. And for you, I'm going to buy the orange socks."

211

She turned around and gave me a smile.

"There was an assistant there, dyed blonde hair, friendly, a bit cagey. But she was the only person working. I started asking her how much things were, I tried a few things on . . ."

"And?" I interrupted, really getting fed up.

"Sorry! Don't get upset! Okay, so the door at the back opened, I guess the door to the warehouse, and a girl walks in, twenty-five-ish, brunette, her hair short and boyish, a bit green about the gills, kind of androgynous but at the same time really feminine, and she had these very long fingers."

"And?"

"She was carrying some blue and grey American-looking workshirts, they looked like they were out of a Sears catalogue, really seventies . . . She folded them up and put them on this low shelf. She was heavily pregnant."

"And?"

Bela sat down beside me on the edge of the bed.

"It was her, Antón. I knew in an instant. Your description wasn't that precise, but I recognized her immediately. Particularly because of what you said about a flat nose. It wasn't *that* flat, but I could see what you meant."

"Did you talk to her?"

"No—well, yes. It was her I asked if I could try the jacket on. She's such a bad saleswoman, it actually means she's good at it. She has this slightly diabolic smile. And she's highly strung, she's constantly stretching the fingers on her right hand with her left. I think she's left handed."

"And how are you so sure it's her?"

212

"Because I am. Do you want me to come with you when you go and see her?"

"I don't want to see her. I don't want to find out if she's having my child. I need calm."

"You should. You should meet her."

I looked at Bela, somewhat surprised.

"You said before that I had no right to go looking for her."

"I know."

"You said she was probably crazy and, as well, that I wasn't ready to tackle any more problems."

"I know, but I've changed my mind."

"Fickle woman."

"And you? Are you always coherent? I don't think you can go on turning it over and over in your head for the rest of your life. Knowing you, that's exactly what you'll do. What would Uncle Juan have said? What would he have advised, not in words, but just with his presence?"

I knew this time my sister was right. I was running away from too many things. I had been running away for too long. I'd decided to keep my head down, thinking the world around me would stop too. But the woman and child had come to me, through Bela. It would be ridiculous to try and resist. And my duty, if I am really the father, is to tackle the thing head on, face up to it, offer myself in case the future baby needs me.

"Fine," I agreed. "I'd like it if you came with me."

"Tomorrow?"

"No, Saturday."

"Okay," said Bela seriously. "Saturday."

And up she got. Looking at her now, in her pajamas and her Swiss Army jacket, I felt an overwhelming love for her. Nosy, beloved Bela. Then it was just me. I couldn't read. Or sleep. I spent a little while chatting with you, Vidor. Remember? We talked about children, about the five you had, about the three of them that died before the age of five, about your daughter, who lost her mind, and your son, my great-great-grandfather, who inherited both your anger and something of your head for business, but not your joie de vivre.

*Thursday, February 25, 2010*

> "A happy man is not he who others believe to be happy, but he who believes it himself."
>
> MONTAIGNE

Work, then dinner with Bela, Zoltan, María and the twins. The moment Maks saw me, as he's done every time since my episode in the Retiro, asked me, very solemnly, whether my stomach was feeling all right.

*Friday, February 26, 2010*

> "The moment a man questions the meaning and value of life, he is sick."
>
> FREUD

Bhutan, Druk Yul, "Land of the Thunder Dragons": a small country situated between India and China in the Himalayas. It has a very pretty flag, divided diagonally into two triangles, one orange, one yellow, and a sweet-looking dragon in the middle. In Bhutan farmers and Buddhist monks live side by side with yaks, red pandas and snow leopards. For its isolation and for the peacefulness and purity of its peaks, temples, valleys, forests and fortresses, some consider it the true and last-remaining Shangri-La. Since 1972, at the behest of the then King, Jigme Singye Wangchuck, living standards have been judged according to the Gross Happiness Index, GHI. I kid you not. The truth. None of your Gross Domestic Product, GDP. None of your supposedly objective statistics. Subjective ratings only: delight and happiness. I have no idea if this came about through fair motives, if the idea was to promote citizens' happiness in the kingdom, or if the whole thing was some ploy to cover up corruption. Is the Dragon King a poet or a thief, or both? Are there any poets left these days, or only thieves? Anyway. This has all come up because today Fran burst into my office, with all the delicacy of a buffalo, to propose, in all seriousness, that we spend the summer in Shangri-La.

"Let's go, Antón! To Shangri-La, to Bhutan!" he said, hands propped on my desk, leaning over me, his face red with excitement. "A month, a proper trip, none of your weekend break nonsense. To fucking paradise, with the monks, up in magic mountains, drinking yak milk! You know they couldn't give a shit about GDP there, or inflation, or unemployment? All they care about there is

215

happiness, everything's looked at from that perspective . . . What do you say?"

I told him to go ahead and look into it, that I'd think it over, hoping that he'd gradually come off the idea and it would he forgotten, end up in the land of the unrealized dreams, our own personal Shangri-La. Sad—deeply sad— to see a friend so happy, so animated, so close to the brink. Hysterical happiness in a middle-aged man is a clear sign of tragedy in the home front. I'm convinced that Fran's had long talks with his secretary about Shangri-La and his naïve paradise. It could even be that she was the one who told him about it, after having come across it in some tabloid magazine.

*Saturday, February 27, 2010*

> "... As long as our species continues, those who
> are best acquainted with the human condition
> will continue seeking and promising themselves
> happiness, until the day they die."
>
> LEOPARDI

I had orange juice and some wholewheat toast for breakfast, and went for a run in the Retiro. It was a cold, sunny day, the kind of winter's day when the air actually seems clean, as if there wasn't any pollution, and the trees, naked, very still, reached up like compassionate giants from some prehistoric age—a gentler time. I'm getting fitter all the time; my body doesn't wobble like crème caramel with every step. At a few points I even overtook other runners, the ones that, like me, panted and sweated more than was reasonable, pulling all kinds of faces, running none too stylishly and crying out for someone to make them stop before they had a heart attack.

Bela was ready when I got home. There was no way out. What was I going to say to Lucía when I came face to face with her? How was she going to react? Was I doing the right thing? I took a shower and, for the first time in a long while, couldn't decide what clothes to wear. I went for a blue shirt, jeans, my olive green V-neck, the gray wool jacket and, when I thought of you, Vidor, in your honor, my Hungarian shoes. I though they might bring me luck; even I, every bit the rationalist, have sometimes resorted to superstition in order to overcome my lack of self-assurance. Bela looked me up and down affirmatively, nodding.

"*Lop ez, lop az . . .*" she said.

" *. . . és minden frankó lesz.*"

This was a fun Hungarian saying that imitated the musicality of Spanish ("A liar is López, a liar is Gómez, but after all everyone is hon-est") and that, ever since we were young, Bela and I would intone before facing unpleasant situations or ones that struck us as in some way surreal. We headed out on foot and, in my expectancy, I thought it felt akin to special occasions when we were children and Uncle Juan would take us, also always on foot, to an exhibition, a concert or the cinema. The feeling of ants scurrying around in my stomach, making tracks in the lining, was the same. But no, I wasn't a child any more, and Uncle Juan wasn't here, and what the morning had in store for me was even more unpredictable than the most unpredictable of red letter days in my life to date. We got to Calle Almirante and Bela stopped in front of a shop window with a headless mannequin in it.

"There it is in front. They've put an ugly jacket on in place of mine, German army I think. Oh, by the way, her name's not Lucía, it's Leia."

"What? Now you tell me?"

"Mm, I just remembered."

"Leia? Like Star Wars? Is there such a name?"

"Seems so. Shall we go in? Have you worked out a plan, some strategy I should know about?"

"No. Let's go."

Leia. On hearing her real name, or nom de guerre, a door opened somewhere in my memory; certain details from the night of the crime came into my thoughts, undermining my spirits still further. We went in. The soft winter sunlight was filtering through the window, and the back of the shop was in semi-darkness. It was crammed with clothes. I could make out two figures leaning over a small counter. One of them latched onto my gaze. It was her. She struck me as both fragile and powerful at the same time and, seeing her swollen belly, taut beneath her black sweater, I felt a sudden and unexpected emotion: I realized that that bump, that very simple shape, was protecting another, far more complex, in motion, for now utterly dependent but almost ready to set out on its own. My child, perhaps. I went closer.

"Hello," I said, with someone else's voice. "Good morning."

Leia looked at me without seeing me, but then something changed, her eyes flashed, then a veil passed over them, a shadow, then a flicker of panic, and before I knew it she was gone. The other figure turned out to be a middle-aged woman, strong and focused-looking, hair dyed an almost white blonde, expensive glasses with blue frames and, whilst not ugly, she looked hard, with craggy features and an angry look in her eyes.

"What have you done to her, you?" she spat, almost shouting. "Who are you?'

Angry woman went out of the shop as well then and, for a moment, I felt dirty, as though guilty of something, dirty in the way only a man—the penetrator, the invader—can feel dirty. But fortunately it didn't take me long to see the funny side. Now Bela and I were alone in the shop, like we were the owners.

"No orange socks for me then," I said, totally seriously, without irony.

"And no dress for me." said Bela. "It was her, wasn't it?"

"It was her."

"Don't let it get to you, Antón. Bear in mind that the first time she saw you you were drunk and on drugs, in some shithole club, and the second time she brought on one of your episodes. Guess for her it's like seeing some kind of monster."

"Thanks, Bela."

Neither of us said anything for a few moments, me with no idea what to do, Bela looking around half-heartedly. No sign of Leia or angry woman.

"That was weird, wasn't it?" I said.

"Yes, you gave them a fright. Sure you didn't do anything . . . unusual that night?"

"What's that supposed to mean?"

"I don't know, anything . . . like anything violent."

"Have you lost your mind?"

"I don't know, even just if you were verbally violent, or offensive, what should I know. Or if the sex was hard, like Zoltan with María, anything perverted . . ."

"Don't talk nonsense, sis. What shall we do?"

"Get out of here, I say, scoot, vanish in a puff of smoke. Or would you rather wait for them to come back?"

"No. I'm going to leave my card."

I took a business card out of my wallet and left it on the counter.

"Not going to write her a note?" asked Bela, slightly reproachfully.

"What do you want me to write? A love letter? A marriage proposal? To say let's go ASAP for a couple of babies, a boy and a girl? Sometimes, Bela, I swear, I don't get you!"

Annoyed, I got a pen and wrote on the card: *I'm Antón Mallick, the alleged father of your child, as you know. We need to talk.* It sounded ridiculous when I read it back, too restrained, and fake somehow as well. I suddenly felt like telling her I'd had enough of her, of trying to find her, of her maybe being about to have a child of mine, of her cowardly, childish reactions, and of myself and this whole shitbag of a world. But the card didn't quite have space for all that. Plus it would hardly be the act of an optimist. I crossed out *We need to talk* (*why did I think she* needed to?), and instead wrote: *I need to talk with you. No more running away, Leia, please.*

Bela, reading over my shoulder, appraised my effort and gave me a pat on the back.

Leaving the shop, we looked left and right along the street, but they were nowhere to be seen. We headed in the direction of the Paseo del Prado. The question of the search for Mystery Woman was turning into a mindbender. The first time I'd found Lucía, it wasn't her, but some crass blackmailer instead. The second time, her name wasn't Lucía, but Leia, a sci-fi comic book name, and she'd fled at the sight of me.

"Where now?" Bela said.

"How should I know? Somewhere far away—far, far away."

"Poor Antón. Take a look in the left hand pocket of your jacket."

"What?"

"Just look, shrimp."

I put my hand in the pocket and felt a soft ball. I took it out. It was the orange socks.

"They're cashmere. Hand-wash only."

"You stole them?"

"Sharp as a tack, Antón! Anyone ever told you you're possibly the cleverest human being in the whole wide world? She stole your ID, right? Well then, you get to keep those. At least you'll have got yourself a pair of socks out of this whole sorry affair."

Bela put her arm in mine, and the morning followed its course. Unreal to begin with, strange, with the not-encounter still fresh, and soon afterwards turning a normal morning, mellower, because, as you know, Vidor, in the end what we all like best is peace and quiet, and we love to forget. In the afternoon, I read. In the evening, a DVD, Spike Lee's *25th Hour*. Masterpiece.

NOTES ON BELA'S BOOKS

*Diapsalmata* (1843) by Kierkegaard (1813–1855)

Sören Kierkegaard was Danish and, like most people who are exceptional, sensitive and strange, was often ridiculed. They laughed heartily at him, sometimes in the street, and in newspapers as well. I feel a great affection for Kierkegaard and his elegant melancholia. In terms of the book, I like the fact he seeks poetic truths, that is, he doesn't set out to make a point, he stays intuitive. Unlike other thinkers, the repetitive bores who make such painfully slow headway, the ones who believe their works should be set in stone, the contrived heroes in the history of thought, he, as well being profound, also has a lightness to him. And what are his ideas on happiness? What does the Dane have, what does he offer me? Kierkegaard is a glum man and he is a pessimist; faith cannot staunch his wounds; life to him is all a bitter cup. Is it, Leia? Do you find it so? Seeing as you're already sufficiently powerful to pop up in my thoughts, I include you in my notes on books too. Are you an optimistic woman? Thousand to one you are not. Are you happy? Thousand to one you are not. Are you going to call me? Thousand to one you are not.


*Sunday, February 28, 2010*

> "Now has the cloud put off its alluring face,
> wherefore without scruple my life drags out

222

its wearying delays. Why, O my friends, did ye so often puff me up, telling me that I was fortunate? For he that is fallen low did never firmly stand."

BOETHIUS

I got up early, worked until one o'clock in the afternoon, and went for appetizers with Carlos and Bela in El Cantábrico, shellfish and tap beer. At one point Carlos got a call on his mobile, and I thought I saw him and my sister look knowingly at each other. Excusing himself, as Carlos went out he placed his hand on Bela's shoulder. She reached hers up, their hands touched. I have a suspicion that the brush of her fingers over the back of his hand was her spelling out the word LOVERS on his skin. Am I losing it? Are Bela and Carlos fooling around? Are they an item? Is Fran really sleeping with the secretary? Or am I paranoid, or jealous, simply suspicious of everyone because of the fact I'm alone, alone, alone?

It also struck me today that it's been two months since I slept with a woman (I looked up an old girlfriend in December, Vidor—shame I didn't share that one with you, you would have enjoyed the details). Anyway. That afternoon the three of us went to the cinema together, to the Ideal multiscreen. When we came out of the film, Bela had a date with Carlos, they were going for dinner somewhere. In her words, she's on vacation and ought to be making the most of it. Back at home, I've locked myself up in my room to read. Of course, between one paragraph and the next, I've been thinking about Leia. An alarmingly mercurial woman—and that's putting it kindly. A column of smoke or, better, a cloud of dust, an irritant, a nuisance, the kind that gets in your eyes, making them itch.

NOTES ON BELA'S BOOKS

Giacomo Leopardi (1798–1835) *Thoughts*

Giacomo Taldegardo Francesco di Sales Saverio Pietro Leopardi. Take that. The son of a learned, tightfisted count and a pathologically miserly society lady—to the point that she rejoiced in the death of one of her babies because of the money they'd save as a result. He was a hunchback, but it would be facile to put his inveterate pessimism down to this. Why had I never heard about this fabulous collection of "thoughts"? Why is it not required reading in high school, rather than books like *Platero and I*, a book about a donkey, for goodness' sake? Has the world gone completely crazy? Have you read it, Leia? What about you, Vidor? Did you ever hear anyone mention him, or were his books banned in Spain? I imagine that, Leopardi being so ahead of his time, very few people here will have been able to understand his work. Even though he has an altogether bleak view of the human condition, I've been crying with laughter, I've had to use my bedsheets as handkerchiefs, I woke Bela up at three in the morning to read her one or two extracts (my somewhat hysterical irruption into her room didn't go down massively well), I reread it as soon as I'd finished it, worn out though I was . . . What's this happiness now? Why do I enjoy reading about desolation so much? Is there something wrong with me? Am I depraved? Or, worse, bitter? No, I feel it can't be that. Cause to consider my reaction to Leopardi. Anyway. Viva the aristocratic hunchback!

*Monday, March 1, 2010*

> "Nature, with her usual benevolence, has ordained that men shall not learn to live until they lose the motives for living."
>
> LEOPARDI

Leia hasn't called. Today was a big day at work: we've finished drafting the contract of the insurance policy. When it's signed, on Thursday, the client will pay the premium deposit, which is 13.5 percent of the total. In parallel with my work, the building of "the creature" (aka *Transat*, the satellite) is coming along in time. On the other hand, Bela has met up with Carlos again. They've been to a couple of exhibitions and to a PARTY that, naturally, I wasn't invited to. I must confess I'm not in favor of the Bela-Carlos axis. He's incapable of keeping a relationship together for longer than four months, and my sister could get hurt. She and I are going to have a talk.

*Tuesday, March 2, 2010*

> "Everybody has heard the tale of the Picard, to whom, being upon the ladder, they presented a common wench, telling him (as our law does some times permit) that if he would marry her they would save his life; he, having a while considered her and perceiving that she halted: 'Come, tie up, tie up,' said he, 'she limps.'

> Another answered his confessor, who promised
> him he should that day sup with our Lord, 'Do
> you go then,' said he, 'in my room; for I for my
> part keep fast to-day.'"
>
> MONTAIGNE

Leia hasn't called. Work, a run in the Retiro, chat with my mother (particularly affectionate: must remember to look into why), reading and bed.

*Wednesday, March 3, 2010*

Leia hasn't called.

*Thursday, March 4, 2010*

> "Buddhism had tried to quiet a sick world
> with anesthetics; Christianity sought to purge
> it with fire."
>
> SANTAYANA

> "Only the despairing can be happy, for hope is
> the greatest torture, and despair the greatest joy."
>
> SAMKHYA SUTRAS

Leia hasn't called. If she doesn't call over the weekend, I'm going to go and track her down. Enough of playing hide and seek. It's a good way of putting it, an apt definition, but, really, in this game, she's the only one hiding. If this were a fairy tale, she'd be the elegant cat treated harshly by life, and I the little mouse, so disoriented that it mistakes itself for the cat, and possible father to the litter, or something nutty like that.

We celebrated the signing of the policy today with a copious, ridiculously expensive dinner in "a well-known Madrid restaurant," as they would put it in the society pages. Those present: Gorostegui, Gozalo (aka the go-go's), Ramon Llorente, Fran (there as the representative of the legal department but, mainly, ravenous and eager to take part in the banquet), and me. The surprise was the presence of Llorente, the aerospace engineer. He hardly goes in for the whole "together, we're better, boys," "we're the greatest" corporate bullshit. He's a polite man, with a gentle manner, elegant in a scruffy kind of way, with a pair of blue eyes that only look at you when the conversation interests him. Between toasts and cheap jokes he told us about the writer Arthur C. Clarke, the "father" of communications satellites, and about his visionary article "Extraterrestrial Relays," published in 1945 in the magazine *Wireless World*.

While Ramon held forth on Clarke, on orbits, on receivers and on microwave transmission towers, Gorostegui, as usual, giving the impression that he knew this all already, every now and then gave a "I know, I know," or "I found that really interesting when I read about it too, yes, I know." A point came when Llorente couldn't take it any more and invited Gorostegui to go ahead and finish the story. Gorostegui, credit where it's due, showed balls by giving it a go though he didn't have a clue. And he's nothing if not savvy: realizing his ignorance was about to be exposed, he took advantage of the entrance of an attractive woman to change the subject, and then, turning back to Llorente, said: "You finish it, you're the technician after all. All I'm good for, really, is to bring a bit of human feeling to the story, isn't that right, guys?"

Sometimes a working lunch, with your colleagues, giving and receiving a few slaps on the back and a few well-dones, is great, from the very moment you sit down until they bring the bill (you're not paying). Gorostegui, asking for the bill, found it necessary to get all *pompous*, reminding us about the "pressing need to tighten our belts in this exciting, risky project, given the weakness of the markets and the intensity of the global economic crisis, which looks like it could well become endemic." And for the rest, I should note the fact that Bela's gone from being depressed and shut up in the house the whole time, to being in suspiciously high spirits and going out every single night.

*Friday, March 5, 2010*

> "Blessed are they that mourn: for they shall be comforted . . . Blessed are they which do hunger and thirst after righteousness: for they shall be filled . . . Blessed are the pure in heart: for they shall see God."
>
> St Matthew

Leia still hasn't called.

"If you marry, you will regret it; if you do not marry, you will also regret it; if you marry or do not marry, you will regret both; Laugh at the world's follies, you will regret it, weep over them, you will also regret that; laugh at the world's follies or weep over them, you will regret both; whether you laugh at the world's follies or weep over them, you will regret both. Believe a woman, you will regret it, believe her not, you will also regret that; believe a woman or believe her not, you will regret both; whether you believe a woman or believe her not, you will regret both. Hang yourself, you will regret it; do not hang yourself, and you will also regret that; hang yourself or do not hang yourself, you will regret both; whether you hang yourself or do not hang yourself, you will regret both. This, gentlemen, is the sum and substance of all philosophy."

KIERKEGAARD

Leia called yesterday, Vidor. But that's not nearly all, Saturday and the early hours of Sunday held an awful lot more, maybe too much more, and now, at six o'clock in the morning and only just home, when I sat down at the computer to write my diary I had no idea where to begin. Do I begin at the end, with my attempt to climb the spiked fence at the Retiro, little under an hour ago? How to describe a day which BEGGARS DESCRIPTION?

The thought of speaking with you, Vidor, came into my head beneath the branches of the ahuehuete tree, which as you know is my favorite tree, a species of Mexican cypress and the oldest tree in the park, planted in 1631. Strangely, the tree with the thickest trunk in the world, one hundred and eighteen feet in diameter, belongs to the same species, and it was under another such specimen, known as "The Tree of the Sorrowful Night," that Hernán Cortés wept on the July 10, 1520, after his defeat at Tenochtitlan. But now I'm starting to sound like Bela, right, Vidor, your beloved great-great-great-granddaughter—rambling, getting lost in forest and desert. We were on the subject of my having come home, zigzagging all the way, and it having occurred to me to speak to you under the tree, to ponder a little, to draw a few conclusions, and it having struck me as a fun thing to do (?) to hop the park fence—the gate being locked at night. Yes, I was drunk (you guessed?) and I'd come along to the Alcalá Gate, turned right on Calle Alfonso XII, such a stately street, and then, when I got to the Felipe IV gate, opposite the Casón, began sizing up that fence.

Alcohol can sometimes make you feel young again, almost a child—a child, of course, that's been led astray, innocence lost, not really very childish at all. I clambered up on the bars, with some difficulty, had no qualms about grabbing hold of the golden spikes, got a leg up and, I have no idea how, leaped over to the other side. On getting to my feet and seeing, yes, I was *on the other side*, and that if I held any hope of getting out of the park before it opened I was going to have to jump back over, I felt in little doubt as to what an idiot I was. "Now what?" I said to myself. I climbed the stairs and walked along the flowerbed as far as the ahuehuete, an enormous, mysterious somber presence, and I felt peaceful, peaceful to be in the park all alone, like I owned the place, or, at least that I was its one and only nightwatchman, to put it more humbly. I touched one of the branches of the tree: it still had leaves on, though they were dry and wrinkled, a dun orangy color. I sat on a bench, took a deep breath, lit a cigarette and relaxed. It could be, Vidor, it could be that I might have thought of Ana, and that I was still madly in love with her, for all she's been dead a year, even if I know I'll never see her again, or smile at her, or touch her, or hear her voice. It could be that I thought, with some amazement, that you can go on loving someone who is dead with the same intensity as someone alive—*passionately*. And the awful thing is not, as the saying goes, that they leave a void in us, but the opposite: they occupy such a large space in our thinking, a territory so vast and crowded, solid, almost, that the rest of the universe diminishes, grows smaller, feels stifled, lacks air.

Then, while taking a puff of my cigarette, I noticed I was bleeding, that I'd injured myself when I jumped. Blood was trickling over my left hand all the way down to my little finger. "Hand or arm?" I thought, because I couldn't feel a thing, and when I rolled up my sleeve found the cut to be on my forearm, and a decent gash it was. "Mallick," I said, standing beneath stunning, silent shadows, beneath the stars, "Mallick, it's all over." If in the first place I'd jumped the fence in a spring-like manner, so to speak, the return was most autumnal. The only thing on my mind was making it home in one piece. But before that I went by the Clínico Hospital, where they gave me stitches ("You were lucky, an inch lower down and you'd have bled to death"). Anyway. Time for bed.


It's five o'clock in the afternoon and I've just got up. My stitched-up arm hurts. There are no lights on in the house, I think I'm home alone. I don't feel up to much. For the first time, I'm finding this diary exhausting; I'm now aware of the discipline, the persistence, required. I am not an exhibitionist, neither by profession nor as a hobby, might be one way of putting it. Up until today, it was a way of talking to you, Vidor, you with all your vitality, a way of bouncing my redeeming experiences off you, my will to survive. It was an escape, a cathartic experience, but I have the feeling it's going to become a burden.

I'm currently a day and a half behind, and this faux red notebook (really a file on a computer) already looks outdated to me, I'm not the same as I was, let's say, on December 24. But when it comes down to it, this is no big problem, just a small inconvenience. No point trying to kid myself. The real issue is that now, if I want to update the diary and be even slightly faithful to the truth—mine, that is, the one I turn a blind eye to—I'm going to have to be more sincere than was my original intention when I began writing. *Let's be honest*, Vidor, this diary, logically enough, *has not been entirely sincere*, it is a tool for me and no one else, not even for you, to whom it's addressed, given that you're dead and buried, and hardly yesterday either. The diary format doesn't in itself mean that the writer will reveal any more about his or herself than, say, when he writes a shopping list. There have been deliberate, self-protective omissions in certain entries, until now. I didn't want to say everything. It scared me and it still does. It was a post-Ana diary, a without-Ana diary. But now I can't keep silent, it's not fair. Ana has sneaked into in these pages, and I owe it to her. That's just the way it is.

To recap. On Saturday, at eleven o'clock in the morning, as Bela and I were finishing off a late breakfast, Leia called. The moment I picked up the phone I knew it was her because there was no noise, not even heavy breathing, or a sigh, or gentle wailing, nothing.

"Hello? Yes? Is anyone there? Leia, is it you?"

A few seconds passed, Bela looked up from her toast at me, alert, and then I made out a faltering, uncertain whisper.

"Can I speak to Antón Mallick, please?"

"Speaking. Who's that?"

And another prolonged silence, again the intuition of having to tread carefully, as though walking into a haunted house with glass walls and knowing not to touch the hand offered by the lady there, an ice princess, because the second she touched your big, clumsy, warm fingers, she'd melt.

"Yes it's Leia, you know . . ."

"Ah, Leia, thank you for calling," I said nervously. "I'd like it if we could arrange to meet and talk, if it's ok with you."

"I don't know . . ."

Another agonizing silence, and suddenly I began to sweat, I felt horribly hot, considered taking my sweater off, but wasn't wearing one, I had a shirt on, shitty telephone, there's nothing worse than having a difficult conversation on the telephone.

"Hello? Leia? Are you still there?"

"In El Bandido Doblemente Armado, at eight."

And she hung up. My shirt was soaked. I lit a cigarette.

"Strange girl" said Bela, and took a bite out of her toast. "What did she have to say?"

"Nothing," I said, still in something of a trance. "We're meeting in a café in Malasaña, at eight o'clock this evening."

"Well I'm coming with you. You never know."

"She's very fragile, almost a child. And she has this strange way of speaking."

"That's to my advantage. Watch out for fragile women, we can be dangerous. Children are very cruel, and the ones with a strange way of speaking tend to be very strange indeed."

"You're not fragile, Bela."

"That's what you think. Piece of toast?"

It felt like eight o'clock would never come: more than eight hours to go and that's a hell of a lot of minutes. Bela went out. I tried to quiet my mind, to hurry time along, but at four o'clock I found myself in the bathroom, looking in the mirror. "I don't like you," I said, out loud. "I don't like you at all, Antón Mallick." And I meant it. Daily I was finding myself more fed up with myself, with thinking everything over and over, with trying to understand my sick mind, with trying to be a better person, to seem like a fortress, built of the very thing I lack, to the people around me, with my pathetic ambition to become an out and out optimist, with . . . And what hurt most was admitting my innermost hope in relation to Leia, Mallick-Carrier Woman. Yes, why deny it, I still hoped that this woman with her short hair and her elusive gaze would fall in love with me, and I with her. That we'd have a healthy, happy boy, or a sweet, vivacious little girl, and that we'd find happiness, the three of us together, the two stray puppies who came together in a den of iniquity, plus the lovely fruit of that infernal encounter. Yes, I'd dreamed that Leia and the child were exactly what I needed, the main ingredients in the recipe of my future emotional stability. "What a fool you are, Antón Mallick. You poor fool." The mirror gave me back a faithful image of what I was: male, dark-haired, thirty-two years old, neither ugly nor handsome, with a cut to the eyebrow, a flat nose and an uncertain gaze, very light-colored eyes, faded light blue. I had an urge to punch the mirror, but wasn't able to. Instead of taking action I thought about it first, and thinking about smashing the mirror anesthetized me—too theatrical, too exaggerated, I thought—precisely my problem, always thinking before doing, being so very unaristocratic. It's seven o'clock in the evening now, I've put two whole hours of this Sunday into writing about six hours of Saturday. Hardly a difficult six hours to describe, either. I'm going to get myself an orange juice.


A fresh, revivifying orange juice, and skip to Bela and I entering the café. I spied Leia sitting at a table in the small cafeteria space situated at the front of the bookshop area. She was with her guardian or friend, the stern or ill-humored lady. I smiled to myself: we'd both decided to come accompanied, protected, as though we were teenagers on a first date, or as though this were another era and we were courting, each with our respective chaperone. We introduced ourselves. The sullen woman's name was Marian. Not Mary Anne, not Marianne, not Mariana, not Ana María, not Marián. Marian, no accents, which would be the normal way to spell it in Spanish, another "anything goes" name, post-postmodern, in the Leia, stellar princess mold. Anyway. Right from the start, it didn't go well. I was too naive. The meeting wasn't, as I'd thought, to get to know each other, but for her to defend herself against me. Marian took the lead, and she was at pains to point out, right from the get-go, that the child wasn't mine and that if I carried on hounding Leia they were going to call the police. But let's hear her, Vidor, seeing as we can, let's hear the guardian.

"If you keep on bothering her, we'll hire ourselves a lawyer, and that'll be it for you, got it?" Add to her words a tense glare, and a tense jaw, and hands with fine fingers that might seem to belong to someone else if they weren't jabbing and agitated, gesticulating aggressively to emphasize every word. "A judge wouldn't take much convincing that you assaulted her in that bar and forced her to go to the hotel with you, got it? Who's going to believe you?"

Yes, of course I got it, Marian dear; you express yourself well, I freely admit it, though sensitivity isn't your strong point, got it? Not one question, no interest in finding out anything from me, you didn't even let me get a word in, right? I saw I'd lost before the game had begun, and I gave up trying, possibly I'd spent all my energy on the false Leia, on Lucía of the Hideous Skull Rings and Unemployed Private Investigator Husband. Yesterday I only dared look at the real Leia out of the corner of my eye, asking myself how she could put up with this, I had a hunch your friend was feeling embarrassed, ashamed and intimidated by your howls and accusations—know what I mean, Marian? I tend to give people a chance, a few minutes at least, before I go on the offensive. But, though we carry on listening to you, I'm going to cease addressing you directly now, I find you most distasteful, Marian: adieu, until never, up yours.

"And this meeting, I say again," continued Marian, "is so that you'll leave Leia in peace, it isn't her fault she ran into you, if you've got drug problems and you're an addict, that's your and your family's issue . . . Get it?"

It was right then that I decided I'd had enough. Also, Vidor, I needed a cigarette and had run out. Bela had had enough too. She'd been listening to Marian with infinite patience, but perhaps the drug addict accusation hurt her— the fact she would even use that as an insult, ignoring any possible context. Maybe John, Bela's very own alcoholic, came to mind, I couldn't say. Or our family.

"What did you say?" shouted Bela, and good on her. "What did you say about my brother? Calling him a drug addict? And that's an insult, is it? Even if he was, so what? For your information, my brother isn't an addict, and I've had it up to here listening to your ravings, *get it?*"

While Bela stood up for the Mallick name, I made myself scarce. I came out onto Calle Apodaca, found a bar and bought some cigarettes. I asked for a light at the bar, and I must have taken such a big first drag, every inch the addict, that the barman gave me a knowing smile.

"Drink?"

I ordered a shot of whiskey. This calmed the nerves. The second had me feeling like silk. I was in no hurry to get back. I smoked a few more cigarettes, looked around at the clients' faces, most of them poor, unemployed jerks addicted to daytime reality shows, and I only left, twenty minutes after I'd gone in, when it dawned on me that my behavior, above all with respect to Bela, was a little out of the ordinary. Surprisingly, the three of them were still together; I found them out in the street, across from the bookshop. Marian and Bela were squaring up, barely a streetlamp separating them. Leia, sensibly keeping her distance, was listening to them scream.

"You whore!"

"Slut! Bitch!"

"Say that again! Go on, if you have the balls, I dare you!"

This was more or less the level of the conversation. Anyway. Insults were flying, and the only thing left was whether it would come to blows or not. When Leia looked at me, I looked away. I was about to tell my sister that I was back when, as I came past Leia, the latter took hold of me. Her face was like something out of a comic book, a cartoon character somewhere between tender and tenebrous. *Comic.* But she did have papery skin, like soft white paper, velveteen, high quality. Black eyes—India ink? Her accent, I don't know if it was put on or not, but it was unplaceable, and her voice was cracked, as though she'd drunk too many Irish coffees when she was younger.

How old could she be? Twenty? Thirty? Difficult to know, particularly as it was night, and raining, in the streetlight was dim at best.

"Antón, wait! I . . . I'm sorry."

"Me too," I said, very nobly. Marian and Bela were still tearing into each other, though they'd moved onto choicer phrases, more personalized insults, and then Leia addressed me with the following:

"Do you remember? You poured your heart out, and I felt terrible for you, and . . ."

I froze. Yes, of course I remembered the accursed night, though I'd got some way in my determination to forget. It had all come flooding back when Bela released Leia's name, but on that occasion I'd managed to divert my thoughts, not dive into memory, keep myself on the sidelines. I'd opened up to her. I'd poured my heart out, for sure.

"This is not right," said Leia, in reference, I suppose, to Bela and Marian's screams, or to the fact it had just begun raining and we were getting soaked, or life in general, or all the people who live in precarious situations, or the children who are being sexually abused every hour every day, or the country we live in, or the fact that many of us know what an insecticide named Zyklon B was used for, what the hell . . .

I heard her without listening to what she was saying, and when I saw her without looking at her, she was crying, propping herself up against a building wall, cowering, but I failed to be moved, no, I'm not a melodramatic kind of person, I have my limits, one emotion every couple of hours, for example, and I'd had my fill for the day. Bela

239

and Marian noticed us, and the scene, Leia crying in the rain, and me, cigarette dangling from my lips, trying to light a match, must have looked like pure poetry, pure cinema, pure something, a religious tableau perhaps, because they stopped screaming, which was something at least. Marian tried to deal one final blow, but she was exhausted too, maybe deep down she was unhappy with the role she was having to play, and it was raining too, raining fists, and rain, water in such amounts, tames wild beasts, soothes the spirits, douses fire, and all that. The worst she could come up with was the following, spoken without conviction:

"Now what? Go and get a fix, did you? Well then?"

A nice note to end on. I grabbed Bela's arm and set out towards Calle Fuencarral, and we didn't look back.

"Why do we always forget to bring an umbrella?" said Bela, after a little while.

"So we won't lose it."

I knew it. I knew it would come. Bela began to cry, and when my little sister begins to cry without being in a state of utter depression (when she cries much more softly, as I've now learned), it's a fountain, it's the Flood, it's sighing and wailing and whimpering. Quite the couple we made, arm in arm, soaking wet, one guarded, cagey, the other an inconsolable wellspring. It was turning into a tradition, the two of us venturing into the unknown and it being the two of us leaving together too, still and always alone, bewildered, set adrift. I stepped in a puddle and my shoe sank, I felt the consistency of the water, how dirty it was, the cold, my foot squelched, and I said to myself: "This is it, Antón Mallick, this is where we've got to."

"What's the time, Bela?"

My sister, choking back a sob, consulted her mobile phone. "Nine."

"Fine. Let's get something to eat. And stop crying, please. It's wet enough as it is."

Fortunately the bar at El Bocaíto wasn't packed. I ordered some tapas and two cañas. It was warm in there and I could almost feel my clothes drying out, the steam enveloping me like a shroud. We ate our food in silence. My sister was chewing a piece of battered hake slowly and her eyes, red-rimmed, were fixed on a certain point on the wall, maybe they'd come to rest on the tiles with their atrocious pictures and even worse proverbs. I've always hated proverbs, considering them opportunistic wisecracks. I don't know what would have been on Bela's mind. John? Me? Herself? Whatever it was, it would hardly have been happy thoughts. I went to order a couple more cañas, and when I handed Bela hers, she broke the silence.

"She spoke to you after all, right?"

"She did. She told me I'd opened my heart to her. About Ana, that is."

"But I thought you hated talking about that."

"I do. I don't go shouting from the rooftops that I'm a widower. You know me, I'm not really one for the whole victim thing," and after a pause, I added: "Widower. It feels like such an antiquated word, so sad. I don't know why but I associate it with 'dinosaur.'"

"Maybe because they became extinct?" joked Bela.

"When Leia said that, I felt totally defenseless. I didn't know what to think. I've always considered Ana a secret I don't talk to anyone about, and least of all to strangers."

"So why did you tell her?"

"No idea. Maybe I saw myself reflected in her, as in a mirror. Maybe I thought she and I were alike. I caved in."

"Had she told you something about herself?"

"Leia? No. She wasn't in a good way either, but I don't know why. Whatever it was, she felt sorry for me. Being pitied is horrible."

"Totally. Better to be hated. Her friend Marian, that bitch, was protecting her from you, but there's something else there, I'm sure of it. Like they were afraid to speak. We'll see."

We ordered some more tapas and more cañas, and around half past ten we went our separate ways. My sister wanted to keep me company, but there was something I needed to do on my own. The piece of the Saturday puzzle I'm yet to put in: my visit to Luisa. But first, I'm going to make myself a sandwich. Bela's in, she's having a shower. She never interrupts me when I'm writing, Vidor. Not even now, in spite of being desperate to find out about my latest movements and the blood-stained shirt on top of the washing machine. Maybe she imagines I went and dismembered Marian. No one would ever bother you either when you took refuge in the attic, to calm down after one of your fits, or to think; not even your wife would dare to knock on the door at such times. Sometimes you'd break things, throwing them against the wall in there. Or sit yourself on the dark red pouf you were particularly fond of. And when you came back into the house proper, you'd always have your head hung low, ashamed, with your right hand hidden in the pocket of your velvet jacket. You'd be embarrassed because of having shouted at someone, or having punched a wall, or having given an hour to your thoughts. Because the way you saw it, Vidor, to think was to be weak. The call of the abyss.

Bela and I have been chatting for a little while, Vidor. Part of what I was telling her I ought now to commit to the diary. But we also talked about a more distant past, that past that you didn't enjoy going back to. You, Vidor, preferred forgetting—forgetting understood as liberation—you elected to forget so you could always wake up refreshed, ready to start the new day with a smile. You forgot the hunger of the Hungarian serfs, your mother's varicose veins, your father's putrid breath, the taste of rotten meat, the tears of your abandoned lovers, the beggars' empty looks, the cries of your insane daughter . . . But, after all, even you ended up writing your *Counter-memoir*, you too needed to come to terms with the past. It's impossible to be coherent, isn't that right, Vidor?

Bela reminded me about the day she met Ana, five years ago, at Uncle Juan's house, on the occasion of one of my sister's visits from the US. Ana and I had been going out for about six months. She was twenty-five at that time, she was dark-haired, medium height, and working as a journalist for a press agency. She struck Bela as a good-looking woman, intelligent, direct and in possession of a dazzling smile. Yes, she was surprised at Ana's plumpness, that she had a few pounds to spare. It didn't take me long to admit to her my antisocial aesthetic tastes, my passion for a bit of flesh, my distaste for bones. Bela was amused to see how completely Ana had won our uncle over, to the point that, that same evening, after dinner, he made mojitos for everyone, a sure sign that he felt comfortable in her company. Uncle Juan, hardly a spring chicken at that point, flirted with her, and Bela liked the fact that Ana accepted the game happily, she wasn't outraged and didn't expect us to join in in any way either. This game, innocent and genial, was a good way of allowing for witty repartee, a jibe every now and then, veiled shows of affection. I remember that night, Vidor, I remember how happy I was the next morning when Bela said she liked Ana. As far as I was concerned, everything was perfect. I was in love, and my uncle and my sister liked my girlfriend.

But back to Saturday. On Saturday, out of the four of us who'd drunk mojitos five years earlier in the apartment on Calle Velázquez, only Bela and I were still alive. Uncle Juan and Ana are nothing but ghosts, like you yourself, Vidor, memories that jump out at me, or caress or clobber me, or bring a smile to my face. Bela and I said goodbye outside El Bocaíto, and I walked to Calle Bravo Murillo. That's where Luisa, my mother-in-law, lives. Although, is she still my mother-in-law? Do widowers have mothers-in-law? And if they marry again, do they get assigned another mother-in-law? Is a widower always a widower, or does he cease to be one if he remarries? Could you say, introducing yourself, that you are three times a widower, married a fourth? Can we widowers collect mothers-in-law? How did Henry VIII manage the whole thing? Anyway. Who cares.

I stopped for a whiskey on the way. As I drank, it occurred to me to phone ahead, to tell Luisa I was coming by, but I didn't. I had another whiskey. There was no need to check if she'd be in either, because since the death of her one daughter she barely left the house. Really, I was tempted to call because I knew she'd insist I didn't go, she'd say there was no need, she was totally fine, and that way she'd save me from the bitter pill. A social call that I found terrifying. One more drink. I'd gone seven months without seeing her, and more than two without picking up the phone to call her. Yes, I know, Vidor, these calls to my mother-in-law have gone unmentioned in my diary. Why? They were *personal*. As for Luisa, it's altogether possible that she didn't want to see me either. So why was I going? Out of a misguided sense of guilt? Out of compassion? No. I went because, at times, when you want a door to be firmly shut, you first have to open it. If I want to accept or get to grips with Ana's death, I can't pretend she never existed, her or her mother, any of it. I can't simply forget. Also, even if both of us would rather not see each other, I owed Luisa a courtesy call, to fill her in on what was going on in my life, to show some interest in hers. Anyway. My mother-in-law lives near the roundabout up at Cuatro Caminos, in a neighborhood made up of small business, neighborhood bars and pensioners, and where the immigrants bring a splash of color. Her building, built in the sixties, is a house with six floors, somewhat impersonal, with large balconies. I got there around midnight and smoked a cigarette before going up.

Luisa opened the door and smiled at me. She's an attractive, vital woman, though in the last year she's aged considerably. She was wearing a white blouse, jeans and flat shoes, she had a pair of reading glasses on a cord around her neck and some documents in her hand.

"Come in, Antón. I was just reading through some work papers."

Luisa works at the City Council, in the Municipal Housing Department, in the Buildings office, and she's one of those rare civil servants who does not only her own work but that of her colleagues and bosses as well. She lives on her own; her husband, Ana's father, died midway through the nineties and, though she's had boyfriends, she's always kept her independence. We made ourselves comfortable with a couple of beers in the living room. Whenever I've been to her place, since the very first time, the moment I walk in the door, Luisa has poured one for me, one for herself. Chilled glasses, kept in the freezer. Belgian beer, brewed by monks. I was reminded of how well we'd always got on, our conversations, and I realized that all that, the good times, were now something that separated us, rather than bringing us close. Ana's death stood between us like an invisible wall. I didn't know what to say. Luckily, she went first.

"The trial's two months from now."

"Really? About time. I don't know how they expect people to get over things if the case stays open."

"I don't expect to get over anything, Antón. That option isn't available to me. And you, how are you getting on? Last time we spoke you'd gone back to work."

"Yes," I said, after swigging the beer, with a somewhat ridiculous, put-on cheerfulness, given the circumstances. "I'm a lot better. A few months ago I decided to become an optimist, to be happy, and slowly I'm really getting there. It's all about establishing the things in life that make it worth living, and . . ."

"Oh-ho! And what might they be?" Luisa said, interrupting me, interested but not overly convinced.

"Bullfights, soccer, a good side of ham from Jabugo, women . . ." I joked. But Luisa carried on looking at me steadily, gravely. "Anyway. Now I'm just trying for a little bit of calm, to be able to look at myself in the mirror, more doing, less thinking, particularly about death, not spoiling other people's lives . . . Although, honestly, it's impossible for me to talk about happiness and optimism here," I confessed, waving a vague hand at the room. "Here . . . Words come apart before they're even spoken."

Luisa got up without a word, picked up the two unfinished beer glasses, and vanished into the kitchen. I thought she was kicking me out, but she came back a couple of minutes later with a bottle of whiskey and two glasses with ice.

"I think we could both do with something a little stronger, right?"

I smiled. Luisa put on a CD of a Mozart sonata for piano. The music gushed into the living room, tracing the furniture's contours, brightening the walls, sweeping clean the parquet, giving a sheen to the glass of the family photos. I was on the verge of tears, but, fortunately, Luisa came and sat down again, facing me, and we carried on the conversation.

"And love?" asked Luisa, half-smiling. "I've only been fully happy when I've been in love."

"I wish I could fall in love again, but . . . You know, love isn't all it's cut out to be, even when it is requited. It's like a drinking spree followed by a nasty hangover. To begin with, everything's pretend, and then 'reality' hits you, and it devours you, and it delights in your misery."

"What a disaster," chuckled Luisa. "Quite the optimist, Antón! You're going to have to try a little harder to be happy."

"Mm. Possibly you've caught me on an off night."

Neither of us said anything for a little while, we drank and listened to the music. When the whiskeys were finished, Luisa poured us two more.

"My lawyer's saying the most likely thing is that he won't go to jail, that he'll stay on in the psychiatric hospital. It would appear that he chose her because of her bag, because of the color. 'I saw she was wearing the color of the chosen ones, and I brought her salvation.' Ana died because she was carrying a red bag."

Luisa handed me the whiskey and I drank half down in one go.

"I don't want to know anything about him, Luisa," I said, emphatically. "To me, he doesn't exist. I got to the point of being obsessed, asking myself how someone could possibly do something like that, but not any more. The day I want to know about him will be the day when I become a functioning part of society again, and I don't know if that day will ever come."

"I don't follow you."

"Doesn't matter. There's no question that the guy's a lunatic. And to die at the hands of a lunatic, without there even being any hate, without intent, or any reason, is truly a terrible thing, because it places you outside of history. It's senseless, grotesque, it leaves you in a kind of limbo, in the most absolute nothingness. It's so horrible that everyone looks the other way. An illness is a logical cause, a dreaded but at least comprehensible enemy. Dying in war, the same.

Even Auschwitz is at least something, because it must be remembered, it has some moral value. A maniac who pushes a woman in front of a train in a fit of insanity, no. It has to be forgotten, erased, annihilated from the memory, it's merely an annoyance—it isn't even tragic, because there's nothing grand about it, nothing truly evil, or cruel: it is representative of nothing. It's an empty, random, chance act, a kind of flaw in the manufacturing. And the victim doesn't represent anything either, or anyone, or any country, or association, or team, or historical current, or a group of people, or goodness knows what. She's simply an anonymous unlucky wretch, her identity is lost completely, she doesn't register as part of the statistics, large or small. It's a double death, and also leaves the loved ones out of the picture, like they're on the other side of the fence, over the border."

"I don't know if I follow you, Antón."

I drained the whiskey and poured myself another.

"I'm following me, Luisa. Haven't you been left out of the picture? Does that sicko really matter to you, how many years they're going to lock him up for, how his brain works, if he's guilty or not, the conclusions the trial comes to? Not to me. Ana's dead. End of."

I got to my feet and stood, motionless, breathing hard. I wanted to get out of there. I'd had too much to drink. But Luisa took the bottle and poured me more whiskey. This was her way of saying stay. We weren't done yet.

"Come on, sit down. I know how much you loved my daughter. And she loved you."

My head was spinning. I sat down.

"You have to keep going, get over it. Ana was the best thing that happened to me in my life. You have no idea what it is to have a child."

I kept to myself what I did know about it. Or what I imagined. I took the whiskey and, on autopilot, took a gulp. It seemed like cement, I couldn't get it past my throat. And the music, how long had that been on for? Would that piano never shut up? What's going on in the world?

"Plus there's one thing we've never talked about."

Luisa must have been waiting for a remark from me, or a question, but I said nothing.

"My daughter was nine weeks pregnant, correct?"

I was struggling to breathe, to keep my head up, to see.

"No," I said. "That's not true. Ana wasn't pregnant."

"You're lying."

Luisa got to her feet. For a few moments, I have no idea how long, I lost myself in the music, in the piano, I managed not to think. Luisa came back holding a document, which she put down on the table.

"It's the autopsy report. There's no need for you to lie to me. You knew, didn't you?"

"It didn't have a name yet. Now it's nothing but one more ghost, like your daughter."

Luisa doubled over and began sobbing. I felt nothing. No sorrow, no anything. I had thoughts of Ana, I remembered her face, but it vanished, replaced by that of another woman, some stranger. I finished the whiskey and collapsed on the couch. I heard Luisa's sobs, and the piano, and my own breathing. I fell asleep. When I woke, I looked at my watch: three o'clock in the morning. Luisa had put a blanket over me and left a pair of pajamas on the table. I unfolded them. They must have belonged to Federico, Luisa's husband. They were very small, with gray and white stripes. Clearly Federico must have been a small man. I pictured myself trying to get into his pajamas, trying to button up the shirt, the trousers tight on my thighs, riding up around my ankles. I pictured Luisa dying, the police showing up, finding this suspicious, hefty man dressed in a dwarf's pajamas, a strange drunk, or a very strange drunk dressed in pajamas belonging to a ghost. I laughed. I folded up the pajamas and quietly let myself out.

Out in the streets there were a few cars going around, driving fast with the music up. It was cold, I fished my scarf out of my jacket and put it on. All the taxis were taken. I walked down along Calle Bravo Murillo as far as Quevedo where, without thinking about it, I turned along Calle San Bernardo. The icy wind was gradually bringing me to. All I wanted to do was get home. I picked up the pace. I came past a group of tipsy youngsters singing the anthem of the Spanish Republic. I hummed along. And then, looking up, there was a surprise for me. I'd come to the entrance to Metro San Bernardo, on the Ruiz Jiménez roundabout.

Because I'm an idiot, because I'm absent-minded, because of being drunk, I found myself in the one place I'd avoided going anywhere near for the past year. I began laughing hard. Here was an off-the-scale night: Antón Mallick's Big Night. First Leia, then Lucía, and finally Ana and her pregnancy. No, it really wasn't worth collapsing, or making a song and dance about it. I sat on the Metro steps and took out a cigarette. Down there, down in the depths, underneath the concrete, on October 3, 2008, at around half past eight in the morning, one Ramiro H. L., forty two years of age, pushed onto the tracks one Ana M. S., thirty, just as a train was pulling in, resulting in sudden death. Ramiro was mentally ill and unemployed. Ana M. S., a journalist, was on her way to work. I received a call at around noon. I was at work. Now, as I type, I remember my trip to the morgue to identify the corpse. The smell. The morgue table. The feeling of unreality. Ana. The bewilderment. But there, on the Metro station steps, all I did was smoke, my brain gave me a break, it disconnected as I breathed in and out, I felt nothing, neither cold nor pain, all I did was smoke. Here endeth diary entry for the Day that Beggars Description.

Enough writing now.

### FURTHER ADVICE AND CURIOUS PHRASES FROM
### *CONFESSIONS OF A ONCE-HUNGARIAN SPANIARD*

"Many are those who, in all their life, have only one idea but, out of sheer want and inability, express it in such a range of ways that it is said that their minds are rich and varied."

" . . . ordinary people love the idea of overcoming obstacles, preferably the moral kind. When other people overcome, that is. They like it when someone manages to come out of the rut he was stuck in and turns into a saint. 'Redeem' is their favorite verb, it flicks off of their tongue like the crack of a whip. This is why I always acknowledged my vices—in spite of never confessing them—or at least the classic ones: wine, women, money and gambling. That way, all I could do was get better, and people adored me, and they respected me. Anyone who's good to begin with—and this happens everywhere in the world—is hated until the day they die, as is only natural."

"In order to love people you only have to keep them at the proper distance. With a lover, at the outset, the distance must be short. With family and acquaintances, moderate to far. And with people in general, infinite."

"'What are you Hungarians like?' Señora M. asked me, as she stroked my hair in an incredibly annoying way. 'Extremely dishonest,' I said. She stopped caressing my mane and put her hand to her pearl necklace, slightly taken aback. 'Apart from being dishonest, we are whiners, entrepreneurs and know-it-alls, we're courteous, we're unpredictable, we're individualists, suspicious, disorganized, candid and we're hospitable . . . and the most wonderful lovers!' Señora M. shortly forgot about my hair, and I her cheekiness."

"May none of my descendants ever forget that my grandfather raised pigs, and my father, fleas."

"There's always a way out."

## Tuesday, March 9, 2010

> "When sadness and suffering become intense and intolerable, know for certain that a new era is going to dawn bringing signal progress."
>
> SWAMI RAMDAS

The satellite launch date has been brought forward by a week. It's to be April 15 now, in the legendary Baikonur Cosmodrome, in Kazakhstan. That's where Korolev's *Sputnik* was launched, the first orbital flight, manned by Yuri Gagarin, also the spaceship that made Valentina

Tereshkova the first woman in space. Karl "The Whale" Richter told me about it, also telling me at least ten times that it was top secret, and that it was going to be a real slap in the face for Transat's competitors. When I mentioned to him that it would be my first Baikonur satellite, since the previous ones had been launched from French Guyana, Richter told me the story of the cosmodrome's name.

Baikonur is situated in the southern central part of the country, one hundred and twenty miles east of the Aral Sea. The Soviet Secret Services named it after a mining town one hundred and ninety miles northeast, to confuse the West. Nowadays the Russians have leased the space station to the Kazhaks until 2050, and tourists go there (a fact very much of our time, tourists invading everything; top secret places aren't what they used to be). It spreads fifty miles north to south, and eighty miles east-west, on a treeless plain buffeted by winds. Comprised of a road grid, oil pipelines, and motorways to provision the fifteen launch pads, it also features a city with tens of thousands of inhabitants on the shores of the river Syr Darya. Anyway. The sooner the contract's firmed up, the better. Now my job is to mediate between the operator and the lead insurers, and everyone's getting more and more nervous as the light (and the money) at the end of the tunnel come into view. There's bound to be a few more twists along the way. Today, like yesterday, I got home at ten in the evening, having gone for a bite with Fran on leaving work. The cut on my arm is bothering me less.

*Thursday, March 11, 2010*

"Wretched fate! In vain do you prink up your wrinkled face like an old prostitute, in vain do you jingle your fool's bells . . . Come, sleep and death; you promise nothing, you hold everything."

KIERKEGAARD

It had to happen. I went by the house at lunchtime, without calling ahead: I'd forgotten my phone. The second I went in, I sensed something odd. I sensed an outside presence. I stopped in the middle of the living room. Bela's bedroom door was shut. I knocked. I got no answer, but I knew my sister was in there, and not by herself. I came across a pair of black jeans under a chair, the kind that fall down over people's backsides, crumpled in a pile. And then, strewn on the floor by the drinks cabinet, a pair of blue and white striped underpants. The kind of jeans and underpants Carlos would wear. I got my phone and left. Bela, Bela, Bela.

At about seven in the evening Bela rang me at work to see if I was going to be having dinner at home. I said yes standoffishly, failing to dent Bela's good mood. It was the first time in a couple of weeks that she'd asked me if we could do something together. Later in the evening, when I got back, she was there waiting with a smile, the table set, and a vegetable lasagne (a favorite of mine) in the oven. She's a clever one, that sister of mine. She didn't wait for me to open fire, or to try to pump her for information.

"So what do you think?" she said the moment I sat down, serving me a sizeable portion.

"Great, sis. You know I love lasagne, just like Garfield."

"I don't mean the food. I mean me and Carlos."

What cheek, I thought. Not one bit ashamed to be sneaking around my house, jumping in bed with one of my two best friends; she was the picture of calm. I got angry.

"How long have you been in Madrid, Bela?"

This caught her off guard.

"Not sure . . . Two months, I'd say . . ."

"And you were planning on leaving when?"

Bela put her fork down on her plate, and looked at me, first of all with surprise, but then that became pure anger. Good, I thought. Now the conversation's where it ought to be.

"You pig, Antón! You're kicking me out?"

"Your words. I'm only trying—now that we're living together and all—to get an idea of your plans."

"These are typical Zoltan tactics!"

"That's low, Bela! Fine: I'm a pig. But you know very well I've never resorted to degrading interrogation techniques like Zoltan. Take that back!"

"No! Not a chance!"

"Take it back!"

"No! You're just like Zoltan!"

Sometimes we react to one another like we're still children. Not so strange, Vidor. It happens to everyone, even genuinely serious people, or very boring people.

The tragedy would be if we never acted like children, if we had no life left in us. I took my glass of water and threw the contents at my sister. In her face. She didn't hang about either. Jumping out of her chair, she rounded the table and came and slapped me hard. There was nothing I could do to stop her. Then I grabbed her wrists and twisted one of them backwards, bringing her to her knees.

"Take it back! Take it back Bela!"

"No! Zoltan, Zoltan, Zoltan!"

I twisted the other wrist.

"Take it back!"

"Let me go, you brute!"

I let go. After the storm came the calm. Bela, after going to the bathroom, came back to her seat, and I mopped up the water with a flannel. We carried on eating, in silence now, not looking at one another. Both of us felt genuinely ashamed. Bela had tears in her eyes.

"Don't worry," I said, trying to be calming, show solidarity. "No one saw us."

"Good thing you don't have a dog. Imagine how horrible it would be if your dog had witnessed that. We'd have had to sacrifice it."

"Or if Mom had seen us."

"Or Father."

"Or Zoltan," I said, smiling now, starting to enjoy the conversation. "All his suspicions would be confirmed."

"Yes, he'd love it. He'd give us the whole thing about it not being his fault he's the older brother, or that he has to take *all* the responsibilities, given how pathetically immature we are."

"Absolutely. And it would give him all the justification he needs for never having let us play with his toys. We were always too infantile in his book."

"He was the childish one! He couldn't take losing! Remember when we used to play guess the cup, or dice? He'd always end up hitting us."

"We did cheat, Bela."

"So? That didn't give him the right to hit us. He never actually caught us when we swapped the dice under the cups, or when we'd make signs to each other. He accused us of cheating, but he was so thick he never actually came up with any evidence."

"He split my lip once. Look, remember?" and I leaned forward to show her the little scar, white and brilliant, beneath my bottom lip.

"Such an animal! Then he'd blame you. Breaking his model airplanes and saying it was you. Father punished you and not him."

"Without even asking any questions, as always. The whole summer with no bike to ride. Good thing summers with them were twenty days at the most."

"And it would have been far worse to lose guess the cup to Zoltan."

"Definitely."

We finished the lasagne and I got dessert, a couple of very healthy pieces of fruit.

"So then," said Bela, not looking at me, as she peeled her nectarine. "What do you think about Carlos and me?"

"Not much, sis. Do what you feel like."

"Fine. Will do."

"What strikes me as a little bit sad," I added, "is all the sneaking around, as though you were fifteen-year-olds and we were living in a provincial town two centuries ago."

"No one's sneaking around. Carlos is a bit afraid of you, is all, and I am too."

"You, afraid! Come on! Since when?"

"Since always. In eighth grade, when I was in love with your friend Ricardo ..."

"Bermúdez? You were in love with that loser?"

" ... I was, as it goes. So when you found out he and I were going on a date to the cinema, you took me there on your motorbike, to scare him."

"Makes sense. Couldn't have him thinking he could take liberties with my older sister."

"Carlos told me yesterday he's always been in love with me."

"Too bad for him. Because for you it's just a fling, right?"

Bela said nothing to this, and after dinner we watched Kurosawa's *Dersu Uzala*, an intensely beautiful movie. Watching it, it gives you the feeling of genuinely wanting to become an optimist, it really does. That film fills you with more hope than a thousand sermons, or hundreds of self-help books. The hunter with his crystalline soul makes you believe in the possibility that there exists a certain harmony between man and nature. If there are men like Uzala, you say, all's not lost, it might actually be worth getting out of bed in the morning. And it isn't that Uzala is a happy guy, no. He loses his family, he's a lone wolf and when he goes blind and can't hunt any more, that's it, he loses his place in the world. But such films do reconcile you with reality.

When we said goodnight, I gave Bela a hug, which is somewhat out of the ordinary for us. She understood that my criticisms of her affair with Carlos weren't in jest, but also that I respected her freedom—yada yada.

*Friday, March 12, 2010*

> "Candide, terrified, amazed, desperate, all bloody, all palpitating, said to himself: 'If this is the best of possible worlds, what then are the others?'"
>
> VOLTAIRE

On Monday I'm going to London. I'm meeting the Anglo Saxons to try and get them to be more flexible and to see eye to eye with the French. It turns out, Vidor, that my job is that of moderator, I'm some kind of empathetic *madame* caught between *prima donnas* caked in makeup. Bela and Carlos have gone to Barcelona for the weekend. House all to myself. It's eight o'clock in the evening. What a treat, master of my own time again. I've grabbed a book, collapsed on the living room couch (unheard of since the Bela Invasion), and, gazing at the ceiling, smoked a perfect cigarette. But some unresolved issue always has to come up, something to shake the long desired calm. It occurred to me to check my emails (the fault is mine, all mine—when will I ever learn just to let go?), and I was confronted with an angry email from Zoltan that I felt compelled to reply to immediately:

**From:** Zoltan Mallick
**To:** Antón Mallick
**Subject:** Still alive—what about you two?

Hello, hello, hello? Anyone there? IT'S ZOLTAN, YOUR OLDER BROTHER. In case you care, I'm still alive, and María and the kids are fine. Still helping people with all kinds of problems at my highly successful practice . . . Fifteen plus days and not a word from you two. How on earth do you expect to overcome your enormous array of emotional imbalances with all this navel gazing? Our parents are extremely concerned about you both. I've told them you aren't answering my calls (yes, that Withheld Number is me, I'm opting for privacy in this uncensored and noisy society of ours, which makes intimacy such an impossibility), and they've asked me to intervene. I'VE HAD IT WITH YOU TWO. Got to go now. The twins are screaming. By the way, María is very annoyed.

Yours sincerely, Zoltan

**From:** Anton Mallick
**To:** The Neurotic
**Subject:** Fed up with you as well

Brother: you aren't the only one who has a job. In case you care, the satellite's launching soon—given that it's confidential, and given that I seriously doubt your ability to keep a secret, I won't tell you where or when. I've been on twelve hour days for weeks now, and Bela's preparing her conference on Lope de Vega (have you ever read him? Might you make an exception? Do you even know who Lope de Vega is? Ring any bells? Do you even know he's Spanish? Where would you say he's from? Mexico? A Wetback? A cruel Conquistador?) Anyway. Sorry if we've offended you. What you say about María troubles me, and I'd very much like to see the boys. Dinner at yours on Saturday? Bela's in Barcelona. I'll continue ignoring your Withheld Number calls—I'm not hugely up for surprises at this particular moment in time—you know I'm still undergoing treatment.

With love, Antón

That's where things are, Vidor. If everything carries on as it is, it looks like I'm going to be saddled with one family I never chose to be part of (Father, Mom, Zoltan, Bela), plus a second one (Leia, the baby) which I find myself tangled up in, and yet avoids me. The only thing genuinely mine, of my own making and sustaining, are my ghosts. Whereas you left your family behind (did you at least send them money?) and started a new one that you watched develop cracks, before your very eyes, in a foreign land, a country just as brutal as the one you left behind. I don't envy you, Vidor. I don't envy your blind optimism, or your excesses, or your sins. Or your cowardice dressed up as cruelty. I do admire your ability to take things on the chin, your infectious gaiety, your indomitable rebel spirit, your radical individualism. I'll leave you now. Back to the couch, to read.

*Saturday, March 13, 2010*

> "It is not frolicking and merrymaking that makes people happy, nor laughter and jokes, frivolity's playmates. People are happy often even when sad, if they are steadfast and true."
>
> CICERO

Day with the Zoltans. When we were eating, my brother once again did the thing of pouring the wine but not asking if I wanted any. María's booked herself on a cookery course and is going to learn to make the (according to her) famous three-colored eggs. Anyway. The best thing about the evening was the boys. I played Gogos with them—nothing to do with Go Go Girls . . . These are small, colored figurines, Italian made but clearly Japanese-inspired. The game consists of trying to knock over your opponents' pieces by throwing yours at them. Maks, the eldest and heir to the Hungarian family traditions, tried to cheat (lining up his pieces very far apart, and mine close together, so he could knock over lots of them at once), and he's an awful loser. He scratched my face a couple of times, making me bleed the second time, and giving his father a chance to show his magnanimity and practical attitude by, instead of punishing the little Hungarian tiger cub, cutting his nails instead.

And in the evening, some sex. I needed it, Vidor—luckily, so did she. I won't go into details, I don't want to. Just because you're a ghost, I wonder if you think that means you get to find out everything. Prick.


*Sunday, March 14, 2010*

Another revelation! The good news is that the idea of having another one of my anguish attacks didn't even cross my mind. I heard Bela come in at two o'clock in the morning (I always sleep badly before travelling). There was my sister, drunk, barefoot in the middle of the living room, eating an unpeeled carrot. Apparently, the flight back had been delayed, and she and Carlos landed in Madrid at about ten in the evening. Seeing as they're in the wine-and-a-dozen-red-roses phase, they had no qualms about going for

263

dinner and, after that, for cocktails in a bar on Calle Jesús, not far from the house. Mojitos. Daiquiris. More mojitos. No such thing as Sundays as far as they're concerned, and even less Mondays. Bela was in a sorry state, but there was also something fascinating about her. With her cheeks flushed and her eyes hazy, her lips bright ... When she saw me she came and subsided onto the sofa, somewhat elegantly, imitating one of her favorite actresses.

"Hello, brother! Boring or what? You all right? Why don't you grab us a couple of beers, darling?"

The mere mention of beer at two in the morning was enough to turn my stomach. Hats off, too, for the "darling" touch, oh so mundane; that wasn't bad either. I'm no partypooper (at least not always), so I got her a beer and myself a Diet Coke. Bela, sprawled on the couch, lifted one leg and began stroking her ankle and the sole of her foot, like that was the most normal thing in the world to be doing. I asked her what she was doing drunk in the wee hours of a Sunday, and she answered me like she was sleepwalking, without really paying any attention.

"So how was Barcelona?" I said—trying to liven up the conversation, feeling a bit marginalized, even though it was just the two of us.

Bela didn't answer straightaway. She was in a world of her own, all there was was the alcohol in her veins, and her foot, which she was massaging with genuine tenderness.

"You have no idea how good the sex is, Antón. No idea."

Those were almost her last words. I thought about leaving her on the couch, but I know from personal experience how unpleasant it is waking up in the living room with a hangover and all your clothes on, especially after you reach a certain age. I took her in my arms and carried her to her bedroom. She was heavy, Vidor. Women tend to weigh more than you think, or than they say. I laid her on her bed and undressed her. It was the second time I'd done this—the first after she'd been dumped by some boyfriend or other. I put her under the sheets, went to the kitchen and came back with a glass of water and an aspirin. Sitting down next to her, I gave a few gentle slaps to the face—then, enjoying it, a few slightly harder ones. If I'd have known what was coming, I'd have foregone the pleasure of shaking her up like that.

"Mmmm," she groaned. She opened one eye, then the other, then she sat up and drank. "Eugh! Yuk!"

She was like a little girl. Sister of mine, I thought, beloved Bela. She drank down the potion, and just before diving under the duvet, delivered the bombshell:

"You're an angel, Antón," she began, slurring her words, eyes closed. "Such a shame you don't get it. Should maybe have told you sooner. The thing with Leia—it couldn't be more obvious. She's a lesbian."

And under the goose down she disappeared, protected by warmth and darkness, drunk, blameless, forgetting all about me, embracing the world of dreams.


*Monday, March 15, 2010*


> "The animals are happy; their king alone is miserable!"
>
> ROUSSEAU

265

It's almost midnight. I got to London first thing in the morning. The day was spent in meetings at the Apri office with the lead insurance brokers. Our meeting was more productive than usual. Three of the most contentious clauses were resolved. We're onto the fifteenth version of the contract, and now, for the first time, it's beginning to look as though I might win the office wager. I bet on nineteen versions, and I was one of the most optimistic—that's the new me all over. Fran, for example, big-mouthed as usual, bet twenty-five. I went for Italian food with some of my colleagues and, when someone suggested going on for drinks, made my excuses. Back at the Chamberlain Hotel, I changed and went for a run in the area, in the rain, dodging the few passersby. Following a restorative shower, it was time for the most important moment of the day: the call to Bela. It was eleven o'clock in the evening. Swaddled in the fluffy hotel dressing gown, I lay back on the bed. Bela had left me three voicemails, each one more conciliatory than the last, almost grovelling.

"Hello? Who's there?

"It's Antón."

"Antón, finally! Do you forgive me? Please, say you forgive me!"

A little bit melodramatic, my sister: a woman after Leia's own heart. The crisis with John is giving me the chance to discover previously unknown-to-me Belas: playful Belas, irascible Belas, cruel Belas, theatrical Belas, voracious, brazen Belas. New masks for new situations. I reassured her. Nothing to forgive. When she told me Leia was a lesbian, I knew instantly that she was right. She had somewhat overlooked any niceties in delivering the news, she hardly picked her moment, but . . .

I've told you a few times, Vidor, that my sister is more or less infallible when it comes to the questions that call for intuition over and above proven facts. In that regard Bela resembles our great-great-great-grandmother, who, according to you, needed only to observe someone for a few seconds to uncover all their defects and all their good points. You took her along to work meetings several times so her "eagle eye"—as you termed it—could be of use to you. And in terms of you, she always knew what was really going on with you, she knew your pathetic secrets, she put up with your (numerous) imperfections and she loved you for your (few and far between) virtues. Even after you discovered that one of the maids was a Hungarian spy—the one you got rid of immediately—the dwarf-like, tenacious, ugly informant, a bad tempered and allegedly mute woman, and believed the dwarf to have been "the eagle eye," and that your wife was a charlatan, you ended up having to swallow your suspicions, because she could still see what was going on inside you even with fewer hard facts at her disposal.

Bela, like your wife, tends to keep her mouth shut, prefers not to use her special gift, probably because it frightens her a little, makes her feel a bit like a witch. In fact, yesterday, I was the one who had to stand up for her observation of Leia's sexual or love preferences. According to Bela, "it was the alcohol talking." But it wasn't. Leia's lesbianism doesn't explain everything, but nearly. Or it explains nothing, but it could. It would make Leia a woman in her twenties, gay, wanting a child and seeking an inseminator in the wilderness of the night (not the best place, clearly). She went to bed with me because I seemed as lost as she was, but with acceptable genes, promising even (the blue eyes?), and a moderately nice guy (my tragic past?). After that, once pregnant, already having blundered, she was/is frightened, she looks for me/she avoids me, she does/n't want the baby to have a father, she does/n't want to confess that she used me, she does/n't want to bond with me, she does/n't want to find out if I have as low an IQ as she suspects, she does/n't want to face facts and a situation that is, let's just say, peculiar, brought about/not brought about by her.

Her indecisiveness, very much of our time, shadowy and ghostly, is in her case related, I suspect, to her pertaining to a so-called marginalized group in society, or persecuted, or inadequate, or hermetic, or insecure, or wary, or slightly underground. If anyone had said to me a couple of years ago that I was going to have a child with a lesbian (a stranger, after a chance encounter, not a woman who having passed through my hands and after thinking we were in love discovered she was gay, which isn't the likeliest scenario but, honestly, more likely than what has in fact happened), if someone had told me this at a dinner, say, or out on a stroll, or shopping, or in a Hawaiian bar, all I'd have done was laugh. Yes, I'd have laughed my head off, like I thought it would be impossible to be that unlucky, or that things like that could never happen to me, they only happen to everyone else, to others, to jinxed people, to raving lunatics, to people who fail to see what's really going on around them.

"Mm, I'm not sure, Antón . . . You think Leia's really a dyke?"

"Gay, Bela, let's not be nasty. Watch your mouth."

"Sorry, Antón. I'm so crude, I'm past saving."

"I'm not saying she *might* be; I'm one hundred percent sure she is. I trust your intuition. Remember in the shop? And the meeting? It didn't occur to me at the time, but Marian . . ."

"Mm. Girlfriend, blatantly. That's why Leia was buying the *Lethal Weapon* movies."

"What?"

"Nothing? This is 2010, right?"

"By which you mean . . ."

"That it's a pretty standard story nowadays. Lesbian wants baby. Sleeps with first knucklehead in need of sex, or a friend, or gets artificially inseminated, and bingo!"

"It must have happened in the past as well. I bet it happened in Egyptian times."

"Egyptian times?"

"It's no bad thing that it happens, what's bad is that it's happened to me."

"That's right. So forget about your pipe dreams, your idea of impregnating a stranger on some wild night out in the town and then having, as well as a child with her, the most romantic love story of all time."

"Thanks for that, Bela."

"Welcome."

I'm not going to complain. It would be ridiculous. If my intention is to be a textbook optimist, indisputably empty, flat, unfractured, a cruel optimist, I ought to "look on the bright side," as people say. After all, Vidor, I'll end up thanking my lucky stars. The best option—Leia, not pregnant, vanishing from my life—isn't an option. Forget about it, goodbye. How many times must fate have smiled on me (not getting a woman pregnant, and other equally inconvenient outcomes) without me being thankful for it, just thinking it was the norm, or even what I'd somehow earned. Plus if Leia had been straight, our relationship would have probably been even more tense, and the idea of becoming a couple (for our sake, or for the baby's, or our families, or for the tax breaks couples with children get, or whatever) would always be there, it would have been the most bothersome temptation. And what's more we'd demand passion, love, perfection. But not in this case. Now the objective (genuinely ambitious, don't you think, I'm not kidding now) is to get on well together, be friends, in a position, in the case that nature follows its course, to bring our child up well, to show it love and support. Simple as that.

"And how do you plan to break it to Leia that you know she's a lesbian?"

"With tact, but without touching her."

"Mm. I hope you can. I don't like how she's been with you, but I also don't like what you're now in a position to do to her."

Bela and I talked on into the night, but when the conversation began meandering in what increasingly resembled concentric circles, I said goodbye and turned the TV on, drawn in by the anesthesia promised by a bit of foreign station channel-hopping.

*Tuesday, March 16, 2010*

Today it was back to contract negotiations again and only at about seven o'clock in the evening, when Peter Farrar and I managed to give the others the slip and head to his pub, the Ship, did Leia the Rebel Princess come into my thoughts. As I ate a leathery piece of lamb with potatoes, my friend Peter (I've realized, yes, I consider him a friend, I even went so far as to invite him to come and stay in Madrid) gave enthusiastic accounts of his utterly wonderful holidays, always featuring gardens and flowers (he's a member of a floral society). Before we knew it, we were both sated and a little drunk, gin and tonic number three in hand: the perfect context for exchanging confidences.

Peter told me about Mary, his beloved, the woman who makes him sigh and toss and turn in bed, and who inspired his interest in growing beautiful flowers—who'd have thought it, deep down, Peter's soul is full of flowers, not sarcasm. "Mary, Mary, Mary," said Peter, with a wistful smile, gazing up at the ceiling. Mary and he are neighbors and, unfortunately, she's married. Anyway. Then it was my turn, and I cleared my throat. I felt bad for Peter. Not because of his platonic, or incomplete, love story, not just for the story itself, which was genuinely sad, not only because of that, but also because his tale had been brief, and mine was bound to be anything but. I gave him a rundown of the vicissitudes of my time since Ana's death (a summary, I say, Vidor, don't make fun of me, I was short and to the point, no sob story, kept it cool, also because I was sure he'd already heard some reports of my misfortune), and when I got to the end, to the point where, glancing at him, I delivered the last turn of the screw ("*Peter, I'm afraid that Leia is a lesbian*"), the Englishman made a comment, simple and brilliant, that I could do nothing but rejoice in.

271

But before hearing what Peter had to say, a little analysis, a little context. Farrar's vision of life is what you could call sporting, something genuinely English. It isn't the easiest thing to explain. To understand it you need to have read a good number of English novels, Somerset Maugham and the like, English gentlemen and true sportsmen, and it would also help to have watched countless hours of sport on TV alongside a little Englishman, always with a beer to hand, and rarely uttering a word to one another. They have this ability to step back and observe the universe and its inhabitants, us, as though we were strange and fascinating objects, and not people who are royally fucking them over. Just like in sport, there are certain rules, and with that as your starting point, whatever happens, happens. In a way, as they well know, they're Martians (for them, *The Island* is further from Getafe than from Mars, for instance), which makes their lives fairly sad, but also makes them able to take things on the chin (it's as though the blows don't land, as though everything halts in mid-air just before making contact with them). The nice part is that their irritating, frosty aloofness, their kinship with amoebas and possibly also jellyfish, their cold bloodedness, overall makes them respectful at the same time as subtly disdainful. Their terrifying emotional isolation enables them to be very tolerant, they understand to a tee what is meant by the freedom of others, because of the fact they live trussed up to their own shells and shelters. Let's not forget, either, that they are the ones who were lucky enough to invent the concept of irony, but not out of geniality, nor as a result of an excessive flair for linguistic pirouetting, but because of the difficulty they have, the circumspection, when it comes to expressing in a straightforward manner whatever it is they mean, what they're feeling, and what pains them. Unlike them, we Spaniards are attracted by hyperbole, by excess, which is hardly a straight line either, let's be honest. For an English person life and fox hunting and cricket aren't all alike, but they could be. Which is why, when I saw that Peter was about to comment on my life story and the news that Leia is gay (glancing at me, tinkling the ice in his gin and tonic, slowly licking his upper lip), I leaned closer in so that I wouldn't miss a word of what he was about to say.

"Come, my friend," and after a deliberate pause, he added, smiling lightly: "It's not the end of the world."

"What?" I growled.

"It's not the end of the world, Antón."

I must admit I nearly punched him right then and there (which would have been my first act of aggression since nursery school). Not the end of the world? Ho-ho, little English man! Laughing at me, was he, at my misfortune? Swine, I thought. Son of a fucking bitch. We moved on to talking about soccer, had one last cocktail and, when I was back in my hotel room, on my own, as I was putting on my pajamas, it hit me that Farrar had a point. It's not that bad. In effect. How accustomed we are (or I am) to exaggerating, to overreacting all the time. It's already quarter past midnight. Time for bed. But first, I'm going to send Leia a text message. In it, I paraphrase Peter: "I know you're a lesbian. It's not the end of the world." Message Sent. In my family, Vidor, the first person who made any money happened to be a Hungarian (you). And in my life, the first to give me a wise piece of advice, an Englishman. It's not that bad. Of course it isn't.

How I'd love to be a member of that select "It's not the end of the world" club. Now, sleep. Tomorrow, Madrid.

*Tuesday, March 16, 2010*

Madrid received me like an old aunt, who smiles ironically so as to hide the affection she feels deep down and cannot express. Bela is still immersed in her research of Golden Age authors, who shed a light so brilliant that even today we still find ourselves blinded by its glare. At work, we're into the opening skirmishes of the sixteenth draft of the contract. Fran, unsettled, wants/doesn't want to talk to me about something, and has been gazing at me long and hard, slack jawed; I worry that it's the flirty secretary issue. Tonight, back to my books.

NOTES ON BELA'S BOOKS

*The Book of Disquiet* (1913–1915), Fernando Pessoa (1888–1935)

What a character, that Pessoa. Lisbon, his beloved city, acclaims the dead poet nowadays to the same extent that it disparaged the clerk, the secret genius, when he was alive. I read the closing pages of *The Book of Disquiet* today and, in spite of the brilliance of so many of those phrases and reflections, when I came to the words "The end" felt I could breathe again, felt the same relief as waking up from a nightmare. The book is so crammed with detail, it suffocates you; so full of visions, you come away drunk. In

Pessoa happiness and pessimism are all one, which means there's simply no such thing as sadness. With him there's no morality, only pure esthetics, which makes his ideas on life flickers of genius, and are only useful to give us a glimpse—and that's more than enough—of what he, Pessoa, is like. It's an inwardly-opening idea of the universe, a funnelling impossibly down. The strange thing is that reading him doesn't (by contrast, to drag yourself out of the unpleasant sense of ecstatic affliction, of chronic fatigue) make you want to do something, to wallow in earthly pleasures, to enjoy physical ones, it doesn't make you want to take to the streets, scream and shout, but rather to tuck yourself up in bed and dream dreams in fast forward.

Pessoa's disdain for certain mystics is funny, really—the fact he criticizes them because the only way they'd found to combat the brutal indifference of the universe was to deny it. It's funny because he, Pessoa, is himself every bit the mystic, just disguised as an esthete (or affected by a different kind of madness); he came to the same conclusions as the mystics about both the meaning of life and the reason for writing what he wrote: his is an existence circumscribed by his creativity, which happened not in the world but isolated from it. In the final analysis, anyone who flees pretending he is seeking definitive wisdom or plenitude or beauty or glory or the right word can be considered a coward, even if only for not accepting that the weaponry of intelligence, which is man's lot, is insufficient for getting to grips with life. And for that he has taken to his heels. It is not art that creates Pessoa, but rather fear and bewilderment, wounds, blood and death, worms and

275

the taut skin of the woman he never met, the eyes of the child he never fathered. The place where Pessoa is brave, even extremely brave (the blind courage of the demented), is within himself, in his writing, in thought, be as it may part of an escape, an out-and-out flight. By being a coward, he is also anything but. Reading him forces you to take a step back. My thoughts turn to this diary, which is no more than another incomplete truth, and I ask myself if I too am on the run, for all that I uphold the esthetic of lucidity and the artificial beauty of rational thought when I read others. And me, will I be a coward by not being one?

It's always interesting to read immortal authors (to read them, not to talk with them as though . . . ), because it serves to shatter the sweetened ideas we've been sold about them. Pessoa, thank goodness, is anything but the nutty professor, the scatterbrained dreamer from Lisbon that many would have him be. There is, as with any genius, a tiger in him, a cruel creature, a brute. Pessoa is neurotic, proud, arrogant to the point of nausea, obsessive, repetitive, wearying, unbearable, egotistical . . . as well as being a NUTCASE. He rails against travelling, sex, cohabiting, solidarity, revolution, progress. He is a misogynist and pretends he is asexual. He considers it absurd to discuss the existence of God, and he hates reading (he can't abide others, because for him, only he exists). And on top of this, he's an apologist for pedophilia: "Those among us who are not paedophiles would love to have the courage to be." A monster, in brief, our dear Fernando. Or does anyone still believe the thing about lambs knowing how to write? Who was the pedant writer who said to you, Vidor, that "only he who dares to delve in the most abysmal chasms of his soul may call himself a writer." Was it a Spaniard? A Hungarian? Where did you meet, why? Pessoa delved, and what he found down there was shit, and he transmuted it into gold. No small thing. Many magicians have tried the same, in vain.

His magnificent "Our Lady of Silence" would be apt for inclusion in an anthology of nightmarish gem-texts along with "Qué más da" by Pedro Casariego Córdoba.

*Wednesday, March 17, 2010*

> "Life is the hesitation between an exclamation mark and a question mark. After doubt there is a full stop."
>
> PESSOA

> "Misfortune depends upon fortune.
> Fortune conceals misfortune.
> What has a definite delimitation?
> Or abnormality?
> The normal reverts to strangeness.
> Goodness reverts to perversion."
>
> LAO TZU

"The good thing about Wednesdays is they always fall *just* two days before Fridays." This quip came courtesy of Leia, among others, when we talked today. I find irritating the way she pops up out of the blue, her assumption that I'll be there the second she clicks her fingers. I know this is a bit nonsensical, bearing in mind our almost non-existent relationship, how hit and miss our connection is, but ... It's one of an endless number of things we're going to have to work on. Another being prejudice, our great enemy at the start (even though I consider myself a staunch defender of much-criticized prejudice, something that intelligent minds invented as a wonderful way of saving energy). When I showed up today at a terrace bar on the Plaza San Ildefonso, in Madrid's supposedly "alternative" neighborhood, where we'd arranged to meet, seeing me dressed in suit and tie she wasn't able to suppress a look of disgust, of downright disappointment. Anyway. I was in a videoconference when she called, mediating between French and Germans. I said to Leia that I was tied up, but she, it would appear quite the drama lover, said it was urgent, and that she had to see me right away. Three o'clock, we said. The sun was in the sky—a lukewarm sun that very soon will dare to warm up. There was a busker in the Plaza San Ildefonso, warding off the cold with a wool coat, sad songs, cracked voice and Spanish guitar. Hearing him, I forgot all about the satellite, I became aware that I wasn't in the office any more but among people reading newspapers, having a beer, chatting, scratching an ear or watching sparrows pecking at crumbs. People who could allow themselves to kill a little time while that same time, more slowly, was killing them. I got there late and Leia was waiting for me, sitting at a table, so very young, so very pregnant, drawing. "Why can't she be my daughter, instead of mother to my child?" I thought. How much better it would be to be expecting a mischievous grandchild, maybe a bit slow witted, to have already sorted out the issue of having a child.

"Hello," I said.

"Hi."

"And your bodyguard?"

Leia put down her felt tip pen, closed the sketchbook she was holding and put it to one side, before I could get a look at what she was drawing. In daylight she looks just as fragile as she does by night, but there's also a determination in her dark eyes, an impatience, and a touch of the imp about her, a cruelty, possibly. I was expecting a more insecure woman. Her paunch was showing the due proportions by now, though she was still slim overall. Her nose, less flattened than my own, prompted the thought that our child is going to resemble a midget boxer, or a baby who received the first punch of its life as soon as it was born.

"How old are you?" I asked, point blank.

"Twenty-three. You?"

"Thirty-two."

I ordered something to eat. All Leia wanted was water, she's one of these young people who live on air, or gas, or three pieces of fruit a day, or who feed themselves by looking in the mirror, satisfied, more by what they've denied their bodies than by their bodies themselves. She was wearing a faded leather motorcycle jacket, loose fitting T-shirt, pregnancy jeans and tennis shoes. I felt tired, or old.

"When are you due?"

"End of April."

"And what's with this fixation on having a baby at twenty-three?"

She laughed at this. Which was a good thing, Vidor, because until then I hadn't got a look at her mischievous, congenial smile, her uneven teeth.

"Dunno. My biological clock must be fast, right?"

She picked up a fork and began drawing invisible pictures on a napkin.

"I liked your message."

"The not the end of the world one? Thanks."

My bread and *croquetas* came, and as the food went down, my bad mood gradually subsided too. But only gradually.

"What's on your mind?" she asked me as she watched the way I was eating, my good manners shattered by anxiety.

"About how lucky we've been. The child means we have this wonderful opportunity to get to know each other—with your friend Marian's permission, of course."

"With her permission, right," she conceded, in jest.

"And how are you so sure it's mine?"

"You're the only guy I've slept with since I was sixteen."

"I see. So that makes it a possibility, or a probability, or highly probable, or even a certainty. And why me?"

"The look in your eyes, when you came close to me. I felt sorry for you. And your story—it broke my heart."

There we are: pity.

"So I was a bit of a trophy for you, is that right?" I said. "Downtrodden, pathetic man deserves a child though in principle he's never going to get to know it, that kind of thing."

"Or it was a curse," said Leia, shifting uncomfortably in her seat. "It could also have been a curse, right? How should I know. I was totally out of it that night as well, remember?"

"And is that something you did a lot, going looking for fathers in after clubs?"

"It is. When I got drunk, if I'd had a fight with my girlfriend, bad days . . . But when men started coming on to me, I'd feel disgusted and just go home. Or as soon as I went into a bar, I'd turn around and leave."

"Mm. We're pretty disgusting, us men, some in particular. And why did you rob me?"

"You're a bit of a dickhead, aren't you?" exclaimed Leia, who'd had enough of my aggressive attitude.

"Maybe I am. Apologies, I'm not used to meetings like this."

She took out a cigarette and lit it.

"That night was a different case. You struck me . . . like you were the ruins of what had once been a nice guy. But a nice guy, deep down."

"Maybe I am. Some of my family think so. Actually, only my sister Bela thinks that. You and she have met, she's the one who called your friend Marian a "slut" once or twice. But then my parents and Zoltan, that's my older brother, they suspect I may well be son of the number one bitch."

"This isn't going to work," said Leia, shaking her head.

"What isn't?"

Leia took a sip of water and passed her gaze over the square, which was deserted by now.

"Where do you live?" I asked.

"In Marian's house, for now. And these pretty names of yours? Are you foreign?" she asked, not looking at me.

"Not in the slightest. The names are Hungarian, but we're Spanish, though not all of us, because Zoltan's half Yank. But that's another story. You shouldn't be smoking."

"You don't say! Who do you think you are, my Dad?"

"No, I'm the Dad of the creature you're currently turning into smoked baby."

Leia pushed her seat back and scowled at me.

"I was right, you are a total dickhead."

"Fine, but put it out."

The next bit of food came, octopus Galician style with two sets of cutlery. I put it half way across the table and held out a fork, though one had already been set for her. She took it not all that willingly, but she took it. We tried the octopus.

"It's delicious" she said.

"Can I put my hand on your belly?"

"No."

"Okay. Why the urgency to meet up?"

"Do you always ask so many questions?"

"Only when I've had such a hard time trying to meet up with someone I seriously want to talk to. Plus there's the issue of the child, wouldn't you say? That gives a slightly different feel to things."

And on we went, Vidor. Initial contact. That it was. Naturally enough, we didn't reach any conclusions. We didn't make any firm plans to meet again, we didn't hit it off, we didn't understand each other, and we didn't even begin to get to know one another. But me, I'm an optimist. Oh yes. Big time. Relationships that get off on a hopelessly bad foot have this advantage, as do ones in which it's inevitable, for whatever reason, that the other be given a second opportunity. They can get better. I have increasing faith in disasters, maybe I'm starting to navigate turbulent waters with something approaching agility. I had another meeting I had to go to at quarter past four. It was a clumsy goodbye. I threatened a kiss, but she jumped and stood away from me, and I got caught neither here nor there, leaning in, looking like an idiot, mushy smile on my lips, slack-jawed, meek, annoying. That smile's been persecuting me ever since, and it's night now. All afternoon in the office, whenever it came to mind, I grimaced at the computer, grim grimaces, forcing the expression as far as it could possibly go, inflicting a singularly pleasurable pain on myself.

Now I find myself eating a chicken and lettuce sandwich and, with each mouthful, I bite down hard, I try to obliterate the memory, I try to forget, to grind it out, to overcome the shame filling me. And Leia, what must she think of me? Because *it all comes down to that smile.*


*Friday, March 19, 2010*

> "Thus, we never live but we hope to live; and always hoping to be happy, it is inevitable that we will never be so."
>
> PASCAL


Friday, so full of promise, Thursday behind us, Saturday nearly here. Fran didn't show up at work today, a first in all the time I've known him. I tried calling him but he's got his phone switched off. My friends have been vanishing into thin air of late, leaving me to the mercy of my family, my ghosts, myself, this diary. I took the afternoon off, went for a run, and when I got back at around six o'clock, Bela was at home, reading.

"Not going to the library?"

"I was there this morning, but I started nodding off, it's too peaceful. You can hear people turning the page, chairs being scraped back, uncertain steps, people's brain's crackling, creaking in slow motion . . ."

"And Carlos? He doesn't call me these days."

"Carlos?" Bela frowned, as though it was an effort to remember who he was. "He's away on a teambuilding weekend at some hotel with a convention center in Barcelona. You know the deal, team building, all for one, suits and ties, organized entertainments, booze, buckets of repression, itching for action secretaries. He's there for the weekend. Guess what, Antón? I saw Laura Puerta yesterday."

"Hot Laura Puerta?"

Laura is the only hot friend Bela's ever had, which, far from being an issue for me (my sister's insecurities, which mean she only makes friends with women she thinks are less attractive than her), has always been a blessing, because from a young age it's helped me appreciate the relative beauty of most women, or see some beauty even in ugliness, and this, as it were, has made me more open, or wiser, or possibly just more easy to please.

"The very same. Well, now she isn't only hot, she's a lesbian."

"You're shitting me! We're surrounded."

284

Bela told me about getting to know the lesbian university scene in Boston and finding it all fairly relaxed. Apparently, *Boston Marriages* was a term used in the nineteenth century to refer to women who lived as couples without men, and the origin of the expression, according to her, has to do with *The Bostonians* by Henry James, though I don't remember why. Massachusetts was the first North American state to legalize gay marriage, in 2004. She also said that a University of Boston study published in the *American Journal of Public Health* drew the conclusion that lesbians have more of a tendency towards being overweight than straight women, suggesting that this was because they accept their own bodies, that is, they overcome the social pressure to be thin. "So? Where's this all headed, all these unconnected and unimportant facts to do with Boston and lesbians?" you'll be asking yourself, Vidor, you'll suspect that your clown of a great-great-great-grandson has officially lost his mind, but the thing is that my sister, when she takes the floor, doesn't advance, she goes in circles, around and around, she pesters you, doesn't get to the point, and it worries me quite a lot that this defect of hers is only going to get worse, she's got all the makings of an un-bear-able old woman, the eternal, the insufferable monologist, and no one's ever going to want to play cards with her in the old people's home.

"But Bela, would you possibly mind getting to the ..."

"It could hardly be any clearer, Antón! You're so stupid sometimes. I rang Laura up as research, to find out a bit about how it goes with lesbians round here."

This is Bela to a tee. Inquisitive. Tireless. I should say that I kissed Laura once, when I was sixteen, in some bar, or, to be precise, she kissed me, followed by a slap to my face, and then we carried on chatting like nothing had happened, and I never got my head around it, though it was interesting and mysterious and sexy, and now of course it makes sense, but at the same time I still really have no idea what it was about. Bela arranged to meet Laura and her girlfriend in Lavapiés, the barrio that's the beating heart of Madrid, where bars serve sweetbreads and there are wholesale Chinese stores and exotic restaurants and residents who have lived there forever and lost their spirit, as well as off-the-boat residents from places I wouldn't be able to place on the map. Laura and Rosa did internships in the US, have a penchant for wearing green, claim never to argue, are constantly on their guard (the only time they don't go out carrying a raincoat is in summer), avoid all physical contact, finish one another's sentences, don't care for Chueca, have produce from their respective home towns hanging from the kitchen ceiling, they're regularly getting mugged and they come across as being one single entity rather than two.

"They're like Tweedle Dum and Tweedle Dee, Antón. But they're happy, more or less, they love each other and they're going to adopt. They'll be like a double mother with two heads, but a good one, I'd say."

"Could well be, Bela, could well be. But I'm failing to see what Tweedle Dum and Tweedle Dee have got to do with Leia or me."

"What?" said Bela angrily. Now, the new Bela can sometimes fly into a rage without prior warning. She has sharp edges, the new Bela. She's doing much better. "What do you mean what have they got to do with you? They're lesbians, Antón, and you are utterly ignorant when it comes to lesbians! They exist, they're right there! We can't just forget about them! They hide away because they're doubly marginalized—by the fact they're women and because of their sexual preference! Get it? Thank goodness that young people nowadays—according to Laura and Rosa—are more open-minded, God. They hold hands in the street, they kiss in public, and they couldn't give a shit what people think. Plus their relationships last longer than men's. Which is because you guys, men, gays too, you're all complete bastards! D'you hear, Antón? Bastards, all of you!"

I went into the kitchen, got two beers, opened them, went back through into the living room and handed one to my sister. I wanted to give her the chance to apologize, to acknowledge she'd just overstepped the mark.

"Thanks," she said, calmer now, though her eyes were still smoldering. "And what's up with you? Don't you find lesbians interesting? Aren't you interested in Leia?"

I took a sip of my beer and looked at my sister. I asked myself how much longer we'd be living together, when she might be going back to the US, and it struck me that I'd miss her. Maybe not straight away—not in the first months or years—but later on, for sure.

"I find lesbians, as lesbians, neither interesting nor uninteresting," I said. "I have the same thing with them as with heterosexuals, or with hermaphrodite insects, if you see what I mean. Individuals are what interest me. When it comes to Leia, I'm interested to know what she's like, to see if we can get on. Full stop. Shall we go and catch a film?"

We went to the cinema, Vidor, and I enjoyed it, the popcorn, the coca cola, the darkness, being surrounded by people not talking, concentrating, determined to have a couple of hours of escape. Back at home, we had a light dinner. I've lost 9 kilos now, and I was tempted to take a photo of myself and send it to my mother, to make her happy—sad as it may be that one of the things that makes her feel happiest, or less wretched, is having slim children. After that, I was reading Cioran's work, only to be interrupted by a phantasmagoric phone call.

## TRANSCRIPTION OF CONVERSATION WITH MY FATHER, LAJOS MALLICK, THIS VERY NIGHT, AND OF THE FOLLOWING ONE WITH JOSEFA, MY MOTHER

I was in bed, reading, and laughing to myself, almost hysterically, when the computer rang—a Skype call. Bela didn't get it (she must have been asleep, she finds it impossible not to rush for a phone and answer it before it's rung twice) and I had to get up, annoyed by the interruption, by having to keep up another inane conversation with my mother.

"Hi, Mom?"
" . . ."
"Mom? Can you hear me?"
" . . ."
"Mom? (Pause) If you can't hear me very well, hang up and call again, ok? (Pause). I'll hang up, ok?"
"Don't hang up! (Not my mother, but my father, the man I haven't spoken with for months and months, the

288

Great Houdini, the escape artist, someone who has the greatest difficulty giving a hug, or even a smile, the tireless reader in History and Everything That's Worth Knowing, the Great Enigma).

"Father?! Is that you?"

The sound of breathing, agitated, convulsed, slightly cowardly.

"Hello, son. How are you?"

"Me? (Pause, trying to assimilate how warm the question sounded). I'm well. You?"

"Fine. Your mother told me it isn't long now until the satellite launches. Baikonur? Guyana?"

"Baikonur, father."

"I see. They say it's all dromedaries and space junk out there. Abandoned Buran shuttles. An interesting spot, no doubt."

"Yes. I don't know if I'm going to get to go."

"Fine. I'm glad you're well. The washing machine broke yesterday."

"Really? What a pain . . ."

"Your mother insists we call a technician, when I say she already has a technician in the house."

"Well, it's not the end of the world, I guess."

"Not the end of the world? Where did you get that idea from? It's the pump, there's no question. Now, I'm putting your mother on. Take care, son."

"Father?"

Noises. Then, the slightly shrill voice of my mother.

"Antón? Can you hear me? Son?

"Hi Mom."

"I don't know what you said to your father, but he's just shot out of here."

"Nothing, Mom. I didn't say anything."

"Well he's shot out. What did you have for dinner?"

"Hamburger, fries, deep fried onion rings and a pot of ice cream the size of Zoltan's ego."

"Goodness! Mary and Joseph!"

"I'm onto chocolate doughnut number three—guzzling it down."

"You are incorrigible, Antón! I almost believed you then! You almost gave me a heart attack, son! Why do you have to be so awful? You've always had this harsh side, even though you're a sweety."

"How's Father?"

"From when you were really little, you'd always be up to something, giving Zoltan a hard time, or us, or the ants. Your father always said it, you didn't know what respect was; with you, everything got questioned. There's something perverse about you, son, I hope you know."

"Many thanks, Mother. Probably learned it from you guys, my elders."

"And your geraniums? Are they still going? Have you managed not to kill them?"

"They're fine, yes, clinging on to life most indecorously, they're out of their minds, I say, for not wanting to commit suicide. Hey, Mom, I'm really tired, I was reading, let's talk tomorrow shall we?"

"Whatever you say, Antón. You're a very sweet boy, but you've given your father the cold shoulder today, and now me . . . And poor Bela?"

"She's fine. Big kiss, Mom. I'm hanging up."

Click. The end.

NOTES ON BELA'S BOOKS

*The New Gods* (1969), Émile Cioran (1911–1995)

I can't sleep—thanks to that damned phone call. What a drag my mother can be. But I know that's not important. The worse thing is knowing my father and I will never understand one another, and time is hardly on our side. There are some psychologists—Zoltan amongst them—who need just a few such words, nothing more, and they'll have you in sessions for years to come, until you're utterly fed up with their manner, their nose, or the cologne they use. Cioran, the masterly Romanian philosopher, was told by his mother that if she'd known he was going to turn out to be so unhappy, she'd have had an abortion. Take that. Three or four psychologists could live off that one sentence right there—working full time. Naturally Cioran rose above those words, which is to say, he transformed them into anecdote, they were buried in his vision, which had a far more devastating, far richer effect that that simply sad little phrase.

In Cioran's world, pessimism is an achievement, a trophy, though poisoned. If you stay lucid, you uncover it, you observe it, you receive it as a gift and you get to keep it for ever more. Perhaps some might tend to see Cioran as bitter, an unhealthy pessimist, a mere destroyer, but this isn't quite right. Everything comes at a price, trophies included, and if you dare to think, if you are courageous like Cioran, there's every likelihood that all you'll see will be devastated fields. The good news is that at least *you see them*. There are no laws, there are no systems, humankind is not HUMANKIND, nor HUMANKIND, there is only bewilderment, non sequiturs, and, as well, discoveries, intelligence. Because intelligence is capable of reinventing hope, of making it into something familiar, into the pleasure of thinking, or into going for a stroll hand in hand with someone else who also thinks, or conversing with that person, even if it might mean the destruction of what you yourself think.

I can be tickled both by Wodehouse (a humorist who creates depictions of an innocent, paradisal, unreal universe), and by Cioran and Leopardi (masterly, card-carrying pessimists, a breed of rational visionary). What this means, where it puts me, I don't know, and don't care. Maybe it would be better if I identified with Bertrand Russell, or some other pure-blooded optimist, but some things are not of our choosing. My feeling is that optimism can also be cruel, or else egoistic, or cowardly, or self-seeking, unless it's truly genuine, that is, unless it's down to a person's character and not born from a vision of the world they come to through experience. I've only had dealings with a genuine optimist once in my entire life (he could *almost* make you believe he was one), an extraordinary guy called Miguel Azor who I went to school with, intelligent, funny, a true gem. If I were mayor of Madrid, I'd put his name in lights on the Paseo de la Castellana, because until I met him I could never have imagined that his kind existed. As for the rest, converted optimists or optimists out of practical self-interest, when they make the case for optimism as an intellectual choice, the fruit of thinking or of observation, and when they peddle it as the sole truth, their perspective is one that disfigures, that wishes not to see, it is in a sense a stingy vision, refusing a part of life or reality that also exists and one has to accept. It's good to want to be an optimist, above all because it makes you less of a burden on others, but it's pretty obvious that life isn't actually a bed of roses. On the other hand, unadulterated pessimism, chronic, shut up in itself, with nothing grand about it, that of the embittered person or the neurotic, and arising not out of the fascination and bewilderment and horror that living assumes, provides nothing either. Whereas happiness often has an oxygenating effect, it is an impersonal gift that we receive and we give, a magnificent gift; happiness is something I do sign up for. Cioran, Leopardi, Montaigne and others (writers, artists, film makers, or, what do I know, good run-of-the-mill conversationalists, unnamed creators of exceptional moments, the kind of people you *don't* come across much), bring about in me an intellectual happiness, a lust for life and, why not, a certain secret pride (very very secret) at being a part of the human species.

*Saturday, March 20, 2010*

> "I like to think of life as half light, half darkness. I'm not a pessimist. I don't complain about the horror of life; I complain about the horror of *my* life."
>
> PESSOA

I got up at two o'clock in the afternoon (insomnia attack previous night). Bela was making pesto. In the confrontation between my sister and the basil, which she was trying to pulverize with pestle and mortar, there was no clear winner. Bela was flushed, tilting into fury, not exactly a domestic goddess. While we ate, I told her about my conversation with our father, thereby ruining her weekend altogether.

Something's clearly seriously wrong with Father. It's the first time in years that he's asked how I am. From here, the afternoon flowed by under a shroud, like the Madrid skies. We tried calling the United States, but Mother and Father must be crouched down somewhere, hiding behind their porcelain countenances and their chatter, nothing more than articulated noise, barricaded behind their talent for being garrulous mutes, waiting for our response, convinced we'll grasp their unfailingly cryptic and absurd messages. At about six o'clock in the evening it struck us that we couldn't put off the call to Zoltan any longer. We flipped a coin and I lost, like I almost always do. Zoltan immediately demanded a snap family reunion. At my place. My guess is that, in spite of the circumstances, he likes the idea of getting away from his own house, a few hours away from María and the twins. Zoltan is going to turn out to be human after all. He's coming over at ten o'clock, and he won't have had dinner, and of course he won't bring anything with him.


It's strange to have laughed so much the day after finding out, or suspecting, that your father has one foot in the grave. Maybe this is one of the ominous things about maturity—finding out that such things can and are going to happen to you. Zoltan showed up at ten o'clock in the evening, having—oh my God!—had dinner, and bringing with him—OMG!—an excellent bottle of malt whisky. A patient gave it to him, but still a nice gesture. As older brother, he felt he had to show himself more affected than us. He gazed off into unknown recesses of the living room, answered our questions monosyllabically, combed his hair back with his fingers every five minutes, and poured himself larger whiskys than either of us (this in spite of the fact he barely drinks). Bela, for her part, seemed simply glum. I didn't know exactly how I was supposed to act. We're all clear that it isn't Father being a hypochondriac this time. In fact, the worrying thing is that he hasn't complained about anything for almost two months, according to Zoltan, who speaks with him a couple of times a week. Two months without worrying he's seriously ill, and without going to the doctor's. Very odd.

"And then there's the fact he was really affectionate with you, Antón," said Zoltan, semi-blubbering. "He must be *really* sick."

"Can't he also miss his youngest child?" said Bela. But seeing the looks Zoltan and I gave her, she dropped the hypothesis. "No, you're right. All is really not well with Lajos."

"Why on earth do you call Papa 'Lajos'?" exclaimed a hypersensitive Zoltan.

"What would you have me call him? Matías? Juanito?"

"No, 'Papa.'"

"Well, on the phone, which has been our usual mode of communication, 'Papa' feels forced, and 'Father' really harsh. Anyway, up yours. I'll call him whatever the hell I feel like calling him."

"Bela! How dare you speak to me like that?"

"Cool it, you guys—more whisky anyone?" I said, intervening just as I was about to burst out laughing.

One of the peculiar things about our family meetings is that only rarely do we make binding decisions, ones that are ever carried out. We come together to form something akin to a commission (everybody knows, Vidor, how futile commissions are) in which the members are always the same, the items to be discussed make no difference (we'll end up fighting about other things), and the positions taken up by each member have stayed fixed since childhood. On this occasion we came to a consensus: that one of us ought to go to Hudson, and that this should happen no later than ten days from now. We're all prepared to go, but no one suggested a date, or to buy the tickets. Zoltan went on and on about our Father in the past tense, as though he were already dead and buried, game over. He drank at pace, not a drunkard's pace, not a connoisseur's pace, rather that of the teetotaler, that is, like a suicide, respecting neither time nor the effects of alcohol. On top of this, he got so misty-eyed that Bela and I, to compensate, were obliged to seem somewhat cold and detached.

"Remember his barbecues?" said Zoltan. "His chicken in beer! What a *legend*! If it flamed up, he'd use the beer to put it out, and that would make it even tastier."

"His chicken wasn't that tasty, Zoltan," I said. "Father didn't know the first thing when it came to cooking. No one in Spain would dare serve chicken like that, not even in a roadside diner. He didn't cook the breasts properly sometimes."

"That was why you," added Bela, pointing at Zoltan, "always gave yourself wings and legs, am I wrong? And with those revolting turkey burgers he used to make, you'd give us the first ones, the ones that had gone cold. Ever since I was young the sound of a turkey squawking has been enough to make me puke."

"Oh you are heartless. No—you live on a different planet, is what," pronounced my older brother, slurring his s's now and pouring himself more whisky. "If I say Papa's chicken in beer was spectacular, it was. He didn't cook much, but he was good at it, he had skills, a gift, whatever you want to call it. I've never known such a complete person. He was . . ." and Zoltan opened his eyes wide, which is Zoltan-speak for total concentration, and would get coeds hot at certain Yank universities, goodness knows why. " . . . He was a Renaissance man! That's what he was! A modern Leonardo, he knew more about any subject you care to name than the rest of us put together."

"Okay, Lajos knows a lot of stuff, but about chicken, not a clue."

"Nor about turkey."

"Nor about Hungary."

"Nor about comparative literature."

"Nor about Spain in the last twenty-five years."

"Nor about us."

The meeting could easily have ended badly, fists flying, Zoltan being sick on my glass coffee table, but at about midnight I got a text message from Leia: "Fulanita de tal? With Marian." After a couple more messages back and forth, I grasped that 'Fulanita de tal' is a bar on Calle Conde de Xiquena, and Leia was asking if I wanted to come for a drink with her and her friend. "Perfect," I thought. "Family reunion over."

"I'm going out," I announced.

"Why?" asked Zoltan, who was maybe hoping he'd spend the night at my place and we'd watch the sunrise together.

"There's no more to drink, you've seen to that. And we've covered the thing with Father, haven't we?"

"Where are you going?" asked Bela, like me enticed by the idea of going out and putting the reunion aside.

"I'm meeting someone," I said, giving them to understand that I preferred the prospect of phase two of the evening alone.

"Well Zoltan and I will come with you! Right, Zoltan!"

"Of course! How can you go out in this state without your older brother to look out for you?"

My siblings looked at me like I was holding tickets for Rolling Stones' (actual) last ever concert, the one where they're going to die on stage, at last, complete with ovations and death rattles. Something like that.

"Okay," I said, not wholly enthusiastically. "But when we get there, no complaining."

They both clapped their hands, we headed out, and Zoltan offered to drive us in his family hatchback.

"You diabolical creatures, both of you!" he said as he dismantled the twin's child seats. "My little bro, and my little sis, de-vils, yes sir. Do you realize? This is going to be our first ever time going out drinking together. You do realize that?"

I hadn't counted on Zoltan's enthusiastic attitude. The drink drive campaign was not such a thing as could trouble him, nor were his wife's questions when he came staggering into their bedroom later on, nor were hangovers, nor the possibility of a bad conscience. He bounced between worrying about Father being so gravely ill, wistfulness, and a huge urge to let his hair down, to let go. A little time out from all the constant scheming. As we drove, he put on an Amy Winehouse CD, full volume. Zoltan and Amy Winehouse, a nonsense cocktail—very much of our times. When we got to the bar, he paid for all of us to get in.

Fulanita de tal is a pub with a couple of different bars, a corridor, unisex bathrooms and Spanish music playing. When you come in, the first thing you notice is that it's full of women, very few men. And you hardly need telling: if a place of that description isn't a brothel, the only thing it can be is a gay bar. But let's not get mixed up, Vidor. It wasn't murky, or strange, or sinister, but well-lit, pleasant, innocent. Normal. Myths are merely that, myths. I guess Leia chose to meet there as a test. We were lucky: She and Marian were sitting together at the bar and, as soon as we got in, after the introductions, we were able to order drinks. Seeing Leia, so heavily pregnant, at that hour of the night, brought out the father in me, as though I were the future father of the child (which I was, but also wasn't): I immediately felt an urge to protect, or to prohibit, or to control. Bela and Marian chatted like lifelong buddies, the conversation between Leia and I wasn't overly fluid, and Zoltan kept casting little looks at my sister and me, asking what the hell we were doing in that place, making exaggerated grimaces of disgust. It wasn't long before he pulled me to one side.

"What do you call this?" he spat, all enthusiasm forgotten. "Weren't we going to go out the three of us?"

"I told you, I was meeting someone."

"Trying to impress me or something? I have lots of lesbian patients. Bringing me here like it's some kind of zoo is incredibly disrespectful, Antón. Cruel, and out of order, even by your standards."

"Wrong end of the stick, brother," I said. "This is no outing to the zoo. I brought you to meet the future mother to my child."

"You what?"

"Leia. The pregnant one."

"Jesus!" exclaimed Zoltan, after scraping his hair back so hard he almost tore it out. "You aren't pulling my leg? No? Jesus! I'm so sorry, Antón, really! You . . . and her! Her . . . and you! So the thing about the woman was true! Fuck! I'm sorry."

"Try not to be," I said, calmly. "There's been quite enough feeling sorry: for my situation, for Father's, for Bela and John, everything. Tonight's for not feeling sorry about anything, okay? Far better to carry on killing yourself with booze. I'll keep you company."

I left him on his own, deep in thought, and I went over to Leia, took her by the arm and led her to one side. I'd wanted to say something to her for days, and I'd finally mustered the energy to do so . . .

"Leia . . ."

"Yes?" she said expectantly, sensing it was something important.

"I want you to know that I'd love to help out with the child." Leia was going to say something, but I stopped her. "Say nothing, please. Just promise me you'll think about it."

That was a weight off my shoulders. We went back over and joined Marian and Bela, and ordered another round. The atmosphere relaxed, and Bela and I laughed hysterically at every joke, we were in fits, we had a ball. But the night had become too much for Zoltan, who kept himself apart, drinking at high speed, making it impossible for me to put the reunion and all my problems behind me.

I wonder, Vidor, whether sibling relationships are easy for you to understand. How many did you have? I can't remember exactly. I know two died as babies, and that you were the first born. There was a girl, wasn't there? Your sister didn't talk very much, or almost not at all, and she was the very image of your mother, she was robust like her and had forward-slumped shoulders, she stooped and had expressionless, watery blue eyes. According to you, she had spinster written all over her face. I can't remember the names of the male children who survived, the ones you left behind, and whether there were two or three of them. I know you all used to fight a lot, and that you, being the oldest, used to give them a thrashing. When you were in Spain, I know there were no letters, you never had any news, though I don't know whether you yourself tried to keep contact with them. Your positions on the board stayed fixed: You in Spain, them in Hungary. An altogether Mallick arrangement. I find it difficult to understand how you could have broken the bonds like that, or that there weren't such bonds. I find it difficult to understand how someone can bury a childhood, erase it from memory, however tough that childhood might have been. In your case, optimism was anything but genuine; it was one more mask. Anyway. I chatted with Leia and Bela and the rock-like Marian, and when I went downstairs to the toilet at one point, found Zoltan there. He was at one of the urinals and said for me to come past. When we came out he took me strongly by the arm and gave me a hard look. For the first time I felt a little afraid of Zoltan.

"How long have you known about Leia?"

"I'm sorry, Zoltan," I said, trying to get him off me.

He let me go and began swaying back and forth, the alcohol taking hold.

"You should have told me about it. Dickhead."

"It's nothing to do with you, Zoltan," I said, forcing a smile. "I'm not up for sermons, and I'm not all that keen on turning into some kind of news agency with myself as the sole topic, either."

"You will never get it, Antón. You tell me things, and I give you sermons. That is how things work, or how they ought to work."

"Fine. I'm sorry. Shall we go up?"

"Admit you're a dickhead?" he said, bringing his face close up to mine. Our noses were almost touching.

"I admit it."

"So, you admit it?"

"I said I do, Zoltan, fuck. I admit it."

"Good," he sighed, and that crazed look in his eye faded, making way for another, still crazed, but less dangerous. "If you admit it, in that case, with you I shall come."

We went upstairs, rejoined the group, and soon after decided to call it a night. It was around three o'clock in the morning. I don't know if I passed Leia and Marian's test.

We put Zoltan in a taxi and told him to call us when he got home. Bela and I got in another.

Back at the apartment I smoked a cigarette on the balcony. It wasn't cold. Some of our neighbors were having a screaming match. A young couple. Their window was open, and through the quiet of the night the insults came, the hurtful phrases. Bela had gone to bed. I got a message on my phone. Yes, Vidor, it was the woman I've been sleeping with from time to time. But you'll never find out whether I went to see her or not.

*Sunday, March 21, 2010*

"Every childbirth is suspect: the angels, luckily, are unsuited to it, the propagation of life being reserved to the fallen. The plague is impatient and greedy; it loves to spread. There is every reason to discourage generation, for the fear of seeing humanity die out has no basis: whatever happens, there will be everywhere enough fools who ask only to perpetuate themselves, and, if they themselves end by flinching from the task, there will always be found, to devote themselves to the cause, some hideous couple."

CIORAN

I've spent this Sunday working in my study at home. There are four outstanding clauses still to be agreed, barely one out of the fifty pages that make up the whole contract, but Richter's set April 6 as a deadline for the signature—

nine days before the launch. If I manage it, as well as a bonus, I've been promised I'll get to go along to Baikonur with him. The other launches I've watched at the Palacio de Congresos, alongside politicians, military men and other mainstream weirdos. As it turns out, everything's in order with the manufacture; it's just me that's going to be behind schedule. And if I set up a meeting in New York? That way I could visit Father, but the problem is that the meeting would be more effective if held in London or Paris. Zoltan called. He says he's going to go to Hudson next week, possibly Wednesday. He doesn't mind going on his own, he says. He feels ashamed about his drunken antics last night. How fortunate to feel bad about things like that.

Bela spent the day with Carlos. When she got back, after dark, we looked at flights to New York on the internet, just in case. Then, Playstation for an hour, and reading. I haven't managed to reach Mom by Skype (Status: Offline) or on her mobile phone (disconnected).

*Tuesday, March 23, 2010*

> "No one is so completely disillusioned with the world, or acquainted so thoroughly with it, or has such hatred for it, that if it regards him benignly for a while, he does not feel somewhat reconciled to it. Similarly, no one is known by us to be so wicked that if he greets us courteously he does not seem to us less

wicked than he was. These observations serve to demonstrate the weakness of mankind, not to *justify the wicked* or the world . . ."

LEOPARDI

I'm at work and Zoltan has just called. He's spoken to Mom. Our fears have been confirmed: Father has been in bed for several days, he won't get up. He's admitted that he's been having severe migraines for months now and can't see very well out of one eye, but refuses to go to the hospital. And Mom's putting up with it, maybe she's run out of oomph or maybe she's just as frightened as him. How can they be so irresponsible, those two? Don't they realize it could be something serious? Do people like them really exist? Anyway. What a mess.

Bela's leaving tomorrow morning. She's bought her ticket. We're having dinner together later.

I can't focus. Shit. Luckily I'm not so important, I'm not the only one at work on this, but just a mere malfunctioning cog in the machinery.

It's one o'clock in the morning and Bela's packing. She might be coming back, but, just in case, she's taking everything with her. Whenever visitors leave I have the feeling that I'm never going to see them again. And, in a way, that's true. Bela, these two months in Madrid, this Bela, will never be again. If I see her again soon (I'm hoping it doesn't come to that), in a few days, in Hudson, she'll be a *totally different* Bela. After all, her stay here with me, our confused wanderings, the search for Leia, her fling with Carlos, all of it, is already in the past, and soon enough it will be another group of memories that rears up and surprises us some day, the kind of thing you'd have difficulty believing ever happened to you, a dream within a dream. Strange, but, if we lived trapped by anything, it's by the present moment.

Three o'clock in the morning. I worked for a little while, and when I went to get a Coke, I came past Bela's suitcase in the living room, next to the front door. It's dark blue, plastic, large with little wheels, functional. It looks like a larger version of the ones used by Iberia airlines flight attendants. It has a Celtics sticker (John's contribution, I expect), and one from the Bahamas. And it is covered in dents and scuffs.

*Wednesday, March 24, 2010*

> "Happy the man who demands no more from life than what life spontaneously gives him and who guides himself with the instinct of cats who seek the sun when there is sun and, when there is no sun, find what warmth they can. Happy the man who renounces his life in favor of the imagination and finds pleasure in the contemplation of other people's lives, experiencing not the impressions themselves but the external spectacle of those impressions. Happy the man, then, who renounces

everything and from whom, therefore, nothing can be taken or subtracted."

PESSOA

I went to the airport with Bela first thing this morning, we took the Metro. She checked in (and got charged for excess baggage, such a pain, it's all about not letting you breathe), we had a cup of coffee and said goodbye outside passport control. At work, Fran, who's been so focused (on his family life, according to him) over the last month, has suggested we have lunch together, "and have a little chat." Whenever anyone says they want to meet "for a chat," it's advisable you gird your loins and at least choose a restaurant where the food is worth it. As far as the contract goes, there's no chance it's going to be tied up on schedule.

Leia, Leia, Leia. Seeing as she's never going to make me fall madly in love, is she trying to make me go mad full stop? Is she a young woman, or a woman-to-be? Work in progress, or wreck? Does she still think that the way you get to know someone is by putting obstacles in their way, rather than observing the way they negotiate the ones that come up naturally? I suspect, Vidor, that you wouldn't be able to stand her, at least to begin with (lionesses were more your thing than butterflies, if you see what I mean), though it's also true that I'm not you. At two o'clock in the afternoon she called asking me to meet for lunch. "It's urgent, Antón. Please don't let me down."

I cancelled lunch with good old Fran, who will just have to carry on talking to himself, and made my way to a pizzeria on Calle Infantas. I went unprepared for another

Rendezvous from Hell with Macabre Joke Thrown in for Good Measure. Vidor, there was honestly a point there where I thought my life can't be real, like *The Truman Show*, and all the people in my life actors being paid, I don't know, by some crazy millionaire with the most perverse sense of humor, some guy whose toe I stepped on as a kid and he has held it against me ever since. This could even be a good way of describing God (crazy millionaire) and Man (me). We play in different leagues—isn't that right, Vidor? Yours is that of control, that of the captain of the ship, taking the helm during the storm, putting the compass between his teeth; and mine is . . . Mine is? Anyway.

And what was I confronted by in that pizzeria? LEIA, CHAPERONED BY HER PARENTS, WAS WHAT I FOUND. Don't laugh, Vidor. Don't be unpleasant—really, there's no need. There's more. LEIA INTRODUCED ME AS HER BOYFRIEND. The father, Ramón, is a practising locksmith in his fifties, dark-haired with a monobrow, dead pan, and who doesn't speak, or at least not when I'm around, or when his daughter's around, or his wife, or when it's a combination of the four of us. The mother, Petra, as well as being slim and good looking, is a mother, though apparently non practising, and who talks nonstop without saying anything at all (who might she remind me of, Mom?). They're from Toledo (nothing to say on that front, good or bad). Leia was lucky: she has (it would appear) inherited the best of each of her parents, or, in any case, not the worst. The pregnancy didn't come up in conversation, nor our supposed relationship, and they asked me no questions, nothing. And when I say nothing, Vidor, I mean *nothing*. NOTHING.

I went from feeling surprise to irritation, from irritation to surprise, and surprise to curiosity. We didn't discuss the weather, but the whole thing was as though we were discussing the weather. The reassuring thing is that I suspect a first meal with Mr. and Mrs. Somoza Senior could be exactly the same, say, as a last meal, twenty years down the line (different décor, different food, each of the people eating of a different age, the grandchild included, who by this point will have become a deeply purposeful young lady, or a youngster with sideburns). I paid (the father thanked me with a slight and elegant nod). The meal was, you could say, very similar to a Sunday lunch in Britain. Ha. At four, before coffee, I got up to leave. Since no one asked the reason why I had to leave on such a red-letter day, me, the boyfriend, the father-to-be, found it necessary to come out with the truth, saying that I was very sorry but I had a lot of work and a father on his death bed. This they understood perfectly, the mother becoming all smiles, the father shaking my hand. Leia left with me. Alone with her in the street, that real place with real concrete and real passers-by, I felt irritated again, but the Galactic Princess has something disarming about her, it's impossible to get your Darth Vader mask and the light sabre out and cut her head off.

"Nuts, right?" said Leia, smiling mischievously.

"Couldn't agree more."

"They don't understand what's going on, my folks."

"Yeah. Maybe if you were to actually tell them something . . . By the way, why . . ."

"Was that true about your Dad?"

"It was. As was the thing about the pizza being good, and about lemmings, a kind of rat that sometimes commit suicide en masse. Leia, your parents, exactly how much do they know about this?" I said, pointing at the bump.

"They know and they don't know ... Can I walk you to work? I've got an hour before I have to be back at the shop."

"Fine. You like walking?"

"Sometimes. You?"

"Almost always."

We walked. She was used to walking more quickly. My pace is still half way between my own and Ana's. Leia looked in shop windows, and at the faces of passersby, and, out of the corner of her eye, at me. I felt an urge to tell her a few things about the baby, and about responsibility, and about the lunch with her parents, but I kept my mouth shut. Leia had the enormous sketchbook with her again, the one I'd seen when we ate in the terrace bar on Plaza San Ildefonso. She noticed me looking at it and stopped, opened it and showed me the contents.

"They're drawings for my T-shirts. Before I was selling them at university, now I'm gong to sell them in Marian's shop."

It was pictures of children and women and man-like creatures. They had malformed heads and almond-shaped eyes and they were laughing, writhing, like someone had told them a macabre joke. They were drawn in the style of a dirty comic, but in fine lines and with the forms not totally finished, as though they were disappearing, as if the material was escaping from their gaping mouths. They were funny and depressing. Or only depressing?

"Like them?"

"I do. How often do you see your shrink?"

Leia laughed, put the drawings away, and we set off again.

"Anyway, they sell pretty well. I've got a website. And the thing with the shop, that's sure to be good . . . I also make cloth dolls and sets."

"Sets?"

"Sort of scale models in boxes. Inside there are different cloth dolls, little families who live in these cute little clean and perfect, and really ugly houses. They always seem to be having a great time, I don't exactly know why. I'm having a show at a gallery next week. You'll come?"

"Count on it."

We got to my office, on Calle Mejía Lequerica, Leia said "what a beautiful building," and we said goodbye, saying we'd see each other soon. Now it's nine o'clock, I haven't had any dinner, and the phone's ringing.

It was Bela. She managed to take Father to the hospital in Hudson. They're doing tests, but it doesn't sound good. It isn't that he can't see well out of one eye: he's *blind* in one eye. Mom's basically lost it, keeps on saying Lajos is just fine. How did you deal with things, Vidor? The same as them? Crude and cowardly? Unfortunately, I think you probably were. You barely mention your family's illnesses, or your own, though it's also true that when it came to your daughter you showed genuine bravery, to the point that you even allowed her to leave the house, as long as she had someone with her. Luisa, crazy Luisa. What was her condition—how would they diagnose her nowadays?

Would they be able to cure her, or to make her life moderately pleasant? She used to hit you. Never smiled. She couldn't look after herself. Smelled like cologne. You never say it, but you felt responsible. You thought you'd carried madness with you from Hungary, in the little bundle you'd brought as luggage, along with your jokes, your voraciousness, your exuberant charm, and the memory that, once, you'd had an animal for a mother. Did your fits of temper scare you, Vidor? Did you use to beat my great-great-great-great-grandma? Your children? The servants? Were you a monster, Vidor? Were you a wounded monster, like me, like my neighbor downstairs, like the child who forces itself to smile, like the old woman who's nice to people only out of fear of being abandoned, like the gardener who has love only for his plants? Bela said she'll call as soon as she knows something. I have to talk to Zoltan.

Zoltan's furious with our parents. How could they do this to him? Why did they trick him? Half an hour harping on it, until I told him to fuck off. We've agreed to have our bags packed and ready to go, and I've got seats held on various flights to NY tomorrow and the day after. It's ten o'clock at night. I don't feel like having any dinner. I'd rather finish reading *Ecce Homo*, though I don't know why. At least the texts are short.

NOTES ON BELA'S BOOKS

*On the Genealogy of Morals* (1887) and *Ecce Homo* (1888) by Friedrich Nietzsche (1844–1900)

Father, hospitalized. It's three o'clock in the morning here, which makes it nine pm last night in Hudson. Bela isn't picking up her phone. I suppose the results won't be ready until tomorrow. I'm reading through my notes on *On the Genealogy of Morals* and *Ecce Homo*, written on the pages of the book itself, in pencil, in hasty capital letters. Notes in each of the books I've read these last months, including Bela's and Zoltan's copies, which are now, with any luck, about to be recycled. Notes and notes and notes and more notes and phrases underlined and still more notes, and all for nothing. I'm finding it impossible to draw *conclusions* today, pick out the main points, as I usually try or claim to do. I can't and don't want to think. I can't sleep and I want to. I can take a pill and I don't want to. I can drink a couple of whiskeys and I want to and do. I can leave the house and go to a bar and look at the people and I don't want to. I can't run into the plump blonde dog walker and fuck her in the middle of the street and I want to. I can and I don't want to, I want to and I can't.

Anyway. What do I do with all of this now? Admit defeat and transcribe my notes into my diary, and leave it at that? Will they tell me anything about my quest for happiness? Do I carry on looking for it? Or put the books back on the shelf with the rest, forever, or until I pick them up again some day, in the next twenty years, if I'm still here, to remind myself of these last months, this last year, my life, *utterly alien to me*? It isn't *precisely* that I might be thinking about my father (terrified, in his pajamas, with my mother by his side, the two of them hand in hand, his bathed in sweat), or about you, Vidor, or about myself, or anyone at all. Tonight is a deep night, endless and teeming, and four o'clock's come around already. And so? The only notes of any interest to me are the ones I wrote on the final page of *Ecce Homo*, this very night:

"Nietzsche, as well as being a great thinker (sic), captivatingly profound, is also a great writer (sic), not for the beauty or elegance of his style, but for the conviction and brilliance of his texts and the concepts he comes up with. He opens fire on everything and everyone, and that has meant his ideas are open to manipulation (appropriation by the Nazis, therefore earning him a reputation as anti-Semitic, etc), to having parts of his work mistaken for the whole. Anyone who reads him (pessimists, for example) will find themselves insulted on one or another of his pages, or on several, but that's not the point. Whatever it is, Nietzsche is against it; he doesn't go in for ideology, only action, only the battle. His strategy is to fight against all preconceived truth. Nietsche's thinking is permanently on a war footing, and in this respect he's courageous, unsettling, luminous, striking and unique. His is one of the most magnificent intellectual adventures, transmitting energy and joie de vivre (the desire to think and to act). Reading Nietzsche, one takes pleasure in his daring, in his idea that thinking itself can be a risky undertaking. If he became great, if there is something scintillating about him, it's because he has the drive and the courage to seek truths that he himself then contests, even at the risk of coming across as fool and at times being truly pathetic. And there is humor as well. It's occurred to me, reading Nietzsche, that, at their loftiest, ideas incorporate humor. And how interesting are the ideas that, like life itself, avoid political correctness, injure and bite and lacerate and make us tremble and devour us and force us into an awareness of the loss of this very second, of all seconds, of not currently stroking or biting or licking the skin of that woman whom perhaps we never have and never will meet, much as we might want to, much as we might have laughed fleetingly at her jokes, but who is life in its unadulterated form, is all pulses and smiles and drinks coca-cola and has the most perfect skin and *is*, and to have only a moment with or within her is and isn't enough because she is lost and, at the same time, fully realized, she cannot be repeated and you are losing her, yes, you've been losing her since the day she was born, you fool, you were losing her when you were with her and you are still losing her now that you are without, at least have the courage to accept it, and she is no goddess, don't even put her on a pedestal, see her for what she is, resplendent and broken, and you know her whole past though she might not tell you it, and she's miserable, yes, like you, though it's masked by happiness, but she doesn't inspire sadness or pity, and it is not love that I speak of, after all love is a fog that obscures the blue sky, love is nothing but a four-letter word, too short, not in the least bit everlasting, an abstract, and you learned with her that thinking is sometimes a road too long and you ought always to be inside her, in every moment, and even then it wouldn't be enough, and if she looks at you with her brown eyes, apprehensive of you, wanting you, off limits, not the slightest bit mysterious, then you're already in the abyss, peering out, all your cells in motion, some of them dying, some of them leaping up, all of them feeling that you and she are alive, together and apart, the two bodies,

315

fucking quietly, never to be alien again, feeling they were made to find one another, to link together, to dissolve, to laugh at death, to turn finally into dust motes that will bear no resemblance to the instant in which she looked at you and you her, or the one when you confused your sweat with hers and her black hair was about to explode between your fingers and her wound was not a wound but a door, or the time when both of you couldn't decide what to order at an Italian restaurant and you lost your appetite and became worried that you'd never be able to eat again, or the time you were on a beach in Crete, just the two of you, and you looked up from your book and saw her in the sea, motionless, far from you, or when she came into a bar having recently got out of a cold or possibly ice cold bath, and you asked yourself who the hell had decided to turn on *all the lights in the universe* just then, and if they'd done so in order to *annihilate you once and for all*. Because, how many letters are there in your name, Ana, and why can't I spell it out? In the end, yes, Nietzsche experts are going to be proved right: for him, as for all of us, everything depends on whether, on that afternoon, walking in the countryside, you dared to kiss that woman or not."

And so? Where does that leave you, Antón Mallick? Have you moved forward? Have you matured after reading all that? Are you going to carry on being so innocent as to look for the answers about happiness in books? Did you reach any conclusions, you poor fool? Will you look on the damned bright side now, for once? Go on, off you go to the kitchen, take a pill from the second drawer, take it, sleep. Go on. Please, go. I need a break from you.

*Thursday, March 25, 2010*

"How high I had leaped both above and away from the wretched flathead-chatter of optimism versus pessimism!—I was the first to see the essential contrast—the degenerative instinct, which turns itself against life with a subterranean vengefulness . . . as opposed to a formula of the highest affirmation, one born out of abundance, out of superabundance, a Yeasaying without reserve to suffering itself, to guilt itself, to everything questionable and alien in existence itself . . . Perhaps I am even envious of Stendhal? He took away from me the best atheist joke that precisely I could have made: 'God's only excuse is that he does not exist . . .'"

NIETZSCHE

"Truly man is a marvellously vain, diverse, and undulating object."

MONTAIGNE

It's five o'clock in the afternoon now. We are flying over the Atlantic. There is a huge amount of water down there, such a large quantity that it bears no resemblance with a glass of water, or the water that comes out of the tap, or with the shower, but, in some way that I struggle to express (I'm not talking about the water cycle), it is still related to rain, when we see it fall, when it drenches us. There are fish and jellyfish and salt and algae and seahorses down there, but from up here there's no way of knowing that, that and so many other things. Now, finally, I'm in a position to do what I planned: write a list of my ghosts. First of all, yes, I have to carry out my duties. Relate how I got here. Follow through on this diary.

I hardly slept—maybe two or three hours at the most. At eight o'clock in the morning, I was at work. There are only two clauses outstanding now, though that doesn't actually mean anything. I stopped by Fran's office at about noon. I was feeling bad for not paying him much attention recently. When I came in he gave me a nervous, guilty-looking smile. Next to his desk stood two voluminous suitcases. I looked at Fran, did the math . . . I didn't have time for him, not today, Bela could call at any moment. Why today, Fran?

"Leaving your wife?" I spat, skipping the niceties.

"I am. I wanted to talk to you about it, but . . ."

"Moving in with Yaiza?"

"I am," he said, more firmly now, looking me in the eye. "I left Sandra a note."

"When?"

"This morning."

"And has she read it?"

"What's the time?" he said, looking at his watch. "Not yet. She'll go by the house at lunch."

"And Yaiza knows you're moving in?"

"Not yet, but we've talked about it many times. I'm going to tell her at lunch," he said, his Saint Bernard face lighting up. "I've booked a . . ."

"Shut up," I said. "You've still got a chance to avoid destroying your life, or at least avoid making it demonstrably worse. The whole thing is a dream, an impossibility, a mirage, you want strawberry-lollipop flavored happiness and it just doesn't exist. You'll wish you hadn't done this. Do you want to spend the rest of your life with your kids, or on your own in the confessional, weeping in front of the priest?"

"Don't know."

"Well you ought to know. Go home, tear up that note, come back to work and be done with the pantomime."

"I don't know, Antón."

"How old's Yaiza?"

"Twenty-two in September."

"And you are?'

"Forty-two, in July."

"Christ! She could be your daughter if only she were uglier! She's going to freak out when she sees the suitcases. What's she going to do with some old eunuch, and all he's got is problems? Take a look at yourself: you were raised to believe in certain things that you still really believe, but that you've come to doubt these last few months, and it's too late. Take a trip to Shangri-la with Sandra, or wherever, wherever you like. Leave the kids at home. Now, I'm sorry, but I've got a hell of a lot of work on."

I gave him a hug and a kiss on both cheeks, and left him. I hope my shock therapy has an effect and I'm sorry not to have been a better help. Poor guy, so irresponsible, so suicidal. At half past twelve Bela finally called. The doctors have looked at the MRI scan and the other tests they did on Father. A brain tumor the size of a tennis ball. Mom is going to have to decide whether they operate. He could lose his speech, movement . . . And they're not even sure that would save him. A death sentence. We'll never know if he's going to die at the age of seventy-one because of being a total idiot, or if he was going to die at seventy-one anyway (being an idiot anyway). I called Zoltan. There was a flight to New York at four o'clock in the afternoon. We said we'd meet in the airport at two.

> "All the members of your family are God. Love
> them and always treat them well."
>
> SWAMI RAMDAS

Zoltan, it would appear, always travels in suit and tie. For him it's a question of appearances, it shows good manners. I found it quite moving, seeing him there, surrounded by the crowds of Hotentots in flip-flops. He showed up with red-rimmed eyes looking sleep deprived, a shaving cut on his chin, sucking a mint, an Ipod with headphones, a feminine-sized (gigantic) suitcase, a leather document holder, silver fox style, the newspapers and an adventure novel. I have no idea why, but something about him brought James Bond to mind.

"We have to go to the pharmacy," he announced, by way of hello.

"Fine. Have we had any news?"

"No. Father could die at any moment. Aren't you going to ask me why I need to go to the pharmacy?"

"No, I'm really not."

"Are you really that heartless, Antón? Flying terrifies me. You haven't got any Lexatin, have you? It's the only thing that does it for me. How could *I* forget?"

Surprise, surprise. My older brother's a bona fide collector when it comes to neuroses. I've only ever flown with him when we were younger but, apparently, his mental health, like everyone else's, is wearing a little thin. Being forty isn't like being twenty. We checked in, came through passport control and headed for the pharmacy. The assistants there were two young, serious women, wearing white lab coats, their hair up in pigtails: all as should be. One of them, the taller of the two, a kind of down-in-the mouth crane, addressed my brother. I asked myself why it is he always gets served first when we go into shops.

"Can I help you?"

"A box of Lexatin, please."

I shot Zoltan an interrogating look, who returned it with a death stare. I was sure he didn't have a prescription, and that he was about to make an idiot of himself. And I wasn't wrong.

"Here it is."

"Thank you."

Zoltan went to pay and the girl, not smiling, asked for the prescription. My older brother fished artificially around in his wallet, putting on a fake smile, just like the awful actor he is.

"I can't understand it, honestly . . . Heavens! I must have forgotten it!"

The pharmacist grabbed the Lexatin as though it were a packet of heroin. Which, in a certain sense, it was.

"Wait, young lady! Don't put it away!"

Zoltan carried on pretending to look for the prescription. I swear, he looked in every single pocket. Every single one. Not forgetting the super stylish leather document holder. Hopeless.

"Where could it be? Where the . . ."

"I'm sorry but I can't sell Lexatin without a prescription."

My brother suppressed a snort.

"Young lady, I am a psychologist, and I give you my word that I need it to fly. Look."

He showed her one of his business cards. They're hideous—bone colored, the lettering in a bombastic, antique font.

"I'm sorry," said the incorruptible crane. "I can't give it to you. And, as I'm sure you well know, psychologists aren't authorized to hand out prescriptions."

Zoltan looked deflated. He'd started to sweat, and it isn't exactly what you could call warm in Barajas Airport.

"For the love of God! I need Lexatin! Don't you get it? Please let me have one, just one pill, please, I beg you!"

"Sorry, sir, I'm not allowed."

The other pharmacist, a little rat wearing too much makeup, came over, and the pair glanced at each other knowingly. Another pain in the neck, the look said.

"We don't give out single pills, sir. You have to understand that."

"Fuck this!" burst Zoltan, losing it. "I've spent my whole life getting prescriptions from colleagues, God! Every single day I treat unhinged people, people who in their least exciting dreams fantasize about defecating on women wearing pharmacist's lab coats! I need Lexatin!"

I thought the day had come when Zoltan would be locked up for some public disorder, but no. He sobbed a little, covered his face with his hands and managed to get a hold of himself. The crane and the little rat looked at him, half-disdainful, half-disconcerted.

"It's okay," said Zoltan, calmer now. "My father, Lajos Mallick, is on his death bed in a hospital in Hudson, New York, in the United States of America. He has a tumor in his brain the size of a tennis ball, according to my poor sister. We found out this morning. I'm terrified of flying, and there's no way of controlling it. I went to night classes to try and cure myself, but there's nothing for it. Would you please give me a pill, please would you be so kind?"

The crane doubted for a second, but the little rat did not. This was her big moment, and there was no way she wasn't going to grab it with both hands. This was why she wore that lab coat, to make it clear that she was a lady in uniform and that she wielded sufficient power that someone would find it pleasurable to defecate on her.

"Sir, I'm sorry."

Zoltan gave her the same look he gave me when we left the bathroom in the Fulanita. An assassin's look, demented. But she was a bold pharmacist, that little rat, and she held his gaze.

"Right, give me some Valerian, if it wouldn't be too much trouble."

They brought out a small yellow box of Valerian and, I swear it, Vidor, even before he'd handed over the money, Zoltan tore open the pack, took out the little bottle, unscrewed the top and drank straight from it, downing the whole thing.

"Sir!" squeaked the little rat. "What are you doing? That's dangerous!"

Now the crane and the little rat were looking at Zoltan with a certain amount of respect, if not downright fear. Good for him.

"Be quiet, you little sewer rat!" I interrupted, fed up. "Didn't he say he needed Lexatin? What did you expect, that he'd have just a little drop?"

I left a ten-euro bill on the counter and got my brother out of there. I went and bought some more of his mints (I didn't want to ask him for any, given the state he was in), set him up on a seat in our gate's departure lounge and there he stayed, listening to Amy Winehouse or some other equally rebellious and magnetic and self-destructive singer. I headed for a café that had wifi, and did some work. We still had an hour and a half before boarding. I talked to Farrar (he wants to come visit this summer, he adores Spain, now what do I do, how I hate my spontaneous and over-the-top display of kindness), wrote a report for Richter, spoke to Gorostegui and, when my phone rang and I saw Zoltan's name come up on the screen, paid and headed to the gate.

> "The great Tao (or way) is very level and easy; but people love the by-ways."
>
> LAO TZU

> "Whatever is alive, the most repellent animal or insect, shudders with fear—does nothing but. Whatever is alive, by the simple fact of living, deserves commiseration."
>
> CIORAN

I've just eaten the blandest chicken with tasteless carrots and lifeless beans. I spent a moment considering the life of the chicken I'd just ingested, realizing that if it had been capable of writing a diary (dipping its beak in the blood of another chicken, surprised by its own capacity to abstract from its immediate experience, discovering itself, feeling it absolutely necessary to make reference to its experiences), its testimony would be a merited inclusion in an anthology of Truly Awful Lives. I've got a seat next to a curt and bitter woman who keeps on giving me scornful looks, but I can't complain. I boarded the plane alongside Zoltan and that, yes, that was a test. He was truly hysterical. Mouth flapping like a fish out of water. His hands were sweating more than a teenager in the cinema before his first ever kiss. Eyes the size of a lemur's. We sat down next to the emergency exit next to a girl who had had no idea yet what was in store for her.

"That Valerian is a piece of shit. Sure you haven't got any Lexatin on you, Antón?"

"Arent we lucky? We're right by the emergency exit. If we crash, we'll be the first ones to get to throw ourselves in the sea."

Zoltan crunched the mints with true violence, like a polar bear eating its first seal after months of a winter fast. I'm running out of comparisons (why always of animals, what's wrong with me?). Zoltan was really in a bad way. While we were waiting for clearance to take off, an airhostess came by (a heron with a sprightly, liberal look, about forty years old) and he grabbed her by the arm.

"Got any Lexatin?"

The heron studied us for a moment, a professional and experienced gaze. On the plane layout we'd already been noted with the red dot that indicates problem passengers.

"Calm down, sir. We'll be taking off in just a few minutes."

"Got any Orfidal? Valium? A whiskey?"

She smiled mischievously.

"What's your name?"

"Mallick, Zoltan Mallick."

"I beg your pardon?'

"ZOLTAN MALLICK! FUCK'S SAKE!"

"Please, no shouting. You're not going to give me any problems, right, Zoltan? Promise?"

"I promise. Are we going to die?"

The air hostess disentangled herself from my brother and made her way to attend to some other psychopath, or dissatisfied client, or mother with twins. Everything carried on along more or less the same lines as we waited for take off, except that the young girl sitting in the same row as us, averted her gaze. Keeping herself turned away, almost turning her back to us, her nose pressed up against the window, she pretended to be entranced by the ecstatic, apocalyptic mesa landscape outside. When the motors began to roar, Zoltan got some kind of electric shock, his whole body tensed up and he grabbed me by the hand.

"Pray with me, Antón, please!"

"What the?"

"Pray with me, fuck!"

"Are you out of your mind?"

When he saw I wasn't going to join him in his prayers, he began reciting the Lord's Prayer at the top of his voice.

"OUR FATHER WHO ART IN HEAVEN!"

"Keep it down, bro," I hissed in his ear, starting to lose it myself. "Down!"

"HALLOWED BE THY NAME!"

A few laughs went around, along with a prickle of fear in the other passengers, the ones who could really have done without a lunatic in their midst.

"THY KINGDOM COME!"

"Quiet or you're dead, you jerk!"

"THY WILL BE DONE, ON EARTH AS IT IS IN HEAVEN ...!"

What to do? How do you deal with a situation like that? Violence is the only way. But, how ...

"GIVE US THIS DAY OUR DAILY BREAD ...!"

I pinched him hard on the side, making him jump out of his seat, only the seatbelt stopping him from smashing his head. He carried on praying, but now in lowered tones, quickly, in a horrible, distorted voice, sounding like Donald Duck. The tranquilizing effect of the pinch: noted. The aeroplane picked up speed and, gradually, like an old pelican with its bill full of fish, managed to ascend. I shut my eyes for ten minutes so as not to have to see whatever my brother was getting up to. It was only a few seconds before I stopped hearing the singsong laughter of the cretins behind us. When I opened my eyes, Zoltan was writing something in a notebook as if he was possessed by the devil.

"Now what are you up to?" I asked, intrigued.

"I'm leaving a note, for my parents, for your sister, and for you."

"Why for me?"

"Because you, like all evil creatures, always manage to save yourself, you're a survivor, damn you."

"And what are you saying to us?"

"That, in spite of everything, in spite of myself, I love you. And not to sell my part of the office to my business partner for a cent under a million euros."

"Nothing's going to happen, Zoltan, calm down. Remember, you're the older brother."

"Older brother? I'VE HAD IT UP TO HERE WITH BEING THE OLDER BROTHER! I'D LIKE TO BE . . . ITALIAN!"

I knew then there was no way I could bear seven plus hours next to him, not without killing myself first. My plan had been to do some work, write my list of ghosts, and sleep a little.

"Why don't you listen to some music? Something upbeat, a little Amy Winehouse or something. What do you say?"

"To hell with that junky! I want to be wide awake when we crash! I want to see my own death!"

Anyway. An hour later (Zoltan did not stop praying for a moment), I got up and went in search of the air hostess. She was on her own in the air-hostess-zone, or whatever it's called, putting colored sweets in a basket.

"Hi."

"Hi," she recognized me straightaway. "How's your colleague doing?"

"He isn't my colleague, he's my older brother. He was what I wanted to talk about. He needs some Lexatin."

"Really sorry," she said, smiling. A real witch, and shrewd, I could tell. "This isn't a pharmacy."

"And I want to change seat too."

She laughed.

"Will that be all?" she asked, flirtatiously, hands on hips, scoffing at me.

"No. Will one hundred euros do?'

Incredulous, she backed away from me, on the defensive. I held her gaze, inexpressive. When a crafty smile appeared on her face-cream flattened face, I knew I'd won.

"You're bribing me?"

"One hundred and fifty."

"Done."

We both glanced around, I gave her three fifty-euro bills, and went back to my seat. My brother was onto the Ave Marias now, and the young girl was staring into her lap, lost in thought.

"Be strong," I said to Zoltan, patting him on the back. "Be strong, big boy."

After about a quarter of an hour, the avaricious air hostess appeared. She was holding something in her closed fist, and she leaned over me, placed four tablets in my hand: white and red and lovely. How many boxes of Lexatin were there on this flight, I asked myself? She also gave me a glass of water.

The young girl had witnessed the handover. I winked at her, and showed Zoltan a pill. Never has my brother given me a look of such unadulterated love. He took the pill and a minute later the heron appeared with a timid, pale guy of about thirty.

"Here it is," the hostess said to Zoltan's new victim.

I got up, gathered my belongings, and followed the airhostess to my new seat, next to the sourpuss woman. Sometimes, I said to myself, in really critical moments, everything can turn out all right. I've just been brought a whiskey on the rocks, prompting a look of displeasure in my seat-mate, a most unsightly grimace, crinkling her

329

sickly, sullen cadaver mouth. This airline's service is perfect, if a little expensive. Now I can turn to my ghosts.

LIST OF GHOSTS PERTAINING TO ANTÓN MALLICK, MARCH 2010
(ARRANGED CHRONOLOGICALLY BY DEATH OR VISITATION)

1. Ancestors (with special mention for Vidor Mallick)

My mother's family hail from Salamanca and Santander. Apart from that, I don't know much. I never knew my grandparents, and my great-grandparents only through anecdote, the kind that it's difficult to believe have been passed on orally. Proverbially mediocre types, possibly honest, unimaginative, stubborn, frugal, with robust jaws and beady eyes. I don't believe they would have been able to understand ideas like "landscape" and "photography" until midway through the twentieth century. Their ghosts never visit me, though they're around somewhere, making a nuisance of themselves, or looking for someone to make a nuisance of themselves with, forgotten. It makes me feel slightly dizzy thinking about them. As for my father's family, I am one hundred percent sure they endured various centuries' servitude. Dismal and dreary lives, closer to those of pigs than our image of a human life. You were the one to leap into the spotlight, it was you, Vidor, who waged the battle against forgetting, making sure your name would be remembered beyond the confines of some tiny stinking village. This makes you a kind of magus, or something akin to the father who comes back at Christmas from a long trip, arms full of presents, promises, and wild tales to boot. For sure, the spotlights fall on the lead actor, leaving the cast in shadow (your wife, as well as almost all the other ancestors on my father's side). You, Vidor, were the first and only ghost I've consulted, and I did it, moreover, in a selfish way: to let off steam. And little by little you've disappointed me. I now find the fact that your name translates as "happy" to be a sick joke. I don't need you any more. After you, the Spanish Mallicks turned to study, got in on land grabs, earned money, lost money, and had the effrontery to think they'd been chosen or selected or made for something, anything other than spreading their seed and dying alone. The only exception being, of course, Uncle Juan, but I'll come to him soon enough.

2. Luis (Luisito) Mallick

My little brother. If he hadn't died, I wouldn't be the youngest, with all that it entails (he didn't even have time to take proper possession of his role as "the baby of the family," or to be called 'Luis' without the diminutive 'ito'). I think I have memories of him, though they could just as well be second hand memories from photos or from the little I've been told about him. He was blond, had green eyes, fairly good-looking, a bit weedy. He died in an accident, in the swimming pool at my parents' house. He tripped and hit his head on the pool edge, and goodbye. When he hit the water he wasn't Luisito any longer. My sister says that when he died Mom locked his room, leaving everything inside exactly as it had been. He was two. I was three and a half. Apparently I was playing with him when he died, though I have no memory of it. Maybe, though I'll never understand it, his death was the main reason my parents went to the US with Zoltan and left Bela and me in the care of Uncle Juan. There are several photos of him in the house in the US, and in all of them he's smiling; very uncomfortable, slightly frightening photos, like a child that's both dead and not dead. When I was small I used to tell my classmates and adults I met about my brother's death to make them feel sorry for me. I also fantasized that he was still alive, and that he was my best friend. One day I stopped doing it.

3. Juan Mallick

I've filled you in on him already, Vidor. A man in full, the kind you don't get many of, not that they're non-existent. One of these people who show us that values, properly understood

331

and assimilated, applied to actual people and conversations, help, along with character, in making good men complete. Juan Mallick was broadly at peace with the world up until the point when his wife, María, died in childbirth, as well as the child she was carrying (they were going to call the child Juan, after him, not at all Hungarian, curiously enough). After that he buried himself in his books, in the law, in maps of Hungary, in habits and mysterious daydreams. But Bela and I showed up and I like to believe that in a strange way, as he felt his way blindly, callowly, sheepishly, Uncle Juan dared to discover the world anew. We owe him so much, he was so giving, that in fact his greatest gift was managing to make us not feel indebted. I'm not idealizing him; he was also only a man. He learned to hide the beast that we are all of us obliged to live with. He was a mysterious man, he needed time alone, to face his personal ghosts with no one around. He looked down on my father, though he never spoke badly of him. He was drawn to my mother, in the way that only gas-filled balloons can create a draw, the ones that know only how to rise, escape, and that sometimes end up trapped in the branches of a tree. I was with him when he died. Only in the very last moments was he afraid. In his case, yes, it's true, I swear it. His soul departed his body through the mouth, along with his final breath.

4. Ana Alonso, and the child she was carrying when she died

To describe anyone is to diminish them, it is a jail, complete with bars, door, and bolt, along with that puerile desire to try to understand, to trap. I might have the temerity to dedicate a sentence, or a thousand pages, to Ana, but sometimes the best thing is to accept that, truly, even being prison wardens is beyond us. Let's let her be free. The only thing left to say is that, for me, *she is not her death*, nor the way she died, but rather all the years in which . . . And as for the person that was going to be our child, that person-to-be, it is nothing more than an idea, sufficiently cruel and shameless as to leap out at will, though its power over me is limited. Another ghost that didn't get much time—whose claws never even grew.

5. Lajos Mallick

I include you, Father, even if you are still alive. I have no qualms about diminishing you, of being unfair with you. You and I have forever been playing hide and seek, childish old men that we are. You are a coward and you are bitter, two failings I have no time for. But then, if I had to pick a word to define you, it would be "idiot": an idiot with a brain full of facts, a dry, dusty, sterile master of conventional wisdom. You abandoned us, and your excuse—a job offer you couldn't turn down—still seems to me like a bad joke. I don't think I'm better than you. Nor worse. You taught me that not all fathers love their children and I learned, after much trying and too many disappointments, that I would always love you, in my way. When you die, you'll still be on my list. Father, we ran out of time. A long time ago. A long, long time ago.

6. ????????? Mallick Somoza, my son

Until very recently you've been nothing but an aggravating, destabilizing ghost. There was a moment there when I feared you might be named Dragosi, but we're through that now. In less than a month you'll be a screaming, supposedly weak baby, my son. We'll see.

There are other ghosts apart from these, but they're benign, marginal, easy to dispel, or wallow in. There are ghosts of me as well, all the Antóns I've ever been, that is, or couldn't or didn't want to be, but these, now and forever, couldn't be more beside the point. We're still flying over the Atlantic, three hours to go till we touch down in New York. I'm off to check on Zoltan.

A day without end—a life in a day. Now we find ourselves on a silver corrugated Amtrak train, destination Hudson. We boarded at Penn Station—a grandiose place, built in the early 1900s by McKim, Mead and White, demolished in the 1960s and replaced by an ugly modern one, which is about all you can say about it. What would the world be like if everything beautiful that's been destroyed had been conserved instead? A pastiche, I suppose. A drain. An absurdity.

Zoltan sleeps, happily under the influence, and I look out across the land. We're traveling along the wide, fast-flowing Hudson River, *upstate*, headed north. Boulders, bridges, boats, a tributary, football pitches, stately homes clinging to the hillsides. And trees, thousands of trees stretching away over the hills. Spring still hasn't showed up here. The best thing is feeling again this sensation of vast spaces, of wide horizons. In which sense, there couldn't be a better place to die than in the US.

*Friday, March 26, 2010*

> "Happy the man,
> And master of himself, who can
> Each day say: I have lived. Let Jove
> Tomorrow fill the sky above
> With clouds, or pure sunlight."
>
> HORACE

Spring. Yet another convention cooked up to save energy, to see without looking, to give general guidance, to be unspecific. It's five o'clock in the morning, I've had coffee and wholewheat toast for breakfast and I'm in the living room, by the window that looks out onto the garden. Once I've finished writing this, I'll make a couple of work calls and see to my emails, and then I'm going for a run. I haven't seen Father yet. When we got to the house last night Ana stormed into my mind. Pretty strange to feel her so strongly, here of all places—though the last trip we made together, it's true, was to Hudson, and I also haven't been back since she died. Mother came in her SUV to pick us up from the station in town at around eleven o'clock last night. I expected Bela would come, but it ended up being my sister who spent the night at the hospital. "She really wanted to," my mother said, by way of explanation. She's got a nerve.

Mom said she thought I looked "magnificent" (not as fat as she'd expected), whereas Zoltan she said looked "not so great" (he was having trouble staying upright, poor bastard). Not a word was spoken about Father until Mother felt she'd got us properly installed in the house. Until then, she stuck to dizzying us with countless minor details about logistics. She is, as is to be expected, quite affected; she seemed old to me, fragile, the worrying side of thin. She's given the go ahead to the operation (Father has apparently been asking what he's doing in hospital, though he's also been asking them to keep the morphine coming). It's set for the day after tomorrow. When we asked Mother about the chances of a successful operation, and what exactly they defined as success, she didn't want to say anything. Bela will tell us soon enough. I suspect none of it will make sense, as is usually the way.

It's seven o'clock and I've just got back from my run. I'm bathed in sweat. Zoltan's still sleeping, fingers crossed he hasn't overdone it with the pills. Mom's in the garden, sitting on her heels weeding by the pond, in full garb, kitted out in straw hat and gloves. For a moment I wondered what had happened to my phone, briefcase and papers, before I quickly realized that Mom must have "tidied up."

Before embarking on my run, just as it was getting light, I went over to the annex. It has the same white weatherboarding as the main house, with a black slate gabled roof and unshuttered sash windows. The door was unlocked. It's my father's den. It's where he keeps all his excruciatingly practical gizmos, things he's bought online that my Mother won't allow in the house. It also has a little library containing his technical manuals (the rest, along with my mother's romantic novels, are in the living room), the tools, the lawnmower, other contraptions, a filing cabinet, his easy chair and the table with his computer and the printer on it. The easy chair is one of my father's most prized possessions—a huge, unsightly thing, complete with headrest and outsize arm rests. The corduroy upholstery is in tatters, and the original green has now gone a faded sickly yellow. My father, not without irony, maintains that it is a feat of engineering, plus he got it for next to nothing, ten years ago now. Why a technology-obsessed engineer with endless back problems uses an old chair to work at his computer, all hunched over, rather than just getting a modern office chair, I've never understood.

I sat in it, for the first time. It is comfortable, maybe a bit too much give. Smell of his aftershave. There were sheets of paper on the table, piles of his online "research," and a beaker etched with the silhouette of an Algonquian Indian and holding his gold fountain pen, packets of mint gum, a used up Nolotil blister pack, a compass and a broken mercury thermometer. I turned on the computer. It had a password. Of course, I might have guessed. I typed in "Hell," but no joy. Turning it off, I began opening drawers.

The original notebook of your *Confessions of a Once-Hungarian Spaniard* was in one. Why did I feel nothing finding it, holding it in my hands? Why did Uncle Juan leave it to his brother, and not to Bela, or me? How did the two of them feel about each other, what went on between them? The heavy, yellowing pages, the black ink, the careful handwriting. I held it up to my face and inhaled. I can't find words for the smell. Putting the notebook back in the drawer, I went back outside. It had grown light enough now to go on my run. I did some stretches looking back at the house, its lines simple like a child's painting, with its stone chimney set to one side, and the maples, the spruces, the pines, the willow and the flower beds, and I thought that if anything bad ever happened in such places, it could only be out of sight, in the basement or in closets.

Mother was going back over to the house, and I said hi. She came over, we kissed and I told her I'd found your notebook, Vidor, and that I was thinking about asking Father if I could have it. Mom didn't respond to this, said she had to get some clothes ready for Father, and off she went. I walked as far as the road, Quin L.A. Road it's called, and I looked in number fifteen's gray mailbox. Empty. No post for the Mallicks. The air was fresh but not cold. I set out running, keeping to the grass verge. Incline, brown wooden house and big garden and black dog barking, woods, farm to the left with one dappled horse and one gray, got to a crossing, took the left, one mile, lake with a few small boats, incline, a blue pickup truck came past, the landscape opened up, prairies and farms and horses and cattle, *Warning!* signs stuck to the trunks of trees, a garden with toy sets and a basketball net, uphill, a fat, deep red farm almost bursting with grain, two miles, now I was breathing hard.

At another crossing I turned right onto Merwin Lake Road. Suddenly I saw flashing between the trees and heard quacking. Panting, I stopped. A house, a lake. No one to be seen. A wooden jetty, thirty or so feet away, half hidden by the trees. I peered over at the shore. The huge lake glistened. There were hundreds of large ducks bathing quietly between the water lilies, sliding around like unhurried ballerinas. And then suddenly the ducks began beating their wings powerfully, making a racket, taking to the air, churning up the water, and then flying low to the surface for a few seconds and landing, and all was calm again. A red dragonfly came to rest on my shirt, and then on my head. More quacking, and the ducks moved in unison over to the other side of the lake. I thought how much I'd like to commit to memory the image of the ducks in flight over the lake, and the din, and the golden crests in the water, how I'd like this to be one of the memories I'd always keep from this trip, or from my life, and I shut my eyes and concentrated until my head hurt and all I could see were glistening drops of water and the ducks had gone and I began shuddering and I opened my eyes and it wasn't the same any more, it wasn't the same lake or the same ducks or the same water lilies or the same house or the same jetty or the same woods and I kicked the trunk of a tree and said to myself "This is it, Antón Mallick, this is where we've got to," and I set off running and didn't look back and I ran possibly five miles and I still feel that one day I'll remember that lake, just as it was when I first saw it, in that vital moment, and I am not lost or defeated or dead, only desperate, it will take an awful lot more to finish off Antón Mallick, and I have no idea why my mother interrupted me just now and gave me a tender kiss on the cheek, just now, while I was still writing, while my fingers fly across the keyboard not wanting not able to stop djgncms5fsadfmzáertccxkdke5gfdx,záq¡4osdfdgg-fmwdcmctoewwp5470r°s'.c,djszsjdjfnxzaxcc+flsmKWK-JD............................................................................................

..................................................................

...............................................

*Saturday, March 27, 2010*

> "Our power resides in our incapacity to know
> how alone we are. Blessed ignorance, thanks to
> which we can act, or at least act up."
>
> CIORAN

It's nine o'clock in the morning and I've just got back from a run. I found it impossible to write last night, I took a downer at about one in the morning and slept deeply. Zoltan, Mom and I went to the hospital at about eight yesterday morning. It's situated on a hill in Hudson, composed of a series of modern brick buildings. Bela was with Father, Room 103. When Zoltan and I went in, my father asked what we were all doing there, and I looked over at Bela who smiled back weakly. Mom established shifts and certain rules, giving no reasons. One person maximum with Father at a time. Her, two hours, and then each of us, one hour. When Zoltan and I were on our own with Bela, we asked about the operation. The doctors weren't all for it, she said, but they weren't totally against either. There was a slim chance it would give him two or three years of a reasonable standard of life, and a far bigger chance it would be curtains. Wonderful. Zoltan went to see the doctor, and Bela, after a coffee with me, headed back to the house to sleep (she had four "free" hours, according to Mother's schedule). When Zoltan got back, he claimed Bela had not understood a thing, though the information he gave was very much the same our sister had given us. I suggested a walk around Hudson, but he said he'd rather stay, "keep watch."

The town of Hudson is set out on a grid and has a feeling of spaciousness to it, with a wide main street, Warren Street, where you can find most of the shops. The houses are wooden, with big windows and high ceilings, there's a firefighter museum, a couple of decent coffee shops, a school, a few banks, art galleries and a preponderance of antiques shops. I bought a coffee and a half kilo cookie and walked on into the more depressed parts of town, where one or two whites and a lot of blacks live. At eleven I was back at the hospital. Zoltan, ashen, came out of the room, and I went in. Father was lying on the bed, half-sitting up, awake, in a gown, and had a drip in his left arm. He greeted me with a nod, and shut his eyes. Physically, he and Zoltan are very alike. I kissed him on the cheek. It scratched. I tried talking with him, but he didn't open his mouth. I told him about me, about the last few months. Every now and then Father protested, let out a whimper. The thought of the operation came into my mind and I shuddered. When Bela came to relieve me, I went and sat with Zoltan in the waiting room. Mother had gone to do some shopping. She wanted to make us her famous roast beef and mashed potatoes.

After Bela's turn, she and I spent the next few hours talking. My second shift came round, and was endless, me talking non-stop, my father clearing his throat and weeping and protesting and me holding his hand and him, in moments, suddenly taking his away, or gripping mine, and the nurses coming in and out, and it carried on that way, the universe reduced to one room in semidarkness with a dying father and views over the Catskill Mountains, purple silhouettes against the horizon, and at the end of my third shift, between nine and ten o'clock in the evening, as I was saying goodbye to my father, he opened his eyes and gave me a hollow look, black, sunken eyes, a look like a well that had no water at the bottom, and he grabbed me by the shirt and pulled me close. We looked at one another for a few seconds, no defiance, no understanding, until his contorted face relaxed and he let me go, and taking his hand I gently placed it in his lap, and he shut his eyes. I kissed his forehead and saw, or perhaps I'd like to believe I saw, a tired half-smile, and I smiled too, though he could not see me, and I told him everything would be all right, we were all there with him. I was finding it hard to breathe, I was feeling smothered and at the same time so full of air that I wanted to vomit, and when I left the room my mother, Zoltan and Bela were arguing at the end of the corridor, and Mother raised her voice, and Zoltan did too, and then Bela, and I felt one of my anguish attacks hit, I unfurled. But it was only an everlasting instant. I came back to myself, the blood must have drained from my face judging by Bela's frightened look, but Mother carried on shouting, she was hysterical, all I wanted was for her to shut her mouth immediately, and then a phrase arose in my mind which in that moment I believed to be an incantation, a spell, how absurd, anyone who understands the brain get in touch, and I said to my mother that I was having a child and that I liked fat women—just like that, out of the blue—and Mother was quiet then, baffled, before coming back with a similarly demented answer, very Mallick, in spite of not being one herself, and she shouted fine, great, she'd already suspected it and, now everyone in the family was for airing secrets, she could tell me with a clean conscience that Uncle Juan had written *Confessions of a Once-Hungarian Spaniard*, that Father had found it when Uncle Juan died and left him the notebook, and how he'd taken it to a Hungarian who said, this isn't Hungarian, it's a made-up language, with its own grammatical rules and twists and made up words, and I could do what the hell I liked with the notebook, and I guess Uncle Juan wanted to tell my father something with the manuscript, it was a coded message, it was a watershed in the brothers' mute war, and Uncle Juan clearly wanted it known that the memories were made up, Mother said, calmer now, and that, according to Father, you, Vidor, could barely read, and then a very large black hospital porter came and threw us out, no more shouting, and we noisy little Spaniards went outside, upset, downcast, and I took out my cigarettes and Bela and Zoltan both asked for one, and I offered Mom one, which she said no to, and I was already breathing easier, how strange, and my heart beating normally, and we stood there for a long while not saying anything, looking off into the darkness, our backs to the hospital, and at the very moment that it occurred to me to point out that we'd left Father on his own, a doctor appeared and placing his hand on my mother's arm said Lajos Mallick had just passed away.

Bela and I looked at each other. Zoltan put his head in his hands. Mother said thank you to the doctor. Like in a dream. The three of us went to hug Mom, and got all in a tangle, clumsily grasping one another, and Mother broke down crying, all she could manage was: "Now what?" and I want to think that that commotion was the commotion of a united family, and not just of a shaken, bewildered, broken family. The funeral is at midday. It turns out Father left everything in order, he did it without telling anyone, four years ago.

"It is the stillest words which bring the storm."

NIETZSCHE

The service was simple, just us and the gravediggers, in the cemetery at Zinder, five miles from the house, in an area with gently rolling hills, prairies and corn fields. I'd never been there before. It's on a plain between two small motorways, across from a dairy farm. And it isn't big, fifty metres by one hundred, and totally open. Gray stone gravestones. There are a number of obelisks, and there are flowers, and American flags billowing over the graves of World War Two veterans. There are also gravestones from the end of the eighteenth and nineteenth centuries, Dutch and German surnames. I asked myself what my father had in common with these soldiers, or with these Northern European settlers with their unpronounceable names. Maybe he was always a foreigner, like people who have fought in wars, or those who have tried to find their place in faraway lands, or those who don't manage it in their own. As the coffin was lowered, I exchanged looks with each of my siblings. I think we were all having the same thought, another of those thoughts that, in such moments, make you feel not terribly proud of yourself. We are next. The tombstone read: "Lajos Mallick. 1935–2010."

And that was all.

*Sunday, March 28, 2010*

Yesterday, after the funeral: meal at the house. Mother swears she's feeling better. TV. Mother, kitchen and garden. Zoltan, sleeping. Roast beef.

Today: to Old Chatham with Bela, and the world-despised Wal-Mart (Mom: "It's *hell* in there, always full of bad people"—read, fat people). Wrangler Jeans, like the ones we wore as kids, five dollars. Bela says she and John are getting back together, and that she wants to have a child. Good news, bad news? Three-siblings-cinema—with Mother too, all together in the living room.

*Monday, March 29, 2010*

I'm sitting on the flight back to Madrid, flicking through the pages of *Confessions of a Once-Hungarian Spaniard*. Zoltan's asleep, doped up. I can just see him taking a liking to the drugs he prescribes his patients. Bela stayed with Mother, who doesn't yet know what she's going to do with herself. It's all been very odd. Next to me is a music professor from New York called Mike, big-bottomed, sixtyish. I have a healthy dislike for conversations with strangers on airplanes, but we went through some turbulence and, when it was over, he began talking at me about himself, about his family, his work, with an altogether American openness. When he'd finished he asked me, bluntly, if I was happy, if I believed in happiness, to which I said no. I told him that I aim not to be miserable, that I'm a happy pessimist, and that's what I've always been and always will be (the pessimist part, that is; the happy part, we'll just have to see about). When I admitted that I'd found Kafka, Cioran and Nietzsche funny, he smiled like he understood. He said he considered himself an optimist, but burst out laughing when I told him about Richard Bentall, an English psychologist who published an article in the *Journal of Medical Ethics* entitled "A proposal to classify happiness as a psychiatric disorder." He then made the comment that researchers only carry on looking into optimism because the funding's much better than if they try to look into pessimism. It's all a question of target *markets*.

They're bringing the food.


*Saturday, April 3, 2010*

I've been back in Madrid for nearly a week. I'm at home, I've just had dinner and I'm about to go out and meet a lady friend. Goodbye, Vidor. Or should I say, goodbye Uncle Juan? Maybe it's high time I accept that I've been talking to myself all along, wouldn't you say? And time to leave you in peace, in whichever nether region you happen to be floating in. Time to stop complaining, to face the facts. Great knowing you. Anyway. Here are a few last phrases from you, selected by me.

### FINAL ADVICE AND CURIOUS PHRASES FROM *CONFESSIONS OF A ONCE-HUNGARIAN SPANIARD*

"If you observe a child you will see that it laughs a hundred times a day. An adult, fifteen. This gives you an idea of the effect of the passing of years. To laugh, therefore, is a marvellous rebellion, a celebration of life."

"I don't understand people who deny the existence of ghosts. A ghost is a person who now exists only in our memory."

"A gentleman asked us in the discussion who we were afraid of. Someone said thieves. Another said wicked people. A third, tax collectors. 'And you, Mallick?' I thought about it for a few moments before replying: 'Bitter people.' I don't know if they understood what I meant."

" . . . and one morning my eldest son came into the playroom without knocking and happened upon me in tears. He looked terrified and shot out. I sent for him, and when he was brought back to me I sat him on my knees. 'Now,' I said to him, 'you know all the secrets that there are. Now you're a man. Laugh, or I'm going to beat you.'"

"I am, and have been, happy. I swear it. Goodbye."

*Wednesday, April 7, 2010*

The satellite launch has been put back another fortnight. The solid rocket busters were damaged in transit, and it's going to take them a month to rebuild them, though there's also the option of buying from our competitors. Richter, despite the problem, and the fact the contract still has a few loose ends, is happy. He's taking me to Baikonur. I'm going to see the room where Korolev slept, his space monk cell.

*Wednesday, April 14, 2010*

I finally got round to seeing Leia's exhibition (on its last day, yes). She was going to show me an ultrasound scan, but forgot to bring it. She's sold quite a lot, mostly drawings and the little cloth families. She's mad as hell. She wanted to sell *everything!*

*Sunday, April 18, 2010*

It's been raining since this morning. Steadily. It's strange. It doesn't tend to rain like this in Madrid. Things here are usually so extreme.

Someone's calling me.

# ACKNOWLEDGMENTS

To A. Mac Kay, for kindly filling me in on "special" kinds of insurance.

To J. L. Gallero, for book recommendations and for sending me quotations on optimism (and pessimism).

To A. Fernández Rubio, a constant help.

To J. L. López, for talking to me about his work as a private investigator.

To S. Sesé, for encouragement and patience.

To everyone who reads my early drafts, for their advice.

To M. and M., for putting up with me though you didn't even know what I was writing.

# ABOUT THE AUTHOR

NICOLÁS CASARIEGO is author of the novel *Dime cinco cosas que quieres que te haga* (Espasa Calpe, 1998), the books of stories *La noche de las doscientas estrellas* (Lengua de Trapo, 1999) and *Lo siento, la suma de los colores da negro* (Destino, 2007) and the essay *Héroes y antihéroes en la literatura* (Anaya, 2000). In addition, he has published stories in various anthologies and newspapers, travel articles for *El País* and *El Mundo*, and is co-scriptwriter of several feature films.

*Cazadores de luz* (Destino, 2005), his second novel, was finalist for the Nadal Award 2005. He is also author of the children's series *Marquitos detective* (SM, 2007), *Marquitos caballero* (SM, 2009) and *Marquitos ladrón* (SM, 2012).

After the Spanish original version of this novel, published by Destino in 2010, his latest title is *Carahueca* (Temas de hoy, 2011), a movie tie-in book of the screenplay he co-wrote for Clive Owen's project, *Intruders*. The film has been directed by Juan Carlos Fresnadillo and produced by Universal Pictures.

In 2008 he was awarded the Writers Omi residence fellowship for international writers at Ledig House, New York.

# ABOUT THE TRANSLATOR

THOMAS BUNSTEAD is a writer and a translator. He has had short stories, reviews, interviews and essays featured in publications including the *Times Literary Supplement,* the *Independent on Sunday,* The Paris Review Blog, Words Without Borders, www.3ammagazine.com and www.killauthor.com. A mentee with the British Centre for Literary Translation in 2011-12, working with Margaret Jull Costa, he has translated novels by writers including Eduardo Halfon and Enrique Vila-Matas, and short stories and non-fiction by writers such as Yuri Herrera, Willy Uribe and Juan Zúñiga.

CPSIA information can be obtained at www.ICGtesting.com
Printed in the USA
LVOW06s1607140714

394267LV00002B/404/P